HUNGRY LIKE THE WOLF

Salvatore allowed his hands to skim up her bare thighs, his gaze drinking in the sight of her delicate face framed by the fall of golden hair, the shimmering hazel eyes.

The male in him reacted with predictable desire to her beauty, but the stirring of his wolf was unexpected. He'd never experienced having his animal so close to the surface during sex, and he was caught off guard by the violent excitement that pulsed through his blood.

She sucked in a sharp breath as his eyes glowed with the inner fire of his beast, filling the room with a golden light. But it wasn't fear that rippled over her features. It was the same raw need that clawed at him.

He needed to mark her with his passion, with his scent, with his very essence.

As if sensing his possessive animal instinct, Harley nipped his bottom lip.

Salvatore sucked in a sharp breath as Harley planted a path of wet, demanding kisses over his chest.

"Harley."

His plea was cut short as she wiggled down his body, the tormenting kisses heading ever lower.

Unaware of how close he was to the edge, or perhaps simply enjoying her power over him, Harley continued to drive him mad, her lips sending tiny shock waves through his body . . .

Books by Alexandra Ivy

Published by Zebra Books

Beyond The Darkness

Guardians of Eternity

ALEXANDRA IVY

ZEBRA BOOKS
KENSINGTON PUBLISHING CORP.
http://www.kensingtonbooks.com

ZEBRA BOOKS are published by

Kensington Publishing Corp.
119 West 40th Street
New York, NY 10018

All Kensington titles, imprints and distributed lines are available at special quantity discounts for bulk purchases for sales promotion, premiums, fund-raising, educational or institutional use.

Special book excerpts or customized printings can also be created to fit specific needs. For details, write or phone the office of the Kensington Special Sales Manager: Attn.: Special Sales Department. Kensington Publishing Corp., 119 West 40th Street, New York, NY 10018. Phone: 1-800-221-2647.

ISBN-13: 978-1-4201-0298-7
ISBN-10: 1-4201-0298-2

First Printing: April 2010

10 9 8 7 6 5 4 3 2 1

Printed in the United States of America

Chapter One

It wasn't his finest day, Salvatore Giuliani, the mighty King of Weres, had to admit.

As a matter of fact, it was swerving toward downright shitty.

It was bad enough to regain consciousness to discover he was stretched out in a dark, nasty tunnel that was currently ruining his Gucci suit, and that he had no clear memory of how he had gotten there.

But to open his eyes and use the perfect night vision of his werewolf heritage to discover a three-foot gargoyle with stunted horns, ugly gray features, and delicate wings in shades of blue and gold and crimson hovering over him was enough to ruin a perfectly horrible mood.

"Wake up," Levet hissed, his French accent pronounced and his wings fluttering in fear. "Wake up, you mangy dog or I'll have you spayed."

"Call me a dog again and be assured you'll soon be chopped into bits of gravel and paving my driveway," Salvatore growled, his head throbbing in time to his heartbeat.

What the hell had happened?

The last thing he remembered, he'd been in a remote

cabin north of St. Louis to meet with Duncan, a cur who'd promised information regarding his traitor of a pack leader, and the next he was waking up with Levet buzzing over him like an oversized, extremely ugly butterfly.

God Almighty. When Salvatore got out of the tunnel, he was going to track down Jagr and cut out his heart for sticking him with the annoying Levet. Damned vampire.

"You will not be doing anything unless you get up and move," the gargoyle warned. "Shake your tail, King of Slugs."

Ignoring the grinding pain in his joints, Salvatore rose to his feet and smoothed back his shoulder-length raven hair. He didn't bother knocking the dirt from his silk suit. It was going in the nearest fire.

Along with gargoyle.

"Where are we?"

"In some nasty tunnel."

"A brilliant deduction. What would I do without you?"

"Look, Cujo, all I know is that one minute we were in a cabin with an extremely dead Duncan, and the next I was being dropped on my head by a gorgeous but *très* ill-mannered woman." Bizarrely, the gargoyle rubbed his butt rather than his head. Of course, his skull was far too thick to harm. "That female is fortunate that I did not turn her into a beaver."

"It had to have been a spell. Was the woman a witch?"

"*Non.* A demon, but . . ."

"What?"

"She is a mongrel."

Salvatore shrugged. It was common among the demon world to interbreed.

"Not unusual."

"Her power is."

Salvatore frowned. He might want to choke the

gargoyle, but the tiny demon possessed the ability to sense magic that Salvatore couldn't.

"What power?"

"Jinn."

A chill inched down Salvatore's spine and he cast a swift glance up and down the tunnel. In the distance he could sense the approach of his curs and a vampire. The cavalry rushing to the rescue. His attention, however, was focused on searching for any hint of the jinn.

A pure-blooded jinn was a cruel, unpredictable creature who could manipulate nature. They could call lightning, turn wind into a lethal force, and lay flat an entire city with an earthquake. They could also disappear into a wisp of smoke. Thankfully, they rarely took an interest in the world and preferred to remain isolated.

Half-breeds . . .

He shuddered. They might not possess the power of a full-fledged jinn, but their inability to control their volatile energy made them even more dangerous.

"Jinn have been forbidden to breed with other demons."

Levet snorted. "There are many things forbidden in this world."

"The Commission must be told," Salvatore muttered, referring to the cryptic Oracles who were the ultimate leaders of the demon world. He reached into his pocket, coming up empty. "*Cristo.*"

"What?"

"My cell phone is gone."

"Fine." Levet threw his hands in the air. "We will send a memo. For now we need to get out of here."

"Relax, gargoyle. Help is on the way."

With a frown, Levet sniffed the air. "Your curs."

"And a leech."

Levet sniffed again. "Tane."

Expecting Jagr, Salvatore's brows snapped together. One vampire was as bad as another, but Tane's reputation for killing first and asking questions later didn't exactly warm the cockles of a Were's heart.

Whatever the hell a cockle was.

"The Charon?" he demanded. Charons were assassins who hunted down rogue vampires. God only knew what they did to lesser demons. And in a vampire's mind, every demon was lesser.

"An arrogant, condescending donkey," Levet muttered.

Salvatore rolled his eyes. "Jackass, you idiot, not donkey."

Levet waved a dismissive hand. "It is my theory that the taller the demon, the larger his conceit and the smaller his . . ."

"Continue, gargoyle," a cold voice cut through the dark, abruptly lowering the temperature in the tunnel. "I find your theory fascinating."

"Eek."

With a flutter of his wings, Levet dashed behind Salvatore. As if he was stupid enough to think Salvatore would keep him from certain death.

"*Dio,* get away from me, you pest," Salvatore growled, swiping a hand at the gargoyle even as his gaze was warily focused on the vampire rounding the corner of the tunnel.

He was worth focusing on.

Although not as large as many of his brothers, the vampire was dangerously muscular, with the golden skin of his Polynesian ancestors, thick black hair shaved on the sides, and a long Mohawk that fell past his shoulders. His face was that of a predator, lean and hard with faintly slanted honey eyes. At the moment he was wearing nothing more than a pair of khaki shorts, obviously not sharing Salvatore's own fondness for designer clothes.

Of course, the big dagger he was holding in his hands made sure that no one was going to question his taste in fashion.

Not if they wanted to live.

There was the sound of footsteps and four of his curs came into sight, the largest of them rushing forward to drop to his knees and press his bald head to the ground in front of Salvatore's feet.

"Sire, are you harmed?" Hess demanded.

"Only my pride." Salvatore returned his attention to the vampire as Hess rose to his feet and towered at his side. "I remember nothing after entering the cabin and finding Duncan dead. No, wait. There was a voice, then . . ." He shook his head in aggravation as his memory went blank. "Damn. Did you follow us?"

Tane absently stroked the hilt of his dagger. "When we found the cabin empty, Jagr assumed you were in trouble. Since your clueless crew seemed incapable of forming a singular coherent thought, I agreed to come in search of you."

Not surprising. Unlike purebloods who were born from full Weres, the curs were humans who had been bitten and transformed into werewolves. Hess and the other curs were excellent killers. Which was why he kept them as guards. Using their brains, however . . . well, he did the thinking for them. It solved any number of problems.

"So what happened to our captors?"

"We've been gaining on you over the past half hour." Tane shrugged. "They obviously preferred escape over keeping their hostages."

"You never caught sight of them?"

"No. A cur escaped through a side tunnel a mile back, and the demon simply disappeared." Frustration flashed through the honey eyes. Salvatore could sympathize. He was anxious for a bit of blood and violence himself. "There're only a handful of demons capable of vanishing into thin air."

"The gargoyle thinks it's a jinn mongrel."

"Hey, the gargoyle has a name." Stepping from behind Salvatore, Levet planted his hands on his hips. "And I do not think, I *know*."

Tane narrowed his eyes. "How can you be certain?"

"I had a slight misunderstanding with a jinn a few centuries ago. He zapped off one of my wings. It took years to grow back."

Tane was supremely unimpressed. "And that's somehow relevant?"

"Before the demon dropped me and did her disappearing act, she left a little present." Turning around, Levet revealed the perfectly shaped handprint that had been branded onto his butt. Salvtore's laughter echoed through the tunnel, and the gargoyle turned to stab him with a wounded glare. "It is not amusing."

"That still doesn't prove it was a jinn," Tane pointed out, his own lips twitching with amusement.

"Being struck by lightning is not a sensation you easily forget."

Tane instinctively glanced over his shoulder. No demon in his right mind wanted to cross paths with a jinn.

"How do you know it isn't a full jinn?"

Levet grimaced. "I am still alive."

The vampire turned to Salvatore. "The Commission must be warned."

"I agree."

"This is Were business. It's your duty."

"I can't lose the trail of the cur," Salvatore smoothly pointed out. Ah. There was nothing better than getting the upper hand with a leech. "He's proven a danger to more than just Weres. I'm sure the Commission would agree that my duty is to put an end to the traitors."

A blast of frigid air filled the tunnel. Salvatore smiled, releasing his own energy to counter the chill with a prickling heat.

The curs stirred uneasily, reacting to the power play between two dangerous predators. Salvatore never allowed his gaze to stray from Tane. Few Weres could best a vampire, but Salvatore wasn't just a Were. He was king. He wasn't going to back down from any demon.

At last, Tane snapped his fangs in Salvatore's direction and stepped back. Salvatore could only assume that the vampire had been ordered to keep the bloodshed to a minimum.

"This will not be forgotten, dog," Tane warned, turning on his heel and silently disappearing down the tunnel.

"Good riddance, leech."

Waiting long enough to make sure the vampire didn't have a change of heart and return to rip out his throat, Salvatore turned back to his waiting curs to discover them battling back their urge to shift.

He grimaced. As a pureblood, he had the ability to control his shifts unless it was a full moon. Curs, on the other hand, were at the mercy of their emotions.

With a shudder, Hess at last gained control and sucked in a deep breath.

"Now what?"

Salvatore didn't hesitate. "We follow the cur."

Hess clenched his meaty hands at his side. "It's too dangerous. The jinn . . ." His words broke off in a squeal as Salvatore's power once again reached out, striking the cur like the lash of a whip.

"Hess, on how many occasions have I told you that if I want your opinion I'll ask for it?" Salvatore drawled.

The cur lowered his head. "Forgive me, sire."

"The cringing cretin is not entirely wrong." Levet waddled forward, his long tail twitching. "It had to have been the demon who killed Duncan and knocked both of us out."

"No one is asking you to join us, gargoyle," Salvatore snapped.

"*Sacre bleu.* I am not going to be left alone in these tunnels."

"Then chase after the vampire."

The damned gargoyle refused to budge, a sly amusement entering the gray eyes.

"Darcy would not be pleased if something was to happen to me. And if Darcy is not happy, then Styx is not happy."

Salvatore snapped his teeth. Darcy was one of the female purebloods he'd been searching for over the past thirty years, and while he didn't have the least fear of her, she'd recently mated with the King of Vampires.

Styx he did fear.

Hey, he wasn't stupid.

Muttering a curse, Salvatore led the way down the tunnel, his already pissy mood plunging to foul.

"Get in my way and I'll chop you up and feed you to the vultures. Understood, gargoyle?"

He sensed his curs falling into step behind him, with Levet bringing up the rear.

"Mangy dogs can smooch my posterior," the gargoyle muttered.

"A jinn is not the only creature capable of ripping off a wing," Salvatore warned.

A blessed silence filled the dark tunnel, and at last able to concentrate on the faint trail of cur, Salvatore quickened his pace.

It was moments like this that he regretted leaving Italy.

In his elegant lair near Rome, no one dared treat him as anything other than Master of the Universe. His word was law, and his underlings scrambled to do his bidding. Best of all, there were no filthy vampires or stunted gargoyles.

Unfortunately, he'd had no choice in the matter.

The Weres were becoming extinct. Pure-blooded females could no longer control their shifts during pregnancy, and more often than not lost their babies before they could be born. Even the bite of Weres was losing its potency. A new cur had not been created in years.

Salvatore had to act, and after years of research, his very expensive scientists had at last managed to alter the DNA of four female pureblood babies so they could not shift.

They were a miracle. Born to save the Weres.

Until they had been stolen from the nursery.

He growled low in his throat, his anger still a potent force even after thirty years. He had wasted far too much time searching through Europe before he at last traveled to America and managed to stumble across two of the female Weres. Unfortunately Darcy was in the hands of Styx, while Regan had proven to be infertile.

During his trip to Hannibal, however, he'd managed to discover that the babies had at some point been in the hands of Caine, a cur with a death wish who'd convinced himself that he would be capable of using the blood of the females to turn common curs into Weres. Moron.

Salvatore had been in a cabin to meet with one of Caine's pack who'd promised to reveal the traitor's location, when he and Levet had been knocked unconscious and kidnapped.

It had to have been Caine who attacked him.

Now the bastard was leaving a trail straight to his lair.

A smile curved Salvatore's lips. He intended to savor ripping out the traitor's throat.

A near half hour passed as Salvatore weaved his way through the winding tunnel, his steps slowing as he tilted back his head to sniff the air.

The scent of cur was still strong, but he was beginning to pick up the distant scent of other curs, and . . . pureblood.

Female pureblood.

Coming to a sharp halt, Salvatore savored the rich vanilla aroma that filled his senses.

He loved the smell of women. Hell, he loved women.

But this was different.

It was intoxicating.

"Cristo," he breathed, his blood racing, an odd tightness coiling through his body, slowly draining his strength.

Almost as if . . .

No. It wasn't possible.

There hadn't been a true Were mating for centuries.

"Curs," Levet said, moving to his side. "And a female pureblood."

"Si," Salvatore muttered, distracted.

"You think it's a trap?"

Salvatore swallowed a grim laugh. Hell, he hoped it was a trap. The alternative was enough to send any intelligent Were howling into the night.

"There's only one way to find out."

He moved forward, sensing the end of the tunnel just yards in front of him.

"Salvatore?" Levet tugged on his pants.

Salvatore shook him off. "What?"

"You smell funny. *Mon Dieu,* are you . . ."

With blinding speed, Salvatore grasped the gargoyle by one stunted horn and yanked him off his feet to glare into his ugly face. Until that moment, he hadn't noticed the musky scent that clung to his skin.

Merda.

"One more word and you lose that tongue," he snarled.

"But . . ."

"Do not screw with me."

"I do not intend to screw with anyone." The gargoyle curled his lips in a mocking smile. "I am not the one in heat."

Hess appeared beside Salvatore, halting his urge to rip off the gargoyle's head.

A pity.

"Sire?" the cur demanded, his thick brow furrowed.

"Take Max and the other curs and keep guard on the rear. I don't want anyone sneaking up on us," he commanded.

It was unlikely the cur would recognize Salvatore's disturbing reaction to the female's scent. Hess hadn't even been transformed when the last mating had happened. Not to mention the fact that he was as thick as a stump. But Levet was certainly annoying enough to let the cat out of the bag.

Waiting for the curs to grudgingly shift back, he gave the gargoyle a shake before dropping him onto the ground.

"You—not another word."

Regaining his balance, Levet glanced upward, his wings fluttering and his tail twitching.

"Um. Actually, I have two words," he muttered. Then, without warning, he was charging forward, ramming directly into Salvatore and sending him flying backwards. "CAVE-IN!!!"

Momentarily stunned, Salvatore watched in horror as the low ceiling abruptly gave way, sending an avalanche of dirt and stone into the tunnel.

Because of Levet's swift action, he had avoided the worst of the landslide, but rising to his feet he was in no mood for gratitude. Hard to believe this hideous day had just gotten worse.

Moving to the wall of debris that blocked the tunnel, he sent out his sense to find his curs.

"Hess?" he shouted.

Levet coughed at the cloud of dust that filled the air. "Are they . . . ?"

"They're injured, but alive," Salvatore said, able to pick up the heartbeats of his pack, although they were currently unconscious. "Can we dig our way through to them?"

"It would take hours, and we risk bringing even more down on our heads."

Of course. Why the hell would it be easy?

"Damn."

The gargoyle shook the dirt off his wings. "The tunnel is clear behind them. Once they recover they should be able to find a way out."

He was right. Hess might have a brain the size of a walnut, but he was as tenacious as a pit bull. Once he realized he wouldn't be able to reach Salvatore, he would lead the others back to the cabin and return overland to dig them out.

Unfortunately, it would take hours.

Turning, he glanced toward the stone wall that marked the end of the tunnel.

Whatever exit the cur had used to get out of the tunnel was now buried beneath the rubble.

"Which is more than I can say for us," he muttered.

"Bah." With a flagrant disregard to the thin sliver of ceiling that hadn't yet fallen on their heads, Levet gingerly climbed up the side of the tunnel. "I am a gargoyle."

Salvatore sucked in a sharp breath. A ton of rock and dirt falling on his head wouldn't kill him.

Being buried alive with Levet? That would be the end.

If he had to rip out his own heart with his bare hands.

"I'm painfully aware of who and what you are."

"I can smell the night." Levet paused and glanced over his shoulder. "Are you coming, or what?"

With no other legitimate options, Salvatore awkwardly scrambled behind the gargoyle, his pride as tattered as his Italian leather shoes.

"Damn lump of stone," he breathed. "Jagr should rot in hell for sticking me with you."

Nearly flicking Salvatore's nose with the tip of his tail, Levet continued upward, sniffing the air. He paused as he reached the edge of the ceiling, his hands testing the seemingly smooth rock until he abruptly shoved upward, revealing the cleverly hidden door.

Levet disappeared through the narrow opening and Salvatore was swift to follow, grasping the edge of the hole and pulling himself out of the tunnel.

He crawled through the dew-dampened grass, heading away from the opening before at last rising to his feet and sucking in the fresh air.

Weres weren't like most demons who enjoyed being

hidden in damp, moldy caves and tunnels for centuries on end. A Were needed open space to run and hunt.

With a shudder, Salvatore glanced around the thick trees that surrounded him, his senses reaching out to make certain there was no immediate threat.

"Ta-da." With a flutter of his wings, Levet landed directly in front of Salvatore, his expression smug. "Shove it up your ear, oh ye of little faith. Hey . . . where are you going?"

Brushing past the annoying pest, Salvatore was weaving his way through the trees.

"To kill me a cur."

"Wait, we can't go alone," Levet protested, his tiny legs pumping to keep pace. "Besides, it is almost dawn."

"I just want to find his lair before he manages to cover his trail. I'm not losing him again."

"And that is all? You promise you will not do anything stupid until we have front up?"

"Back up, you fool." The sweet scent of vanilla invaded Salvatore's senses, clouding his mind and stealing his waning strength. "Now be quiet."

At a glance, Harley was the spitting image of a Barbie doll.

She stood barely over five feet, her body was slender, her heart-shaped face was delicately carved with large hazel eyes that were thickly lashed, and her golden blond hair that tumbled past her shoulders gave her the image of a fragile angel. She also looked far younger than her thirty years.

Anyone, however, stupid enough to dismiss her as harmless usually ended up injured.

Or dead.

She was not only a full-blooded Were, but she took her training in combat skills to a level that Navy SEALS would envy.

She was working out in the full-scale gym when Caine returned to the vast colonial home. She continued lifting the weights that would crush most men as she absently listened to his bitter tirade about the ineptitude of his cur pack and the injustice of a world that contained Salvatore Giuliani, the King of Weres.

At last, Harley moved to take a swig of bottled water and wiped the sweat coating her face. She glanced toward Caine, who leaned negligently against the far wall, his jeans and muscle shirt filthy, his short blond hair tousled. Not that his bedraggled appearance dimmed his surfer good looks. Even beneath the fluorescent lights that made everyone appear like death warmed over, his tanned skin glowed with a rich bronze and his blue eyes shimmered like the finest sapphires.

He was gorgeous. And he knew it.

Barf.

Harley's lips twisted. Her relationship with Caine was complicated.

The cur had been her guardian since she was a baby, but while he'd protected her and kept her in considerable luxury, she'd never truly trusted him.

And the feeling was entirely mutual.

Caine allowed her to roam the house and the surrounding lands with seeming freedom, but she knew she was under constant surveillance. And God knew, she was never allowed to travel away from the estate without two or three of Caine's pet curs. Caine claimed he was concerned for her safety, but Harley wasn't stupid. She knew his motives were far more selfish.

It might have been tempting to escape her golden

cage, save for the knowledge that a lone wolf, even a pureblood, rarely survived. Weres were by nature predators, and there were any number of demons that would be eager to rid the world of a Were if they could catch one without a pack's protection.

Besides, there was always the fear that the King of Weres was out there somewhere, anxious to kill her as he had her three sisters. Caine might be determined to use her for his own purpose, but at least that purpose meant he had to keep her alive.

Tossing aside the towel, Harley sent her companion a mocking smile.

"Let me see if I have this straight. You went to Hannibal because Sadie created some mysterious mess that you had to clean up after, and while you were there, you brilliantly decided to kidnap the King of Weres, only to drop him like a hot potato when you were nearly caught by a vampire and pack of curs?"

Caine pushed away from the wall and prowled forward, his gaze skimming over her tight spandex shorts and sports bra. The cur was nothing if not predictable. He'd been trying to seduce her for years.

"You have it in a perfect little nutshell, sweet Harley." He halted directly before her, toying with her ponytail that had fallen over her shoulder. "Do you want a reward?"

"And your pet jinn?"

"Slipped from her leash. She'll be back." His smile was taunting. "Like you, she has nowhere else to go."

Harley jerked from his touch. Bastard.

"So now you've lost half your pack and your demon, and you've left behind a trail that will lead the pissed off King of Weres and his angry posse directly to this lair."

Caine shrugged. "I'll call for one of the local witches.

My trail will be long gone by the time the almighty Salvatore manages to get out."

"Get out of where?"

"I collapsed the tunnel on top of them."

"God. Are you even barely sane?"

"Once they manage to heal enough to dig out of the rubble, they'll discover the entrance has been completely blocked. They will have no choice but to turn back."

"You're pretty damned cocky for a cur who has just pissed off your royal master."

"I don't have a master," Caine snarled, revealing a glimpse of resentment at being a lowly cur instead of a full Were, before he smoothed out his expression. "And besides, the prophecies have spoken. I'm destined to transform the curs into purebloods. Nothing can happen to me."

Harley snorted. Caine wasn't a complete loon. He managed to control his large pack that he had spread throughout the Midwest with an iron hand. He was a Harvard trained scientist who made a fortune with his black market drugs. He regularly kicked her ass at Scrabble.

But at some point in his very long life, he claimed he'd been visited by an ancient pureblood who had given him a vision. Harley didn't pretend to understand it. Something about seeing his blood run pure.

Being a scientist, he naturally assumed this miracle would be performed in a lab, which was why he kept Harley as his permanent houseguest. He thought by studying her blood he could find the answers he sought. Moronic, of course. Visions were the stuff of mist and magic, not glass beakers and microscopes.

"Look, if you want to get yourself killed because of your delusions of grandeur, I don't give a shit." She narrowed her eyes. "But I'm not going to be happy if you put me in the firing line."

Caine stepped forward, reaching to trail his fingers over her shoulder. His touch was warm, experienced. She shook him off.

A woman would have to be dead not to find Caine attractive, but Harley needed more than simple lust. She needed . . . hell, she didn't know what she needed, only that she hadn't yet found it.

Besides, her skin was suddenly feeling hypersensitive. As if it had been rubbed raw by sandpaper.

"Would I ever put you in danger, sweet Harley?" Caine goaded.

"In a heartbeat, if it meant saving your own hide."

"Harsh."

"But true."

"Perhaps." His gaze dipped downward, studying her sports bra. "I need a shower. Why don't you join me?"

"In your dreams."

"Every night. Do you want to know what we're doing?"

"I'd rather yank out your tongue and eat it for dinner."

With a laugh, he snapped his teeth near her nose. "Naughty Were. You know how it makes me hard when you threaten violence."

Spinning on her heel, Harley headed for the door. "You'd better make that a cold shower or you won't have to worry about Salvatore Giuliani slicing off your balls. I'll already have them dangling from my rearview mirror."

She tuned out Caine's low laugh as she headed toward the front of the house.

It was late and she was tired, but she ignored the carved wooden staircase that led to the bedrooms as she entered the paneled foyer.

What the hell was wrong with her?

She felt restless and on edge. As if there was a looming thunderstorm and she was about to be struck by lightning.

Telling herself it was nothing more than frustration with Caine and the mysterious games that were being played around her, she yanked open the door and stepped outside.

What she needed was a walk.

And if that didn't work, then there was always cheesecake in the fridge.

There was nothing in the world that couldn't be cured by cheesecake.

Chapter Two

Salvatore crouched in the bushes and studied the large home that was stuck in the middle of nowhere.

Like most colonial homes, it had a lot of bricks and fluted columns, with a double row of tall windows that would give a vampire nightmares. There was a large front terrace with a sweeping drive that was lined by oak trees, and a covered pool behind the four-car garage.

A nice crib for a mere cur, but Salvatore's interest wasn't in architecture.

Instead, he tested the late spring air, futilely attempting to ignore the pervasive scent of vanilla that seeped through his body like the finest aphrodisiac, and concentrated on the bastard who had dared to try to kidnap him.

He might have escaped, but he wasn't the forgive-and-forget type.

"The cur's inside," he said.

"Holy cow." Levet flapped his wings, standing on tiptoe to glance over the bush. "Do you pay all your curs like AIG executives or do the lunatic fringe receive special bonuses?"

Salvatore's retort died on his lips as the door was suddenly pushed open and a female pureblood stepped into the night.

She was stunningly familiar. As one of quadruplets, she possessed her sisters' pale blond hair and slender body. A body that was deliciously revealed by her stretchy shorts and tiny bit of spandex that passed as a top. He would also bet his Rolex her eyes were a perfect emerald.

But that's where the similarity ended.

Both her sisters, Darcy and Regan, possessed the electric energy of all Weres. But this woman. *Cristo,* he could feel her vibrant power charging the air a half mile away.

His wolf stirred beneath his skin, straining to be closer to the female that called to him at his most primitive level.

"Salvatore?" Levet snapped his fingers in front of Salvatore's eyes. "Hellllooo. Anyone home?"

"Don't bother me, gargoyle," Salvatore growled.

"You promised you would find the cur's lair and then we would wait for . . ." The three-foot pest sucked in a sharp breath as he at last caught sight of the woman strolling toward a marble fountain. "Oh. Darcy's sister."

"Si."

"Salvatore, you are not going to do something stupid, are you?" Levet stomped his foot as Salvatore rose and stepped around the bush. "*Mon Dieu.* Why do I even ask? Of course you are going to do something stupid. And who do you suppose is the one who is going to get hurt? *Moi.* That is who."

"Return to the bushes," Salvatore snapped, his attention never wavering from the woman who had suddenly stiffened and turned in his direction.

"Do you never watch horror films, *stupide*?" Levet squeaked. "It is always the one who stays behind who Jason or Freddie or Michael Myers chops in half."

Salvatore made a Herculean effort to ignore his companion as he slid forward. The female had sensed his presence and was preparing to bolt.

That was unacceptable.

And not just because he'd been searching for her for the past thirty years.

Hell, that was at the very bottom of the list.

Way below getting her naked and into the nearest bed.

She took a wary step back as Salvatore neared, and he forced himself to come to a halt, raising a hand in a gesture of peace.

"Wait."

Her eyes narrowed (not emerald, but instead a stunning hazel with flecks of gold), and her expression hardened, but there was no fear. His fascination ratcheted up another notch.

There was nothing sexier than a woman who knew she could take care of herself.

"Who are you?" she demanded, her low, husky voice brushing over him like a physical caress.

"Salvatore Giuliani."

Recognition flashed through her eyes. Unfortunately, it wasn't the good kind of recognition. Not like finding the perfect silk tie to match his new Armani suit. More like a woman who turned over a rock and didn't like what crawled out.

"God," she breathed. "Caine is an idiot."

"What's your name?"

"Harley."

He stretched out his hand. "Come to me, Harley."

"I don't think so."

"I'm not going to hurt you."

"And I should believe you, why?"

Salvatore frowned. She wasn't acting like a Were who'd been kidnapped and held captive by a deranged cur.

"I'm here to rescue you."

She shook her head, her hair shimmering with pale beauty even in the darkness.

"Hip-frigging-hooray for you. Who said I wanted to be rescued?"

"You aren't being held against your will?"

"No one holds me against my will." She flicked a dismissive gaze over his less than pristine suit. "Especially not a man."

Salvatore growled low in his throat. He didn't get dismissive glances from women. Women drooled and panted and sometimes fainted when he entered a room.

"It doesn't matter," he rasped. "You're coming with me."

"Very smooth, Romeo." Levet moved to stand at his side. "It's no wonder the Weres are nearly extinct."

Salvatore glared at the gargoyle. It didn't improve his mood to know the miniature demon was right. He could seduce a woman with a mere glance, so why was he barely restraining his urge to snap and snarl?

Because the female was his, a voice whispered in the back of his mind. And she was damned well going to admit it.

"Levet," he warned as the demon waddled forward.

"Shh. Allow the master to work." With a flick of his tail, Levet halted directly in front of Harley, and performed an awkward bow. "Please forgive my oafish companion, beautiful Harley. He is never troubled by the need to display good manners." He heaved a dramatic sigh. "Royalty, you cannot live with them, cannot slice off their heads. Well, not without a great deal of stupid fuss." The delicate wings fluttered. "What Salvatore intended to say was that we would be deeply honored to have your company so we can converse with you over a lovely meal." He licked his lips. "Perhaps a roasted ox. Or two."

A reluctant smile curved Harley's lips and Salvatore swallowed a sigh. Men wanted to drown the gargoyle on sight, women inevitably found him charming. It was as unfathomable as black holes.

"I like you," she murmured.

"But of course you do, *ma belle.* I am quite irresistible to the opposite sex. It is a blessing . . . and a curse."

"Enough." Salvatore scowled. "I have been searching for you for a long time, Harley. You're not going to escape me now."

"Oh, yeah?" A slow, taunting smile curved her lips. "Then come and get me."

She whirled on her heel and with startling speed, was headed toward the side of the house.

In less than a heartbeat, Salvatore was giving chase, his brain shutting down as his predatory nature took over.

He didn't know what he intended to do when he caught her. Bite her, bed her, or toss her over his shoulder and lock her in his lair. But it was going to be deeply satisfying.

"Salvatore . . ." Levet called, his voice nothing but a distant annoyance.

His only thought was catching the slender form that was rounding the corner of the house.

Had he been in his right mind, he would never have given chase. *Madre del dio,* it had trap written all over it. As it was, his only thought was sweet vanilla and warm woman.

Cutting the corner around the house, he had a nanosecond to realize that Harley had come to a halt and was standing with a smug grin on her lips. Then the earth beneath his feet began to shift and he was falling through empty air.

"Sucker," the woman called, adding insult to injury as Salvatore hit the paved floor and the top of the silver cage slammed shut above him.

Harley's heart was thundering in her chest as she paused at the entrance to the basement.

A part of her was damned proud of herself.

After years of having Salvatore Giuliani's name used as her personal boogeyman, she hadn't panicked when he'd suddenly appeared. In fact, she'd coolly stood her ground, and even lured the mighty King of Weres into her trap.

Piece of cake.

Harley blew out a sigh and wiped the sweat from her brow.

Liar, liar.

Her seeming composure had been nothing more than shock and temporary insanity.

The shock had been a result of the realization that the powerful Were who wanted her dead had finally tracked her down, and was standing just a few feet away.

The insanity was the raw, undeniable reaction to Salvatore's presence.

Frigging hell.

Caine had warned her that Salvatore was a powerful beast. Werewolves didn't have hereditary royalty. They fought and schemed and bullied their way to the top. Like *Top Model,* only with a lot more blood and less boobs.

What Caine hadn't mentioned was that Salvatore was drop-dead, mouthwateringly gorgeous.

A shudder shook her at the thought of his lean, darkly handsome face and eyes like liquid gold. His features were pure Latin, with a long aquiline nose and full lips. His hair was a rich wave of raven satin that flowed just past his shoulders. And his body . . . yum. Even beneath the filthy suit, she could tell it was lean and hard in all the right places.

Still, she'd seen handsome men before.

Caine was no slouch in the looks department.

So why hadn't any of them made her blood sizzle and her palms sweat?

It was like he possessed some sort of electric charge that was the precise current to push her buttons.

All her buttons.

She knocked her head against the wall, telling herself to stop being an idiot.

So, Salvatore had an animal magnetism. No doubt being the king gave him an extra umph or something. That didn't mean she was about to forget the fact that the bastard had killed her sisters.

Or that he'd been hunting her for years.

Damn his black soul.

She wished he'd never shown up, she told herself sternly. But now that she had him caged, she wanted answers.

Hiding her unease behind a mocking smile, Harley pushed open the door and stepped inside.

The basement was divided in half, one side being a high-tech lab where Caine practiced his scientific voodoo, and this side being an equally high-tech prison. Usually the three silver cages were used for curs who were stupid enough to piss off Caine, but over the past months Caine had installed the triggered traps in the yard to discourage intruders.

Her mouth went dry as she spotted Salvatore standing in the middle of the closest silver cage.

If he was dangerous before, now he was nothing less than feral.

The golden eyes glowed with a tangible heat, his lips curled to reveal the white teeth that could grow to lethal fangs in the blink of an eye.

"Let me out of here," he demanded, his voice thick.

Harley forced her reluctant feet forward, refusing to be unnerved by the choking power that filled the room. God Almighty, she'd never felt anything like it.

"But I just went to so much effort to get you in there," she taunted. "Well, maybe it wasn't *so* much effort. Like all men, you see a woman and assume you naturally have the upper hand."

Salvatore stilled, his fury morphing into something far more dangerous. With a slow glide, his gaze seared over her body, taking his sweet time in memorizing her every curve before lifting back to her face.

"Let me guess, you're a woman who likes to be on top?"

"Always."

"Come in here and I can show you the benefits of being on the bottom."

A disturbing shiver raced through her body. "Being royalty really has gone to your head if you think a lame-ass line like that would ever work on a woman with half a brain."

"Then there must be thousands of women with half a brain," he drawled.

"The plastic blow-up kinds don't count."

"*Cara,* I could make you roll over and beg."

Harley tilted her chin. Damn, what was it about this Were?

She should be getting a gun and shooting him in the

head, not imagining his precise technique of getting her to roll over and beg.

"I'd rather do the gargoyle."

Salvatore tilted back his head and delicately sniffed the air. He chuckled.

"Liar."

Shit. Harley abruptly turned on her heel and studied the numerous torture devises hung on the cement wall.

"You said you've been searching for me," she rasped.

"*Si.*"

"Why?"

"Because you're a very special Were."

"Special?" Her sharp bark of laughter echoed eerily through the room. "Don't you mean defective?"

"You're perfect," he smoothly countered, his voice brushing over her skin like warm velvet. "Just as you were intended to be."

She abruptly turned back to stab him with a furious scowl. "As my sisters were before you killed them?"

Salvatore flinched, feeling as if he'd just taken a punch to the gut.

He'd been accused of a number of despicable things, many of them true. But this . . .

"Dio," Salvatore breathed. "What the hell are you talking about?"

"Did you think I didn't know you hunted down my sisters and murdered them in cold blood?"

Salvatore's lips curled in a humorless smile, his shock being replaced by a grim comprehension. He'd wondered why Harley was treating him as the enemy rather than being desperate to flee Caine's clutches.

"Clever bastard," he muttered, stepping close enough

to the silver bars to feel the painful prickles crawling over his skin. Weres were deathly allergic to silver. In fact, it was one of the few things that could actually kill a pureblood. Silver through the heart, or decapitation. "I'll admit there have been any number of occasions Darcy and Regan have inspired thoughts of homicide, but I've risked my life to protect them, even after they were stupid enough to choose vampires to act as their guardians. The only danger to your sisters is Caine."

Her eyes narrowed. "You're lying."

"If you don't believe me, then let me go and I'll take you to them. Darcy is in Chicago with Styx and Regan was headed there to join her, the last I heard. I'm certain by now Jagr's hot on her trail. Besotted idiot."

"Yeah, right." She folded her arms over her chest, but Salvatore didn't miss the uncertainty that flashed through her eyes. Her faith in Caine wasn't absolute. "I suppose you also have a bridge you're trying to unload? I'm not buying."

"I have no reason to lie."

"Are you frigging kidding me?" She deliberately glanced over her shoulder at the splendid collection of whips, daggers, swords, and even a good old-fashioned mace. "You have *every* reason to lie."

"Use your brains, Harley. If I wanted you dead, we wouldn't be having this conversation."

Her lips tightened in annoyance. She couldn't deny the truth. If he'd attacked to kill, she wouldn't be standing there.

"You murdered my sisters."

"Why the hell would I murder pure-blooded females I invested millions of dollars and decades of my life to produce?"

"Because you didn't want the Weres to know their king

had failed in his Frankenstein experiments. You had to get rid of the evidence."

Salvatore had intended to kill Caine before ever arriving at the estate. Now he intended to kill him slowly.

With as much pain as inhumanly possible.

"My only failure was allowing you to be stolen from the nursery. You . . ." His gaze skimmed over her beautiful, heart-shaped face, his body humming with a constant awareness. "Are flawless."

"Bullshit." Her expression hardened. "I can't shift."

Her smoldering frustration filled the air. Ah. Now at least now he understood a portion of her thorny personality.

"Is that why you overcompensate? Because you can't shift?"

Lifting her hand, she flipped him off. "Overcompensate this."

Salvatore chuckled. It was insanity. He'd allowed his hormones to overcome his common sense, and now he was locked in the cage of his archenemy with no immediate hope of escape. He should be infuriated. He should be using his powers to attempt to bend the female to his will.

Instead, he was hot and bothered and barely able to think of anything beyond this female who was swiftly becoming an obsession.

"To keep you from shifting was precisely the reason for my Frankenstein experiments, as you call them. Female Weres have lost their ability to suppress their shifts during the full moon. It has made it nearly impossible for pregnant Weres to carry their young to full term." He caught and held her gaze. "We are vanishing, Harley, and you hold the hope for our future."

She licked her lips, caught between the urge to tell him to go to hell and a grudging need to know more.

"So you're saying you cooked me and my sisters up in your lab to save the Were species?"

"You were genetically altered, *si*."

"And my sisters? Are they out producing the children you're so desperate to have?"

"Regan was unfortunately barren, although it hardly matters since she was busy falling in love with a leech the last time I saw her. And Darcy . . ." Salvatore grimaced. "She was a disappointment as well."

"Why?"

"She had the same pathetic taste for the living challenged."

Her brows lifted. "I assume you mean a vampire?"

"Not just any vampire." There was an edge to his voice. That happened a lot when the walking dead entered the conversation. "She mated with the Anasso, King of Vampires. May his cold soul rot in hell."

Harley paced the cement floor, her expression distracted as she pondered his words.

"Darcy." She softly tested the name. "Regan."

"They are very much alive and anxious to meet you."

She continued pacing, refusing to meet his gaze. "Caine said there were four of us."

"There's another sister who I haven't yet found. I suspect Caine knows where she is."

She halted unconsciously close to the cage, her eyes troubled as she shook her head.

"No. I don't believe you."

Salvatore was a Were who firmly believed in grasping opportunity. Especially when that opportunity included a gorgeous female who set his blood on fire.

"Then believe this." He reached through the bars, grabbing the straps of her sports bra and yanking her close enough to kiss her. A groan rumbled deep in his throat. She tasted of exotic spices and danger. He shivered as wild lightning streaked through him. "You're mine," he whispered against her lips.

For a breathless minute she softened against him, seemingly as indifferent as Salvatore to the painful silver between them. Then with a muttered curse, she pulled away, her eyes dark with alarm.

"Caine's right. You're a lunatic."

With a glare that would have seared the skin off a lesser man, Harley stormed from the room and slammed the door behind her.

Lunatic.

Salvatore shoved his fingers through his hair.

He couldn't agree more.

Harley reached the top of the stairs when Caine appeared in the hallway, a pair of faded denims riding low on his hips, his hair still damp from the shower.

"I heard the alarm." His eyes darted to the door she'd just closed behind her. "What the hell is going on?"

Harley blocked the door, her emotions in an unpleasant jumble. And all because of that stupid Were.

Wasn't it bad enough that he'd managed to make her question everything that Caine had ever told her? Not that she had ever been fully on board with Caine's smooth stories. They had changed too often over the years to be completely believable.

But to use his kingly mojo or whatever it was to make her melt beneath his kiss.

It was despicable.

She lifted a hand and pressed it to her lips. They still

tingled with pleasure. And they weren't the only thing tingling.

It had to be that damned musky smell of his. It was some sort of Were aphrodisiac or something.

Stirring up her anger to cover the craving that still prickled through her body, Harley pointed a finger in Caine's face.

"I warned you that your delusions of grandeur were going to get you killed," she snarled. "Salvatore has dropped in for a visit."

"Shit." Caine's face paled. "Did you get him? Is he caged?"

"Do you mean did I save your ass from certain death? Yes, I did."

Caine glanced toward the closed door to the basement, his brow furrowed.

"I need to make a phone call."

A phone call? Harley narrowed her gaze. The cur was acting strangely, even for Caine.

"Fine. I'll keep an eye on the prisoner."

Like a striking snake, Caine reached out to grab her arm. "No."

"Why not?"

His smile was strained. "You think I would risk you being in the same room as a rabid Were who has sworn to kill you?"

"He's locked in a silver cage. For the moment he's helpless."

"A pureblood is never helpless."

Harley studied the too-handsome face. Caine didn't want her near Salvatore. The question was, why?

"If you're afraid he might escape, that's all the more reason I should keep watch on him."

The blue eyes glowed in the dim light of the hall. "I

have curs to take care of guard duty. You have better things to do with your time."

She shrugged. "Not really. Besides, I want to talk with the Were."

"Talk to him about what?"

"Does it matter?"

His fingers tightened on her arm. "Of course it does."

"Why?"

"I don't want you exposed to the filth he's bound to spew."

Harley snorted. Like most nonhumans, Caine managed to adopt the social norms that flowed and changed with the passage of time, but every so often he showed his age. The older demons were even worse.

"Spew?"

The glow in his eyes shimmered with blue fire, revealing he was hanging onto his wolf by a thread. Curs were always at the mercy of their emotions.

"Salvatore is notorious for fabricating lies that hide his evil nature. The Weres would never have allowed him to stay in power otherwise."

She yanked her arm out of his grasp. "Do you mean lies like the fact that two of my sisters are alive and well, and currently living in Chicago?"

Chapter Three

Harley watched the anger ripple over Caine's face before he clenched his jaw and studied her with a wary gaze.

"You already spoke to Salvatore?"

"It was a brief discussion."

"What else did he say?"

"He mentioned that far from wanting me and my sisters dead, he has been trying to save us." She deliberately paused. "From you."

His false laughter echoed through the hallway. "That bastard. He would say anything to save his worthless hide. You weren't stupid enough to believe his lies, were you?"

"Of course not." Harley smiled, able to lie with the best of them.

At the moment, she didn't know what she believed.

She didn't trust Caine. And she sure as hell didn't trust Salvatore.

All she knew for certain was that she wanted answers.

"Good." He brushed the back of his hands down her cheek, allowing his fingers to linger on the curve of her neck. "He's dangerous, Harley. You need to stay away from him."

"If he's so dangerous, why don't you just kill him?"

"And have every Were in the world wanting to nail my ass to the wall?" he smoothly demanded. "No, thank you."

Yeah, right. She narrowed her gaze.

"Holding him captive isn't going to make the Weres any happier."

"Who will know that I'm holding him?" His hand deliberately encircled her throat. "He was alone, wasn't he? I assume you would have mentioned if he had his pack of curs with him."

Harley abruptly recalled the tiny gargoyle. After capturing Salvatore, he'd slipped her mind.

She knocked Caine's hand from her throat. "Yeah, completely alone."

"There you go then."

"The vampire chasing you will suspect you're involved in Salvatore's disappearance."

She could sense him scrambling for a suitable lie. "Not if I force the dog to call his pack and assure them that he's fine and on my trail. By the time they figure it out, we'll be long gone."

She snorted at his ridiculous boast. Caine might be a bad-assed cur, but he was a pale imitation of Salvatore Giuliani.

"You think you can force the King of Weres to do anything?"

Without warning he moved forward, his pride clearly pricked by her patent disbelief. He crowded her against the wall and lowered his head until he was speaking directly against her mouth.

"Never underestimate my powers of persuasion."

She lifted her hands and pressed them against his bare chest. "If you want to keep those lips, then you'd best remove them."

He stepped back with a mocking smile. "Someday, sweet Harley."

"Don't you have a phone call to make?"

"I want your promise you'll stay out of the basement."

She met his gaze squarely. There was something going on, and she suspected she was involved, whether she wanted to be or not. She intended to discover what the hell it was.

"Fine."

"Your promise."

She brushed her fingers over her chest. "Cross my heart and hope to die."

"Be careful of your words." His low voice was thick with warning. "Death can lurk in the most unexpected places."

Her eyes narrowed. "That sounded very much like a threat, Caine."

"More of a friendly warning, pet."

"Don't call me that."

He patted her cheek, his smile insulting as he turned to make his way down the hall.

"Behave yourself."

"Creep," she muttered.

Waiting until she heard Caine climbing the staircase to his study on the second floor, Harley turned to shove open the door behind her.

She didn't give a damn about her promise.

If Salvatore had answers, she wanted them.

* * *

Salvatore was seated on the cement floor in the middle of the cell, as far from the silver bars as possible.

Not that it truly mattered.

The silver was a bother, but the true danger was the debilitating weakness caused by Harley.

Cristo. He understood the scientific logistics of a Were mating. Although the attraction was mutual, it was always the female who had the final choice of whether or not to accept the bond. The male's power was restrained to prevent him from taking the female by force.

Of course, when the powers returned after the mating was complete, it was rumored they were even more potent. He became the perfect weapon to protect his family.

It all made perfect sense.

And it was a royal pain in the ass.

Why him? And why Harley? And why now?

The matings had faded away, along with the Weres' ability to control their shifts during the full moon. No doubt a biological necessity for females to mate with as many men as possible, in the hopes of obtaining a viable pregnancy.

Salvatore groaned as the scent of vanilla flooded the air, warning of Harley's imminent return.

His brain might not comprehend the inconvenient mating, but his body was fully on board with the program.

Just having her in the same room was enough to make him hard and aching.

Rising to his feet, he watched as Harley slipped into the room and closed the door, leaning against it with a resentful expression.

A slow smile curved Salvatore's lips. Harley might consider him the enemy, but she was as helpless as he was to deny the smoldering attraction that crackled between them.

Her awareness filled the air like the finest perfume.

"I knew you'd be back," he drawled.

"Right." She rolled her eyes. "Because you're so frigging irresistible?"

"I am to you." His smile widened as her fists clenched and she looked like she was considering punching him in the nose. Dangerous women turned him on. "Besides, you have questions that only I can answer."

"Did you ever consider the possibility I came back to kill you?"

"No."

"So arrogant."

He shrugged. "You wouldn't want me if I were a doormat."

"I don't *want* you, period."

Salvatore arched a brow at her blatant lie. "You've never been around another pureblood, have you?"

Her eyes narrowed. "Why?"

"Because if you had, you would know I can smell your physical response." He breathed in deeply, his body tingling in response. "It fills the air."

An astonishing blush touched her cheeks before she was roughly pushing away from the door and pacing toward the cage.

"Why doesn't Caine just kill you?"

He paused, struck by her pertinent question. "I don't know."

"I thought the King of Weres knew everything?"

He cast a disgusted glance toward the locked door of his cage.

"Obviously not."

She unconsciously rubbed her arms, as if trying to rid

herself of the tangible electricity that pulsed between. His lips twisted.

Ah, if only it were that simple.

"You said that my sisters and I were stolen from a nursery?" she demanded.

"*Si.*" Salvatore grimaced. Far too late he realized he'd been played the fool. "At first I assumed it was traditional baby snatchers who were out to make a quick buck on the black market. Now I suspect it's a calculated plot intended to destroy the Weres."

"And you think Caine's involved?"

"Without a doubt."

She nodded, as if not particularly surprised by Caine's treachery.

"What happened in Hannibal?"

"Short or long version?"

"Short."

"After years of searching, I tracked your sister Regan to a psychotic imp named Culligan who'd been torturing her for the past thirty years." He shrugged. "Not surprisingly, she went a bit homicidal when I released her, and she tracked Culligan to Hannibal where Caine's minions first tried to capture her, and then tried to kill her."

"Which minions?"

She was testing him. Whether it was to discover if Caine was lying or he was, it was impossible to say.

"Sadie was the leader. Regan killed her. Then there was Duncan, who intended to lead me to this lair." His jaw tightened. "Unfortunately, Caine and his pet jinn got there first."

Her lips parted, no doubt with yet another question, then there was the sound of a click and abruptly she was spinning on her heel and rushing back to the door.

She grasped the door handle and futilely attempted to pull it open.

"Shit," she muttered.

Salvatore was on instant alert. "What?"

Before his companion could answer, the sound of Caine's voice echoed through a speaker set in the corner of the ceiling.

"I did warn you, sweet Harley," the cur mocked. "I wanted to keep you out of this, but you wouldn't listen."

"No . . ." She pounded her fists against the steel door. "Caine."

"Harley, what the hell is going on?" Salvatore demanded.

"Damn you." She pointed a finger toward Salvatore. "This is all your fault."

Salvatore snorted. His fault? He was locked in a damned silver cage in the middle of nowhere, and it was his fault?

It wasn't until he caught the first whiff of gas that he at last understood Harley's outrage.

Something was being pumped into the basement.

Something powerful enough to make his knees buckle and the world go black.

Although the large wooden cabin was less than fifty miles north of St. Louis, it would have taken more than a GPS to find the house.

Not only was there acres of thick trees and a high fence that protected the estate, there was also a spell of Concealment that had been woven by the local coven of witches. If that wasn't enough, there were large lethal wolves that prowled the outer perimeter and ate anyone who accidentally stumbled too close.

Caine had deliberately chosen this cabin to hide his unconscious prisoners. Beyond being close enough to his previous lair not to have to worry about Salvatore waking up prematurely, it was his most heavily guarded compound.

He could no longer trust Harley, or what she had told him.

If someone had been with Salvatore, then he wanted to make damned certain they couldn't follow.

No one, absolutely no one, could sneak up on him here.

Of course, he would feel a great deal happier if he weren't currently standing in the cramped tunnels that ran beneath the estate. He was tired, stressed on an epic scale, and in no humor to meet with the ancient Were who stood in the depths of the shadows, his eyes glowing an eerie crimson and his body wrapped in a heavy cape.

Christ, the man was nasty. Caine shivered, for the first time realizing that rather than the usual heat that radiated from Weres, the air was filled with an unpleasant chill.

Like his companion was a damned corpse.

Or a bloodsucker.

Clearing the fear from his throat, Caine tilted his chin. The Were had demanded this meeting the moment Caine had revealed that he had captured Salvatore. He had no idea how the Were had arrived so swiftly, and in truth, he didn't want to know. But since his arrival, the arrogant dog had done nothing but complain and criticize.

Typical.

The bastard was never satisfied with Caine's efforts.

Which was precisely why Caine tried to limit the number of reunions to one or two a decade.

"I told you I would take care of Salvatore and I did," he said, tired of being a whipping boy for the Weres.

"You also promised you would make sure that he

didn't find the female Weres until I was prepared to act," his companion taunted, his voice oddly hoarse, as always.

"It wasn't my fault."

"It never is."

Caine's skin prickled as he battled against his snarling wolf. When he was tense, it was always more difficult to control his shifts.

"If you think you can do better, then you take him."

"It's not time yet, you fool."

"Time for what?"

"Destiny to be fulfilled."

"Well, screw it. I've waited thirty years for this supposed destiny to happen," Caine snapped. "I'm getting tired of empty promises."

The Were released a warning growl. "Are you questioning my authority?"

Caine bit back his angry words, realizing he had gone too far. Swallowing his pride, he knelt in a gesture of submission.

For now, he needed the disturbing Were.

But someday . . .

"No."

"Remember this, cur, if something happens to Salvatore before my plans are complete, I'll skin you alive and feed you to the vultures."

There was a blast of cold air and a hair-raising scent of evil, then the Were seemed to simply melt into shadows.

Caine counted to one hundred, then added another fifty just in case.

Once he was certain he was alone, he turned his head to spit in the dirt.

"Someday, I'm going to kill that bastard."

* * *

Harley woke to a pounding head, a dry mouth, and her body wrapped firmly in the arms of a warm, delicious Were.

For a demented moment, she snuggled closer, lured by the heat and rich male musk that would entice any poor woman into helpless stupidity.

It was only when Salvatore's hands slid down to cup her ass and he pressed her against his hardening erection that she painfully came to her senses.

Was she completely mental?

With a shove that sent Salvatore flying onto his back, she scrambled to her feet and glared down at his smug smile.

"Do you always grope unconscious women?"

He folded his hands over his stomach and crossed his legs at the ankle. He should have looked ridiculous lying on the cement floor, with his raven hair tousled and his expensive suit wrinkled. But he didn't.

He looked . . . edible.

The bronzed, stunningly beautiful features. The full, sensual lips. The whiskey-gold eyes.

A delectable male, from the top of his raven hair to the tips of his Italian leather shoes.

"Only those who crawl all over me in their sleep," he said. "If anyone was violated, it was me."

The worst part was that Harley couldn't be certain she hadn't been violating him. Her body seemed to have lost its connection to her brain.

"God," she muttered, as annoyed with herself as with Salvatore. "Get over yourself."

In one fluid movement, he was on his feet and standing directly in front of her.

"I'd rather be over you."

"Enough." She abruptly turned from the smoldering

invitation in his eyes, her palms sweating. "I have more important things to worry about than a dog in heat."

She felt him step back, although it didn't help much. His power swirled through the small space with crushing force.

"Do you know where we are?" he demanded.

She turned and glanced around the six-by-six cage made of silver bars that was set in the middle of a barren cellar. There was nothing to identify the cramped prison beyond a narrow door and bare lightbulb in the center of the ceiling. There were no windows, no furniture, not even a blanket, but the muted scent of wooden logs gave away their location.

"In Caine's cabin near St. Louis."

Salvatore closed his eyes, testing the air. "It's dusk."

"Do you have a point?"

"Levet becomes a statue during the day." His eyes opened, a hint of frustration shimmering in the golden depths. "He should be waking any moment to follow our trail."

Harley shook her head, Salvatore's frustration echoing deep inside her. She might be furious with Caine, but she wasn't stupid enough to underestimate him.

"There won't be a trail to follow."

"What do you mean?"

"One of Caine's lovers is a witch. He never moves from one lair to another without her casting a spell to cover his scent, as well as anyone with him." She grimaced. "No one's going to be able to find us."

"*One* of his lovers?" Salvatore arched a brow, ignoring the most pertinent point of her explanation. "How many does he have?"

She made a sound of impatience. "I've never bothered

to keep count. Why? Are you interested in joining the bimbo brigade?"

"My only interest is in knowing whether or not *you* share his bed."

"It's none of your damned business."

His lips twisted, an odd yearning flaring through his eyes. "Ah, if only that were true."

A melting heat threatened to weaken her knees and Harley gave a sharp shake of her head.

She wasn't going to be distracted.

"I don't know what your damage is, but in case you've failed to notice, we're in a little bit of trouble here. Can you focus on something other than trying to get into my pants?"

His lips curled. "I can multitask."

No crap.

"Fan-frigging-tastic," she groused. "Then get us out of here."

Chapter Four

Salvatore glanced toward the locked door of the cell, folding his arms across his chest.

"And just how do you expect me to perform that particular miracle?"

"I thought you were some sort of uberking," she taunted. "Don't you have any special powers?"

Salvatore smiled, unruffled by her sharp tone. She could snap and snarl all she wanted, but she couldn't conceal the scent of her arousal.

And when he'd awakened to discover her snuggled in his arms . . .

Dio, it had almost made this whole kidnapping thing worthwhile.

Almost.

"None that involve B and E," he admitted.

Her gaze narrowed. "B and E implies entering. We want to exit."

He folded his arms over his chest. "What about you?"

"Me?"

"You obviously know Caine . . ." His jaw tightened as a flare of savage possession speared through him. "Intimately.

You better than anyone should be familiar with the weaknesses in his security."

"I know nothing about Caine." Her lips curled in a sneer, but Salvatore didn't miss the bitterness that edged her voice. "He's done nothing but lie to me since I was a baby."

He was petty enough to be pleased at the thought of poisoning any relationship between Harley and the damnable cur, but within that perfectly logical reaction was an unexpected stab of regret. The woman was clearly distressed by the realization that her life had been a lie.

Risking life and limb, Salvatore grasped her hand, half-expecting to be tossed across the cell. She stiffened, but she surprisingly didn't go homicidal on him. A step in the right direction, he told himself, savoring the feel of her warm skin that eased the sense of weakness that plagued him.

Cristo, he needed to mate her.

The sooner the better.

"He told you that I murdered your sisters?" he asked.

"And that I was next on your list to die." Her expression assured him that she was grimly clinging to her suspicion he intended to harm her. "He swore he was the only one who could protect me."

"A clever means to keep you in his power."

"Bastard."

"Did he ever reveal why he was so anxious to keep you so close?"

"He's been using my blood in his experiments to change curs into full Weres."

Salvatore shook his head in disgust. The conceited fool. The Weres' power was a mystical force, not a scientific one. A clever man might be capable of making small alterations, as he had done, but what made purebloods immortal was pure magic.

"He can't seriously believe in such nonsense?"

"Oh, he believes." Her fingers unconsciously tightened around his. "Allegedly some ancient werewolf came to him and revealed a vision that his blood would run pure."

"Ancient werewolf?" Salvatore frowned. A Were had given Caine the crackpot vision? It made no sense. "Are you certain?"

"That's what he said."

"Blood runs pure. What the hell does that mean?"

"Hey, it was his vision, not mine."

Salvatore muttered a curse. He felt like he was trying to put together a puzzle with half the pieces missing.

He hated puzzles.

"Did he ever say how he managed to get his hands on you?"

"No." Her eyes narrowed in suspicion. "I suppose if you're telling the truth, and I'm not entirely on board with that theory, then he must have stolen my sisters and I from your nursery."

"It was humans that broke into the nursery."

"Caine could have hired them." She shrugged. "He's never been anxious to put his own neck on the line. Not if he can convince some other schmuck to do the dirty work."

"It's possible."

"You don't sound very convinced."

Because he wasn't.

"There's something I'm missing," he muttered, his gaze lowering to her slender fingers clasped in his hand. Absently he brushed his thumb over her knuckles, relishing her silken skin.

He'd give his favorite Porsche to discover if she was so soft and smooth all over.

Easily picking up the heat stirring in the air, Harley yanked her hand free and glared at him with an impatience that didn't entirely mask her flare of awareness.

"Yeah, you're missing a way out of here. Can you please concentrate?"

"Are you always so bossy?"

"Do you expect me to kneel and kiss your feet?"

He chuckled softly, stepping close enough to wrap his arms around her waist and brush his lips lightly over her mouth.

"You're welcome to kneel, but I have something better for you to kiss."

"Stop that," she muttered, shivering as his lips skated over her jaw and down the curve of her neck. Her fingers grabbed the lapels of his jacket. "Dammit, Salvatore, we're being watched."

Lifting his head, Salvatore glanced toward the tiny hole drilled above the door. He sent out a flare of power, smiling as he heard the small pop, and a whiff of smoke floated through the air.

"Not anymore." Mission accomplished, he returned his attention to more important matters. Nibbling the tender skin at the base of her throat, he shuddered at the need that blazed through him. "That scent is driving me mad."

"Would you . . ." Whatever she had to say was forgotten as Salvatore bit the tender spot where her neck and shoulder met, allowing his fangs to grow long enough so she could feel his mark. She shuddered, her vanilla scent flooding the room. "God."

"You even taste good," Salvatore muttered.

Her fingers clutched his jacket, and her head tilted back to allow him full access to her satin skin. Salvatore didn't hesitate.

He hadn't become king by being slow to grasp opportunity.

Tightening his grip until she was pressed against his thickening arousal, Salvatore nuzzled a path down the line of sports bra, slowing his pace as he reached the soft swell of her breasts.

"What did you do to the camera?" she husked, as if attempting to devise some means of distracting him.

Good luck with that.

It wasn't that he lied when he said he could multitask. The responsibilities that lay heavy on his shoulders meant he could never put aside his duties. Not even when he was enjoying a bit of extracurricular activity.

In this moment, however, the world and his duties could go to hell in a handbasket.

No doubt because this wasn't extracurricular.

This was the main event.

The life-altering woman he hadn't even known was waiting out there for him.

"I can disrupt small electrical devises," he said, his lips moving over her silken skin.

"Great." Her tone was disgruntled, but her fingers had moved to shove into his hair, her heart thumping so loudly he could have heard it even without his inhuman abilities. "You can zap a toaster, but you can't get us out of this cell. A fat lot of help you are."

He chuckled, his fingers skimming up her back. "I have other skills."

"Unless it's picking a lock, I don't want to know about them."

"Yes, you do."

She made an explosive sound of pleasure as he licked the tip of her nipple through the stretchy material.

"Dammit, Caine's going to come down here as soon as he realizes the camera isn't working."

"Good." He nipped the tight bud, growling in pleasure as she quivered in eager response. "I've wanted to have a little chat with him for a very long time."

Without warning she shoved him away, her face flushed as she wrapped her arms protectively around her waist.

"I doubt he'll be in a chatty mood," she rasped.

Salvatore's lips twisted. Under normal circumstances, no Were would have been capable of escaping his grasp. Being king did have its benefits. This whole premating thing sucked.

Well, the loss of his power sucked.

The rest . . .

It was definitely growing on him.

"We'll see." He sucked in a deep breath, attempting to halt any more growing. Time for his own attempt at distraction. "What of the jinn?"

Genuine surprise flashed through her eyes. "How did you . . ." She shook her head. "No, never mind. What about her?"

"What's her connection to Caine?"

"I'm not really sure." The hazel gaze briefly shifted toward the door before returning to Salvatore. A sure indication that Caine had kept his illegal demon under tight wraps. "He claims that he rescued her from a mage who'd held her captive for centuries. I don't know if it's true or not since she always stayed in one of the outbuildings. I only saw her on occasion, and she usually was at a distance."

Salvatore absently nodded. "He must have some means of keeping her hidden or the Oracles would already have hunted her down."

Harley's brows snapped together. "What's your interest in her?"

A slow, wicked smile curved his lips. "Jealous, Harley?"

She turned her head, refusing to meet his teasing gaze. "For God's sake, get over yourself."

His smile remained. "Don't worry. My interest is pure self-preservation. Curs I can handle. I'd rather not provoke a jinn."

"They're so dangerous?"

"Deadly."

She turned back, her expression worried. "Caine said she disappeared in the tunnels. The last I knew, she hadn't returned."

"Then I suppose we'll have to hope for the best."

"Yeah, 'cause that's really worked well so far," she taunted.

"You know, *cara,* when we get out of here, we're going to have to work on that attitude of yours."

"*If* we get out of here, you're not going to have to worry about my attitude. I'll be long gone."

His gaze slid down her slender body. "You can run, but you'll never be able to hide from me." He lifted his head to meet the stunning hazel gaze. "Not ever."

Her jaw tightened. "I've done a pretty good job until now."

Salvatore stiffened. The silver that surrounded him had nearly disguised the prickles of warning that crawled over his skin.

Without thought, he swept Harley behind him and turned toward the door.

"Stay behind me."

"Sexist pig." She punched him square in the back, nearly sending him to his knees. *Cristo.* "I don't need a man to protect me."

He spun on his heel to meet her belligerent scowl.

"This has nothing to do with protecting. I don't want you accidentally stepping between me and Caine."

"Why? What are you going to do?"

"Uberking stuff." Unable to help himself, he caught her face in his hands and roughly kissed her. "Don't move."

He turned back, sighing as he sensed Harley shift so she could see the door. She might be willing to concede his first shot at Caine, but there was no way in hell she was going to hide behind him.

Harley wasn't the cowering sort.

A beat passed before the door was shoved open and Caine entered the room. Salvatore's wolf stirred, instinctively reacting to having a male so close to his mate.

It was his purely human side, however, that was provoked by the man's smooth blond beauty and smug expression.

He wasn't sure what he'd expected when he finally encountered the cur who had been a pain in his royal butt, but it wasn't this slender man dressed in faded jeans and a black muscle shirt, who looked like he should be on the beaches of California instead of leading a cur revolt.

He wanted to smash that too-handsome face.

Or maybe he would just rip off his head and be done with it.

The head ripping off became much more likely as the bastard studied Harley as if she were his favorite bone.

"Harley, my love, you've been a very bad girl," Caine taunted.

"Screw you," Harley muttered.

The blue eyes glowed with a hunger that set Salvatore's nerves on edge.

"Later, pet," the cur drawled. "And only if you behave."

Salvatore stepped close enough to the bars to feel the burn of silver.

"Careful, cur," he warned, his voice thick with warning.

Stupidly confident that Salvatore was contained in his cell, Caine folded his arms over his chest.

"Well, well," he sneered. "If it isn't the glorious King of Weres."

Salvatore glanced toward Harley. "I like glorious better than uber."

She rolled her eyes. "I'll make a note of it."

"Of course, you're not so glorious right now," Caine snapped, obviously not pleased at having his moment of gloating interrupted. "I've seen better looking Ipar demons."

With insulting slowness, Salvatore returned his attention to the cur.

"Easy to be brave when you have me locked in a cage. It would be a lot more impressive if you let me out and faced me like a man."

Caine laughed. "Do I look like a putz?"

"You look like a cur with a death wish."

"Just the opposite. I intend to become immortal."

"Hard to become immortal after I've chopped your head off and fed it to the rats." Salvatore paused, narrowing his gaze. "Still, just out of morbid curiosity, how do you intend to acquire this immortality?"

Caine shrugged. "You aren't the only one with skill in the laboratory."

"Skill and blind hope are two different things. There's nothing in a test tube that can change you into a Were."

Caine tilted his chin, the glow of a true zealot shimmering in his eyes.

"Obviously, there is. I saw it in a vision."

"Did this vision happen to occur while you were indulging in some pharmaceutical pleasures?"

"This isn't a joke," Caine growled.

"Good. I'm not laughing. Where did this vision come from?"

"None of your damned business, Giuliani."

Enough. Salvatore wasn't a patient werewolf under the best of circumstances, and at the moment he was sore, filthy, and trapped in a silver cage. His patience was non-existent.

Without warning his power lashed out, ramming Caine into the wall and holding him there with an invisible but very tangible force.

"It's Your Majesty, cur," he corrected, his voice edged with ice.

Caine struggled, but even with Salvatore weakened, the cur was no match for him.

"Shit."

Salvatore smiled with cruel satisfaction. "How did you get the vision?"

"It was a Were."

"You're going to have to be more specific."

"I don't know." Caine struggled to breathe, his perfect features twisted in a grimace of pain. "Dammit, he didn't give me a name."

"Describe him."

The cur tilted back his head, the veins of his neck popping out as Salvatore's power squeezed his body with brutal force.

"Short," he gritted. "Brown hair, English accent."

"You're keeping something from me." Salvatore cursed the silver bars that prevented him from getting his hands on the cur. The long-distance torture was taking its toll. "What is it?"

Caine's eyes flashed as he struggled to shift. An impossible task so long as Salvatore held him in his control.

"I'm going to kill you," the cur hissed.

Salvatore tightened his grip. "Wrong answer."

The cur's labored breathing echoed through the room as he glared at Salvatore with sheer hatred.

Far preferable to the smug grin.

"His eyes were red even when he was in human form," he at last ground out.

Pure shock gripped Salvatore. *Merda.*

It couldn't be.

He had killed the bastard nearly a century ago.

Still, the description was unmistakable.

"Briggs," he breathed.

Harley moved to his side. "Do you know him?"

"Obviously not as well as I thought I did."

Across the room, Caine snarled in pain. "Release me."

Salvatore gritted his teeth, cursing his weakened state. His hold on the cur was hanging by a thread.

With the last of his strength, he focused on Caine.

"Not until you've offered me a quid pro quo. Get the keys and unlock this cell."

"Rot in hell."

"Don't make me ask you again," Salvatore gritted, but the power behind his words faltered, and with a low growl Caine lurched forward, breaking the invisible bonds that held him.

"Bastard," the cur breathed, reaching behind his back to pull out a handgun he had tucked in the waistband of his jeans.

Salvatore didn't even try to regain command of the infuriated Caine. Instead, he instinctively turned to wrap Harley in his arms, driving her to the ground and covering her with his body.

Chapter Five

It happened so fast, it was little more than a blur to Harley.

One minute she was standing beside Salvatore, and the next she was flat on her back with the damned Were perched on top of her.

She flinched as the sound of a gun firing echoed painfully through the small room, the bullets flying harmlessly overhead, striking the cement wall and filling the air with the bitter scent of gunpowder.

The shooting came to a halt and Harley heard the slam of the door as Caine beat a hasty retreat.

They lay motionless; the rapid beat of their hearts the only sound to break the heavy silence.

Slowly the stench of gunpowder was replaced by Salvatore's rich musk that seemed to seep into Harley's skin, branding her with an awareness that was as unwelcomed as the realization of just how perfect his heavy body felt pressed so intimately against hers.

Damned Were.

He had to be doing some sort of mystical werewolf shit on her.

She refused to believe that his savage magnetism could be anything but a trick.

As if deliberately mocking her desperate theory, Salvatore shifted to settle his hips between her spread legs, his head lowering until his face was pressed against the curve of her neck and the raven hair fell about her like a curtain of warm satin.

A treacherous heat swirled through the pit of her stomach and Harley planted her hands against his chest.

A distraction.

That's what she needed.

And pronto.

"Well, that worked out well," she muttered, her heart slamming against her chest when his lips lightly touched the base of her throat.

"Could be worse," he murmured.

"Get off me."

"Why?" His lips continued to nibble, sending jolts of electric pleasure through her. "We're obviously stuck in here for the time being. We might as well make the best of a bad situation."

Oh . . . God. She squeezed her eyes shut, battling the fierce tug of attraction that flared between them.

Distraction, distraction, distraction . . .

"Did you turn Caine into a cur?" she husked.

He stilled, as if caught off guard by her question. "No."

"Then how did you control him?"

"I'm the king. All curs belong to me."

Harley snorted. Pure arrogance, in all its glory.

"And the Weres?"

"Of course." He nipped the lobe of her ear. "You're mine, *cara*. From the top of your golden head to the tips of your tiny toes, and every delectable curve in between."

Harley felt a flutter of unease as she recalled how Salvatore had held Caine captive.

"No frigging way," she rasped.

He laughed softly, his breath brushing against her skin, making it prickle with excitement.

"In every way." He pulled back to regard her with an unnerving intensity. "And just a word of warning, Harley, I don't share."

Her mouth went dry even as she was shaking her head in denial.

"God, I thought Caine was off his nut."

The golden gaze skimmed down to her mouth. "I make no guarantee of my sanity, but I do promise that my claim to you is very real."

"Salvatore."

"I like the sound of my name on your lips," he muttered, abruptly lowering his head as if unable to resist temptation. "And the taste," he whispered against her mouth. "I especially like the taste."

It was the biting need clutching her body that at last pushed her unease to sheer panic.

Without giving herself time to think, she shoved her hands against his chest, sending him flying off her and onto his back on the cement floor.

"What part of 'get off me' did you not understand?" she rasped, scrambling to her feet to glare down at his amused expression. "What's so funny?"

With a liquid grace he was on his feet, his raven hair tumbling about his lean face and the golden eyes glowing with anticipation.

"I'm a predator."

Like that was some sort of secret?

The man reeked of danger.

"And?"

"And there's nothing I enjoy more than the chase." He smiled, his teeth startling white against his bronzed skin. "Well . . . almost nothing. I have a feeling that on this occasion, the capture is going to be even more satisfying."

Prey? Her eyes narrowed. "You're an idiot if you think I'm some sort of helpless female that's yours for the taking."

"I wouldn't want you if you were helpless. At least not unless you were in the mood to be at my mercy." He reached to stroke a brazen finger down the low scoop of her sports bra. "You might enjoy a night in my handcuffs."

"Yeah." She slapped his finger away. "About as much as I would enjoy having my eyes gouged out."

His smile widened. "I'm going to enjoy teaching you just how many pleasures are waiting for us."

With short, jerky steps, she moved to glare at the door across the room.

"For God's sake, now is not the time or place for this."

He moved to stand directly behind her, the heat of his body searing her back.

"Then when is the time?"

"How does *never* sound to you?"

"Unbearable," he breathed into her ear.

Harley wrapped her arms around her waist. It was either that, or wrapping them around the edible Were. Damn him to hell.

"Can you control Caine even at a distance?" she demanded roughly.

There was a taut silence, then with a faint sigh Salvatore moved to stand at her side, his profile hard.

"Not with you . . ." He sharply cut off his words, sliding a covert glance in her direction. "Not at the moment. The silver disrupts my powers."

She frowned, wondering what he was hiding from her.

"He won't be stupid enough to get that close again."

"He'll be back."

She rolled her eyes. "So now you're clairvoyant?"

"There's no need for clairvoyance. Caine's kept me alive for a reason. Eventually that reason will force him to return."

"It won't help if he's not already in your power. He'll just tranq you or fill the basement with gas like he did before."

He grasped her shoulders, turning her to meet the power of his golden gaze.

"Harley, one way or another, I promise you that we're going to get out of here."

"And you're never wrong?"

"Never."

"Arrogant."

He flashed that devastatingly sexy smile. "Confident."

The fact that she couldn't simply laugh at his egotistical boasts pissed her off. The conceited beast would get them out just to prove her wrong.

She pulled from his grip and eyed him with suspicion. "You know the Were who's helping Caine?"

His smile faded, his expression suddenly grim and forbidding.

"*Si.*"

"I'm assuming from your tone that the two of you aren't BFFs?"

"He was my greatest competition toward claiming the throne."

Harley lifted her brows. "Is there really a throne?"

"Of course." He seemed startled she would even ask. "It's a massive wooden chair with a lot of gilt and velvet cushions. It's also bespelled so that only the true king can sit on it. It helps clear up any doubt as to the next heir."

She grimaced. No doubt there was also a big, gaudy crown with a lot of flashy jewels.

"And your contender's ass wasn't royal enough to fit?"

A feral smile curled his lips. "He wasn't in the mood to try after I ripped out his throat."

"Nice." Harley tossed her head, hoping he didn't notice her tiny shiver of alarm. Salvatore Giuliani would make a very bad enemy. Something to remember. "It's no wonder he's chummy with Caine. They both hate your guts."

"Actually, it's more than a wonder. It's nothing less than a miracle."

"Why?"

"Because, after I ripped out Briggs's throat, I cut off his head, carved out his heart, and burned his carcass." The golden eyes flashed. "He should be dead."

"Yeah," she breathed unsteadily. "You'd think."

Salvatore watched Harley grimace, belatedly realizing that it might not be the best strategy to reveal just how brutal he could be when the occasion demanded. Not if he was to convince her that her only hope of safety was in his hands.

Then he shrugged. Unless Caine developed the ability to think with his brain instead of his ego, Salvatore was going to have to kill him. And anyone else who threatened Harley.

Perhaps it was best she knew the truth from the start.

As if coming to the same conclusion, Harley breathed in a deep breath and met his gaze squarely.

Brave and tough.

Just his kind of woman.

"Have you considered the possibility that maybe the Were who's tag teaming with Caine isn't Briggs?"

Ah, if only it were that simple.

"No, the description fits too perfectly." Salvatore shook his head in disgust. "*Cristo.* I should have known his death could not be so simple."

Her sharp bark of laughter echoed through the cell. "You did everything but eat his carcass for dinner. That isn't simple by anyone's standard."

"Not for most Weres, but I already suspected that he was dabbling in magic."

She took a sharp step backwards, her expression oddly wary. "Weres can do magic?"

His smiled with rueful amusement. If he could do magic, he wouldn't be stuck in this damned cell.

"They aren't born with the ability to perform magic like a witch, but any creature—" He broke off as he realized he wasn't being entirely honest. "Well, any creature besides a vampire can be imbued with magic."

"Imbued? I don't understand."

"There are ancient demons who can share their powers with others."

She considered a moment, her expression dubious. "I haven't met many ancient demons, but they've never struck me as the sort to share anything, let alone their power."

"Very perceptive, *cara,*" he said. "Only the very stupid or the very desperate would agree to become a vessel for borrowed magic. The cost is far too high for whatever reward you hope to gain."

"What's the cost?"

"Your life, if you're lucky."

She hesitated before asking the obvious question. "And if you're not lucky?"

"Your soul."

"Damn." The hazel eyes were troubled as she glanced toward the door, perhaps realizing for the first time just how truly perilous their situation was. "Why would this Briggs be willing to give up his soul?"

It wasn't a tough question to answer. Like Caine, Briggs had always been an egotistical jackass who assumed he was a God-given gift to Weres.

The mere thought he wasn't going to be top dog (quite literally), was enough to send him over the edge.

"He's nearly a century older than myself, and until my birth he was considered the leading candidate to become the next King of Weres."

Harley caught on quickly. "And you stole his thunder?"

"What can I say?" He smiled with a faux modesty. "It was known since I was in the cradle that I was destined for greatness."

"You're impossible," she muttered. "What makes you suspect this Briggs is borrowing some demon's power?"

"Besides the fact he came back to life?"

She waved aside his logic. "You said you already suspected he was dabbling in magic before his creepy resurrection. Why?"

Damn, the woman didn't miss a thing.

"Once a Were reaches puberty and begins to shift, his power is more or less set. It's possible to learn fighting skills or to become more cunning, but the level of power doesn't change."

She considered for a moment, then she gave an abrupt nod. "Okay, that makes sense."

"After it became obvious that I would outrank Briggs, he disappeared from Rome for several years, and when he returned I began to sense he had gained strength that he shouldn't have possessed." Salvatore shuddered. "And, of course, there were his eyes."

"His eyes?"

"They stayed crimson even in his human form."

"What does that mean?"

"That he's more wolf than human. He maintains his intelligence and cunning, but any human morals and ethics have been replaced by sheer animal instinct." Salvatore's smile was sour. "Not that he had many morals to begin with."

"And he has black magic."

"*Si.*" Salvatore's jaw tightened. "He will kill without mercy or remorse."

There was a sharp flare of alarm in her eyes. For all her bravery, Harley had the sense to be frightened when she should be.

Thank God. He had enough soldiers willing to throw their lives away.

"Did you ever confront him about his power boost?"

"It was not my place so long as the previous king still sat on the throne."

She snorted. "I find it hard to believe there was ever a time you didn't assume you were the boss."

Salvatore ground his teeth, recalling those long, dark centuries as the previous king retreated from his duties, leaving his subjects in disarray and vulnerable to attack. It was then that the Weres had begun to falter, and even with all his power, Salvatore had yet to halt the slow decline.

A knowledge that gnawed at him with remorseless need to alter the grinding wheels of fate.

And one he rarely shared with anyone.

He shrugged. "I can be diplomatic when the occasion demands."

"Right," she drawled in blatant disbelief. "So what happened?"

He sucked in a deep breath, crushing his ancient fury before it could cloud his concentration.

He would dwell on Briggs and his past mistakes later.

There were enough problems just a tad more urgent at the moment.

"I tried to keep an eye on Briggs, but then the king died and before I could voice my suspicions, Briggs attacked."

"Obviously, you won."

"I did, but it was much more difficult than it should have been." His tone was flat, his words not revealing the grisly battle that had taken him nearly a month to recover from. "One mistake and I would have been the one in the grave."

Something flashed through the hazel eyes.

Horror? Dismay?

Disappointment that Briggs had screwed up the chance to chop off his head?

"Now he's back," she said.

"So it would seem."

"And with a grudge."

"No, with a plan," he softly corrected.

The grudge was a given. Briggs had wanted him dead since the day he was born. The very fact that he hadn't ambushed Salvatore before he realized the bastard was lurking around hinted that he had some plot beyond murder.

"What kind of plan?" she demanded.

"That, *cara,* I don't yet know."

She stabbed him with a frustrated glare. "Well, thanks a butt-load for dragging me into the middle of your feud."

Salvatore moved to capture her face between his hands. There was no way he was going to be the villain of the piece.

"Ah, no, I won't take the entire blame. Caine was the one to drag you and your sisters away from the safety of my lair."

Her chin tilted to that stubborn angle he was beginning to recognize.

"Oh, yeah? If you hadn't been messing with our DNA, then he never would have taken us."

Salvatore studied her breathtaking beauty with a brooding gaze. "I wonder."

"I'm not sure I want to know."

"If Briggs is responsible for Caine's mystical visions, then he's no doubt the one who convinced the gullible cur to steal you from my nursery," he said slowly, speaking his vague suspicions out loud.

"Why?"

"Just another question with no answer."

"Great."

Salvatore stilled as a familiar scent of granite whispered through the air.

"Damn."

Her eyes widened. "What is it?"

"The cavalry," he muttered with a grimace. "Unfortunately."

"Why unfortunately?"

Salvatore turned his head to watch the drain cover in the middle of the cement floor shoot upward, followed by a small gray form pushing out of the hole.

"Because the only thing worse than being stuck in this cell is being rescued by that."

Once clear of the drain, Levet gave himself a shake like a wet dog to regain his usual lumpy shape, a smirk curling his lips as he met Salvatore's resigned frown.

"Oh, Wilma, I'm home."

Chapter Six

Obviously less conflicted about their rescue, no doubt because she had yet to spend any quality time with the annoying pest, Harley hurried toward the edge of the cell, kneeling beside the silver bars.

"Levet," she breathed, her voice softening in a way that made Salvatore grit his teeth. How the hell had he become the bad guy, while the stunted gargoyle was treated like a long lost friend? "What are you doing here?"

Levet waddled forward, careful to keep a distance from the bars. Even gargoyles were allergic to silver.

"*Ma belle,* you did not believe I would abandon you to a pack of mangy dogs?"

"How did you follow us?"

"Fah." He waved a clawed hand. "As if I could be outwitted by a mere witch."

"Stop preening and get us the hell out of here," Salvatore growled.

"I see that you are in your usual charming mood," Levet sniffed, carefully reaching through the bars to pat

Harley's hand. "I do not envy you, poor Harley, for being trapped with this foul beast."

She shot Salvatore a taunting glance. "You have no idea."

"Levet, do you remember that conversation we had about your wings and whether or not they remain attached to your body?" Salvatore said, his soft tone making the gargoyle take a hasty step backwards.

"Bully." His tail twitched. "If it were not for your lovely companion, I would leave you here to rot."

"Just hurry, gargoyle."

Moving to the door of the cell, Levet studied the lock, his heavy brow lowering.

"Uh-oh."

"What?"

"The lock has been spelled."

"I thought that no witch could outwit you?"

Levet managed to look offended. "I can blast through it, but you are always so testy when I blow things up."

Salvatore muttered a curse. "Perfect."

Levet tilted back his head and tested the air. "There are six curs in the house and three more outside." He stabbed Salvatore with a questioning glance. "Can you overpower them?"

"No."

"Some king you are . . ." Levet bit off his words, his gaze sliding toward Harley as he belatedly recalled the reason for Salvatore's lack of power. "Oh."

"Precisely."

"What?" Harley frowned. "What's going on?"

Salvatore ignored his companion as he concentrated on the small gargoyle.

"Can you reach Styx?"

"*Non,* we are too far away. I attempted both Tane and

Jagr, but I could not locate either of them. I could perhaps reach your curs."

"No, I won't have them rushing here on a suicide mission," Salvatore said without hesitation.

"Oh, but it is fine for me to risk my neck?"

"Absolutely."

Levet sent him a raspberry, but before Salvatore could reach through the bars and rip out the gargoyle's tongue, Harley straightened and sent him an impatient glare.

"Can we just concentrate on getting out of here?" she snapped. "Caine might be a lowly cur, but eventually he's going to smell a gargoyle in his basement."

Salvatore swallowed a sigh of resignation. If it was ever discovered he'd been rescued by a pint-sized gargoyle, he'd never live it down.

"Can you blast a hole big enough for us to get through?" he grudgingly demanded.

Levet glanced toward the thick ceiling. "Not without the possibility of the house falling on our heads."

"Not up," Salvatore corrected. "Down."

Levet paused, sniffing the air. "A tunnel."

"More than one." Salvatore shifted his gaze to Harley. "Do you know where they lead?"

"No." She shook her head. "I was never allowed in them."

"We'll have to risk it," he said, knowing even as the words left his mouth he was going to regret this. The gargoyle was a walking disaster. "Levet?"

The tiny demon lifted his hands. "Stand back."

Wrapping his arms around Harley, he hauled her to the back of the cell, doing his best to protect her from the silver bars, as well as the coming explosion.

"What are you doing?" she muttered. "The silver . . ."

"Trust me, the silver is the least of our worries," he said, tucking her head in the hollow of his shoulder.

He had a clarifying instant to recognize just how perfectly she fit against him before the shocking concussion hit, the air filling with a deadly bombardment of silver shards as Levet burst open the cell. Hastily spinning, Salvatore used his back as a shield, grinding his teeth as tiny slivers of silver lodged in his shoulder.

"Holy shit," Harley breathed.

"Hold on," Salvatore growled, already knowing what was coming next.

There was another explosion, this one sending powdered cement rather than the deadly silver pelting against him, thank God, and tightening his arms around Harley, he braced himself as the floor beneath them disappeared and they tumbled into the tunnel below.

The jarring impact of the landing wrenched Harley from his arms, and cursing the pain of the silver digging into his flesh, Salvatore crawled forward, using his hands to search for his mate through the thick cloud of dust.

"Harley." His hands found her sprawled on the hard dirt. "Are you hurt?"

She coughed, sitting up to brush the dirt from her face.

"I'm fine." The dust began to clear and she glanced up at the gaping hole above. "Levet?"

"I am here, *ma belle*." With a delicate flap of his wings, Levet stepped off the edge of the hole and floated down, landing beside Harley with a small bow. "Your magnificent knight in shining armor in all his glory."

Salvatore rose to his feet, inwardly contemplating the pleasure of roasting the gargoyle over an open fire. The damned demon didn't have a speck of dust on him, while the rescue had left Salvatore covered in a new layer of filth, his back aching from the fall, and a half dozen silver splinters in his shoulder that were already aching.

"Your glorified head is going to be displayed on Caine's trophy mantel if you don't get a move on it," he rasped.

Levet snorted, assisting Harley to her feet. "As if I fear a flea-bitten cur."

Striding forward, Salvatore knocked away Levet's hand and pulled Harley close. His logical mind understood he was being ridiculous. His instincts, however, couldn't bear for any man to be near this woman.

"Caine's working with a powerful Were who has tapped into black magic," he snapped.

Levet's eyes widened in alarm. "*Sacre bleu.* What are you waiting for?"

Salvatore shook his head as the demon scurried down the dark tunnel, his tail twitching in agitation. He turned to regard his companion with a somber expression. Who knew what was waiting for them?

"Stay close," he warned softly.

Her eyes flared in the darkness. "As if I have a choice."

"You never did," he said, leaning forward to steal a short, possessive kiss.

Then, grabbing Harley's hand, he tugged her to him as they strode after the retreating gargoyle.

Salvatore kept their pace slow but steady as they wound their way through the dark tunnel. He wasn't running headlong from one enemy, only to blunder blindly into the clutches of another.

Not that his reasonable caution was appreciated by his companions.

At his side, Levet muttered French curses and behind him, Harley kept herself occupied by comparing him to several body parts of animals, none of them complimentary.

What was the point in being king if he couldn't have a little respect?

Gritting his teeth, Salvatore attempted to ignore the silver that remained imbedded in his flesh, making it impossible for him to shift into wolf form. His wounds wouldn't heal so long as the silver remained.

And worse, it was another drain on his fading strength.

The very thing he didn't need.

He intended to make Caine and Briggs pay for every moment of this misery.

In blood.

Levet broke off his inventive curses, glancing over his shoulder. "The curs have entered the tunnel."

Salvatore's pace never faltered. "They won't be the only ones."

"What do you mean?" Harley demanded.

"If Caine has any sense at all, he'll have sent a few curs overhead to try and cut us off at the exit."

"So you have effectively trapped us down here?" she accused, her angry tone unable to hide the fear he could sense in the air.

"Of course not," he smoothly lied, coming to a halt. The mark of any great leader was convincing others you knew what you were doing, even if you didn't have a clue. Besides, he didn't want to listen to any more bitching. "Levet, can you cut off our pursuers?"

The gargoyle sniffed. "My talents are boundless."

"Can you do it without bringing the entire tunnel down on our heads?"

He lifted his tiny hands toward the ceiling. "We shall see."

Not entirely reassured, Salvatore grabbed Harley's arm and pulled her farther down the tunnel.

"You might want to give him some room," he muttered. Then, as a pulsing shaft of light speared through the darkness, he abruptly turned his head. "And hide your eyes."

"Not again," she muttered, the words barely leaving her lips when the explosion sent them both tumbling backwards.

Rolling on top of Harley, Salvatore protected her from the flying debris, relieved that they were the usual rocks and clumps of dirt to be found in a tunnel. He wasn't in the mood for any surprises.

"Ta-da," Levet chirped, his wings flapping with pride as Salvatore rose to his feet and pulled Harley upright. They all silently studied the seemingly solid wall of dirt that now blocked the tunnel behind them. Then, just when Salvatore hoped that something had actually gone right, Levet glanced toward the low ceiling. "Oops."

"Oops?" Salvatore growled.

"Maybe we should hurry."

Salvatore heaved a resigned sigh. "Damn."

As one, they turned to sprint forward, no longer concerned about what might lie ahead, just as dirt began showering down on their heads.

The dash to stay ahead of the cave-in lasted nearly two miles, but at last the ceiling once again became stable, and better still, the tunnel widened and branched into two separate passageways.

Salvatore came to a halt, waiting for Levet to skid to a stop at his side. Despite his perfect vision in the dark, this cramped and dank place was more suited to a gargoyle than a Were.

"What do you sense?" he demanded.

Levet sniffed the air and pointed his hand to the right. "This tunnel has an opening thirty or forty feet past the curve." There was more sniffing. He pointed to the left. "That one . . ."

"What?" Salvatore prompted.

"It continues on, but I cannot tell more than that. It has not been used for several years."

Salvatore hesitated only a moment before coming to his decision.

"Can you get past any curs who will be waiting?"

"If you are attempting to insult me . . ."

"Can you do it?"

Before Levet could answer, Harley grabbed his arm and jerked him around to meet her scowl.

"Just hold on. What are you planning?"

"We have to split up."

"Split up? Are you kidding?"

"If Levet can get past the guards, he can contact Styx and let him know we're in trouble."

She blinked in surprise and Salvatore smiled wryly. Hell, she couldn't be any more shocked than he was. Before this moment, he would have laughed at the suggestion he would deliberately seek out the leeches for help. So far as he was concerned, the only good vamp was one who stayed in his grave, where he belonged.

Unfortunately, the suspicion that Briggs was still alive changed everything. Lunatic curs he could handle. A Were siphoning black magic meant that he had to swallow his considerable pride.

The vampires were the only ones he could trust to keep Harley safe.

"The vampire?" she muttered.

Salvatore grimaced. "As much as it pains me to admit it, we're going to need his help."

"You're going to use the vampires to kill Briggs?"

"For now, all I want is to get away from Caine and his goons," he hedged.

She tried to hide her shiver. "Then shouldn't we be trying to get out of these tunnels?"

"I don't doubt we could fight our way past the curs, but they'll be right on our tails. I prefer to slip away unnoticed."

Her scowled remained. "What of Levet?"

"The curs have no interest in a gargoyle, and once he comes out the curs will be expecting us to be behind him. Hopefully, it will take some time for them to figure out we aren't with him."

She gnawed her bottom lip, trying to find the flaws in his logic.

"Have you considered the possibility that the tunnel might be a dead end?" she at last demanded. "We'll be trapped."

Salvatore slowly smiled. "Trust me."

She snorted. "Not in a million years."

"We'll see." He grabbed Harley's chilled hand and glanced toward the silent demon at his side. "Go, Levet."

Tossing his hands in the air, the tiny demon stomped his way down the dark tunnel.

"Go, Levet. Come, Levet. Sit, Levet," he muttered, making sure his voice carried back to Salvatore. "You do know I am not the dog around here?"

With a roll of his eyes, Salvatore tugged Harley in the opposite direction.

"*Cristo*. I hope one of the damned curs eats him."

"You aren't very grateful," she predictably protested. The damned gargoyle possessed an unfathomable appeal to the fairer sex. Color him baffled. "He did rescue us."

"I will give you anything you desire if you keep that our little secret."

She laughed. "Is the big bad wolf embarrassed to be saved by the itty bitty gargoyle?"

"That itty bitty gargoyle could drive a perfectly reasonable demon over the edge," he grumbled.

Thankfully, Harley was smart enough to let the conversation drop.

"Always presuming we live long enough to get out of these tunnels, what do you intend to do?" Harley demanded.

Salvatore slowed his pace as the passageway narrowed, batting aside the thick cobwebs.

"First I intend to get you somewhere safe," he said, too distracted to consider his words. Stupid mistake. "Then I'll deal with Briggs."

"Ah. So you intend to unload me on the vampires so the manly man can take care of business without having to tend to the helpless womenfolk?"

He winched at the sugary sweetness that dripped from her voice.

"Briggs isn't your battle to fight."

"You can do anything you want to Briggs, but I can keep myself safe, thank you very much," she snapped. "You aren't my mother."

Salvatore was at least smart enough not to press the issue. She would be going to Chicago with Styx. End of story. But there was no need to argue before he could manage to contact the vampire.

"Be thankful I'm not your mother," he instead distracted her. "Sophia wouldn't have been pleased at being locked in a cell. There's no telling what carnage she would have caused."

Harley stumbled, her breath suddenly ragged. "She's . . . alive?"

Something dangerous, almost tender, stirred in the depths of Salvatore's heart.

"She's very much alive," he said gently. "She's been searching for you and your sisters, just as I have."

"So she's near?"

"The last I heard she was in Kansas City."

Harley abruptly shook her head, obviously disturbed by the realization.

"God."

Salvatore kept his gaze trained on the tunnel that was slowly heading upward, sensing his companion would be horrified if she knew the vulnerability etched on her beautiful face.

"Harley."

"What?"

"I don't want you imagining Sophia as some kind of June Cleaver," he cautioned, not wanting her to think a reunion with Sophia was going to be some fantasy lovefest.

The tough female Were didn't have a motherly bone in her body.

"Who?"

He sighed at her confusion. He forgot she was only thirty years old.

"Let's just say she isn't the maternal type."

"What about my father?"

"One of several donors."

"Donors?"

"Sperm donors."

She sucked in a sharp breath. "Of course. I was brewed in your lab," she muttered. Then without warning, she yanked her hand from his grip. "Holy shit."

Salvatore turned his head to meet her horrified gaze. "What?"

"You weren't one of the donors, were you?"

His sudden laughter echoed through the darkness. "No, *cara,* I don't have a God complex."

"Yeah, right."

His gaze skimmed deliberately down her slender form, allowing his searing awareness to heat the air around them.

"I didn't create you to be my daughter, Harley. I created you to be my queen."

Chapter Seven

Harley was thankful that Salvatore's outrageous claim managed to distract her from the knee-weakening relief that there was no possibility he might be her father.

Talk about ick factor.

"Queen?" she asked. Okay, it was more a squeak, much to her embarrassment.

Salvatore flashed a smile. "It's your fate."

"Don't say that."

"Ignoring your destiny won't alter it."

She should have punched the annoying bastard. She didn't believe in destiny. And even if she did, she would make damned sure that it didn't include becoming a part of this Were's harem.

Queen or no queen.

But oddly, it wasn't fury that raced through her. It was . . . excitement.

"Just shut up," she hissed.

She ignored his speculative gaze as the tunnel split in two, and they halted to study the less than appetizing options.

So far beneath the ground it was nearly impossible to

determine which direction they were headed. Especially for Weres, who depended heavily on their sense of smell.

Salvatore hesitated a long moment, clearly no more confident than she was in knowing the best means of escape. Then, with a shrug, he took off down the left passageway.

"This way."

With little choice, Harley followed in his wake. As soon as they were safely away from Caine, she would decide when and where to ditch the arrogant King of Weres.

For now, she was willing to allow him to keep her from being put back in that damned cell.

"If you get us lost down here, I'm not going to be happy," she warned.

"And that would be a change?"

Ridiculously, his sardonic tone made her smile. "Smart ass."

Silence descended as they continued to wind their way through the twists and turns of the narrow passageway, Salvatore's steps slowing the farther they traveled.

She frowned as she studied the broad width of his shoulders that seemed to droop with weariness, and the blood that stained the back of his once elegant jacket.

When had he been injured? And why weren't the wounds healing?

If they were truly deep, then he only had to shift. Once he was in wolf form he could repair even a grievous injury.

Her brooding thoughts were interrupted as they were forced to bend beneath a particularly low section of the tunnel, the distinct sound of a click echoing through the thick, silent air.

"What was that?" she breathed, already knowing it couldn't be good.

Whirling around, Salvatore grabbed her arm and thrust her ahead of him.

"Run."

"What is it?" she demanded, taking off with as much speed as possible in the cramped tunnel.

"A trap," Salvatore rasped.

On cue, there was the sound of grinding metal, then dust began to filter from the sides of the passageway. Expecting yet another ceiling to fall on her head, or the floor to open up and swallow her, Harley was unpleasantly surprised when silver darts began shooting from hidden slots in the walls.

"Shit."

She crouched low and charged through the dark, hissing as one of the darts sliced through the back of her arm. Two more darts yanked through her ponytail, and one passed close enough to her ear that she heard it whistle.

She lost track of time, focused on dodging the barrage of silver that continued to shoot from the dirt walls.

Not a bad thing to focus on, considering the dart she barely avoided before it slammed into her temple.

It was not until the pelting projectiles had slowed to an occasional unpleasant surprise that Harley at last realized that Salvatore had fallen several steps behind, his beautiful face covered in a sheen of sweat, his hair plastered to his head.

She stumbled to a halt, an odd alarm clenching her heart.

"Salvatore?"

He stabbed her with an annoyed glare, his eyes glowing with a golden light.

"Just keep running."

A stray dart shot between them and Harley heaved a resigned sigh. She couldn't just leave him. Not when he was obviously injured.

Why she couldn't was not something she intended to mull over.

"Crap." Moving to his side, she draped one of his arms around her shoulders and grabbed him around the waist, taking as much weight as he would allow as they continued down the tunnel. "What's wrong?"

"When Levet broke into the cell, it sent a shower of silver in my shoulder," he grudgingly confessed. "It's draining my strength."

That would certainly explain his inability to shift, and his weakness. Still, she couldn't shake off the sensation that he wasn't being entirely honest.

"We have to find some place to rest," she said, her own legs beginning to feel the strain as the tunnel dipped and curved, leading to seeming nowhere.

"No." He sucked in a shaky breath. "This tunnel isn't safe."

She sighed, pretending she didn't notice his musky male scent and the heat of his hard body that was sending tiny flutters through the pit of her stomach.

"Are you always so stubborn?"

He managed a crooked, knee-weakening smile. "I'm charmingly determined."

Charmingly determined? He was frigging beautiful was what he was.

Even covered in filth, with his suit in tatters and his hair tangled, he was drop-dead, mind-numbingly beautiful.

"You're a pain in the ass," she muttered, more annoyed by her potent awareness of this Were than his teasing.

"As long as it's your ass . . ." His drawling words trailed away, his golden eyes narrowed. "Wait."

She frowned, grudgingly coming to a halt. "I thought you wanted to keep moving?"

He reached out a slender hand to press it against the side of the tunnel.

"There's a way out just behind this wall."

Harley squashed the distraction of Salvatore's presence and concentrated on the wall, feeling the echo just beyond the dirt.

"I feel it." She opened her eyes. "Can we get through?"

Salvatore straightened, pulling away from her. "There's only one way to find out."

Before she could point out they were currently absent a pick and shovel, Salvatore whirled in a movement too fast for human sight and kicked his foot against the hard dirt. Harley winched as his foot punched a large hole through the wall, revealing there was indeed an opening on the other side.

Damn. He could knock off a man's head with that kick.

Or the head of a mouthy female.

Dismissing the unpleasant possibility, Harley moved forward, tugging at the clumps of crumbling dirt to enlarge the hole. She had barely started when Salvatore was at her side, his breath rasping as he shoved at a particularly stubborn rock.

"You don't have to be Superman," she said tartly. "I can do this."

His brief smile was strained. "The sooner we get out of here, the sooner we can find someplace safe to hide."

Harley grimaced, feeling as if she had been dipped, dredged, and battered in grime.

"This someplace better have a shower."

Salvatore grunted, managing to shove aside the rock.

Then, without hesitation, he pressed himself through the narrow opening. Harley rolled her eyes as she hurried behind him. Clearly it didn't occur to him to allow her to take lead, despite the fact he looked close to total collapse.

Typical.

He'd rather fall flat on his face than admit he needed a woman's help.

She had always suspected that testosterone sucked any common sense from the male brain.

Entering the cramped chamber carved in the dirt, Harley paused to take in her surroundings. Not an overwhelming task. There was nothing more than a pile of stones in one corner, and across the room, an opening that revealed some roughly carved stairs.

She had, however, heard Caine speak of his various spiderweb of tunnels, and she knew there was more here than met the eye.

"The stairs," Salvatore muttered, heading toward the opening.

"Hold on."

His expression tightened with a weary impatience. "Harley."

"Caine always keeps stashes hidden, in case of a hasty exit," she said, moving to the loosely piled stones. Her kick held considerably less impact that Salvatore's, but it was enough to send the rocks flying to reveal a pile of objects that had been hidden beneath them. "See?"

Moving to her side, Salvatore reached to pluck the two loaded handguns off the ground, surprisingly shoving one into her hand before tucking the other into his waistband at his lower back.

The large ivory-handled dagger disappeared into a holster beneath his tattered pant leg, but he appeared far more interested in the tiny silver medallions that were half-buried beneath the dirt.

Most people would dismiss them as pieces of junk. A stupid mistake.

"I recognize these," he said, gathering the medallions in his hand, a smile of satisfaction curving his lips.

Harley shrugged. "Amulets."

He tilted one of the amulets to display the odd symbol etched into the thin metal.

"Caine's cur pack used these to hide from me while they were in Hannibal."

Abruptly, Harley realized that Salvatore's scent had disappeared. Completely and utterly.

"Holy shit."

"Here." He pressed an amulet into her hand. "Keep it on you."

She absently tucked the amulet into her sports bra, unnerved that Caine had possessed such a powerful tool that he'd never bothered to share with her.

But why should she be surprised? Caine had never been subtle in his obsession to keep her from slipping away from his control.

This amulet would have offered her the opportunity to escape without fear.

"No wonder Caine keeps so many witches on his payroll," she gritted, annoyed that she'd been so easily fooled.

"I thought he took them to his bed."

"Fringe benefits." She shrugged. "Or at least they seem to think so."

The golden gaze studied her with an unwavering intensity. "But not you?"

"I'm not interested in being the flavor of the month." She met his gaze squarely. "For any man."

Without warning, he leaned forward to brush a possessive kiss across her lips.

"Good."

Harley shot upright, frowning at the jolt of pleasure that raced through her.

"I don't need your approval."

Chuckling at her unmistakable blush, Salvatore grasped her hand and tugged her toward the stairs.

"Let's go, sunshine."

With Salvatore's luck running from bad to extremely shitty, it was nothing less than a shock when the stairs led to a narrow exit that was well hidden and cur-free.

Not that he lingered long enough to appreciate his unexpected stroke of fortune.

Keeping a steady pace, Salvatore ignored the fact that St. Louis was less than an hour away, along with a strong Were pack that he could call on to protect him. Instead, he headed directly north, toward the far more distant Chicago and the damned leeches.

Harley's expression was puzzled as they ran past the fields and dark farmhouses, but for once she kept her opinion of his leadership abilities to herself. Or perhaps she simply concluded that Caine was more likely to start his search on the roads leading south.

In either case, Salvatore was relieved not to have to fight with the female. In his current state, he wasn't at all certain he could win.

Devoting the majority of his attention to making sure that nothing leaped at them from the cornfields and thick patches of trees, Salvatore wearily tripped over a fallen log that was hidden by the thick weeds.

"Enough," Harley snapped, an odd anger in her voice

as he smoothly regained his balance and turned to meet her glittering gaze. "We have to find someplace to rest."

He regarded her in a thoughtful silence. Was she concerned for him?

"There's a town just beyond the hill."

"A town?" Her brow furrowed. "I'm not sure that's a good idea. Caine could have spies anywhere, and we don't exactly blend in."

"Then we'll be careful not to be seen." Taking her hand, he pulled her through the field and up the gentle swell that overlooked the small town. "There."

He could feel Harley's tension increasing as they neared the outskirts of the sleeping town, reaching a near panicked level as they traveled through the handful of blocks that made up the business district. Salvatore kept a firm grip on her hand as he headed straight toward the L-shaped motel that promised cable TV and Internet access.

He was too close to the promise of a hot bath and clean sheets to risk having to spend the rest of the night chasing his high-strung companion.

Carefully testing the air, Salvatore rounded the back of the motel, halting at the door nearest the end of the building. There were only a few guests occupying the various rooms, and all of them were human.

"We can't check into a motel like this," Harley hissed, tugging her hand free to indicate his filthy, unkempt appearance. "They'll call the police."

Salvatore smiled, moving forward to turn the knob, easily breaking the lock and shoving open the door.

"I have my own check-in system."

Not nearly as impressed by his ability to find them shelter as she should have been, Harley stepped through the door and flipped on the light. Following behind her, Salvatore grimaced.

Okay, maybe he couldn't expect her to be excessively impressed.

Perhaps not even slightly.

The room was larger than those in newer hotels, with a bed on one side and a pair of chairs and small table set beneath the window on the other. But the cheap furnishings had long ago given up the battle against shabbiness, and the turquoise paint was peeling off the wall. And the carpet . . .

Salvatore shuddered.

He moved across the room to peer into the bathroom, prepared for the chipped shower and vanity in a nasty shade of salamander.

Moving to his side, Harley wrapped her arm around her waist, her expression tense.

"What if the manager rents out this room?"

"Highly doubtful at this hour, even if there was anyone desperate enough to stop here." He slid a challenging glance in her direction. "Do you want a shower or not?"

"And what are you going to be doing?"

He smiled. "Making myself useful."

"Forget it."

"Take your shower, *cara,*" he murmured, stealing a swift kiss before pressing her into the bathroom. "I'm in no condition to scrub your back. At least not with the attention to detail that I prefer."

Her eyes narrowed, her expression defiant. "I'm locking the door."

"I insist, and keep that gun where you can use it," he murmured, pulling the door shut and waiting for her muttered curse and the lock to be slammed into place before turning to head out of the motel room and into the night.

A weary smile curved his lips as he moved silently through the shadows, heading toward the stores that had closed hours before.

He was on the run from a Were who should have died centuries ago, he had no idea what had happened to his servants, he had no money, no cell phone, and the silver digging into his shoulder felt like ragged shards of lava, but there was no mistaking the raw, primitive satisfaction that burned through his blood.

Finding Harley completed him.

It was that simple and yet, that insanely complex.

And it was nothing less than a miracle.

Halting at the back of a dress shop, Salvatore easily dealt with the cheap lock, using his powers to turn off the alarm system. Collecting a few plastic bags, he moved through the darkness to fill them with a change of clothing for Harley and himself, as well as a nightgown that Harley would no doubt insist upon wearing.

He hesitated a moment over the delicate lingerie, ruefully choosing a sports bra and matching undies rather than the silky thongs. Harley would choke him in his sleep with the thong if he brought it back to the motel.

Perhaps someday . . .

He paused long enough to empty out the cash register, making a mental note to reimburse the owner. Not that he particularly cared about a human's business. But if Darcy discovered he'd stolen from the shop, she would pester him for weeks about his corrupted karma. And unfortunately, he might need the tenderhearted Were to convince Harley that he wasn't some rabid monster who was plotting to kill her.

Leaving the dress shop, Salvatore made a stop at the

small deli to scoop up several packaged sandwiches and bags of chips before making a final sweep of the neighborhood and returning to the motel room.

Careful to close the door and slide the bolt, Salvatore turned and . . .

"Dio," he breathed, staring at Harley as she stood in the middle of the hotel room.

Her wet hair hung loosely around her shoulders, the amulet dangled on a thin strip of material she'd ripped from a washcloth and tied around her neck, she wore nothing more than a towel she'd wrapped around her still damp body, and the gun was held in one hand with a casual expertise.

She should have looked ridiculous.

Instead, Salvatore felt as if he'd just been kicked in the gut as he met the hazel eyes that flashed with a smoldering fury.

She was sexy, and dangerous as hell.

"Where have you been?" she demanded, her hand tightening on the gun. As if she was considering the pleasure of shooting him.

He reached down to grasp the bags and piled them onto the bed, clever enough to hide his smile of satisfaction at her annoyance.

"We needed supplies," he smoothly explained.

"And what if you'd stumbled across one of Caine's pack? Or that Briggs?"

He turned to meet her scowl. "Were you worried for me, Harley?"

She stiffened, not about to admit the truth.

"You're in no condition to be out running around."

"Ah, you do care."

"You might have led them here."

"I wasn't followed."

Prowling forward, Salvatore stripped off his tattered jacket and shirt, tossing them on the floor.

Harley instinctively stepped back, although she couldn't hide the manner in which her gaze lingered on his bare chest.

"What are you doing?"

"I need you to dig out the silver in my shoulder."

"With what?" She shook her head as Salvatore reached down to pull the dagger from the sheath at his ankle. "No. No way."

Salvatore plucked the gun from her hand, tossing it on the bed before pressing the hilt of the dagger into her unwilling fingers.

"It has to be done, Harley. I can't reach them."

She clenched her jaw, trapped between her desire to condemn him to hell and the knowledge that his injuries wouldn't heal until the silver was gone.

"Damn." She pointed toward the chair by the small table. "Sit down."

Taking his seat, Salvatore waited until Harley was standing rigidly behind him, reaching over his shoulder to grasp her hand and press it to his lips.

"Just the silver, *cara*."

She predictably yanked her hand from his touch, but Salvatore didn't miss the care she took not to jostle his shoulder.

"If I decide to kill you, it won't be with a knife in the back," she muttered. "Hold still."

Bracing his hands against his knees, Salvatore closed his eyes and concentrated on his breathing. Unlike vamps, he didn't have the ability to go into a healing trance to avoid his injuries. Until he could shift, he had to grin and bear it.

Well, not grin.

It was more of a groan-really-loud and bear it.

Bowing his head, Salvatore clenched his teeth, trying to remember he was a macho king, while Harley sliced through his flesh, searching for the silver shards that had burrowed deep beneath the skin.

Harley cursed beneath her breath as she struggled with a particularly defiant shard.

"Am I hurting you?" she rasped.

"Harley, you're cutting into my shoulder with a rather large knife," he pointed out softly.

There was another searing jolt of pain, then blessed relief as the last of the debilitating silver was removed and his natural powers kicked into gear.

"I think that's it," she muttered, giving a tiny squeak of alarm as Salvatore surged from the chair and with a burst of energy, shifted into his wolf form.

At any other time, Salvatore would have taken smug pleasure in Harley's gaze that clung to his large body with unconscious appreciation, perhaps even have done a bit of showing off to prove the strength of his body and the beauty of his thick raven fur.

Now, he sprawled on the carpet and shuddered as he struggled to heal his wounds, feeling as weak as a pup despite the mystical forces that flowed through his blood.

Any preening would have to wait.

A damned shame.

It was one of his finer talents.

His shoulder cramped as the torn muscles and punctured skin knit back together, the burned flesh being restored, although it remained tender. Tired, hungry, and weakened by the mating bond, it would take some time for him to fully recover.

Allowing himself only a brief moment to savor the

primitive pleasure of embracing his wolf, Salvatore grudgingly shifted back to human, indifferent to his lack of clothing as he shakily rose to his feet.

A Were was rarely modest.

He did pause to scoop the amulet off the carpet. He didn't know enough about magic to know how close he had to keep the thing to hide his scent, but he wasn't willing to take any chances.

"*Cristo.* I need a shower," he muttered, crossing toward the bathroom. "There's food and clothes for you in the bags."

"Are you going to be okay?"

"You're not getting rid of me that easy." He glanced over his shoulder and pointed toward the bags on the bed. "Eat."

She stuck out her tongue. "Yes, sire. At once, sire."

"And behave yourself."

Leaving the door to the bathroom open, Salvatore stepped into the shower, sighing in relief as the hot water poured over his body. He was less pleased by the cheap motel soap and shampoo, but at least it managed to scrub away the grime, and wrapping a towel around his waist, he ripped a strip off a washcloth to tie the amulet around his neck.

He shoved the wet hair from his face and returned to the main room, a small smile curving his lips as he discovered Harley had pulled on the flannel nightgown that fell past her knees.

No doubt she assumed the repulsive garment would stifle his rampant desire. Instead, Salvatore found himself pondering the various methods of stripping it off.

He could do it slow, tugging the ugly fabric upward to reveal the body beneath, inch by glorious inch. He could do it quick, ripping open the gown with a sharp jerk. He could do it using nothing more than his teeth.

Pacing the floor with short, jerky steps, Harley watched as he moved toward the bed, her expression oddly wary.

"Now what?" she demanded.

"Now I eat and we get some rest," Salvatore said, casually tugging off the towel and reaching in one of the bags for a pair of black satin boxers.

With a choked sound, Harley turned abruptly to stare at the wall, her back rigid.

"Can't you call someone to come and pick us up?" she gritted. "This isn't the most secure location."

Pulling on the boxers, Salvatore settled on the bed, leaning against the headboard as he took three of the roast beef sandwiches and wolfed them down.

Literally.

"I intend to be on the move before anyone could reach us. Is there a problem?"

"Do you want a list?" There was a pause, then squaring her shoulders, Harley turned to scowl at him. "Tell me why you don't want to call your pack. The truth."

Salvatore stiffened in surprise. He hadn't expected her to be able to read him with such ease.

It was . . . unnerving.

He wiped his hands and piled the empty wrappers on the nightstand.

"I have no proof, but I suspect that Briggs is capable of controlling the minds of both Weres and curs, if only for a short amount of time," he confessed.

Her brows lifted. "Did he control your mind?"

"No, but before I battled him, I was attacked by Weres who had always been unquestionably loyal to me." His hands clenched in ancient anger. "I was forced to kill more than one of them."

"Maybe they just weren't as loyal as you thought they were."

Salvatore shrugged. He wished she was right. It was easier to accept he'd killed traitors rather than faithful companions who'd been under the compulsion of Briggs.

Unfortunately, he knew his servants too well.

They would carve out their own hearts before betraying him.

"I'm not going to take any chances."

"But you are taking a chance," she pointed out. "For all you know, my mind might be under the control of Briggs."

Salvatore snorted. "You're too bloody stubborn to be controlled by anyone. Besides, I've been with you for hours. I doubt Briggs's power lasts more than a few minutes."

She considered his words, absently nibbling on her thumbnail.

"I suppose it would explain Caine's ridiculous belief he had some sort of vision," she conceded.

"I'd say his outsized ego has as much to do with his visions as Briggs's," he muttered.

She ignored his sour opinion of the cur. "It seems risky to expose vampires to a magic-mad Were."

"The vamps are impervious to mind control. Unfortunately, it's too close to dawn for them to travel. We'll have to wait until tomorrow night to meet up with them." He patted the mattress. "For now we rest."

She licked her lips, abruptly appearing more disturbed by joining him on the bed than his confession that Briggs could control minds.

"Fine. You rest and I'll keep watch," she croaked.

"I already did a sweep. No one knows that we're here."

"You can't be sure . . ." She sucked in a startled breath

as Salvatore slid off the bed, and with fluid speed, had moved to snatch her off her feet. "Dammit, put me down."

"With pleasure."

With two long strides he was tossing her onto the bed and swiftly covering her with his body. A violent pleasure surged through him at the feel of her slender curves that fit perfectly against him.

Dio.

He didn't know if it was the mating bond that made him react with such raw, biting hunger to this particular female, or if it was simply a normal reaction between a man and woman, and in truth, he didn't care.

He wanted her.

Now.

Salvatore watched the hazel eyes darken as Harley reacted to the prickling heat that filled the air, able to hear the sudden leap of her heart.

"Get off me," she gritted, clearly not as pleased as Salvatore by their explosive response to one another.

"We're staying in this bed, Harley," he warned. "It's up to you whether we sleep, or enjoy a more pleasurable pastime."

Chapter Eight

Harley wrenched her gaze from the molten gold of his eyes, feeling as if she were slowly melting beneath the potent heat of his desire.

What the hell was wrong with her?

She was in a cheap motel, on the run because she'd been stupid enough to allow her curiosity to overcome her common sense, and in bed with a king she had been taught to fear and loathe for the past thirty years.

She should be kicking some serious Were butt, not battling the urge to sink her hands in that thick raven hair so she could tug his head down and kiss him senseless.

Of course, in her defense, the man was obscenely beautiful.

Not only his lean, savagely handsome face, but his body that more than lived up to its promise once the ragged clothing had been removed.

His bronzed skin was smooth and stretched tautly over the lean, sculpted muscles that rippled with a fascinating ease. His chest was broad and tapered to a slender waist, his arms were toned without unnecessary bulk, and his hands were perfectly formed, with slender fingers that were currently stroking her shoulders with a tender touch that sent streaks of heat to all her most intimate places.

Yummy goodness from the top to bottom, and every place in between.

Damn him.

"You deliberately picked a room with only one bed, didn't you?" she accused, her voice embarrassingly husky.

"I chose the room farthest from the office and out of sight of the road." A slow, wicked smile curved his lips. "The fact that it only has one bed is a bonus."

"Bonus for you, maybe."

He lowered his head to nuzzle a spot just behind her ear, making Harley's heart stutter in shock. When had that particular spot become so sensitive?

"I could make sure it's a bonus for you as well."

"You're so full of yourself . . ." Her taunting words were completely ruined as his seeking lips found another point of weakness at the base of her throat. "Oh."

"Oh, indeed," he growled, nipping her collarbone. "Do you taste so sweet all over?"

His exotic, musky scent invaded her senses, seeping into her skin like the finest aphrodisiac. The distracting smell clouded her mind, which was the only explanation for why her hands lifted to stroke down the magnificent length of his back.

"What are you doing to me?" she muttered.

His soft laugh brushed over her cheek as he reached down to grasp the hem of her nightgown, and with one smooth motion had it tugged over her head and tossed across the room.

"Do you want a detailed explanation or will a brief

overview do?" he demanded, arching back to run a searing gaze over her body, now covered in nothing more than a pair of white panties.

Harley shivered, the golden gaze a near tangible force as it lingered on her oddly heavy breasts.

"You know what I mean."

"Actually, I don't have a clue."

"You're using some sort of power to . . ."

He shifted, settling between her legs that had instinctively widened. Lowering his head, the raven hair brushed against the puckered tips of her nipples.

"To what?"

"To seduce me."

His tongue flicked over her nipple, the rough stroke wrenching a moan from her throat.

"Power?"

She dug her nails into the smooth skin of his lower back. "Don't laugh at me."

He continued to tease her nipple, his hardening erection pressing with flawless precision against her feminine core. Oh . . . God. It felt good. Insanely good.

"Laughing is not what I want to be doing with you," he said, kissing a path between her breasts.

"Giuliani."

With a low groan, Salvatore surged upward to claim her lips in an openmouthed kiss that was hard with unrestrained hunger. Need blazed through her like wildfire, searing away any hope of resistance.

"I don't know what power you're talking about, *cara,* unless it's the potent appeal of my manly charm," he husked against her lips. "Which I've been told is irresistible."

Her hips arched upward in blatant invitation. "I don't believe you."

"Why?"

"Because I can't want you. I don't even know you."

He chuckled, scorching a path of kisses down her throat. "We have all of eternity to become better acquainted."

She retained enough sense to shy from his possessive tone. The only thing in her life she was certain of was the fact she was tired of being manipulated by others.

From now on, she intended to be in charge of her own life.

"Not likely," she warned, scraping her nails up his back. She reveled in his violent shudder of pleasure. "And if you think this means I'm ever becoming your stupid queen, then you can just think again."

"*Cristo,* Harley," he breathed. "Can't I even kiss you without you arguing?"

"I just don't want you thinking . . ."

His hands skimmed over her body, his mouth planting restless kisses between her breasts and down the quivering plane of her stomach.

"I'm not thinking, *cara,*" he rasped. "And that is supposed to be the point. Let yourself go."

Harley nearly came off the bed when his tongue dipped into her belly button, a shocking bolt of pleasure aiming straight between her legs.

Lord. Salvatore's lovemaking was as intense and ruthless as his personality.

She felt like she was being battered with sensations. The relentless exploration of his hands, the thrilling expertise of his lips, the hard thrust of his erection.

It was like being tossed into the middle of a maelstrom with no idea of how she got there.

"You mean you want me to give myself to you?" she managed to demand.

He lifted his head to regard her with open amusement. "How delightfully Victorian. If you prefer, I can give myself to you."

"Good." Way past the point of no return, Harley decided the only thing left was to take charge of the situation. Running her hands up the curve of his back, she plunged her fingers into his hair, and with one smooth motion she was flipping Salvatore onto his back and straddling his waist. She smiled smugly as she gazed down at his startled expression. "Then you won't mind if I'm on top."

Hell, no, Salvatore didn't mind.

What werewolf didn't like a woman who knew what she wanted—and was daring enough to take it?

Especially if that taking included his body, which was primed and ready to please this female.

Of course, he would prefer if she wasn't glaring down at him as if she was debating between kissing him senseless or breaking his jaw.

Spread across the lumpy mattress, Salvatore allowed his hands to skim up her bare thighs, his gaze drinking in the sight of her delicate face framed by the fall of golden hair, the shimmering hazel eyes. His heart thundered in his chest as his gaze lowered to linger on the perfect breasts tipped with rosy nipples before lowering to the slender curve of her waist.

The male in him reacted with predictable desire to her naked beauty, but the stirring of his wolf was unexpected. He'd never experienced having his animal so close to the surface during sex, and he was caught off guard by the violent excitement that pulsed through his blood.

She sucked in a sharp breath as his eyes glowed with the inner fire of his beast, filling the room with a golden light. But it wasn't fear that rippled over her features. It was the same raw need that clawed at him.

"You wanted to be on top, *cara,*" he said thickly, his hands lifting to cup her breasts, his thumbs strumming her hardened nipples. "Shouldn't you be taking advantage of me?"

Her eyes narrowed at his blatant challenge, her hands tightening in his hair as she leaned down to kiss him with a rough passion that made his wolf growl in pleasure. She tasted of vanilla and woman, magic and power all wrapped in sweet temptation.

Salvatore's hips lifted off the bed, rubbing his aching cock against her. Even through the satin he felt scalded by her heat.

Dio. He needed to be in her.

He needed to mark her with his passion, with his scent, with his very essence.

As if sensing his possessive animal instinct, Harley sharply nipped his bottom lip.

"This means nothing, Giuliani," she muttered.

His hands followed the curve of her waist, ripping off her satin panties.

"Whatever lets you sleep at night, *cara.*"

"Arrogant bastard."

Salvatore sucked in a sharp breath as Harley planted a path of wet, demanding kisses over his chest, her hips rocking against his erection. Arrogant? In this moment he would have happily gone down on his knees to beg Harley to put him out of his misery.

"Harley."

His plea was cut short as she wiggled down his body, the tormenting kisses heading ever lower.

Gritting his teeth, Salvatore shifted his hands to clutch

the blanket beneath him. It was that, or toss her back onto the mattress and take her with a furious hunger.

Unaware of how close he was to the edge, or perhaps simply enjoying her power over him, Harley continued to drive him mad, her lips sending tiny shock waves through his body. Then without warning, her seeking mouth closed over the tip of his cock, the moist heat branding him through the satin of his boxers.

"Cristo." He reached to grasp her arms, hauling her up his body to claim her lips with a force just short of pain. "I throw in the towel, *cara,*" he growled, his accent thick. "I can bear no more."

She deliberately rolled her hips, her smile smug. "Shouldn't a king be able . . ." Her eyes widened with shock as Salvatore reached to jerk down his boxers, and with one smooth motion was lifting his hips to pierce her damp heat. "Oh, God."

Smoothing his hands up her back, Salvatore sucked the tip of her breast between his lips, relishing her low moan of pleasure. She fit as tight as a glove around him, making him tremble with the effort to wait until she was accustomed to his penetration.

"So good," he rasped. "Ride me, Harley."

Planting her hands on his chest, she lifted her hips, drawing him out to the very tip before slowly sinking back down, burying him deep inside her. Salvatore muttered a curse, his hands gripping her hips as he waged war against his looming orgasm.

Dammit. He was famed for his stamina. He could satisfy a woman for hours before claiming his own release. But never before had sex called to both the man and beast inside him.

Sweat gathered on his brow as he concentrated on the mesmerizing beauty of her face. For once her features were unguarded, flushed with passion, and her eyes dilated as she quickened her pace.

His hips lifted to meet her downward strokes, his growl of satisfaction filling the air as her fingernails bit into his chest, drawing blood.

The air was scented with her arousal, her slender body bowing above him as she tipped back her head and lost herself in the pleasure.

"Salvatore," she cried softly, a frantic edge in her voice as her climax neared.

"Cara," he whispered. "Let go."

"I . . ." She moaned in relief as Salvatore tightened his grip on her hips, pumping deep into her with a relentless tempo. "More."

"As much as you desire, Harley," he swore, his hand cupping the back of her head and tugging her down so he could kiss her with savage pleasure.

Their tongues tangled, their bodies moving together with a growing desperation. Then, just when Salvatore feared he was going to explode, he felt Harley stiffen, her cry of completion muffled against his lips.

Salvatore sank his fingers in her satin hair as her climax clutched at his cock, his hips slamming upward as he unleashed his passion in a flurry of unrestrained hunger.

His wolf howled in satisfaction as his orgasm burst through him, the shock waves of pleasure radiating through his entire body.

His.

His woman. His mate.

The other half of himself.

* * *

Salvatore jerked awake, muttering a curse as he realized just how deeply he'd slept.

Not entirely unexpected. He'd been forced to burn through his energy at a dangerous pace while he was injured. His body demanded the time necessary to recover. Even if it left him vulnerable.

Instinctively his arms reached across the bed for Harley. It was one thing to risk his own neck, and quite another to risk his mate.

His eyes snapped open as his seeking hands found nothing but rumpled sheets.

"Harley?" he muttered, his sluggish mind belatedly recalling her smell was masked by the amulet. *Dio.* Leaping from the bed, he tugged on jeans and a white T-shirt as he noted the khaki shorts and shirt he'd stolen for Harley were missing. "Stubborn, ill-mannered brat," he muttered, slipping on the running shoes and shoving his hands through his tangled hair. "When I get my hands on her, I'll . . ." Salvatore stiffened as the scent of cur tainted the air. "Shit."

Gathering the gun and dagger left on the nightstand, Salvatore cautiously slid from the room, avoiding the late afternoon shadows as he inched around the hotel to study the nearly empty parking lot.

Two men stood near the trash dumpster. One was a tall, gaunt human with thinning black hair and a narrow, impressively ugly face. The other was a young cur with clipped brown hair and the muscular body of a weight lifter.

"A blonde, you said?" the human was saying, a cunning light in his pale eyes.

The cur gave an impatient nod. "Traveling with a dark-haired man."

Obviously angling for a bribe, the man cleared his throat. "That's not much to go on."

The cur bunched his muscles, predictably oblivious to the hints. Curs didn't do subtle.

"Don't jerk me around," he warned. "How many strangers do you get in this hillbilly hellhole?"

Stiffening, the man tossed two garbage bags into the Dumpster and headed for the motel.

"Maybe you should just be moving along."

With a low growl, the cur had moved to block the man's path, his hand shooting out to grab his shirt and lift him a few inches off the ground.

"And maybe you should answer my question before I rip out your throat."

"Jesus Christ, what the hell's up with your eyes?"

Muttering a curse, Salvatore was crossing the parking lot. What was wrong with the stupid cur?

The first rule in the demon world was to always avoid the attention of mortals. Those who flaunted that particular law would soon find themselves dead. Or worse, hauled before the Oracles. The ruling Commission could devise punishments that would make death seem like a holiday.

Flowing forward with blinding speed, Salvatore clubbed the cur on the back of the head, calmly stepping over his unconscious form as it tumbled to the cement.

"Forgive me for intruding, but you looked like you could use some help," he drawled.

The human licked his lips, his eyes wide and hands shaking. "Who are you?"

"The man who apparently just saved you from having your throat ripped out."

With a shudder the man glanced down at the unconscious cur. "There's something not right with him."

"Drugs."

"I never heard of a drug turning a man's eyes red before."

"A new designer drug from St. Louis," Salvatore smoothly lied.

The man frowned, but accepted Salvatore's ridiculous claim. "You know him?"

"My partner and I have been tracking him since he escaped from the authorities two days ago."

"You're a cop?"

"Close enough."

Proving he wasn't a full-fledged idiot, the human ran a suspicious gaze over Salvatore's hard features and lethal golden eyes. Not even casual clothes could hide his feral nature.

"Where's your badge?"

Salvatore shrugged. "I'm not here to interfere in your business, I'm just looking for my partner. The blonde this man was asking about."

The man took a wary step backwards. "The blonde?"

"Yes. Have you seen her?"

"I don't want to get involved . . ."

Reaching into his pocket, Salvatore pulled out the roll of money he'd stolen the night before.

"I can make it worth your while." He peeled off a few bills, tossing them at the man's feet. "Where did she go?"

Careful to keep an eye on Salvatore, the human bent down to snatch the money and shove it into his pocket.

"I saw a blonde running up Main Street."

"On foot?"

"Yeah."

"How long ago?"

"Not more than fifteen minutes."

"She was alone?"

The man straightened, shoving the money in his pocket. "As far as I could tell."

With a dip of his head, Salvatore headed toward the street. *"Grazie."*

"Hey, what about this guy on the ground?"

Salvatore's pace never slowed. "Not my problem."

"You can't just leave him here."

"Actually, I can, although I will offer you a word of warning." Reaching the stone wall that marked the edge of the parking lot, Salvatore easily vaulted over it to land on the sidewalk. "You don't want to be nearby when he wakes up."

"Hey . . ."

The human continued to yell meaningless words, but Salvatore was already jogging down the street, forced to keep his pace frustratingly slow to peer in the passing shops.

Cristo. He'd been an idiot to let Harley keep the amulet. It was practically an invitation for the headstrong Were to bolt, knowing he couldn't track her scent. Of course, on the upside, no one else could track her either, he reminded himself. And considering the number of enemies on his trail, that made the amulet a treasure beyond price.

No, if he had a brain in his head he would have let her keep the amulet and instead tied her to the bed.

Salvatore shuddered. Even after hours of sating his rampant desire, his blood still heated and his body hardened at the mere thought of the aggravating woman.

Not surprising.

He'd enjoyed talented lovers over the years, but what happened between him and Harley hadn't been just sex.

It had been a stunning explosion of sensations that had bound him irrevocably to his mate. And he didn't even have the sense to regret the realization that his life was forever altered.

In fact, his only regret was that Harley was obviously not ready to accept their mating.

Reaching the edge of the town, Salvatore took a moment to consider his options. There was always the possibility that Harley had decided to return to Caine. She had to know the cur would be willing to forgive her anything if she agreed to stay with him. There was also the possibility that she'd stolen a car and was even now speeding ever farther away.

His instinct, however, told him that she was still near.

Entering the woods that sprawled north of the town, Salvatore cautiously threaded his way through the thick undergrowth. In the distance he could hear the call of birds and the rustle of small game, but a heavy silence cloaked around him. Not unusual. Animals could sense his predatory nature. It was, instead, the prickle of energy that warned a Were was near.

"Harley?"

Alarm trickled down his spine as the scent of rotting meat filled the air. Whoever was out there, it wasn't Harley.

Swiftly tugging off his clothes, Salvatore prepared to shift. Under normal circumstances there wasn't a Were born who could challenge him. Unfortunately, his unclaimed mating bond made him vulnerable.

Calling his power, Salvatore hesitated as a cold chill blasted from a small clearing just ahead of him and the shimmering outline of a man began to form. His hands clenched as he recognized the short Were with unkempt brown hair and crimson eyes.

He was paler than he recalled, his face thinner, and his eyes an even deeper red. But there was no mistaking the cruel features and whiff of madness that clung to him.

"Briggs," he hissed.

"Ah, Salvatore Giuliani," the man sneered, his English accent as pronounced as it had been centuries ago. Briggs had always been too arrogant to try to blend in with the crowd. Which explained the long black cloak he had wrapped around his slender body. Or maybe his taste in fashion was just that revolting. "You cannot know how long I have waited for this moment."

"I presume you've been waiting since I kicked your ass, tossed you in a fire, and spread your ashes on a dung heap," Salvatore sneered.

The crimson eyes flashed, the chill spreading to bite into Salvatore's skin. *Dio.* What had Briggs done to himself?

"So proud of yourself, and yet here I am."

Salvatore narrowed his gaze. He didn't know jack-crap about magic, but he was certain a Were couldn't suck enough power from his host to pop from one place to another. Briggs had to be projecting his appearance.

Not that it made him any less dangerous.

Or less crazy.

"But not in all your glory," Salvatore taunted, vividly recalling that Briggs's weakness had always been his inability to control his temper. "Afraid to face me like a true Were, magic-sucker?"

"And why should I bother when I have slaves to collect the trash?"

Briggs lifted his arm and Salvatore staggered backwards as the Were sent a crushing command toward the distant curs. The years obviously hadn't taught the Were any restraint. He'd always been a big fan of overkill.

Shaking off the pinpricks of pain, Salvatore studied

his age-old enemy. It wouldn't take long for the curs to arrive. Before then, he needed to know how Briggs was still alive and what the hell he was plotting.

"Surely you can't be idiotic enough to believe your curs can capture me?"

Briggs smirked, confident he had Salvatore cornered. "They are remarkably inept, but they serve their purpose on most occasions."

"Not this occasion." Salvatore shrugged, deliberately nonchalant. "Unless you have a few hundred hidden among the trees."

"As always, you have sadly underestimated me, Salvatore."

"No, Briggs, as always, you've overestimated yourself." Indifferent to the fact that he was stark naked, Salvatore folded his arms over his chest and peered down his nose at the smaller Were. Briggs hated to be reminded of his small stature. "You would think dying once would have taught you that you will never be as good as me. I'm the king, and you're a tainted has-been who has to use black magic because he isn't Were enough to beat me."

"King?" Briggs curled his lips. "You're a pathetic upstart who stole what was rightfully mine."

"If it was rightfully yours, I would never be allowed to sit on the throne. You were found unworthy."

"Bastard." Briggs lifted his arm and Salvatore felt icy bands of power wrap around him, driving him to his knees. "I will make you pay."

"Magic," Salvatore snarled, nearly gagging at the stench of rotting meat. A Were's strength was a warm, earthy force that had nothing in common with the twisted perversion of black magic. "You're pathetic."

Briggs moved toward him, his cloak rippling around him, though the leaves beneath his feet made no sound.

Freak.

"I'm not the one on my knees."

"What do you want?"

"Everything you took from me."

Salvatore spit at the heavy boots that halted mere feet away. "The Weres will never accept a walking corpse who stinks of treachery."

"They will have no choice."

Salvatore's sharp laugh echoed through the trees. "Weres always have a choice."

"I can give them what you cannot."

"And what's that?"

The Were smirked. "A future."

"Future? What the hell is that supposed to mean?"

"Children."

Salvatore sucked in a stunned breath. No. This lunatic couldn't possibly have found the cure to heal the Weres. Fate might be cruel, but it couldn't be completely without mercy.

Briggs was an unstable, power-hungry despot who would lead the Were to certain destruction.

"You think you can produce children with magic?" he demanded.

"I would not be the first Were leader willing to seek help for our people through . . . unconventional means." A taunting smile curved his lips. "How do you think I was first introduced to the power?"

"You lie."

Briggs reached out to run a finger down Salvatore's cheek, his touch leaving a trail of frigid pain.

"I was taken into the king's confidence when it was obvious I was to be his heir." His eyes flashed with pure hate. "Before you were born."

Salvatore gritted his teeth, trying to ignore the unease that stirred in the pit of his stomach.

The previous king had been a reclusive, sometimes volatile beast who too often disappeared for years on end. He'd become even more secretive after Salvatore had come into his powers, rarely mingling among his pack.

But there hadn't been any hint he was brewing up evil in his lair.

That seemed like something Salvatore would have noticed.

"If that was true, then he would have shared the same information with me," he rasped.

"He was warned not to."

"Warned? By who?"

"By the ancient spirits."

"Cristo." Salvatore jerked from Briggs's painful touch. "You're completely nuts."

Fury tightened the gaunt face. "Do not dare to mock me."

"If you're to be the great Messiah, then where are your creations?"

With an effort, Briggs regained command of his temper, smoothing his hands down the ridiculous cloak. "All in good time."

There was no mistaking the Were's smug confidence, and Salvatore was hit by a sudden suspicion.

"God, you can't believe you will change your pathetic curs into purebloods?" He shook his head. "I would expect such stupidity from Caine. But you, Briggs? How disappointing."

Briggs's expression was condescending, reminding Salvatore how much pleasure it had been to cut out his heart.

"I merely offered the cur the opportunity to glimpse

into his future. What he claims to have seen is no concern of mine."

"If it isn't the curs, then where are your supposed children?"

"They will come when the time is right," Briggs assured him. "You interfered too soon."

Interfered? As much as Salvatore wanted to take credit for disrupting Briggs's nefarious plans, he hadn't done anything more than stumble across Caine. And . . . Harley.

A sudden, blinding rage rushed through Salvatore as he struggled against the icy bonds that held him.

"You son of a bitch," he ground out. "You will never have Harley, or her sisters. Never."

"Harley?" Briggs appeared genuinely puzzled. "Ah, Caine's bitch." He shrugged. "She'll no doubt warm my bed, as will all the female purebloods."

Salvatore's rage faltered, his brow furrowed. "You can't fool me, Briggs. You're responsible for stealing the baby Weres from my nursery."

"Of course, I did. And they have proven to be the perfect distraction." He chuckled. "Even better than I could ever have dreamed possible."

"You had four pure-blooded babies snatched for a distraction?"

"I knew how desperately you were pinning your hopes on them and that you would sacrifice anything to retrieve them, even leaving your stronghold in Rome," Briggs drawled, his flagrant conceit etched on his face. "They were mere pawns in your ultimate destruction."

Son of a bitch.

Salvatore shook his head in self-disgust.

Of all the reasons he'd imagined for the theft of the

babies over the past thirty years, he'd never even considered the possibility it had been a plot personally directed at him.

"You deliberately led me here."

"Of course."

"Why?"

"As I said, it is not yet time to reveal my grand scheme," Briggs said, leaning down to better enjoy Salvatore's frustration. "But be assured . . ." He bit off his words as his eyes widened in an unexpected horror. He leaned even closer, sniffing Salvatore's skin. "What is that?"

A savage smile curved Salvatore's mouth. "The mating bond."

Briggs straightened, his pale face becoming downright pasty.

"No. It cannot be."

"Obviously, it can."

Caught in their battle of wills, neither men noticed they were no longer alone. Not until there was the distinct sound of a gun being cocked.

"Checkmate this."

Salvatore's blood ran cold as he caught sight of Harley standing directly behind Briggs, her handgun pointed to the back of the Were's head.

"Harley, no!"

Chapter Nine

Harley was already squeezing the trigger when Salvatore cried out. With deadly accuracy the bullet smashed into the back of the Were's head, the force of the blow sending him tumbling forward.

She instinctively kept the gun pointed at the stranger, her gut clenching as she watched the gaping hole in his skull swiftly knitting back together.

Where was the blood? The gore?

Not even the most powerful Were could be shot point-blank and not take a few minutes to recover.

Well, that was the common assumption.

A pity no one had told the scary Were who was already shimmering with power as he shifted.

Harley's breath disappeared as the lethal animal with russet fur and large razor-sharp teeth turned to regard her with fierce crimson eyes.

Holy shit.

Harley never realized that blood could actually curdle.

Accustomed to curs, she was unprepared for the sheer size and terrifying power of a pureblood. The air thickened, choking her with the heavy sense of danger. Her skin prickled. And her muscles clenched.

Her gut impulse was to flee from the terrifying predator, but Harley possessed enough sense to freeze.

The fastest way to death was to give the big sceevy Were something to chase.

Instead, she steadied her arm and prepared to shoot the beast. It hadn't done much the first time. Okay, it had done *something.* It'd pissed him off. But unable to shift herself, she didn't have much choice.

The Were lowered his head, preparing to attack, but before Harley could get off a shot, a furious howl split the air.

Stunned, Harley stumbled backwards, watching as Salvatore crouched on the ground, his body thickening and his face elongating as a thick raven-black fur rippled over his skin. In the blink of an eye, he was transformed into a huge werewolf.

God, he was beautiful, she acknowledged, her heart squeezing with an odd fear as he crashed into the unknown Were with a violent force.

Rolling across the clearing, the two purebloods ripped at one another with long claws, their jaws snapping. Harley lowered her gun, unable to risk taking a shot as the vicious battle continued.

The scent of blood filled the air, making Harley's stomach clench with dread. Salvatore was the larger, more aggressive Were, but the stranger appeared freakishly immune to his savage wounds.

It had to be Briggs, she told herself. Nothing but black magic could allow the lesser Were to survive Salvatore's brutal fury.

The realization, however, did nothing to reassure Harley.

How was Salvatore supposed to defeat a zombie Were with evil powers?

A pained yelp echoed through the trees as Salvatore at last rolled on top of the squirming Were, latching his teeth deep into his opponent's throat. The fight should have been at an end, but proving his unnatural powers, Briggs continued to claw at Salvatore's back, leaving deep scratches that oozed an alarming amount of blood.

Salvatore couldn't bleed to death, but he would quickly weaken if he wasn't allowed to heal.

Dammit.

Harley found herself moving forward, tired of watching from the sidelines.

She didn't have a clue what would hurt the Were, but she was willing to try anything. Starting with unloading a bunch of bullets straight into his head.

Circling wide enough to avoid distracting Salvatore, Harley waited until she had a clear shot at the Were's head before lifting her arm and aiming the gun.

Almost as if sensing her presence, Briggs shifted his crimson gaze to regard her with a malevolent warning.

God. Her throat tightened with an icy dread, but her arm never wavered. The thing was an abomination. The thought of it creeping around the world would give any sane demon nightmares.

Perhaps reading the determination etched on her face, the Were snarled with fury and Harley was hit with a blast of frigid air. Reeling backwards, she could only watch in horror as the thing disappeared with a loud pop.

Harley ended up flat on her back, more stunned by the Were's vanishing act than by the magical blow. She sucked a breath into her aching lungs, staring at the dappled sun that peeked through the heavy canopy of leaves overhead. Then without warning, her view was blocked by Salvatore's lean, darkly beautiful face.

"Harley?" He'd changed back to human form, but the golden eyes continued to glow with power.

Sitting up, Harley pushed the hair out of her face and studied the hard naked body crouched beside her. It was worth studying at any time, but for the moment Harley's only interest was in the deep wounds that marred his bronzed flesh.

"You're injured," she breathed.

"Nothing that won't heal," he assured her, his expression concerned. "What about you?"

"I'm fine."

To prove her point, Harley forced herself to her feet, knocking the dirt off her khaki shorts as Salvatore moved to pull on his jeans and T-shirt. His movements were stiff, but it was obvious he would recover, and Harley found her rush of adrenaline fading, leaving behind a vague unease.

When she had awoken earlier in the day to discover herself wrapped tightly in Salvatore's arms, she couldn't deny she'd panicked.

It wasn't shock at having so thoroughly enjoyed their night of passion. The man was a flat-out no-holds-barred expert in bed. Even now her body tingled in all the right places at the memory of his skillful touch.

No, it had been the realization that she had so easily forgotten that Salvatore was still little more than a stranger. A stranger that until a day ago she'd believed was her mortal enemy.

For all she knew, he was playing an elaborate game that was going to end with her dead. She'd be a fool to trust him because he happened to be good in the sack.

Besides, for the first time in her life she was . . . free.

There was no Caine with his dire warnings of what would happen to her if she dared to leave his protection. No curs to constantly monitor her every movement.

And with the amulet, not even Salvatore would be able to track her.

So she'd taken off.

Or at least, she'd tried to take off.

Stupidly, she hadn't been able to shake the persistent uncertainty that plagued her as she had headed off to discover her long overdue destiny.

Salvatore claimed that her sisters, and even her mother, were alive. It could be a lie, of course. In fact, it probably was. Still, could she just walk away if there was the smallest chance of being reunited with the family she'd thought she'd lost forever?

Walking alone through the trees, she'd at last accepted that she would never be satisfied until she discovered the truth of her sisters. Her destiny had waited for thirty years. It could hold off a few more days.

So she'd turned around.

Watching the annoyingly beautiful man tie his shoes and collect his gun and dagger, Harley ignored the treacherous leap of her heart.

She was here to find her sisters.

That was the reason she'd returned.

The *only* reason.

It had absolutely, positively nothing to do with Salvatore Giuliani, King of Weres.

Busy reminding herself of that very pertinent fact, Harley was caught off guard when Salvatore whirled toward the trees behind him.

"Curs," he hissed.

Belatedly catching the unmistakable smell, Harley

tightened her grip on the gun. Dammit. The pack was already circling them.

They'd been so occupied with the near-death fight with the zombie Were that they hadn't even noticed the approaching trouble.

"Just frigging perfect," she muttered.

Salvatore cupped her chin in his hand, his expression fierce.

"Run."

She narrowed her eyes. "Don't tell me what to do."

He growled in frustration. "Very soon we're going to have a long conversation about the proper way of following orders."

"Any conversation about following orders is going to be very short and will probably involve bloodshed."

The golden light of his eyes flared, but before he could argue, two curs crashed into the clearing. Turning, Salvatore moved to stand directly before them, arrogantly confident despite the fact the two had already shifted into werewolves that were as large as ponies, and powerful enough to fill the air with a prickling heat.

Sensing another cur approaching behind them, Harley silently slid behind a tree, her gaze still trained on Salvatore as he held out a hand toward the curs. Even from a distance she could feel a painful pressure filling the clearing.

She didn't have a clue what he was doing, but she suspected the curs weren't going to be happy.

She was right.

With agonized whines the animals fell to the ground, their fur-covered bodies writhing. Still Salvatore continued to hold out his hand, his powerful compulsion hammering into the hapless curs.

Harley winced at the sound of bones popping. Somehow Salvatore was forcing the curs back to human form.

A painful process, if their howls were anything to go by.

Fascinated by the macabre spectacle, Harley nearly missed when the cur behind her began to move forward. Pressing herself to the tree, she shook her head in disgust as she recognized the man who was trying to sneak up behind Salvatore.

A red-headed, fiery-tempered cur, Frankie always had more brawn than brain.

And thankfully, that included ramming headlong into a battle without making sure he wasn't about to be outflanked.

Following silently in his wake, Harley pressed her gun to the back of his head.

"Hello, Frankie," she murmured. "Miss me?"

With a foul curse, Frankie whirled around, murder in his eyes. "Bitch."

Before he could guess her intent, Harley hit the idiot on his hard head with the butt of her gun, the force sending him sprawling onto the ground, knocked out cold.

"You have no idea."

"Done playing?" Salvatore asked, a faint smile curving his lips.

Harley shrugged. "What now?"

"Now we leave."

She waved her gun toward the unconscious curs. "What about the Three Stooges?"

"I don't think they'll be in the mood to follow us. At least not for a few hours." He moved to grab her hand, tugging her through the trees.

"What did you do to them?"

"Just a little reminder that I'm their king."

"Little?"

"They're still alive, aren't they?"

Harley grimaced. "I thought you didn't have a God complex?"

He chuckled, lifting her hand to brush his lips over her knuckles.

"I don't like to lose."

"I'll keep that in mind." She pulled her hand from his grip, unable to concentrate when he was touching her. Or at least, she couldn't concentrate on what she needed to concentrate on. Ripping off Salvatore's clothes and taking the gorgeous Were in the bushes wasn't going to help them escape. "So I assume that was the infamous Briggs?"

Salvatore's smile widened, as if he could read her mind.

Jackass.

"A projection of him."

Harley had heard of the trick, but she'd never encountered anyone with the magical power to perform it.

"He wasn't really there?"

Salvatore knocked aside a dead tree leaning across the path, leading her down a steep hill covered with leaves and loose stones. Absolutely perfect for sliding down and breaking her fool neck.

"A portion of his essence was bound in the spell, but his physical form wasn't present."

"He felt solid enough."

"*Si*. It's the risky part of such a spell. Although he's far away, he can allow his spirit to become a solid force. It gives him the ability to travel at will, but it also makes him vulnerable to attack."

"Then he was injured?"

"His physical body carries the wounds he suffered in spirit form."

Satisfaction flared through her heart. She hated to waste a perfectly good bullet.

"I'm glad."

Salvatore's soft chuckle brushed over her skin. "My sentiments exactly." Pausing, the Were sniffed the air. Then seeming to come to a decision, he continued down the hill. "This way."

"The river?" she muttered.

"Curs hate water."

Harley licked her suddenly dry lips. "So do Weres."

"Which means the last thing they'll expect is for us to travel by boat," Salvatore pointed out, stepping through the last of the trees.

Harley's steps faltered as she realized that Salvatore had led them directly to a small wooden dock where a shiny new speedboat was moored.

Damn.

Like any sane Were, she hated the water.

No, it was more than just hate.

She was *terrified* of water.

There was no rhyme or reason to her fear. It wasn't as if she could drown. And as far as she knew, she'd never had a childhood trauma that included water.

She only knew that the only good water was the kind that came out of a showerhead and then disappeared down a drain.

"You also claimed that they wouldn't be able to find us if we were wearing the amulets," she accused, biting her bottom lip as Salvatore nimbly leapt into the boat, and with a tiny surge of his power, had the motor running.

He glanced back to watch her far more cautious approach, his golden eyes sparkling with rueful amusement.

"Why did I know you would throw that in my face?"

"Do you want to be in the middle of a raging river when that demented Briggs attacks again?"

He paused, easily sensing her tension. "You're scared of the water."

Grudgingly she moved down the dock, climbing into the boat with an awkward stiffness.

"I'm not scared. I'm . . ."

"You're?"

"Naturally cautious." The boat rocked and Harley hastily dropped onto the padded seat next to Salvatore. "Have you even driven a boat before?"

He shrugged, reaching over to untie the line. "How hard can it be?"

Harley popped to her feet, her heart stuck in her throat. "No way."

Salvatore pushed her firmly back into her seat, then before she could protest, he was pulling away from the dock and gunning the boat through the water.

"Don't worry, Harley," he said over the roar of the motor. "I'm not going to turn us over."

"Capsize," she gritted. "It's called capsize."

He laughed. "Fine. I won't capsize us."

The river was high and choppy, lashing at the boat as if determined to smash it to tiny bits. Harley's stomach threatened to revolt, and she grimly latched her attention onto Salvatore's finely chiseled profile.

In the late afternoon sunlight his skin glowed with a rich bronze, his raven hair whipping in the wind. He looked hard and dangerous and ruthlessly male.

"And what if Briggs makes a surprise visit?" she demanded.

He flashed a teasing grin. "Then capsizing will be the least of our concerns."

"Not helping."

"*Cara,* I don't know how Briggs managed to find me, but I'm certain it will take him time to heal. This is our best chance to get to Styx."

She clutched the edges of her seat. "I should never have come back."

Salvatore kept his gaze trained on the gigantic barge that was headed in their direction, but Harley didn't miss the sudden tightening of his hands on the wheel.

"Why did you?"

"Come back?" She shrugged. "Does it matter?"

"Not nearly so much as why you left."

"Why wouldn't I leave? You're being hunted by a demented, magically enhanced Were and a large number of pissed off curs," she smoothly lied. No need explaining her fascination with him was what truly scared the heck out of her. His arrogance had already reached epic status. "Only a lunatic would hang around you."

"If that's the reason you left, then you wouldn't have snuck away while I slept."

"I snuck away because I knew you would try to stop me. I didn't want to argue."

He snorted. "Since when?"

"Maybe you should just concentrate on driving."

Caine paced the small clearing, halting before the three curs who knelt in the dirt.

He wasn't surprised he was too late.

In fact, after he'd realized Giuliani and Harley had found the amulets he'd hidden in the tunnels, he was shocked the fools had stumbled across them at all.

Unlike his soldiers, Caine hadn't run blindly after prey he couldn't track. Instead, he had called for the witch who had made the amulets, knowing she could cast a spell to reveal their location.

At least their *general* location.

Magic was never an exact science.

Which was why he preferred not to depend on it.

"Forgive us, master, the Were overwhelmed us," Tio, the cur nearest to him, muttered, his face pressed to the ground. "We failed you."

"His power," a second cur, Drew, muttered. "Shit. I never felt anything like it."

Caine's jaw clenched. He didn't like to be reminded of Giuliani's power. Or how easily he could enforce his will on curs.

"Just tell me what happened, you idiots."

In unison the three soldiers climbed to their feet, the two naked curs still trembling from Giuliani's attack while Frankie was nursing a wound to his head that was swiftly healing. Harley's work, no doubt.

Tio, his dark hair matted with sweat, answered. "We were searching for the prisoners as you commanded, and . . ."

"And what?"

"I don't know what the hell happened. One minute we were near the highway, and the next thing I knew we were here."

"Did Giuliani call you?"

"I don't think so." The cur shook his head in confusion. "He was busy fighting with another Were."

"Harley?"

"No. Some pureblood with red eyes," Frankie said. "Christ, he gave me the willies."

Briggs. Caine clenched his hands at his sides. Damn the Were. He'd gone to great lengths to keep his pack from coming in contact with the magic-wielding pureblood.

Caine might be able to convince the curs he'd been granted a mystical vision of the future; after all, they wanted to believe he possessed the power to offer them the chance to become purebloods. But they'd be far less eager to follow him if they suspected his vision had forced him into a partnership with a traitorous Were who had sold his soul for power.

Even curs had standards.

"What happened to him?"

"Harley snuck up behind him and shot him in the head." Drew said.

"Stupid woman," Caine muttered, his heart freezing at the danger the female had put herself in. Dammit, he *needed* her. Or at least, he needed her blood. "Is she trying to get herself killed?"

"Didn't matter," Frankie said. "Giuliani shifted and attacked the other Were like a madman. I thought for sure he'd kill him, but then the stranger just disappeared."

"Freakiest thing I ever saw." Tio's eyes were wide. "And that's saying something."

"Did Giuliani manage to injure the Were before he disappeared?"

"Mauled the hell out of him," Drew said.

A chill bloomed in Caine's heart. Briggs had always been smugly confident that his power was greater than the King of Weres. Christ, he boasted of it with nauseating frequency.

What if he was wrong?

"Damn."

With a frown of suspicion, Frankie moved forward. "You don't seem surprised that there's a Were out there who can simply disappear."

With a vicious backhand, Caine sent the cur flying backwards, blood dripping from his mouth.

"Maybe you should concentrate on finding the prisoners you allowed to escape before I have your pelt made into seat covers."

Effectively reminded of who was boss, the three curs scrambled to obey his command.

"Yes, master."

Waiting until the curs had disappeared through the trees, Caine turned his attention to the blond-haired woman with plump cheeks and a lush body.

"Vikki."

Dressed in tight denim shorts and a tiny tank top that barely covered her generous breasts, she sashayed across the uneven ground to press against him.

"You need me, lover?"

"You can sense them?"

She closed her eyes to concentrate on the spell she'd cast before leaving his lair.

"Distantly." She pointed her hand toward the river. "That way."

"Go with the curs and keep me informed of their location."

Opening her eyes, she pouted at his sharp command. "I want to stay with you."

He yanked from her clinging touch. "I'm not in the mood for games."

Fury raced through her pale eyes as she gave a toss of her curly hair and turned to join the curs.

"Fine."

"Don't try to capture them. I just want to know where they are."

Without turning, she lifted her hand to flip him off. "Whatever."

There was a faint rustle of brush before Andre appeared at Caine's side. The muscular cur with long brown hair and black eyes was Caine's second in command, and one of the few people that Caine actually trusted.

"How do you intend to overpower two full-blooded Weres who will be expecting you to attack?" Andre asked.

"A worry for later."

Caine bent down, studying the damage caused by the fierce battle between the two powerful Weres. Claw marks gouged the ground, splashes of blood and chunks of fur spread over the broken branches. He touched a tuft of pale fur, knowing it didn't belong to Giuliani.

"What is it?"

"A warning."

"I don't understand."

Caine straightened, his jaw clenched. "A soldier only becomes a hero if he picks the winning side."

Salvatore had always been a predator. Wherever he went, whatever he did, he was the biggest, baddest creature around. And that's exactly how he liked it.

Suddenly becoming the prey . . .

It sucked.

Silently cursing Briggs and Caine and the persistent curs who he could sense in the distance, Salvatore angled toward the Illinois side of the river.

Sitting with white-knuckled tension at his side, Harley shot him a wary frown.

"What is it? Is there something wrong with the boat?"

He slowed as they neared the bank, grimacing at the thick tangle of mud and weeds that lined the river. Thank God his Armanis were safely tucked in his St. Louis lair.

"We're not going to sink, *cara.*"

"Then why are you stopping?"

"The curs are back on our trail."

She shrugged, obviously having sensed already that they were being hunted.

"They're still miles behind us."

"As they have been for the last two hours."

"So . . ." The magnificent hazel eyes widened. "Oh."

"Exactly." Salvatore allowed the boat to idle as they drifted into the muddy shallows at the edge of the river. "They've found a means to track us."

Harley considered a long moment. "It has to be the witch who made the amulets." She at last concluded. "She's the only one who could cast a spell to discover our location."

Salvatore reached to grasp a low-hanging branch, bringing the boat to a halt. Actually, the witch was preferable to the thought that Briggs had recovered swiftly enough to send the curs after them. His own body had healed, but his strength was ebbing toward low.

He was hoping to put off round two until he could recharge his mojo.

"All the witch can sense is the amulets?" he asked, a plan already forming in his mind.

"Yes."

"Does Caine have any hunters?"

"Only Duncan."

Salvatore's lips twisted. It was Duncan he'd been scheduled to meet in Hannibal. The same cur he'd found murdered on the floor of the cabin just minutes before Caine had attacked him.

"Then Caine was an idiot to kill him."

She narrowed her eyes. "So you say."

"Harley . . ." He swallowed his protest. Only time would ease the suspicions that had been drilled into her. "Someday you'll trust me."

"I don't trust anyone."

He held out his hand. "Give me your amulet."

She readily untied the amulet and placed it in his outstretched palm. Salvatore hid a satisfied smile as he yanked his own amulet from his neck. Harley might not realize it, but on some level she did trust him.

"What are you doing?" she demanded as he threw both amulets on the floor of the boat and then vaulted over the side to land in the waist-deep water.

"If the witch wants to chase the amulets, the least we can do is keep her entertained."

"Why don't we just toss the amulets overboard and keep going?"

"They realize by now we're following the river north," he said, waiting for her to clamor out of the boat and stand at his side. Reaching forward, he thrust the throttle in gear, shoving the boat away from the bank and toward the middle of the river. "If they have any intelligence at all they'll have sent a few curs ahead to ambush us."

Harley watched the boat zip away, her color slowly returning. Obviously the muddy water and slimy moss that slithered around her body was preferable to continuing their boat ride.

"They'll eventually stumble across our scent," she pointed out.

Salvatore's expression hardened. He would do whatever necessary to protect Harley, but this division between Weres and curs had to end.

Damn Caine.

Briggs was deliberately using him to weaken Salvatore's power base.

"Let's hope for their sake that they don't."

Chapter Ten

Harley climbed the bank, relieved to discover that the Illinois side of the Mississippi River was a flat expanse of recently plowed fields, rather than the rolling bluffs she was accustomed to. She wasn't a wuss. She could run for hours without breaking a sweat. Hell, she could do it carrying a few hundred pounds on her back.

But at the moment her cheap canvas shoes were covered in slimy mud and her wet underwear was crawling into places it shouldn't be. The last thing she wanted was to slog up and down endless hills.

Besides, she didn't have to be a psychic to sense that Salvatore wasn't running on a full tank.

Big surprise there.

He'd been caged, pelted with silver shrapnel, attacked by a zombie Were, and forced to discipline the curs chasing after them.

She doubted any other Were would still be on his feet, let alone be fully alert and on guard as he led them northward, choosing a path far enough from the riverbank to avoid the tangled overgrowth, and yet far enough from the farmhouses that dotted the patchwork of fields to avoid being easily spotted by a curious human.

They walked for nearly half an hour, the distant scurrying of animals and whisper of leaves rustling in the wind the only sounds to break the silence. Harley sucked in a deep breath, appreciating the firm ground beneath her. Despite her nasty shoes and unruly underwear, she'd rather hike for hours than spend another minute in the damned water. That's why she had feet, not fins.

Of course, she'd always wanted to try flying. Now that looked like a fine way to travel.

Private jet, sipping champagne, and relaxing in plush seats, a yummy steward who specialized in introducing a woman into the mile high club.

Her heart skipped a beat as her fantasy of the blond Nordic steward morphed into a dark-haired, golden-eyed Were with a touch that could make a female howl in pleasure.

She sucked her thoughts away from the inevitable flashback. She didn't need a slow motion replay of Salvatore lying beneath her, his eyes glowing with a searing pleasure and his bronzed skin covered in a sheen of sweat.

Sex, even fantastic oh-my-God-don't-ever-stop sex, was a complication she didn't need right now.

Returning her attention to their surroundings, Harley caught sight of the glint of steel beams of a large bridge spanning the river just visible over the top of the trees.

A bridge meant a town, thank God.

She'd kill for dry clothes and something to eat.

A very large something to eat.

A side of beef sounded just about perfect.

Her mouth watered, but her visions of a medium rare sirloin were shattered by the sound of an approaching car. Expecting Salvatore to ease back into the shadows of the trees, Harley lifted her brows as he instead crossed his arms and waited for the elegant black Mercedes to come to a halt in the middle of the dirt road.

"Now what?" she demanded.

Salvatore sniffed the air. "Imp. The scent is familiar."

"A friend of yours?"

"I make it a rule to spend as little time in the company of imps as possible." A smile touched Salvatore's sensuous lips as the door of the car opened, and a tall woman with perfect curves and a stunning mane of shimmering red hair stepped out. "Of course, there's an exception to every rule."

"Creep," Harley muttered, astonished by the pang of envy.

Okay, the woman was drop-dead gorgeous with her pale skin and slanted emerald eyes. But what woman with a brain larger than a pea drove around country back roads in a skimpy black gown that barely covered the essentials and three-inch heels?

Slut shoes out here? Really?

Harley had never fantasized about becoming one of those upmarket women who bartered beauty for wealth. She liked women who kicked ass.

Give her Lara Croft over Cinderella any day.

"Don't worry, *cara*," Salvatore drawled. "I have quite unexpectedly become addicted to one particular female. There's not another who could possibly tempt me."

Yeah, right.

She rolled her eyes. No man acquired Salvatore's talent in bed by reading how-to books.

"Does that bullshit work on your harem?" she mocked.

He managed to look surprised. "I'll let you know if I ever acquire one."

"The King of Weres without a harem? I don't believe it."

"Being king isn't just a figurehead position, Harley." His shoulders lifted in a restless motion, as if in response to the heavy burdens he carried, his expression suddenly bleak. "The entire Were race is depending on me to save them from extinction. That doesn't leave a lot of time for collecting women."

Sashaying—yes, she actually sashayed—around the front of the car, the imp tossed her long mane of crimson hair, the scent of plums filling the air.

"Your Majesty?" She dipped her head in an oddly formal manner. "I am Tonya, sister to Troy."

"Cristo."

Tonya chuckled at Salvatore's horror. "I take it that you remember my twin brother?"

"He's difficult to forget."

"It's his gift."

"Not the word I had in mind." The golden eyes narrowed to dangerous slits. "How did you recognize me?"

Tonya pointed a finger in Harley's direction. "I recognized her. She's the spitting image of her sister."

Harley forgot her unreasonable dislike for the imp. "You know my sisters?"

"I worked in Chicago until last month, when I transferred to Viper's club here."

"Viper opened a club in this backwoods?" Salvatore glanced around the quiet farmlands. "It hardly seems a mecca for demons."

"We have a specialty coffee shop that caters to humans, and a connected building for our more exotic clientele." The imp sent Salvatore a smoldering smile. Bitch. "You offer the right scratch for someone's itch and they'll drive miles to find you."

"And your job entails roaming the back roads for potential customers?" Harley snapped.

Tonya ran a deliberate hand down the curve of her hip, her eyes holding the knowledge that there wasn't a woman alive who wasn't jealous of her outrageous beauty.

"The only thing that would bring me to the back roads is a command from Santiago. Oh, and the promise of some lovely cha-ching, of course." The imp actually purred at the mention of money. "There's a cash reward for whoever finds you first."

A perilous heat blasted through the air as Salvatore grabbed the imp's arm.

"Who's offering this reward?"

The imp had enough sense to step back in alarm. "The Anasso. He sent out a BOLO for the King of Weres and his mate's sister after he received some sort of mental text from a gargoyle. Since it was still daylight, Santiago sent out his nonflammable servants to keep watch."

Harley licked her lips, bombarded by a muddle of emotions. A growing confidence that her sisters were indeed alive. A relief that Levet had seemingly made it out of the tunnels. And a vague impulse to take off running and never look back.

Her life had always been predictable. Caine might move them from lair to lair, and the curs guarding her had changed throughout the years, but her days were pretty much the same no matter where they were.

Now . . . not so much.

Amazingly, being thrown into the middle of an adventure wasn't quite the exciting buzz she'd always assumed it would be.

Salvatore waved a hand toward the waiting car. "Take us to Santiago."

Tonya pouted. "What about my reward?"

A dangerous smile curved Salvatore's lips. "I won't leave you tied to a tree for the hungry pack of curs chasing us. Good enough?"

"Party pooper." Turning on her heels, an impressive feat considering the rutted dirt road, she returned to the car. "Let's go."

Harley lifted her brows as Salvatore led her toward the car. "Charming as always."

A smile filled with wicked promise shimmered in his eyes. "I need a good woman to teach me manners."

"Don't look at me."

"Oh, I intend to do more than look."

"Watch it, Salvatore, or I'll kick your royal ass."

He reached to pull open the door to the backseat, whispering in her ear as she bent to climb inside.

"Promises, promises."

Heat swirled in the pit of her stomach, making her stumble and sprawl awkwardly across the leather seat.

Damned Were.

Straightening, she glared as Salvatore slid smoothly beside her, but his attention was on the imp as she turned a wide circle through the field before bouncing them back onto the road.

"Do you have any werewolves as customers?"

Tonya glanced in the rearview mirror. "Those of the furry persuasion tend to avoid vampire establishments. A pity." Her voice lowered to a husky invitation. "They always make the best strippers."

Salvatore slid a glance in Harley's direction. "Stripping is not all we do well."

"Amen," Tonya breathed.

Harley could have added a few amens of her own, but instead she gritted her teeth. The imp and her femme fatale act was wearing on her nerves.

"Are you done?"

"Not nearly . . ." Salvatore began, only to grunt in surprise when she nailed him in the ribs with her elbow. "Ah, I'm done."

"Good choice," Harley muttered.

His smile widened. "At least for now." He returned his attention to the imp. "We need food. Any drive-thru will do."

"I can prepare you a meal at the club."

"I prefer my dinner hex-free."

Harley frowned in confusion. "I thought purebloods were immune to hexes. It was one of the numerous things Caine used to bitch about."

"Tonya is not just another imp if she's related to Troy. She's royalty. Which means her hexes are considerably stronger."

Tonya batted her annoyingly long lashes. "I'm not allowed to hex Santiago's guests. Only the customers."

"The drive-thru," Salvatore commanded.

Tonya shrugged. "Suit yourself."

Harley settled back in the leather seat. "He always does."

Briggs was wrenched violently from his healing sleep.

He groaned, the pain of his wounds thundering through his stiff body.

Damn Salvatore. The bastard was going to pay for every second of his suffering.

With interest.

For a moment he savored the image of Salvatore on his knees before him, his pride crushed as he begged for mercy. Then the lovely fantasy was interrupted by the savage pull of his master.

Shuddering at the sensation of an icy hand clutching

his heart, Briggs tumbled off the narrow cot that was set in the back of a bleak cave.

He paused long enough to throw cold water on his face from a ceramic pitcher and pull a clean cloak from the carved chest set next to the bed before leaving the cave to enter the tunnel that led through the vast catacombs.

Briggs didn't know who had originally burrowed beneath the graveyard that was attached to the abandoned Victorian church outside of Chicago. Or even who had kept the ancient catacombs maintained during the years. He had been led here only a few weeks ago by the ruthless call of his master.

Until that moment, his contact with the demon lord had been through the former Were king's amber pendant that Briggs had stolen after it became obvious Salvatore Giuliani was destined to become the heir. Or the painful process of the demon speaking directly into his mind.

Something that always left him regretting his blood oath to the bastard.

Then, without warning, the demon lord had commanded that Briggs leave behind his very comfortable lair in Kansas City to squat in the barren caves like a forgotten hermit. Even worse, the inner chamber that had once been an altar to the dark lord allowed the barriers between dimensions to thin. Briggs had traded his morals for power long ago, but even he had to shudder at the throat-clogging evil that crawled through the air.

He moved through the tunnels that headed ever lower, struck as always, by the smoothly polished stones beneath his feet that were unmarred by so much as a speck of dust or stray cobweb.

Not even vermin would dare disturb the malevolent shadows.

Bypassing the caves that had once been prisons for

immortals, with their silver chains and walls lined with lead, Briggs entered the inner chamber, his nose curling at the lingering stench of human blood.

More than one sacrifice had been made in front of the forgotten altar in the middle of the floor.

And very soon there would be one more. Although this one wouldn't include worthless humans.

The knowledge was almost enough to compensate for the wounds that were taking far too long to heal.

Almost.

Gritting his teeth, Briggs forced himself to kneel before the altar, flinching as the gold brazier flared to life next to him and a frigid blast filled the chamber. Above the altar, the air began to shimmer with a warped rip in the fabric that held the worlds apart, the odor of rotting flesh spilling into the cavern.

"Master," he said. "You have need of me?"

"You have proven to be a sad disappointment, Briggs, just as your father before you," the hollow voice echoed through the cavern, biting into Briggs's flesh.

Father. Briggs curled his lips.

Among purebloods, the pack superseded any family connection. Cubs were kept in the same lair and fiercely protected by all the adults. The concept of two parents and siblings was a human tradition.

Briggs, however, had barely been out of puberty when the king had taken him aside to claim him as his son and heir.

At the time he'd been busting with pride. He'd suspected even as a cub that he was destined for greatness.

It was only after the birth of Salvatore and his father's growing madness that he realized he would have to take matters into his own hands.

Even if it meant bartering his soul.

"I have done all you requested."

"And did I request that you interfere with Giuliani?"

"You wanted him close at hand, as the time of your return draws near. I merely sought to prevent his escape."

"Liar." The icy power washed over Briggs, bringing with it the sensation of being flayed. "It was your overweening pride that led to your attack, even after I specifically commanded that you keep your presence hidden. You were famished for the opportunity to prove your worth against the King of Weres."

"Caine had already revealed my miraculous return from the dead." He readily dumped the blame on his pet cur. Shit was intended to roll downhill. "Giuliani needs to be contained before he can start sticking his nose where it doesn't belong."

"I will decide what needs to be done. And the first order of business is reminding you that your continued existence is entirely at my mercy. And in this moment, I am not feeling particularly merciful."

Briggs didn't have to fake his shudder of agony. "Forgive me."

"I forgive nothing," the voice hissed. "I have waited for centuries to be released from this hellhole. I will destroy you before I allow you to threaten my destiny."

It was a threat that Briggs accepted as gospel. Unlike his dear departed father, he'd never been stupid enough to assume he was anything but expendable to this powerful demon lord.

"Yes, master."

"You will stay away from Giuliani until I give you the order to bring him to me. Do you understand?"

"I think it's a mistake to . . ."

His words cut off as the chamber shook, the shower of stones from the ceiling pelting him on the head.

"You dare question me?"

Briggs swallowed the bile that rose in his throat. He'd died once. It was an experience he didn't intend to repeat.

On the other hand, he wasn't about to allow Salvatore to steal his glory when he was so close to success.

"Please. You must allow me to speak."

"Must?"

"It's Giuliani," Briggs rasped, his head pressed to the cold stone floor as the crippling pain threatened to consume him. "He's a danger."

"What danger?"

"He's begun the mating ritual."

The frigid pressure abruptly disappeared, as if Briggs had managed to truly shock the demon lord.

A relief to be rid of the pain, but not particularly reassuring.

Briggs had bet everything on the mysterious demon lord who promised him the throne that had been stolen by Salvatore. The damned creature should already have sensed trouble.

"Impossible."

"Impossible or not, he's returning power to the Weres."

The town proved to be typical for the Midwest.

Settled on the Mississippi River, it was a combination of small businesses, fast-food restaurants, and chain stores along Broadway Street, while the traditional main drag was lined with historic homes that were battling the passage of time with varying degrees of success.

After swinging through Arby's to buy enough roast beef sandwiches and fried mozzarella sticks to feed a football team plus the cheerleading squad—even supposing cheerleaders would come within a mile of a fried mozzarella stick—Tonya drove them to the waterfront, stopping the Mercedes behind a small brick building with a green awning painted with the words TEAS AND CAKES.

Harley briefly caught a glimpse of small tables with frilly doilies and a front counter with a glass case of pastries. There was a mass of humans stuffed into the small space, with a line out the front door, their expressions tense as they waited to feed their unwitting addiction.

A powerful hex, indeed.

With a grimace, Harley followed Tonya into the attached warehouse that looked in dire need of some kindling and a match to put it out of its misery. There was a faint tingle as they entered the back door, and Harley's eyes widened as she took in the vast lobby decorated in a neoclassical style, with inlaid wood floors and pale green walls with silver engravings. The ceiling was painted with Apollo on his chariot dashing through the clouds, and the handful of chairs were hand-carved.

All extremely elegant and amazingly tasteful.

Belatedly, she realized the warehouse had been wrapped in an enchantment that magically projected an image of shabby abandonment. No doubt it also held an aversion spell that would keep humans from entering.

From the lobby, she and Salvatore had been led to private apartments on the second floor of the warehouse. There were a few raised brows when she'd insisted on separate rooms, but in a thankfully short amount of time she was locked in a bathroom with a lot of black marble and gilt to shower away the hardened mud.

Returning to the attached bedroom, she found a pair of jeans and a turquoise tank top waiting for her on the black-and-gold comforter spread over the jumbo-sized bed. There was also a new set of panties and matching bra, as well as a pair of running shoes.

Yow, vampire hospitality was obviously full service.

The only question was what they charged for that service.

Once dressed, she pulled her damp hair into a ponytail and headed back toward the lobby. She hesitated at the bottom of the sweeping staircase, surprised to discover several large demons entering through a side door and heading directly toward the back of the lobby.

She instinctively shifted so she was hidden behind the elegantly carved banister, keeping a careful eye on the dangerous crowd.

Night had obviously fallen since several of the demons possessed the unearthly beauty of vampires, and at least one was an Ichari demon, a species that remained immobile during the day.

The others . . .

She didn't have a clue. There were some with horns, some with extra appendages, some with wings and razor-sharp teeth. The only thing they had in common was the unmistakable aura of being predators.

Not really in the mood to rub elbows with the motley crew, Harley headed in the opposite direction, opening a door set in an alcove to discover what appeared to be a private office.

Crossing the slate gray carpet, she avoided the heavy walnut desk and wooden shelves that held the sort of high-tech surveillance equipment that would make the CIA salivate. Instead she concentrated on the French Impressionist paintings that were hung on the paneled walls and carefully preserved behind glass cases.

Good Lord. They were breathtaking, but surely they should have been in a museum?

"So the rumors are true."

Harley slowly turned, not surprised to discover the exquisitely handsome vampire with long raven hair and distinctly Spanish features leaning against the doorjamb, studying her with a faint smile. She'd already sensed his approach.

"I'm afraid to ask," she murmured.

"You shouldn't be." Pushing from the door, he slowly moved to stand directly before her. Dressed in a black silk suit and charcoal tie, he filled the room with his cold power. "You are as beautiful as your sister."

"You know my sister?"

"I am Santiago, and it is my honor to call Darcy my queen."

"Queen." She gave a shake of her head. "Unbelievable."

The vampire lifted his brows. "It troubles you that she is mated to a vampire?"

Harley's lips twisted. She wouldn't have been troubled to discover her sisters were mated to tree frogs.

"No. I was told that my sisters were murdered. I'm still wrapping my head around the fact they're alive and kicking."

There was a hint of rueful humor in the dark eyes. "Darcy is very much alive and quite happy to do whatever kicking necessary to keep Styx in line."

"And she's happy?"

"Of course." His gaze deliberately lowered to appreciate the curves revealed by the tank top. "Vampires possess an extensive knowledge of how to please a woman."

Oh, she didn't doubt that for a moment.

Everything about the beautiful demons screamed pleasure.

A pity her taste ran to aggravating, arrogant, outrageously sexy Weres.

"Extensive, eh?"

"Extensive and . . ." His smile revealed a flash of pearly white fangs. "Creative."

"And oh-so-dead if you take one step closer, Santiago," Salvatore drawled, stepping into the room and allowing his heat to blast through the air.

Harley wisely stepped away from the vampire as she turned to appreciate the sight of Salvatore freshly showered and wearing a pair of silky black pants and a sheer white shirt that had been left open to reveal his smooth, bronzed chest.

If there was going to be a fight, she didn't intend to be in the middle of it.

Santiago offered a mocking bow. "Giuliani."

Strolling forward, Salvatore deliberately halted at her side, his hand possessively cupping the back of her neck. The male equivalent of "She's mine, back off."

Harley might have been furious if he wasn't looking so frigging gorgeous, with his hair pulled back with a gold clasp, emphasizing the stark beauty of his face.

And that scent . . .

Warm with a smoky musk that was driving her insane.

Easily sensing her jolt of awareness, Salvatore rubbed his thumb along the side of her neck, his gaze remaining on the vampire.

"Have you contacted Styx?"

"I informed him that Tonya discovered you and the lovely Harley, and that you were on your way to the club," Santiago said. "He'll be heading here now that sun has set."

Harley frowned. "Why is he coming here? I thought you were going to Chicago?"

"Not without back up." Salvatore grimaced. "I assume he's bringing the crow pack with him?"

"Crow pack?"

"His Ravens," Santiago hissed, the dark eyes cold with disapproval. "They are the Anasso's personal guard and worthy of proper respect."

Salvatore shrugged. "How long will it take them to arrive?"

"Four, perhaps five hours."

"What's your security?"

The vampire waved a hand toward the shelves of equipment. "Beyond the enchantments placed on the building, I have everything wired and fully monitored. There are also four guards on duty at all times."

"No werewolves?"

Santiago's lips curled. "I don't trust dogs."

"The feeling is entirely mutual, leech."

"Not to mention the fact they shed."

"Better than being a walking corpse."

Danger prickled in the air and Harley took a sharp step away from both males, her hands planted on her hips.

"Either the testosterone level in this room is taken down a notch or I'm going to show you both what bad things happen when estrogen is let off the leash."

Chapter Eleven

Salvatore's lips twitched as he met Harley's warning gaze, his blood stirring. Damn, but she was hot.

"I heard female Weres were more dangerous than the males," Santiago murmured.

Salvatore nodded. "You should be near one during the full moon."

The hazel eyes glowed with a rising fury. "Do you two want some privacy so you can enjoy your budding bromance?"

Santiago chuckled, heading toward the door. "I need to check on the staff before the doors open. So long as you stay in the building, you should be safe. There is food in the kitchen and drinks at the bar. The entertainment starts in an hour."

The vampire disappeared, closing the door behind him.

"Entertainment?" Harley asked, her eyes abruptly widening as Salvatore roughly backed her against the wall and pressed his body against her. "What the hell?"

Grasping her hands, Salvatore held them over her head, his erection cradled against her stomach.

"You're so damned sexy."

"And that gives you the right to jump me like a . . ."

"A dog in heat?" he finished for her, burying his face in the curve of her neck.

"Yes."

"I *am* a dog in heat."

She shivered, the scent of her arousal spicing the air. "You're also a king. Shouldn't you at least make an effort to be civilized?"

He chuckled, his lips exploring the line of her shoulder. She smelled of soap and woman and smoldering desire.

"You still have your clothes on, don't you?"

She stirred beneath him, her heat wrapping around him. "Salvatore, I'm not going to have sex with you in a room where anyone might walk in."

"Then come to my room."

"No way."

His lips followed the plunging line of her tank top, lingering on the gentle swell of her breast.

"Your room then."

She tried to swallow her groan of pleasure. "No . . . way."

"Oh, there are ways," he promised in low, rough tones. "An endless number of ways. We've already proven that with stunning results. All we need is a place."

She shook her head in denial, but her nipples hardened with unspoken invitation.

"Get over yourself, Giuliani."

Pulling back, he studied her with a brooding gaze. He could hear the rapid beat of her heart, the rasp of her breath.

"Harley, your senses are as sensitive as mine. This

mutual desire is one thing we can never hide from one another."

"Wanting and doing are two completely different things."

He pressed his erection against the curve of her stomach. "I'm painfully aware of the distinction, *cara.*"

For a blissful moment, Harley softened against him, her eyes fluttering shut as the persistent need pulsed between them. Unfortunately, he didn't have time to get her naked before she was roughly shoving him away, crossing the room to stand near the door.

"Tell me what the zombie Were said to you," she demanded.

Salvatore groaned, turning to lean against the wall as his body screamed with frustration.

"Zombie?"

"Zombie. Freak." She shrugged. "Taxidermist wet dream."

With a grudging effort, Salvatore wrenched his thoughts away from seducing his mate and dredged up his encounter with Briggs.

Better than a cold shower.

"Nothing that made any sense," he rasped.

"Flaming psychopaths rarely make sense."

"True enough."

She tilted her head to the side, all too easily sensing the gnawing unease that plagued him.

"There's something bothering you. What is it?"

Salvatore stiffened, battling the instinct to retreat from her probing. Harley wasn't a casual lay to be ignored unless she was in his bed. She was the woman destined to rule at his side.

"He claims that he possesses the power to restore children to the Were."

There was a startled silence as Harley absorbed the significance of his words.

"Easy to claim," she at last said. "Does he have any proof?"

"It is all to be revealed when the timing is right."

"Sounds like a bunch of mumbo jumbo crap to me. Remarkably like the bull that Caine is always spouting."

Salvatore toyed absently with his heavy signet ring, an unpleasant knot in the pit of his stomach.

"They do drink from the same glass of Kool-Aid."

"So why are you letting him get under your skin?"

"Until I know the source of his power, I can't fathom what he's capable of. There's no doubt he's convinced himself that he's the true King of Weres."

"If he was the true king, wouldn't he be sitting on the throne?"

"So I always believed."

With a scowl, she crossed the carpet to stand directly before him, as if afraid he might be oblivious to her annoyance unless they were nose to nose.

"Are you listening to yourself? You're letting that rotting POS screw with your head."

Salvatore arched a brow, startled by her fierce reaction. Was it because she was terrified of Briggs? Or was it more personal?

Cristo, he wanted it to be personal.

Intimately, deeply personal.

Naked wouldn't hurt, either.

Unable to resist temptation, he reached to grab her hand. The mating had stolen a measure of his strength, but touching her offered something just as important.

Peace.

An all too rare sensation in his life.

"He has raised questions that need to be answered."

"What questions?"

Salvatore led Harley to the wide leather sofa set across the room from the desk. Settling on the cushions, he tugged her down beside him.

A part of him was restless, in need of being on the hunt for Briggs and the bastard who was pumping him full of black magic. It was a part easily overwhelmed by his savage need to protect this woman.

Until he knew that Harley was safely in the hands of Styx and his Ravens, he wasn't about to leave her side.

"Whether or not the previous king was involved with the same demon who is controlling Briggs."

She shifted uneasily, but didn't pull away. Progress.

"Is that what the Were told you?"

"Si."

"And you believe him?"

Salvatore grimaced. "I don't want to."

"But?"

He lifted his free hand to rub the muscles of his aching neck. "But I can't ignore the memory of Mackenzie's peculiar behavior the last century of his life."

She flashed a dry smile. "You're going to have to be more specific. I assumed being peculiar was a prerequisite of kinghood."

"Very amusing."

Her smile faded. "Did you suspect anything at the time?"

Did he?

Salvatore didn't have a ready answer.

In many ways, the past had been lost in shadows. After becoming king he had too many troubles to look back. The future consumed his every thought.

Now it was difficult to dredge up the memories without shading them with his growing suspicions.

"He was secretive. Short-tempered. Dangerously unstable," he admitted, recalling his resentment as Mackenzie increasingly ignored his duties to the Weres and remained alone in his lair. "I thought he was battling the Telos."

"What's that?"

He considered his words. "Like all immortals, Weres are vulnerable to the punishment of time," he at last said. "Endless days that become decades and centuries and millennia. Despair can be as destructive as any illness."

The hazel eyes darkened, perhaps for the first time comprehending that immortality had a cost.

"What happens?"

"It's different for each individual." He stroked his thumb over her knuckles, comforted by the feel of her satin skin. It was said that Weres who found a true mate never endured the Telos. "Most complain of a numbing apathy or a lurking darkness they can't escape. Eventually they call on the Vekpos, a mystical fire that will consume a pureblood from the inside out."

"Yikes." Harley grimaced. "We can't do it by accident, can we?"

"No. A Were must be in the throes of the Telos for the power to emerge, and it's a very rare occurrence. Most Weres are too violent not to die in battle long before the threat of ennui can consume them."

She choked back a laugh. "Fantastic. I'm completely reassured."

"You asked."

"The previous king had this . . ." She stumbled over the unfamiliar word. "Telos?"

He shook his head, turning to absently study the pastel paintings hung on the wall.

"That was my assumption. And when his ashes were discovered in his lair, it simply confirmed my theory."

"Sounds fairly cut-and-dry," she pointed out. "Just because Briggs made some wild accusations doesn't make them true."

Intellectually, Salvatore agreed.

Briggs had been an accomplished liar long before he'd ever traded his soul for power. Hell, he'd nearly convinced the Roman werewolf pack to return to the ancient tradition of sacrificing humans to appease the Were gods before Salvatore had stepped in and halted the nonsense.

His instinct, however, refused to dismiss the wild claim. He couldn't afford to overlook any possibility.

God knew his blind assumptions had already led to near disaster.

"No, but even at the time I knew that the Telos didn't completely explain Mackenzie's furtive habits," his voice thickened with self-disgust. Maybe if he hadn't ignored the vague doubts about Mackenzie all those centuries ago, he could have stopped Briggs before he managed to acquire his black powers. Then he gave a shake of his head. There was no going back, only forward. "Those who are committed to death devote their last years performing small rituals to easing the grief of those they'll leave behind."

She squeezed his hand, as if sensing his inner torment. "What sort of rituals?"

"They give away their belongings, they travel to visit the burial grounds of their ancestors, they surround themselves with the pack."

"Grim, but understandable, I suppose." She wrinkled her nose. "What did Mackenzie do?"

"He hid in his lair, refusing my pleas to return to his

throne, even as the Were packs fractured and turned on each other."

She considered his explanation a long moment, then astonishingly, cut straight to the heart of the matter.

"Did the Weres begin losing their powers beneath the previous king?"

Salvatore surged to his feet, hating the knowledge that he was stumbling through the dark, constantly one step behind.

Dio. The fate of the Weres depended on him.

If he failed, they all failed.

"It's difficult to pinpoint an exact moment or even decade, but it was whispered that the decline started shortly after Mackenzie's reign began." His wolf prowled just below his skin, needing a tangible enemy to rip into shreds. "Maybe he sensed the encroaching weakness and turned to desperate measures."

Harley crossed to his side, her brow furrowed. "Or maybe he used the black magic to become king, and that started the troubles."

Salvatore gritted his teeth, wanting to deny that any king would be willing to put his own ambitions ahead of the good of his people, but the lies wouldn't pass his lips.

Magic couldn't force the throne to accept a Were as king, but a corrupt Were could certainly use it to clear the field of contenders.

"It's possible that Mackenzie used black magic to dispose of the true heirs ahead of him."

"Wait." Her eyes widened, as she was struck by a sudden thought. "If he sold his soul to the devil, why wasn't he offered the Lazarus treatment that Briggs got?"

Salvatore shrugged. "Maybe Briggs made a pact with the same devil to make certain Mackenzie *couldn't* rise again."

"Honor among thieves, and all that?"

"Briggs is desperate for the throne."

Harley shuddered, wrapping her arms around her waist. Salvatore didn't blame her. Briggs was shudder-worthy.

"So how does Caine fit into all this?"

Salvatore felt another pang of self-disgust. He'd been following Brigg's false trails for years. Like a particularly stupid hound hunting the chickens and allowing the fox to escape his notice.

"A distraction," he gritted.

She snorted. "He wasn't much of a distraction considering he spent most of his time cowering in his various lairs."

"Actually, you and your sisters were the true distractions," he corrected. "Briggs knew that I would follow your trail anywhere in the world, and that I wouldn't rest until I'd found you." He scanned her beautiful face, his heart whispering it was worth every sacrifice to have at last discovered his mate, while his sense of duty rebelled at having endangered his people. "By dividing the four of you into different locations and constantly keeping on the move, he did a bang-up job of making sure I wasted my time chasing my own tail."

"Distract you from what?" she demanded.

His lips twisted as Harley once again pounced on the most significant point.

He would be a fool to ever try to deceive this woman.

"I don't know," he admitted.

"What do you suspect?"

"I think I was lured from Italy to America for a very specific purpose." He lifted a hand as her lips parted with the inevitable question. "And before you ask, I don't have a clue what the purpose might be."

"Inconvenient."

His humorless laugh echoed through the room at her stunning understatement.

"A little more than inconvenient." He shook his head, resuming his impatient pacing. Tonight he felt every one of his numerous years. "*Cristo,* for all I know, I'm completely wrong about everything. In the past I've blamed the troubles of the Weres on the gods, on the changing societies, and even on the vampires. Perhaps I'm seeking another evil force to accuse so I don't have to admit that my people are destined for extinction."

Silence filled the room, the distant din of Santiago's unruly guests thankfully muffled by the heavy door.

At last Salvatore halted his pacing. He could sense Harley standing just behind him. She hadn't tried to slip away while he was distracted. And so far she hadn't stuck anything in the middle of his back.

Which meant she was thinking.

A dangerous activity.

Turning, he met her guarded gaze.

"Harley?"

"If there's even a possibility you might be right, then shouldn't you be returning to Italy?"

He was caught off guard by her abrupt words. "Trying to get rid of me, *cara*?"

"You don't have to be Ken Jennings to figure out that if the bad guy wants you here, you should be there."

Was she concerned for his safety?

Dio, the sky was surely about to fall.

Salvatore prowled forward, his blood heating as she instinctively backed away. He maneuvered her until her ass was pressed against the edge of the desk, caging her legs between his thighs.

"We'll eventually return to my lair in Rome," he promised

her, satisfaction gripping his heart at the thought of Harley in his classically elegant home. She would add a golden warmth that was badly needed amongst the acres of marble and gilt. "But not until I've dealt with Briggs and whatever demon is pulling his strings."

Her hands landed against his chest. "Very macho."

He claimed her lips in a kiss of sheer possession. "I can be a lot more macho, if only you'd let me," he muttered.

"Stop that." She arched back to stab him with a worried gaze. "I'm being serious. You're the king—you should act like one."

His gaze lowered to appreciate the tight stretch of her tank top. "I'm trying."

"Salvatore."

With a sigh, he lifted his gaze. "What kingly act do you want from me?"

"Tell me what would happen if Briggs manages to kill you and take the Were throne?"

His jaw clenched. "Not going to happen."

"Unless you've been covering up a special ability to read the future, you can't know that." Her expression was stern, unflinching. "Is your pride worth risking the future of your people?"

Salvatore met her unwavering gaze. He was a dominant. An alpha who didn't accept having his decisions questioned.

He'd taught more than one Were that painful lesson.

But oddly, he didn't feel the familiar urge to snarl. Harley wasn't his subordinate. The wolf in him had accepted her as a mate. She was his partner, not one of his pack.

"Harley, Briggs is too dangerous to ignore." His hands stroked up her bare arms to grasp her shoulders. "I can't return to Italy until he's destroyed."

"You don't have royal ass-kickers to take care of your killing for you?"

"Any number, but none who would be immune to Briggs's ability to control their minds."

She couldn't dismiss his logic, but that didn't stop her from finding a new argument.

Women were women, regardless of their species.

"Supposing you do manage to kill him . . ."

"Such faith."

"How do you intend to keep him dead?"

Salvatore didn't have an answer.

And at the moment, he had far more important matters on his mind.

Framing her face in his hands, he lowered his head to brush searing kisses over her cheek.

"A worry for tomorrow."

Chapter Twelve

Harley forgot how to breathe as Salvatore found her lips in a slow, drugging kiss.

No big surprise.

His touch was magic.

With a soft groan, his tongue teased her lips wider, his fingers stroking down her throat. It was Harley's turn to groan. He tasted of whiskey and wolf and wild power. A combination that ignited something untamed deep inside her soul.

A compelling, ruthless heat flowed through her blood, making her hands slip beneath the edge of his open shirt to find the satin steel of his chest.

Okay, she might be responsible for her hands doing the full-body search, but he was certainly responsible for shutting down her higher brain functions. If she'd been thinking clearly, she would have shoved him across the room, not discovered the intimate terrain of his upper body.

His hands shifted to cup her aching breasts, his thumbs circling the rigid thrust of her nipples until she was squirming against him.

"Harley . . ."

His husky words were cut short as Salvatore abruptly lifted his head and glanced toward the door. Harley felt a prickle of energy and the heavy bolt slid shut just as she caught Santiago's approaching scent.

"Go away," Salvatore barked, his muscles coiled and prepared for action.

There was a soft chuckle as Santiago halted near the door, but the vamp was smart enough not to try and enter the room.

Thank God.

"The entertainment is about to begin," he said, his voice deliciously cool and filled with invitation. "I'm certain Harley would enjoy our modest show."

A golden glow illuminated Salvatore's eyes, his rich, musky scent filling the room.

"Santiago, 'go away' is a fairly simple command to understand. Of course, I could come out there and explain it to you."

"I prefer you send Harley out."

"A leech with a death wish," Salvatore growled. "My favorite kind."

Harley heaved the universal sigh of a woman dealing with two stupid men.

"Is this really necessary?"

Salvatore flashed a wickedly infectious grin. "No, but it's always fun."

"Harley, if you are able to slip from your furry leash, feel free to join me. Drinks . . ." Santiago deliberately paused. "And whatever else you might desire, are on the house."

"I'll keep your offer in mind, Santiago," Harley said, her gaze warning Salvatore to keep his mouth shut. She wasn't in the mood for a pissing match. "Thank you."

"My pleasure."

Salvatore's tension eased as Santiago's scent faded. "I

hate vamps. Now . . ." His fingers lightly traced the line of her tank top, the heat of his fingers singeing her skin with pleasure. "Where were we?"

One step away from complete insanity, Harley abruptly realized.

Shoving her hands against his chest, Harley edged enough space to slip away from the desk and Salvatore's oh-my-God touch.

"So what's the entertainment that he's talking about?"

Salvatore squeezed his eyes shut, as if in great pain. Then, sucking in a deep breath, he turned to lean against the desk, his arms folded over his chest.

"Have you ever been to a demon nightclub?"

She snorted at the ridiculous question. "Are you kidding? Caine never let me go anywhere I might be seen by a Were. He told me it was for my safety. Jackass."

"Then I would suggest that your introduction to demon society wait." His brooding gaze slid down her body, not bothering to hide his hunger. "Viper's establishments are always over the top."

"Let me guess—you have your own entertainment in mind."

"Now that you mention it . . ."

The golden eyes flared and the power of his desire smacked into her, nearly sending her to her knees. Holy crap. Her stomach clenched as the vivid image of Salvatore bending her over the desk and roughly taking her from behind seared through her mind.

She rushed toward the door. "I want a drink."

"Do I get a veto?" Salvatore muttered, then as Harley threw the bolt and yanked open the door, he hurried to her side, taking her arm in a possessive grip. "Damn. Wait for me."

She shivered as he led her across the lobby, his mesmerizing, musky scent seeping into her skin as if attempting to brand her.

"There's no need for you to go."

"Trust me, there's every need," he said in dark tones, his brows lifting as she unconsciously rubbed her prickling arms. "Is something wrong?"

"Did you put on cologne?"

An oddly rueful smile curved his lips. "Dolce & Gabbana. Do you like it?"

"It's . . . memorable."

"More like eternal."

She frowned. "What?"

"This way." He ignored her question and pointed toward a set of double doors guarded by a matching set of vampires.

And what vampires they were.

Yow.

Chiseled perfection with the polished golden skin of ancient Egyptians, they had ebony hair that hung down their backs in long braids. Their faces were sculpted masterpieces of high cheekbones, hawkish noses, and noble brows. As she neared, she realized that they had a heavy band of kohl tattooed into their skin to emphasize their almond black eyes, and a hint of color on their full lips.

As if their stunning beauty needed any artificial assistance.

They were mouthwatering enough in their teeny tiny loincloths that revealed the sort of bodies that must have made Cleopatra howl in appreciation.

As they neared, the two silently pulled open the heavy doors, their gazes lingering on Harley with silent invitations of sultry pleasure.

Salvatore swept her past the demons as if they were

invisible, his profile hard as they started down the wide stone steps that led deep beneath the building.

"You're sure about this?" he demanded, his hand tightening on her arm as the air thickened with the scent and sounds of the gathered crowd.

"I've lived with a pack of curs for thirty years. There's nothing that can shock me." Her unfounded bravado lasted until they reached the bottom of the steps and Salvatore shoved open yet another door, this one of steel, and the full force of the gathered demons hit her. "Okay. I might have spoken a little hastily."

"Do you want to leave?"

Harley barely heard his question, her attention focused on the scene spread below her.

In contrast to the airy elegance above, the vast room was circular and made of black marble that terraced downward. On each tier were a series of steel tables and stools that were bolted to the marble, and a series of staircases that led to the huge metal cage set in the lowest level of the chamber.

Overhead, heavy chandeliers spilled pools of light on the crowd of guests, battling back the shadows that twined along the edges, hiding those guests who preferred to remain concealed.

It looked more like Thunderdome than a nightclub.

Salvatore bent to speak directly in her ear, the clamor of the crowd nearly deafening.

"Do you want to leave?"

Her mouth was dry as her gaze skimmed over the demons of varying species. The only thing they had in common was the tangible sense of violence that crackled around them.

She briefly hesitated, torn between good old-fashioned common sense, and the desire to flirt with danger.

She'd always wanted to discover the world outside Caine's lair, hadn't she? Well, here it was. In all its glory.

Or rather, its lack of glory.

"Not on your life," she said, tilting her chin with a display of courage she was far from feeling.

"It just might be," Salvatore muttered, glaring at two hulking trolls who were eyeing Harley as if she were a tasty appetizer.

With a lift of his slender hand, a beautiful female imp with pale red hair and ivory curves on full display in a tiny spandex dress rushed to do his bidding. And if her smile was anything to go by, she was hoping his bidding included taking off that scrap of spandex.

Harley gritted her teeth, but Salvatore seemed oblivious to the woman's blatant invitation.

"A booth," he commanded. "As far from the arena as possible."

"Of course." With a venomous glance toward Harley, the imp wound her way past the tables on the top tier, leading them to a shadowed alcove that held a small booth. Harley slid onto a steel bench seat and Salvatore settled opposite her, his gaze sweeping the crowd rather than focusing on the imp who had practically thrust her breasts beneath his nose. "A drink, lover?"

Harley cleared her throat. "A Bloody Mary," she ordered, her tone warning that her drink wasn't going to be the only bloody thing if the bitch didn't back off.

As if sensing the sudden tension in the air, Salvatore studied her flushed face with a smug smile.

"Hennessy," he absently ordered.

With a flounce, the imp turned and stormed through the crowed, presumably headed to the bar for their drinks. Avidly aware of Salvatore's unwavering gaze, Harley settled back in her seat.

"Isn't Hennessy a little snobbish for a joint like this?"

He reached to stroke his finger over the back of her hand that was lying on the table.

"What can I say? I'm a Were of discerning taste."

Her clever comeback died on her lips as spotlights abruptly flared across the ceiling and the milling crowd erupted into noisy cheers.

Glancing upward, Harley watched as four small golden cages were lowered from the hidden traps in the ceiling. They halted several feet over the large cage on the floor, dangling in the spotlights.

"Holy crap," she breathed, allowing her gaze to shift from one cage to another. "Are those imps?"

Salvatore grimaced. "They're part of the show."

That wasn't reassuring considering the four imps, two male and two female, were completely naked except for the heavy steel collars around their necks.

"Just what is this show?"

"The demon version of *The Dating Game.*"

Harley shook her head. She was addicted to the Game Show Network, and she hadn't seen any show with naked imps hanging in cages.

"Somehow I don't think the human version is even in the same universe. I assume there are a few rules?"

"Rudimentary ones. You pay an exorbitant amount of money for the privilege of joining a dozen other demons in the pit." He pointed toward the huge cage on the floor that could accommodate an indoor soccer league. "The last demon standing is rewarded with a key."

"Key?"

His hand lifted toward the cages, each with a large lock that held the doors shut.

"Once the winner makes his or her choice, the next batch is herded into the pit for their chance at a key."

Outrage flowed through Harley like molten lava. For all of Caine's faults, he'd always made certain that the males in his pack understood the penalty of rape.

Death.

Slow, tortuous, painful death.

"Those are sex slaves?"

"No." Salvatore squeezed her fingers, anxious to keep her from doing something stupid. "I'll admit that I wouldn't shed a tear if someone managed to plant a stake in Viper's unbeating heart, but he would never allow slaves in his club."

"How do you know?"

He leaned close and spoke low enough that not even the most talented demon could overhear him.

"Viper was held as a slave for centuries. He would slaughter anyone involved in the trade."

His reassurances were backed up by the sight of the imps, who happily leaned against the bars of their cages to provoke the crowd below into a near frenzy.

"And you?" she asked.

He chuckled as he lifted her hand to his lips, his tongue tracing the line of her knuckles.

"I don't need such crude methods. My charm is enough to enslave others."

She might debate his charm, but his touch was enough to make a woman beg for more.

"And you call Caine delusional," she said, her words sounding lame as heat curled through the pit of her stomach.

Thankfully the imp chose that moment to return with their drinks, her barely covered boobs distracting Salvatore enough for Harley to jerk her hand free.

Not that it did a damned bit of good.

The excitement bubbled through her blood like the

finest champagne, her skin crawling with a prickling awareness. She shifted uneasily in her seat, suddenly damp and aching.

What the hell?

Waving away the persistent imp, Salvatore shot Harley a knowing smile, easily sensing her stirring hunger.

"You should at least enjoy the warm-up act."

Before she could ask, she caught sight of the naked men covered in nothing more than elaborate tattoos styled into Chinese symbols. They appeared to be human males—except no human was so perfectly ripped no matter how often they worked out, and their skin didn't glow with an oddly metallic shimmer—as they weaved a sensuous path through the tables.

"Frigging hell." Harley drained her Bloody Mary as one of the demons halted in front of their table, performing an erotic dance that had to be illegal in some states. Unable to tear her gaze from the alien beauty of the aquiline features and black, slanted eyes, she struggled to breathe. "What are they?"

"Nozama demons," Salvatore said. "In their culture, the women are the warriors while the males are judged on their sexual prowess."

"Now that is a fine culture," she approved in husky tones, clutching the edge of the table to keep her hands from straying where they didn't belong.

Salvatore growled low in his throat, sending the demon scurrying to the next table.

"Female warriors are respected in Were society, and our sexual prowess is renown throughout the demon world," he informed her, reaching to take her hand in a possessive grip.

"Almost as renowned as your arrogance."

"*Our* arrogance," he corrected, leaning far enough

across the table that his warm breath brushed her cheek. "You're a pureblood, Harley. It is past time you returned to your pack."

A sharp ache tugged at her heart. An unpleasant reminder of the loneliness that had plagued her all her life.

As a Were, she instinctively craved the connection to a pack. Not only for protection, but for the companionship that was as important to purebloods as food and sex.

There had always been a very large part of herself missing.

Still, she wasn't prepared to make commitments to anyone. Not Salvatore. Not her sisters.

"I'll decide if or when I return to a pack," she warned.

Lifting her arm, Salvatore nuzzled the pulse hammering in her inner wrist.

"I could make the decision an easy one if you would let me."

"Not everyone is ruled by their hormones."

The golden eyes flashed with heat. "Ah, if only that were true."

Harley's lips parted as a blast of lust slammed into her.

It wasn't the persistent tug that was always present when Salvatore was near. Or the intense hunger that his kisses so easily roused.

This was a jarring, overwhelming need that felt unpleasantly like drowning.

"Giuliani?" she rasped.

"Relax, *cara.*" He gently massaged her hand.

"What is it?"

"The dancers release a pheromone. It helps encourage more participants to ante up for a turn in the pit."

"Crap." She shifted on the hard bench, her skin coated in perspiration. "I'm about ready to ante up myself."

Without warning, Salvatore surged to his feet, pulling her off the bench and against his hard body.

"No need to fight, *cara,*" he husked. "Unless that turns you on."

In this moment, everything was turning Harley on.

The feel of Salvatore's hard body, his frigging delicious musky scent, the pulse of his outrageous power . . .

Without warning, a hand descended on her shoulder, yanking her around to discover a large Pecoste demon leering at her with yellow eyes, his tusks dripping with venom.

Salvatore instantly bared his teeth, his eyes blazing with the eerie glow of a werewolf a breath away from shifting.

"Remove your hand before I . . ."

Harley didn't wait for the two males to enjoy banging on their chests and blowing a lot of hot air.

With one smooth motion, she kicked the Pecoste demon in the knee, waiting for him to instinctively bend over before she connected her fist with his chin. The demon flew backwards, landing on a table two tiers down. There was a snarl of anger from the demons below and a savage brawl broke out, but Harley didn't wait to appreciate her handiwork.

Instead she wiped her hands on her jeans and met Salvatore's amused gaze.

"When I need rescuing, I'll let you know."

"I'll keep that in mind."

The scuffle had been fun, but the aching lust was still curling through her body. God Almighty. If she didn't have relief soon, she might just explode.

"I've seen enough," she muttered, heading for the exit as she wiped the sweat from her brow.

Not surprisingly Salvatore was swiftly at her side. "Where are you going?"

"My room."

They waded through the crowd in silence, at last reaching the door and climbing the stairs. With every step, the clinging pheromones lessened, easing the choking desire, but Harley's pace never slowed. The artificial lust might be dismissed by a change of location, but the restless hunger that continued to plague her would not be so easily banished.

She didn't know what the future held, but she knew that Salvatore wouldn't wait much longer to go after Briggs. The next few hours might be their last together.

Bypassing the lobby, Harley headed straight for her room on the upper floor, pulling her key card from her pocket and throwing open the door. Then, before she could remind herself of all the reasons why this was such a bad idea, she grabbed Salvatore's arm and tugged him into the room, slamming the door behind him.

Salvatore lifted his brows in wary surprise. "Harley?"

"Isn't this what you wanted?" she demanded, pushing him against the wall and running her hands over the hard planes of his chest.

Without warning, Salvatore grasped her wrists, halting her impatient caresses.

"Wait, *cara*."

Her gut twisted with frustration. "Are you kidding me?"

His eyes narrowed. "I won't be accused of taking advantage of you while you're under the influence."

"Fine." She leaned forward, licking a line from his sternum to the hollow of his neck. "Then I'll take advantage of you."

He shuddered, his heat flaring through the room with the force of a nuclear blast.

"Works for me," he rasped, loosening her wrists so he could pull out the scrunchie holding her hair, ramming his fingers through the thick strands. Harley wasted no time as she grasped the silk of his shirt and ripped it off him. Salvatore laughed with smug pleasure. "*Dio.* Remind me to triple my clothing allowance."

Harley tilted back her head to meet the golden gaze half-shielded beneath his thick lashes.

"Don't be making plans that include me, Giuliani. This is . . ."

"Extraordinary," he interrupted, his hands grasping her hips and jerking her against his rigid cock.

"A temporary madness."

"I'll agree to the madness part." He grabbed the bottom of her tank top, pulled it over her head, and tossed it to the floor. Her bra was next, leaving her breasts bare for his intimate exploration. "Mind-blowing, heart-stopping madness."

She groaned as his thumbs found her hardened nipples, his head lowering to capture her lips in a kiss that demanded utter surrender.

He tasted of aged cognac, his tongue tangling with hers as his fingers tugged at the tips of her breasts, sending jolts of raw pleasure to the pit of her stomach. Harley widened her lips beneath his savage demand, her hands fumbling with the leather belt.

A wildfire was racing through her, and she was eager to be consumed by the flames.

Having dealt with the belt buckle, Harley tugged open the button of his slacks and slid down the zipper, her heart slamming against her chest as her fingers circled his heavy arousal.

Salvatore muttered a low curse, his hips surging forward as a sheen of sweat coated his beautiful face.

"Careful, *cara,*" he gritted. "I'm trying to remember to be gentle."

In answer, Harley balanced on her tiptoes, biting the side of his neck with enough force to draw blood.

"I'm not afraid of the big bad wolf."

With a muted roar, Salvatore was spinning to the side, slamming her into the wall as he dropped to his knees in front of her.

"You should be," he warned, his hands ripping off her jeans, and the tiny triangle of lace beneath.

"Salvatore . . ."

Her breath stuck in her throat as his lips trailed a searing path up the inside of her thighs, while his hands firmly tugged her legs farther apart.

Her fingers dug into his hair, a shudder of sheer delight shaking through her.

"Oh . . . Lord."

"It's too late for prayers," he muttered, giving her legs one last tug so he could find the damp heat he was searching for.

Harley swallowed her scream, her body quivering with erotic approval. She liked having Salvatore on his knees, making love to her with his tongue and teeth.

Her eyes slid closed, her hands stroking through his hair as a sweet tension coiled deep in her womb. She briefly remembered that there had been some insane reason that she wanted to avoid Salvatore's magical touch, but in this moment, she didn't give a crap.

Over and over his tongue teased her clitoris, occasionally thrusting into her opening with a skill that had her charging full steam toward her climax.

Measuring her quickening pants, Salvatore abruptly straightened, kicking off his shoes and slacks to stand before her in his full glory.

And he was glorious.

His lean, perfect features. His luminous golden eyes. His chiseled, bronzed body. His cock, fully erect and eager to please.

Allowing her a few moments to appreciate the sight of his naked body, Salvatore grasped her by the waist and turned her away from him.

"Put your hands on the wall and keep your arms stiff," he rasped in her ear, tugging her leg up and over his thigh, leaving her feeling oddly vulnerable.

Caught off guard, Harley glanced over her shoulder in confusion, her heart jerking at the stark beauty of his bronzed face.

"What the hell are you doing?"

"Trust me," he said, his hand gripping her inner thigh at the same moment his erection nudged at her slit from behind.

"Yes."

Her head fell back against his shoulder, her neck boneless with blistering pleasure as he surged inside her. He was large and angled to thrust deep, each driving plunge hovering between intense bliss and pain.

Leaning heavily against the wall to support her weak knees, Harley groaned as his fingers slid between her folds, stroking through her damp heat in pace with the fierce, relentless pump of his hips.

Somewhere in the dark, a pack of curs was searching for them, Briggs was plotting his evil, and the King of Vampires was rushing in their direction. But the dangers held no meaning for Harley as her body tightened with a near unbearable excitement.

With a growl that was more animal than human, Salvatore buried his face in the curve of her neck, his mouth nuzzling her sensitive skin.

"You're mine," he said, his low words seeming to brand themselves on her soul. "For now and all eternity."

"No."

"Yes, Harley." He thrust deeper, possessing her with every stroke. "There's no going back."

"Dammit, Salvatore . . ."

Her words were cut short as Salvatore sank his teeth into the base of her neck. Shocked by the delectable attack, Harley's body arched, and a scream was wrenched from her throat as the shattering climax clutched at her body . . .

Chapter Thirteen

Caine gripped the steering wheel of the Jeep, heading back to his St. Louis lair at a pace just short of light speed.

He was a good enough general to know he should be with his pack, leading them in pursuit of Salvatore and Harley.

The curs were spooked by Salvatore's display of power over them. It was one thing to hear rumors of the king's ability to force a werewolf to shift, and quite another to experience it firsthand.

And Vikki was certain to bolt at the first sign of trouble. She might be willing to use her magical abilities to impress him, but not if it meant bringing any danger to herself.

Without Caine driving them on, they'd quite likely dillydally long enough to make certain that Salvatore managed to escape.

At the moment, however, Caine was too distracted to launch an all-out offensive against the King of Weres.

He needed time to sort through the doubts that were beginning to plague him.

Predictably, what he needed and what he got were two very different things.

Skimming down the graveled back roads that wound through recently plowed fields, Caine slammed on the brakes as the familiar scent of rotting flesh assaulted him.

"Shit."

Andre shoved his dark hair from his face, his nose wrinkled with disgust.

"What the hell is that?"

"Company," Caine muttered, wishing he had the balls to ignore the unmistakable summons. Of course, if he ignored the summons there was a good chance he wouldn't have any balls to worry about.

"Company?" Andre shuddered. "It smells like he needs to lay down so someone can finish burying him."

Caine shoved the stick shift into park. "Stay here."

"No. You . . ."

Caine's hand shot out to grab his companion by the throat. "Stay. Here."

"Got it," the cur rasped. "Stay here."

Ignoring the bile that rose in his throat, Caine headed for the small cluster of trees. This was what he'd signed up for, wasn't it? A little tit for a little tat.

He just wanted to get his damned tit so he could be done with the nasty tat.

There was an odd shimmer among the shadows, then the outline of Briggs appeared, his crimson eyes glowing like the pits of hell. Obediently, Caine fell to his knees.

"Master."

A blast of cold swirled through the air, crawling over Caine's skin.

"Scurrying back to your lair like the spineless coward you are, eh, Caine?"

"I have my pack searching for Salvatore. It's only a

matter of time before they capture him." The lies tripped easily off Caine's tongue, his head lowered to hide his wary expression. "I need to make sure I have a cell prepared that can hold him."

"There's no need. Our plans have changed."

Caine stiffened. A change in plan usually meant the first plan had gone to hell. Not what he wanted to hear.

"What do you mean?"

"Congratulations, cur," Briggs hissed. "Your day of glory is at hand. Soon you will be transformed, as you always dreamed."

Caine slowly lifted his head, suspicious. Briggs had always been far too vague on how this transformation was supposed to take place.

"How? Harley has escaped."

"Forget the bitch."

"But . . ."

The crimson eyes flared with lethal anger. "I must have Salvatore."

Caine swallowed his demand to know the hows, whens, and wheres of the mystical transformation that had been promised to him for years.

His personal vision had revealed his blood running over barren stone, shimmering with the power only true Weres possessed, but interpreting such a vision was always difficult.

"My pack is on his trail."

"Salvatore will destroy your pathetic excuse for a pack without breaking a sweat."

Caine ground his teeth. "I'm aware of Salvatore's superior strength."

"Then you will pull back your servants and allow me to deal with the bastard."

"Deal with him, or kill him?"

"Oh, I'll kill him in due time." The Were's voice was thick with anticipation. "First, I have need of him alive."

The memory of the violent battlefield he'd left behind spoiled Caine's pleasure at savoring Salvatore's impending downfall. Briggs might boast about his plans for the King of Weres, but Caine was no longer willing to believe that Briggs was invincible.

"You intend to capture him?"

"Yes."

"By yourself?"

An icy power slammed into Caine's chest, stopping his heart.

"Surely you don't doubt my ability to do so?"

Caine's hands dug into the dirt, the pain radiating from his chest through his body in sharp bursts.

"I would never be so foolish," he groaned.

"I wonder." The repulsive smell nearly choked Caine as Briggs moved closer. "Could it be that your loyalty is wavering, Caine?"

Caine pressed his head to the ground. Damn. He'd gone too far. Briggs wouldn't tolerate having his superiority over Salvatore questioned. Certainly not by a mere cur.

Time for damage control.

"No, master, but Salvatore has often joined powers with the vampires. He will be next to impossible to capture if he is protected by the bloodsuckers."

Briggs snorted, not so easily deceived. "Then it's fortunate I have no need to capture Salvatore."

"You believe he'll turn himself over to you?"

"That's exactly what I believe."

"I'm going to admit that would be my last guess." Caine was careful to speak into the mud. Briggs was still too close for his peace of mind. "Salvatore might be arrogant, but he isn't suicidal."

"No, but he's desperate to kill me. Once I offer him the opportunity, he'll be more than eager to join me."

"He'll sense it's a trap."

Briggs laughed. A hollow, sinister sound that made the distant coyotes howl in alarm.

Gallows humor. Had to love it.

"And yet, he'll still come. Salvatore is nothing if not predictable."

Warily, Caine lifted his head, meeting the crimson gaze. "I assume I have some role in all of this?"

"There are a pack of curs camped near your lair, believing you still hold Salvatore."

Caine shrugged. He'd received a call from his pack the minute the curs had surrounded his house.

"They're being watched."

"I want you to bring them to me here."

As the words left Briggs's lips, an image of barren caves below an abandoned Victorian church seared through Caine's mind. Not just figuratively seared, but actually and painfully seared. Like a map had been branded into his brain tissue.

Holy hell. Hadn't the bastard heard of GPS?

"Why?"

"Because I want Salvatore to suffer before he dies," Briggs said, his hatred for the King of Weres pulsing in the air. "There are few things that give me more pleasure than the thought of watching Salvatore's anguish as he's forced to kill one of his loyal servants."

Caine hid his shudder. He'd always considered himself a badass who ruled his pack with an iron fist, but Briggs made him seem like a freaking pansy in comparison.

"Yeah, I can just imagine."

"Ah, but you won't have to imagine," Briggs taunted. "You'll be at my side."

Rising to his feet, Caine covertly stepped back from the biting cold that surrounded Briggs.

"And I'll be given the secret to unlocking the Were's blood?"

"Don't worry, Caine. Soon you'll be given the reward you so richly deserve," Briggs crooned, the crimson eyes mocking. "Don't fail me."

There was a loud pop, and the Were disappeared.

Caine didn't hesitate. Spinning on his heel, he darted back to the Jeep. No way he was waiting around for an encore performance.

Glad he'd taken the doors out of his vehicle, Caine vaulted into his seat and rammed the Jeep into drive.

"Shit."

Andre gripped the dashboard as Caine thundered over a wooden bridge without slowing.

"Are you okay?"

Caine shivered, the nasty cold still clinging to his skin.

"Soon you'll be given the reward you so richly deserve . . ."

He should be delirious. He should be tap dancing on top of the freaking world.

Instead he wished that Briggs had taken his damned visions to some other gullible cur.

"What I am is screwed," he muttered.

Andre narrowed his dark gaze. "Do I need to scout a new lair? The Bahamas? Australia? The Antarctic?"

Caine had to admit it was tempting.

He could keep driving and start over far, far away from the feuding Weres. To hell with becoming a pureblood.

Then he gave a shake of his head. "It's too late to run," he grimly admitted. "There's nothing left but to hope we can survive this fucking train crash."

* * *

Salvatore paced the floor of Harley's bedroom, the disposable cell phone that Santiago had left for him pressed to his ear. Listening to Hess's recorded voice echo in his ear, he halted to gaze down at the black-and-gold bed that was still rumpled and warm from his last bout of mind-blowing sex with Harley.

Cristo, the woman was teaching him a whole new meaning of paradise.

It was more than the raw, feral pleasure that exploded between them. More than the sense of destiny that hummed through his veins. More than the relentless ache to keep his mate near.

It was the simple, uncomplicated pleasure of a man who had just made love to the woman who filled his heart with joy.

The scent of rich vanilla teased at his nose. Salvatore turned to watch as Harley strolled from the attached bathroom, a white towel wrapped around her slender body, her damp hair clinging to her bare shoulders.

He snapped shut the phone and tossed it on the bed, hiding a smile as Harley allowed her gaze to covertly slide over his naked form before jerking back to his face.

"Something wrong?" she demanded.

"I've tried to contact Hess, but I go straight to voicemail."

"You think something's happened to him?"

Salvatore shrugged, not bothering to hide his frustration. He was the perfect example of a control freak. Delegating gave him a rash, and asking others for help, especially the brigade of the living dead, was worse than chewing on silver.

"It's impossible to know, and until Briggs is dead, along with his ability to control the minds of curs, I can't take the risk of tracking him down. I must depend on Styx to send out a search party."

Attempting to appear nonchalant, Harley moved to the bed, burrowing beneath the comforter to hide her delectable body.

"Speaking of Styx, what do you plan to do once he arrives with his Ravens?" she demanded.

As always, Salvatore was fascinated by Harley's odd combination of fierce, brazen desire and blushing female reserve.

Lured like a moth to the flame, he crossed to perch on the edge of the mattress, his fingers toying with a wet strand of hair that draped over her shoulder. Instantly his frustration eased.

"I intend to travel with them back to Chicago."

"And then?"

"Is there a reason for your curiosity?" He leaned forward to plant a kiss just below her ear. "Do you have plans for me, *cara*?"

She stiffened, the scent of her arousal perfuming the air. "Several."

"Several?" His tongue traced the line of her collarbone. "I like the sound of that."

"Most of them include a muzzle and a silver leash."

"Kinky."

She pressed her hands against his shoulders, pushing him back with a chiding expression.

"Does anything deflate that oversized ego of yours?"

He grabbed her hand to pull it to his mouth, nibbling on the pad of her thumb.

"Not when I have you in my bed."

"Salvatore . . ." Her words broke off as she frowned with a sudden distraction, turning her head to sniff at her outstretched arm. "Good God."

"What's wrong?"

"I just took a shower."

"You should have waited for me," he teased, keeping a cautious watch on the glitter in her hazel eyes. Harley didn't have to be able to shift to be dangerous. "I would have scrubbed your back."

"I scrubbed my own back, so the question is . . ." Her eyes narrowed. "Why do I still smell like you?"

"Ah," Salvatore breathed, forgetting the danger as a primitive, wholly uncivilized surge of satisfaction raced through him.

His mating musk had been in full bloom during their rousing bout of sex. She would carry his mark for days.

"What's going on?"

"Have you ever heard the saying, 'That what you don't know can't hurt you'?" he asked, his smile wry.

She jerked her hand from his grasp. "You're hiding something from me."

"No. If you want the truth I'll give it to you, but . . ."

"If you tell me I can't handle the truth, I swear I'll rip your tongue out."

Salvatore studied her in silence. The pale, perfect features. The clear hazel eyes. The full, lush lips.

A face that was forever engraved on his heart.

To tell or not to tell?

He hadn't intended to reveal the mating. Not until he was done killing Briggs and putting the curs back in their place so he had time to concentrate on a full-scale charm offensive.

For all his outrageous arrogance, he wasn't stupid enough to pretend that Harley was ready and eager to be his mate. Hell, she was still trying to decide whether he was friend or enemy.

He didn't want to scare her off before he could do some serious wooing.

Then again, he was beginning to understand this female.

She would badger and pester and be as annoying as possible until she was satisfied he'd revealed what she wanted to know.

"Very well, but don't say I didn't warn you."

Her jaw tightened with impatience. "Giuliani."

He caught and held her gaze. "You carry my scent because you're my mate."

Her face paled, her eyes wide with a stunned disbelief. Salvatore swallowed a sigh. Well, he hadn't expected high-fives and backflips. Still, it would be nice if she didn't look as if she'd just been told she had the ebola virus.

"Mate?" She shook her head. "No freaking way."

He shrugged, disguising his disappointment with indifference.

"You asked."

She scooted to press her back against the headboard, bending her knees and wrapping her arms around them in an unconsciously defensive position.

"I may have been raised by a pack of curs instead of your precious purebloods, but even I know that true matings disappeared centuries ago," she charged. "Caine always claimed that they were nothing more than a myth to begin with."

Salvatore's temper flared. Until the mating bond was complete, even the mention of another male was enough to stir his Neanderthal urges.

"What would a cur know of our history?"

"So he lied when he said that Weres no longer mated?"

With an effort, he reined in his overly possessive wolf.

"It's true that matings were thought to have faded, along with many other Were abilities."

"Then obviously you've made a mistake." She licked her lips, her voice vibrating with unsettled nerves. "We can't be mated."

He smiled wryly. She'd helped him escape from Caine with unwavering courage. She'd faced a demented Briggs without flinching. But the mere mention of being his mate tweaked her out.

Should he be offended or pleased he could inspire such a violent reaction?

"I didn't say we were mated," he corrected, deliberately stroking his fingers up her bare arm. She shivered beneath his touch, her sweet vanilla scent mixing with his musk in a combination that set his blood on fire. "I said you were my mate."

"Is this some sort of trick?"

"More like the irony of fate."

Not amused, she glared at him. "Would you just tell me what's going on? Why do you think I'm your mate?"

"When a male pureblood discovers his true mate, he produces a very specific musk to mark her."

There was a short, dangerous pause. "Mark her?"

"It's a warning to other males to back off."

"You covered me in your scent to scare off other men?"

He skimmed his fingers back down to her wrist, unable to pretend even a token of regret. If he had his way, Harley would be carrying his scent for the rest of eternity.

"It wasn't intentional."

"Bullshit."

He shifted until he was pressed against her hip, able to feel her searing heat through the comforter.

"Harley, as much as I hate to admit it, there are a few forces beyond my ability to control." He brushed his finger over the lush curve of her lips. "Besides, the scent will fade in time."

Her glower remained, but the gold flecks in her hazel eyes shimmered with potent awareness. Salvatore was instantly erect and ready to please.

"You're certain?"

"So long as you don't complete the mating bond or haul me back to your bed."

"It just disappears?"

His gaze drifted down to the pulse hammering at the base of her throat.

"Si."

"And I'm no longer your mate?"

"You will always be my mate, *cara.*" He bent forward, his lips touching that fluttering pulse with a stark yearning. "For all eternity. Nothing can change that."

Chapter Fourteen

For a crazed, breathless moment Harley melted beneath Salvatore's experienced touch. She was beyond denying that she wanted this Were with a hunger that was on the wrong side of obsessive. Even after three first-rate, heart-stopping orgasms, her body was ready to go for number four.

Her mind, however, was in stunned mode.

God Almighty.

Was Salvatore completely nuts?

The mere thought she could be his mate took insanity to a whole new level. Not only were true matings nothing more than an urban legend, but they barely knew one another.

No, that wasn't entirely true. A liquid ache between her legs reminded her that they knew each other intimately. But mind-blowing sex didn't equal soul mates.

So why wasn't she laughing it off as a bad joke? Or sympathizing with his obvious descent into raving lunacy?

This thundering panic implied an emotional reaction she wasn't prepared to admit.

Not even to herself.

With a sharp motion, she pushed off the bed, keeping the damp towel wrapped around her shivering body. In silence she paced from one end of the black-and-gold room to the other, intensely aware of Salvatore's searing gaze following her every move.

At last he rose to his feet and crossed to stand directly in her path, his body gloriously naked and his expression somber.

"Harley?"

She jerked up her head to meet his brooding gaze. "You can't just assume I'm your mate because I smell like you," she abruptly informed him. "I mean, the past few days have been crazy. This could all be nothing more than stress."

"Male Weres produce musk only when in the presence of their mates," he said. "But it's more than just the change in my scent. I knew you were my mate the moment we met."

"How?"

"Here." He grabbed her hand and pressed it to his chest, directly over the steady beat of his heart. "You're stealing my powers. Along with most of my sanity."

She eyed him warily, wondering if this was all some bizarre joke.

"I believe the sanity thing, but I don't know what the hell you're babbling about with your powers. Even if I wanted to, I wouldn't know how to steal them."

A wry smile curved his lips, but the golden eyes remained watchful, closely monitoring her reaction.

"You don't have to do anything but be yourself, *cara*. It's the nature of the mating bond to weaken the male."

Harley abruptly recalled Salvatore's unexpected bouts of weakness during their flight from Caine. And his obvious weariness after being attacked by Briggs.

At the time, she'd put it down to the endless battles and the silver that had been lodged in his shoulder . . .

Now her heart slowly squeezed at the realization that if Salvatore was actually telling the truth, she'd been responsible for the chinks in his considerable armor. For God's sake, she could have gotten him killed without even knowing it.

"What kind of stupid tradition is that?" she muttered sourly. "Haven't the Weres heard of the Darwin theory? Males should get stronger, not weaker, when they have a mate."

A dangerous smile curved his lips as his hands grabbed the top edge of her towel and yanked her against him.

"It's to keep him from taking his mate by force," he growled, his eyes darkening with a slumberous invitation. "The female must be willing or the bond can't be completed."

She studied his lean, beautiful face, searching for some sign of resentment. Surely he had to be pissed at having his powers hijacked?

If he was, he hid it well. At the moment there was nothing but a blazing hunger that smacked into her with delicious force.

Suddenly she was acutely aware of his fingers that curled beneath the towel and branded the upper curve of her breasts. The hard, ruthless lines of his bronzed body. His intoxicating musk that seeped through her skin and flowed through her blood.

With an effort, Harley held onto a thin strand of sanity.

Dammit, Salvatore was being stalked by a crazed psychopathic Were and a pack of crazed curs with regicide on their minds. He should be concentrating on staying alive.

"And once she agrees to the mating, his strength returns?" she demanded.

He lowered his head to trail his lips over her temple, the satin curtain of his hair brushing her cheek.

"It returns even greater than before." His mouth traced the line of her brow. "There's also a legend that ancient mated pairs were once capable of sharing their powers, so they were all but invincible."

The heat shimmered through her body, the potent force weakening her knees. Instinctively she grabbed for his shoulders, her nails digging into his rigid muscles. He growled in approval.

Dammit, he wasn't going to distract her.

This was too important.

"So how does the female complete this mating bond?"

He teased at the corner of her mouth. "I don't know."

She pulled back to glare at him. "How can you not know?"

"It's not a ritual the female performs. She doesn't dance around a bonfire or sacrifice small animals." His lips curled in a smile filled with wicked promise. "Of course, if *you* wanted to dance around the bonfire naked . . ."

"Salvatore."

He heaved a sigh, his hands shifting to frame her face, his gaze stabbing deep into her wide eyes.

"Either the female accepts the male, or she rejects him. It's as mystical and unexplainable as falling in love."

"And if she doesn't accept him?"

"Then he'll devote the rest of eternity to changing her mind." With a powerful motion, Salvatore swept her off her feet and headed to the bed. Harley's stomach clenched at the focused intent engraved on his face. "Like this."

"Wait," she breathed, her voice already thick with a pulsing need. "Your powers . . ."

The golden glow of his eyes spilled through the room. "Are ready and willing to please you."

"I'm serious, Salvatore. You can't go against Briggs while you're weakened," she protested, her breath tangling in her lungs as she landed spread-eagle on the mattress, Salvatore covering her with his heavily aroused body.

"Harley, the last thing I want to think about right now is Briggs."

"This conversation isn't over . . ."

He slid into her with one smooth thrust, and not only was the conversation over, but so was all rational thought.

Wrapping her legs around his hips, Harley closed her eyes in exquisite pleasure, settling for communicating in a more primitive language.

Harley hadn't intended to fall asleep. One minute she'd been floating on a cloud of postcoital bliss and the next she'd been snuggling into Salvatore's arms and drifting into unconsciousness.

She didn't know how long she'd been out when she was awakened by Salvatore whispering in her ear.

"Harley."

"Hmmmm?"

"Harley, I need you get out of bed and dressed as quickly as you can."

It was the tension vibrating in his voice that had Harley's eyes snapping open with sudden alarm.

"Are the vampires here?"

Salvatore eased from the bed and tugged on a pair of jeans. "No."

Harley shook off her lingering glow and crawled out of bed to pull on her own clothes, shoving her fingers through her hair before fastening it back with a scrunchie. No one wanted to face trouble naked.

"What is it?"

Salvatore absently slipped on a black satin shirt, leaving it open as he sat on the edge of the bed and shoved his feet into a pair of black biker boots. A far cry from his tailored Gucci suit, but still sexy as hell.

Lifting his head, he revealed a grim expression. "Briggs."

Harley's blood ran cold. "He's here?"

"Outside."

"Shit."

Standing, Salvatore crossed the room to grab her by the shoulders.

"Find Santiago and stay with him," he commanded. "Styx should be here within the hour."

Her mouth dropped open with disbelief. Did he really think she was going to be treated like some swooning female who had to be protected by her big strong male?

"No."

"*Cara,* don't argue with me," he growled. "Not now."

She stubbornly held her ground. "You're not facing that lunatic by yourself."

"I'll be fine as long as I know you're safe. Do this for me." His jaw tightened, his eyes dark with concern. "Please."

"Salvatore . . ."

Putting an end to the argument, Salvatore wrapped an arm around her waist and tossed her over his shoulder. Then striding across the floor, he yanked open the door and set her down in the hallway.

"Go."

"Dammit." The door was shut in her face, followed by the distinct sound of the bolt being thrown.

She stood for a minute, weighing the pleasure of

kicking down the door and teaching the damned Were a badly needed lesson in pushing her around against accepting that she was wasting time.

Salvatore was just idiotic enough to face Briggs on his own, regardless of the fact that he wasn't firing on all cylinders.

So freaking, typically male.

Turning on her heel, Harley headed down the stairs and back across the wide lobby. It was late, but she could still hear the muted roars from the nightclub below. Obviously blood and sex were a big draw in the ol' demon world.

She was nearing the stairs leading back down to the pit when a female form detached from a shadowed alcove, and the scent of plums swirled through the air.

Tonya, the royal imp.

Or more likely, the royal slut, Harley cattily decided, her gaze skimming over the red microdress that had been lacquered on the lush body, and the heavy layer of makeup on the pale, perfect face.

"You shouldn't be wandering around on your own, sweet thing," the imp drawled. "There are all sorts of beasties roaming around who don't mind if a woman goes furry once a month."

Not bothering to react to the insult or correct the assumption, Harley stabbed the imp with an impatient glare.

"I need Santiago."

"The King of Weres isn't enough for you?"

Harley stepped until they were nose to nose. "Don't. Screw. With. Me. Where is he?"

The woman swallowed, her eyes suddenly wide. "His office."

"You see, that wasn't so hard."

With a pat on the imp's cheek, Harley headed for the

back of the lobby, not missing a step as the angry woman called out behind her.

"Bitch."

Reaching the office, Harley shoved open the door and stepped over the threshold, indifferent to the dangers of intruding on a vampire without invitation.

"I need your help."

Seated behind his desk, Santiago gave a lift of his brows before slowly rising to his feet.

"Of course. I am at your service."

"Salvatore is going outside to meet with Briggs."

"Briggs?"

"A psychotic zombie pureblood who's filled with black magic and sporting a nasty temper." Her voice was clipped with impatience. "He's convinced himself that he should be sitting on the Were throne."

With fluid, almost dizzying speed, Santiago was moving toward a far wall, pressing his fingers to the frame of one of the paintings. With a small swoosh the wall slid inward, revealing a hidden tunnel.

"Wait here," the vamp commanded, disappearing into the dark.

"Where are you going?" Harley threw her hands in the air as the demon ignored her, continuing on to his bat cave and leaving her to twiddle her damn thumbs. "God. Men are so freaking annoying."

She glared at the opening, but she wasn't stupid enough to follow. Entering the private lair of a vampire was a death sentence. Pure and simple.

Instead she anxiously paced the floor, cursing the dampening spell that made it impossible for her to sense whether Salvatore had already left the building.

How had Briggs managed to find them? And how

had he broken through the enchantment to contact Salvatore without alerting Santiago?

Still pacing the floor, her stomach clenched with a fear that sparked her temper.

She curled her hands to fists. Why did she even care what happened to the arrogant King of Weres? Just a week ago he'd been the boogeyman that Caine used to keep her prisoner. Okay, she didn't think he was out to kill her anymore. And he most certainly was the kind of take-no-prisoner lover, one that any woman would have to be an idiot to kick out of bed.

But he wasn't supposed to be anything more than a means to getting to her sisters, right? Ships passing in the night . . . yadda yadda.

Dammit.

She was counting to one hundred and if Santiago wasn't back, she was going to look for Salvatore without him.

She reached twenty when Santiago made a silent reappearance, his long hair tied into a braid, carrying a leather satchel.

A vampire ready for action.

"We're leaving."

"Leaving?" She frowned at his abrupt command. "No frigging way."

His long strides never broke as he crossed to grasp her arm and steer her toward the door.

"Styx and his Ravens are fifty miles north of town. We're driving to meet him."

She dug in her heels. Not just a figment of speech. She might be tiny, but she was all Were.

An irate female Were with combat training.

One of the most dangerous creatures in the world.

"We're not going anywhere until we've stopped Briggs from slaughtering Salvatore," she hissed.

Coming to a grudging halt, Santiago met her angry glare with an unyielding expression.

"My orders are to keep you safe."

"I don't give a crap what your orders are."

"Harley, you are currently my guest, but if you insist on putting yourself in danger, then I'll make you my prisoner."

She didn't miss the silken warning in his dark voice.

"It doesn't matter to you that Salvatore is in danger?"

"Not in the least."

Harley clenched her hands, knowing she couldn't force the vampire to help Salvatore fight Briggs.

"If you don't care about Salvatore's safety, then why are you so determined to protect me?" she snapped.

"You're mate-sister to my Anasso. He was very clear in his command to bring you to him without delay."

Perfect.

The nightclub was overflowing with powerful demons and not a cursed one would lift a finger to help her without the say-so of this vamp.

"Mate-sister or not, he's not my king. I'll decide when I leave." She stepped forward, her temper reaching a critical level. Something or someone was about to get broken. "Get out of my way."

Santiago reached behind his back, pulling a gun from his waistband.

"I am sorry, Harley."

"Don't you dare," she muttered, shoving him in the chest and making a wild dash toward the door.

He wouldn't actually shoot her.

The thought flashed through her mind at the precise

moment she felt a sharp pain in her butt, and the world went black.

Leaving the warehouse, Salvatore followed the sense of Briggs to the small park that had been built near the river. It was late enough to be empty of humans, and the few dew fairies who lingered preferred to dance in the tiny tendrils of fog that lay like a shroud on top of the water.

Prepared for a trap, Salvatore moved past the picnic tables set in concrete slabs and the neatly trimmed bushes, at last coming to a halt as a shimmer broke the air in front of the stone fountain.

He resisted the urge to sweep the area with his senses. For now he had to trust that Harley wasn't going to do something stupid. He couldn't afford to be distracted.

There was a change in air pressure, then with a pop, the familiar form of Briggs was visible in the darkness.

Salvatore gagged at the stench of rotting meat that filled the frigid air.

"You're looking a little ragged, *mio amico,*" he muttered, his gaze skimming over the haggard face and the too-thin body bent beneath the heavy cloak. Even in projection form, the pureblood looked like hell. "And you smell even worse. How long has it been since you got laid?"

"A few of us have priorities that don't involve whores," the crimson eyes flashed. "Of course, once I've taken the throne, I'll have plenty of time to screw your mate. How poetic if she's the first female to birth my litter."

Salvatore's wolf crawled beneath his skin, a brutal fury pumping through his blood.

"You try to bed Harley and she'll rip your black heart out," he rasped.

"Before I'm done with her, she'll be begging to be in

my bed. And if not . . ." The hollow chuckle sent a chill of revulsion down Salvatore's spine. "I don't mind taking my women by force. A struggle always adds a nice spice to sex."

Salvatore's heat blasted through the park, his power a tangible force.

"Being one of the walking dead has obviously putrefied your brain. You will never sit on my throne, and you will never have Harley. The only thing in your future is a long overdue grave."

"Such brave talk," Briggs rasped.

"I'm not the one cowering behind illusions."

"Be thankful you haven't yet faced me in the flesh. You would be dead." A sneer curled the pureblood's mouth. "Just like the worthless king before you."

Salvatore stiffened.

Dio. His suspicions had been right.

"You killed Mackenzie?"

"Are you just now figuring that out?" Briggs mocked. "God, how could fate ever have thought you worthy of being king?"

Salvatore ignored the insult, his thoughts churning. He was playing a deadly game without knowing the rules or the ultimate goals.

"Why did you kill him?"

"Because he was no longer of use to me."

"And no longer any use to your master?" Salvatore challenged, sensing the power behind Briggs was the true danger. "Have you considered what will happen to you once you've served your purpose?"

"I already know my destiny."

"Sitting on a throne that doesn't belong to you? You're a fool, Briggs. You'll be betrayed, just like Mackenzie."

The chill thickened and with a lift of his hands, Briggs struck out, slamming his power into Salvatore.

"You know nothing."

Salvatore reeled from the blow, but he ignored the broken ribs and squared his shoulders. He'd touched a nerve. Briggs could brag and boast all he wanted, but underneath he feared that he was just more useless fodder.

"I know that a demon doesn't share his power without expecting something in return," he ruthlessly pressed. "And that the true cost is always shrouded in lies until it's too late."

A tick jerked beneath one sunken eye, but Briggs smiled with that smug superiority that always set Salvatore's teeth on edge.

There was room for only one arrogant bastard in the pack.

And he was it.

"Don't tell me you're concerned for me, Giuliani," Briggs scoffed. "I'm touched."

"I'm concerned that your damned greed has condemned the Weres to extinction."

"You're the one destroying the Weres. It's my fate to be their savior."

"Very noble, but evil can't create, it can only destroy."

That disturbing laugh once again echoed through the empty park, sending the handful of dew fairies fleeing in horror. Salvatore wished he could join them.

There was something just . . . wrong about Briggs.

Beyond the cold, beyond the hideous smell, beyond the black magic was a sense of twisted perversion.

As if the grave still claimed his soul.

"Did you read that in a fortune cookie?" Briggs taunted.

Salvatore shuddered, wondering if there was anything of the Were left inside the decaying shell.

"Have you ever considered that our troubles began with Mackenzie?" He forced himself to meet the disturbing crimson gaze. "His treachery condemned us and your megalomania has only fueled our downfall. You're like rot that has to be cut away before it can spread further." He didn't bother to hide his grimace. "*Dio,* you even smell like rot."

The frigid power once again flared out, driving Salvatore to his knees. Grimly, he straightened. Another rib was cracked and his lung was punctured, but he'd rather be skinned alive than be on his knees before this abomination.

"Bastard," Briggs hissed. "The only rot among the Weres comes from your tainted blood. Mackenzie should have killed you the moment your claim to the throne was sensed."

Salvatore narrowed his gaze. It was obvious that the mysterious demon had plotted first with Mackenzie and then Briggs to keep Salvatore off the throne. But why? Was there something about him that threatened the creature?

"Is that what your puppet master desires?" he demanded. "My death?"

Briggs snorted. "Who doesn't?"

Good point. Salvatore had never bothered to win friends and influence people. He didn't doubt there was a long line of demons who wanted his head on a platter. But this was more than just the regular run-of-the-mill death wish. This was an attack on the entire Were nation.

"What does my death give him?" Salvatore stepped closer to Briggs, one arm wrapped around his injured chest. "And why use you as a flunky, instead of killing me himself? Is he scared of me?"

"Scared?" Briggs made a dismissive motion, but Salvatore sensed the dark thread of doubt that flowed through the Were. Something Salvatore intended to use to his advantage. At least he intended to use it once he could find the damned coward. "You're nothing more than a mistake that will soon be corrected."

"Empty promises," he taunted. "That's all you can offer."

The Were snarled. "I'm happy to make it a reality."

"Let's do it."

"As you wish. You can find me here."

Salvatore swayed as Briggs roughly shoved the image of barren caves directly into his mind. He'd heard of the trick, but he hadn't realized it burned like a bitch.

"*Cristo.* You could have just given me the directions," he growled.

"I wouldn't want you to get lost." The demented Were smiled, clearly pleased with his cheesy parlor trick. "This way you have no excuse not to join me."

"No excuse beyond the fact that it's an obvious trap," Salvatore drawled. "When we meet, it will be at a location of my choosing."

"You're not making the rules, Giuliani. I am."

"Have you forgotten who is the King of Weres?"

Briggs took a threatening step forward before making a visible effort to control his temper.

"You will join me, or each passing day I will kill one of your curs," he warned, his lips curling in a malevolent satisfaction at Salvatore's growl of shock. "Ah, yes. Did I forget to mention that I've arranged for your bodyguards to join me?"

Alarm mixed with impotent fury as Salvatore recalled

his futile attempts to reach Hess. Dammit. He'd stayed away from his curs to keep them safe.

"Harm them and I swear I will rip you into so many tiny pieces not even your fairy godfather will be able to put you back together again," he threatened, his voice thick with the hatred that poured like acid through his veins.

Briggs backed away, his expression hardening as he realized he'd revealed his instinctive fear.

"Don't tarry, Giuliani," he snapped. "Our reunion is long overdue."

Chapter Fifteen

Harley wasn't entirely surprised when she opened her eyes to discover she was laying in an ivory-and-gold bedroom the size of most apartments. No, scratch that. The size of most family homes with attached garages.

Scooting off the bed drenched in gold satin, she rubbed her butt that was still sore and headed directly to the tray of food that had been left beside a massive fireplace. She didn't hesitate as she demolished the barbeque chicken, the mound of French fries, and coleslaw. She could smell the combination of vampire and Were without even a hint of bloodshed, which meant she could only be in one place.

The Chicago mansion of the Anasso.

The food had to be safe.

Eager to replenish her strength, Harley polished off the entire plate, ignoring the fine bottle of wine and instead downed the pitcher of water.

Only then did she take time to actually study her surroundings.

Holy crap.

Had there been a fire sale at Big Lots on marble? And crystal chandeliers? And Louis XIV furniture?

Or had her sister been punk'd by the guys from *Queer Eye for the Straight Guy*?

She was counting the number of sickeningly sweet cupids painted on the vaulted ceiling when she sensed the approach of a vampire. Turning, she squared her shoulders and prepared to meet her brother-in-law.

Or at least, that was the plan.

She wasn't sure anyone could be prepared for the six-foot-six Aztec warrior with hair braided down his back, dressed in black leather and motorcycle boots. Just for a moment she was speechless as she studied the proud, angular face and dark gold eyes that held the sort of power usually only found at nuclear plants.

He was terrifyingly beautiful.

Then her gaze narrowed and her hands curled into fists.

Dammit. She'd been knocked out for hours and hauled miles from Salvatore's trail.

Someone was going to pay.

"A dart in the butt?" she gritted. "Really?"

The King of Vampires was trained well enough to hide his amusement and instead managed to look just plain arrogant.

"You left Santiago little choice." Was this his lame-ass stab at making amends? "He did insist that I offer his apologies."

"Well, that makes it all better." She tilted back her head to meet his piercing gaze. "I suppose you must be Styx?"

"I am."

"Is my sister lurking nearby?"

"She is downstairs, anxiously waiting for an opportunity to speak with you." With unnerving speed he was standing directly in front of her, his nose flaring as if he were testing her scent. "I asked if I could have a few minutes alone with you first."

Harley stepped back, her hackles stirring at his sudden intrusion into her personal space.

"Watch it, vampire. You might be some sort of relation in our twisted family tree, but that doesn't mean I won't kick your ass."

He folded his arms over his massive chest, not particularly terrified by her threat.

"I only want to ask a few questions."

"What questions?"

He grimaced, looking oddly uncomfortable. "There is no delicate means of approaching this."

"You've already had me drugged and kidnapped," she dryly pointed out. "There's no need to pretend good manners at this late stage."

"Very well. Why do you carry Salvatore's scent?"

She choked at the blunt question. Surely there had to be some etiquette against random sniffing?

"I can't imagine how that's any of your business."

"I'm not trying to intrude into your privacy, Harley."

"No?" Her humorless laugh echoed through the cavernous room that had grown cold with the vampire's pulsing power. "God only knows what you would ask if you *were* trying to intrude. What does it matter to you what I smell like?"

"Because it has been countless centuries since a werewolf has mated." He towered over her; big, dark, and deadly. "You'll have to forgive me if I wonder if this is a miracle or a hoax."

Her brows snapped together. "Why would I try to hoax you?"

"Not you," he gently corrected. "My suspicion is that someone or something is attempting to deceive Salvatore."

She froze, an unpleasant fear settling in the pit of her stomach.

When Salvatore had alleged she was his mate, she had been shocked out of her mind. After all, great sex was one thing, but an eternal commitment was a little more than she wanted hanging over her head.

So why did the thought that Salvatore's bond might be no more than a scam on the King of Weres make her blood run cold?

Gritting her teeth, Harley pretended that an empty ache hadn't bloomed in the center of her heart, and concentrated on the only thing that was important.

Saving Salvatore from his own stupidity.

"Briggs," she muttered.

Styx nodded. "Santiago mentioned the Were. Tell me what you know of him."

Harley ignored her instinctive bristling at his sharp command and revealed the bits and scraps she'd picked up of the perverted pureblood.

Styx listened in silence, his expression settling into grim lines that oddly reminded her of Salvatore.

Or perhaps not so oddly.

They were both leaders who carried the weight of their people on their shoulders.

The heavy sense of responsibility left its mark.

"Only a demon lord should have the power to resurrect a dead Were."

"Demon lord?" She grimaced. "I'm afraid to ask."

Without warning, the ancient vampire turned to pace across the marble floor, his movements surprisingly fluid for such a large beast.

"They are disciples of the dark prince, although few have shown an interest in this world since humans began to crawl from their caves." His lips curled with disdain.

Obviously the vampire wasn't a big fan of demon lords. "And the few who continued to dabble among us lesser creatures were blocked entirely when the Phoenix was called into the Chalice."

"Phoenix? Chalice?" She shook her head. "I don't have a clue what you're talking about."

"The Phoenix is the essence of a goddess who was brought into this world over three hundred years ago by a coven of witches." His eyes flashed with a terrifying emotion. "Her presence blocks the dark prince and his minions from entering this dimension."

Harley took a wary step to the side as his pacing brought him within striking distance.

"That seems like a good thing. What am I missing?"

"The essence is held in a human female who becomes the Chalice of the goddess."

"A human?" She blinked in confusion. "Aren't they a little fragile for such a task?"

"The human is protected by the goddess." His humorless smile revealed a set of kickass fangs. "Although the same coven who conjured the goddess weren't content. They decided they needed a guardian who would never fail the Chalice, so they bound a vampire to her soul."

"Ah." She grimaced. "I assume the vampire didn't jump to the head of the line to volunteer?"

"Not at the time, although he's become reconciled to his position now that Abby is the new Chalice." Styx's expression eased. "They've recently mated."

Harley didn't fully understand the whole goddess and Chalice thing, but she did grasp the most pertinent fact.

"If Abby's carrying this Goddess, then Briggs can't be hooked up with a demon lord, right?"

"I never underestimate a determined demon lord. They have the means to use others to accomplish their goals, and are always swift to take advantage of any weakness." Styx came to an abrupt halt, the cool brush of his power making her shiver. "I need to speak with Abby."

"You think she's falling down on the job?"

He laughed with genuine amusement. "Even if I did, I wouldn't be stupid enough to point it out. Abby has the power to toast demons."

"Literally toast them?"

"Literally."

Harley made a mental note to avoid the woman.

"Why do you want to speak with her?"

"I hope she can convince me that my fears are a figment of my imagination."

Harley's heart plummeted and her mouth went dry at the dark edge of concern in his voice. What the hell would scare the King of Vampires?

"Are demon lords so dangerous?"

"There are many who believe they are our ultimate creators. Which means they could also be our ultimate destroyers."

Without thought, Harley was charging to the door. Crap. Crap. Crap. This was so much worse than a demented Were who refused to stay dead.

"I have to warn Salvatore."

She heard the tiny tinkle of the bronzed medallions threaded through Styx's braid, but she couldn't track his movement until he was standing directly in front of her, blocking her path to the door.

"Hold on, Harley." He grabbed her arms as she attempted to dart around him. "This is nothing more than idle speculation. Jumping to conclusions is worse than doing nothing."

She struggled to free herself from his grasp, her temper exploding.

"You wouldn't be waffling if it was one of your precious vampires in danger," she gritted. "You would be charging to the rescue."

A raven brow flicked upward. "I am not a vampire who waffles. I am attempting to discover who or what is threatening Salvatore, and if it poses a danger to other demons."

"Fine. You do whatever it is you have to do and I'll be on my merry way."

"Where do you intend to go?"

"Does it matter?"

"Yes, it does." He flashed a hint of fang. More out of annoyance than intimidation. Or at least, Harley hoped so. "Salvatore demanded my promise that I would keep you safe. I intend to honor my vow."

"It's not his call. Or yours." She jutted her chin. She'd allowed fear to keep her prisoner for thirty years. She was done hiding from the world. Even if that world was terrifyingly dangerous. "No man's going to tell me what I can or can't do. Not anymore."

His expression tightened, but before he could say anything truly stupid, the door to the bedroom was thrown open and a slender replica of herself walked in.

No, not a precise replica, Harley realized, her gaze skimming over the blond hair that was cut short and spiky and the delicate face that was just a trace more heart-shaped, with eyes that were more green than hazel.

Still, the resemblance was stunning.

Harley watched her sister approach, her stomach twisting with an odd combination of emotions.

What the hell was she supposed to feel?

Joy? Disbelief? Regret?

A raging identity crisis?

With a shake of her head, she decided that she would figure out what to feel later. For now all that mattered was getting out of the marble mausoleum and finding Salvatore.

Clearly unafraid of the towering predator who could easily rip out her throat or simply squash her with one of his massive fists, Darcy crossed to stab her mate with a stern gaze.

"Styx, I wish to speak with my sister."

He dipped his head in instant agreement. "Very well, my love."

"Alone."

The vampire's starkly beautiful features tightened, but astonishingly, he headed obediently toward the door.

"I'll be downstairs. I need Dante to bring Abby here."

Darcy's brows lifted in surprise. "Abby?"

"I have a few questions for her."

Harley's sister pointed a finger at her mate. "Please remember to make it an invitation, not a royal command."

A smile curved the vampire's lips even as he assumed an arrogant expression.

"What is the benefit of being the Anasso if I can't issue royal commands?"

Darcy chuckled. "I'll remind you of a few benefits later."

"You think you can use such a shameless ploy to control me?" he demanded, his fangs extending and his voice thickening with tangible desire.

"Yes."

"You're right." Without the least embarrassment at acknowledging his mate's power, Styx offered Harley a small dip of his head. "Sister-mate, welcome to our home."

Waiting until the frightening vampire had stepped over the threshold and shut the door behind his retreating form, Darcy moved to take Harley's hand in a light grasp, her smile apologetic.

"He promised he only wished to ask you a few questions.

I should have known he'd try to bully you." She rolled her eyes. "Vampires."

Harley's wariness eased at her sister's teasing. Attired in a faded pair of jeans and casual white shirt, with her sweet smile, she didn't look like the Queen of Vampires.

Actually she looked like a high school cheerleader who should be working on her algebra and dating the quarterback.

"Trust me, Weres aren't any different," Harley countered.

"You're right. It's men in general."

"All that testosterone putrefies their brains."

They shared the universal sigh of female resignation at the follies of men.

"I'm Darcy." Her sister squeezed her fingers. "And you're a most honored guest in my home, sister."

Harley pulled her hand free, bothered by the strange sense of connection flowing through her blood at Darcy's touch.

As delighted as she was to meet her sister, she wasn't ready to lower her guard. Darcy was, after all, bound to the vampires. Her loyalty would be to her mate and his people.

"Guest or prisoner?" she demanded.

"Never a prisoner, Harley. I promise."

Unnerved to be staring into a face so remarkably similar to her own, Harley paced toward the tall arched windows. Night had recently fallen, bathing the rolling parkland that surrounded the mansion in velvet shadows, but in the distance Harley could see the Chicago skyline strikingly outlined in lights.

At any other time she might have appreciated the beautiful view. She rarely had had the opportunity to spend time in a large, vibrant city that offered endless entertainment. But not tonight.

There was a disturbing emptiness in the center of her being that was making her twitchy as hell. She needed to be out of the elegant mansion and on the hunt.

Now.

"Is our other sister here as well?" she demanded, as much to know how many others might try to stand in her path as in genuine curiosity.

Later she would appreciate the sisters she thought she'd lost.

"No, Regan left earlier today." Darcy heaved a loud sigh. "Like you, she seemed to believe I was secretly plotting to hold her against her will. I really am a nice person. I only want to get to know my sisters."

Harley turned with a frown. "I thought she was in love or mated to a vampire or something?"

"She'll be mated once she stops running from fate. Poor Jagr." The green eyes narrowed as Darcy studied her with unnerving intensity. "And speaking of matings . . ."

Harley shifted, feeling like a dork as a heat flooded her cheeks.

She hadn't grown up with sisters or best friends. She hadn't gone to sleepovers where she could giggle and talk about boys.

Her private feelings had always been that. Private.

She wasn't ready to discuss whatever was happening between her and Salvatore.

"I'm not mated."

"No, but Salvatore has marked you." Darcy's gaze never wavered. "You know how amazing this is, don't you?"

"It's not something I've given a lot of thought to. We've been a little busy," Harley pointed out dryly.

"Yes." Darcy flashed her sweet smile. "Levet did say you were escaping from the curs who were holding you captive."

"Levet." Harley happily latched onto the opportunity to deflect her sister's attention. "Good God, I forgot about the poor thing. Is he here?"

"No, and to be honest I'm worried about him." There was no mistaking Darcy's genuine concern. "He contacted Shay when he first escaped the tunnels, but we haven't heard from him since. It's not like him to just disappear."

Harley grimaced, a sudden stab of guilt piercing her heart. They should never have allowed the poor little gargoyle to go off alone.

"He might have been captured by Caine."

"Would the curs hurt him?"

Despite his reputation, Caine wasn't completely amoral. But nothing was allowed to threaten his precious dreams of immortality.

"Caine's more likely to hold him captive if he thinks the gargoyle could bring him leverage against Salvatore or the vampires."

They exchanged rueful glances, both knowing Salvatore or the vamps wouldn't lift a finger to save the miniature demon.

"And if there is no leverage?" Darcy demanded.

"Then all bets are off."

"Crap." Darcy wrapped her arms around her waist. "I'm not going to be happy if Levet is hurt."

Oddly, Harley realized she, too, was worried about the gargoyle. He didn't deserve to be caught in nasty Were politics.

"I'll do what I can to discover what's happened to him," she promised.

Darcy bit her lower lip, looking far from reassured.

"Harley, I understand if you want revenge after being held prisoner by Caine for so long, but I can't bear the thought of you putting yourself in danger. If you'll wait, I'm certain we can figure out a suitable punishment together."

Punishment? Harley's brows snapped together. As if she'd waste a minute plotting revenge on the curs.

"Thanks, but I don't give a crap about Caine."

"Then why are you so anxious to leave?"

"Because Salvatore's an idiot and the vampires are jackasses."

"Okay," Darcy said slowly. "I don't disagree, but maybe you could be more specific. Why is Salvatore an idiot?"

Harley's lips twisted in a humorless smile.

Oh, let her count the ways.

She chose the most pressing stupidity.

"He's out there trying to stop some mutant freak who might or might not be a puppet of a demon lord."

"And the vampires?"

"They won't do a damned thing to stop his suicide mission."

Darcy was smart enough not to pretend that Styx possessed any warm and fussy feelings for Salvatore. Or that the vamps would charge to the rescue.

"What do you intend to do?"

"Find Salvatore."

"And then?"

"That's as far as my plan goes."

Darcy grasped Harley's hands and regarded her with a somber expression.

"Harley, will you trust me?"

Harley stiffened. "I've heard those words before."

"Will you?" Darcy squeezed her fingers. "Please?"

There was a short, uncomfortable silence before Harley heaved a noisy sigh.

"Dammit, I'm going to regret this."

Chapter Sixteen

If Caine's nerves hadn't been scraped raw, he might have found humor in the journey through the dark, narrow tunnel that burrowed deep beneath the abandoned graveyard.

It was straight out of a B horror flick.

A brewing storm. Creepy caves. Monsters lurking in the dark.

All he needed was a half-dressed woman screaming at the top of her lungs and a stoner friend wandering off to get chopped in half.

As it was, he didn't find anything remotely funny about leading the four furious curs through the echoing darkness, his skin crawling at the evil that pulsed through the labyrinth of caverns.

He suddenly realized he knew exactly how a condemned man felt walking to the execution chamber.

Clenching his jaw, he held the gun he'd loaded with silver bullets and glanced over his shoulder at the curs who grudgingly followed behind him.

It hadn't been a difficult task to capture Salvatore's faithful servants. Or even to keep them suitably leashed once his own curs had clamped heavy silver collars around their necks. For the moment they were so weak they could barely put one foot in front of another.

But it had taken a whole new level of stupidity to leave Andre to guard the Jeep parked behind the abandoned church and enter the caves.

A damned shame that running away like a freaking puss was no longer an option.

"Salvatore's going to skin you alive and feed your entrails to the vultures," the tall, bald-headed cur growled as he stumbled behind Caine.

"That's the fourth time you've used that same threat, moron," Salvatore snapped. "If you can't think of a new one, then keep your trap shut."

"It's not a threat, it's a promise."

Caine tightened his grip on the gun, sick to death of Salvatore Giuliani.

"Are you so certain?" he sneered. "It seems to me that your precious king saved his own hide and left you swinging in the breeze."

"You know nothing."

"I know Salvatore had plenty of time and opportunity to warn you that he'd escaped and was having a fine time with his current bitch."

The blond-haired cur who Caine suspected had a smidgen more intelligence than the others, snapped his teeth in fury.

"You're wasting your time, traitor. Our loyalty to the king will never waver."

Caine snorted. Okay, the cur was just as brainless as the others.

"Depressingly predictable," he muttered. "I'm sick of curs who are content to be the butt-monkeys of the Weres. Just because you were made, and not born a werewolf, doesn't make you any less worthy. It's your precious Salvatore that has weakened and controlled you to make sure he always has a ready supply of willing slaves. Christ, he's brought us to the point of extinction to keep control. Don't you care that your brothers are dying?"

The bald-headed cur clenched his beefy hands, but the silver poisoning his body made it impossible for him to do more than glare at Caine.

"That recruitment shit didn't work on me when the Civil War broke out, and it sure as hell isn't going to work now."

"But all Salvatore has to do is arrive in America and snap his fingers, and you go running like an eager puppy?"

"He's my king."

"Big yip." Caine resisted the urge to knock the idiot upside the head. "And what does he do for you beyond keeping you on his leash? If you had any pride you would be seeking a means of throwing off the yoke of tyranny. The curs are destined to regain the powers that have been denied them for too long."

The heat of the angry curs blasted through the narrow tunnel, searing away the tainted chill.

"A revolution you intend to lead?" the blond cur mocked.

Caine shrugged. "Someone had to be the Chosen One. It's my fate."

"So you want me to trade being a servant to the true King of Weres to become a slave for a batshit crazy cur?" the larger servant rasped. "No thanks."

Caine considered the pleasure of popping a few silver bullets in the cur's ass, but the sudden stench of rotting flesh was an unpleasant distraction.

It wasn't that he hadn't known Briggs would be waiting for him.

It was the one thing he'd been absolutely certain of.

But that didn't keep his heart from dropping to the region of his shriveled gonads.

As if to mock his sense of impending doom, they stepped out of the tunnel into a large cavern that held three giant cages around a jagged pit in the center of the stone floor. Three torches were set in brackets on the wall, flooding the space with an eerie flicker of orange light, and revealing an even eerier sight of Briggs standing across the chamber.

"Salvatore's pets were always annoyingly faithful," he drawled as his crimson gaze flicked over the shackled curs. "Which, of course, makes them such a joy to kill."

Caine reluctantly shoved his gun in the waistband of his jeans, able to taste the potent fear of his prisoners. He didn't blame them. The sight and smell of Briggs was enough to send the bravest cur screaming in horror.

"Master." Caine bowed, shivering as the icy power curled around him. "I have brought the curs as you requested."

Wrapped in his clichéd black cloak and looking like he'd just crawled from his grave, Briggs waved a dismissive hand toward the nearest cage.

"Yes, I'm capable of seeing what you have done. Lock them away."

Taking more time than necessary, Caine wrestled the weakened curs into one of the cages and slammed shut the door, hearing the lock slide closed. Then with a sick sensation in the pit of his stomach, he fell to his knees in a gesture of humility the pureblood demanded.

"What else would you have of me, master?"

"You have performed your last duty, Caine. Rise to your feet."

Slowly straightening, Caine stiffened as the power in

the cavern thickened, the prickling ice biting into his skin with cruel force.

"What's going on?"

Briggs laughed. "It's time for your reward."

"Here?" A flare of panic threatened to shut down what little brain function was still chugging away. With a grim effort, Caine squashed his fear and forced his leaden feet to inch away from the silver cages toward the opening of the tunnel. "I don't understand."

"No, you don't. And you never have," Briggs taunted, flowing to block Caine's exit. The crimson eyes shimmered with malevolent light, the gaunt face twisted with perverted amusement. "What a gullible fool you've been. I didn't have to do anything more than mutter a bunch of gibberish and call it a prophecy for you to sacrifice everything and everyone for a chance at glory."

"The vision." Caine shook his head, refusing to believe it had all been a lie. It wasn't possible. Not when he had physically felt his blood being altered as it spilled out of his body. He had even smelled his scent changing, becoming Were. It had been a tangible glimpse into the future. "It's my destiny. That can't be a lie."

"Poor Caine." Briggs raised his hand, lashing Caine with his frigid power. "What a disappointment this must be. To have believed that you were the great cur Messiah, and now to discover you are nothing more than a pawn in a Were power struggle."

Caine stumbled to the side, distantly aware of the edge of the gaping pit that loomed dangerously close to his feet.

"Damn you."

A sneer curled Briggs's lips. "At least you can take comfort in knowing that your efforts have led Salvatore straight to his death. Doesn't that warm your heart? I know it makes me all giddy."

"You sick bastard." Caine fell to his knees, his lungs barely capable of drawing in air as the agonizing pain seared through his body, turning his blood to ice. Somewhere deep in his heart, the hope that his growing suspicions about Briggs were wrong died a slow, relentless death. He'd been played like a violin by the pureblood. And now he was going to pay the ultimate price for his stupidity. How fitting. "I hope Salvatore sends you straight back to the hell you climbed out of."

Infuriated by the mere mention of the King of Weres, Briggs sent another bolt of power that slammed into Caine with the force of a speeding semi-truck.

"The only thing Salvatore's going to do is die," he rasped. "Just like you."

The torturous pain dug deeper, shredding through him with unnerving ease. Instinctively, Caine tried to shift, but Briggs's power had taken command of him, refusing to allow his wolf to answer his call.

Laying his hands flat against the stone floor, Caine lowered his head and sucked in short, agonizing gasps of air. So this was it. He'd bet it all and lost.

Pathetic.

But a part of his pride wasn't completely defeated.

He might never become the pure-blooded Were he'd been promised, but he'd be damned if he was going to let the bastard have the satisfaction of killing him.

He'd do the nasty deed himself.

"Screw off, you Salvatore wannabe."

With the last of his strength, Caine shoved against the stone floor, pushing himself to the side until he reached the edge of the pit.

Belatedly realizing his prey was attempting to elude his punishment, Briggs flowed forward, his hands outstretched.

"No."

Caine managed a ragged smile. "See you in hell."

One more shove and he was toppling over the edge and into the waiting abyss, the weightless sense of falling not nearly as terrifying as it should have been.

"Stupid prick," Briggs shouted from above him, his face twisted with fury. "There's nowhere you can hide from me."

The threat would have been a whole lot scarier if Caine hadn't been plunging through the darkness at a speed that threatened a crushing, if not outright lethal, landing. Always supposing the pit ever came to an end.

Perhaps Briggs had a straight connection to hell.

It would explain so much.

Expecting flames and brimstone and imps with pitchforks, Caine plummeted for what seemed to be an eternity. But it wasn't the devil who met him at the bottom of the pit.

Instead it was stark, unyielding stone.

A blinding agony blasted through his body as his bones snapped and his insides turned to jelly. For a split second he had time to actually look death in the face, then a blessed darkness rose up to consume him.

Thank the gods.

The formal salon of Styx's mansion was just as flamboyantly beautiful as the upper rooms.

With delicate furnishings that might very well have come from Versailles, and a Persian carpet that had obviously been woven to perfectly match the gold-and-ivory décor, there was a definite museum vibe to the place.

Across the room the crimson curtains were pulled aside to reveal the towering windows that stretched the length of one wall, overlooking a sunken garden bathed in moonlight. A lovely view, no doubt, but Harley barely noticed. Hell, if she didn't notice the massive vampire dressed in leather who leaned against the marble fireplace, or her twin sister she'd thought dead for the past thirty years, a view wasn't going to capture her attention. No matter how magnificent.

Pacing from one end of the long room to the other, Harley at last came to a halt at the sound of the front doorbell. Darcy tossed her a reassuring smile as she headed into the foyer. Harley caught the unmistakable scent of vampire and . . . human?

Somehow she thought a goddess would have her own unique scent.

Her confusion only deepened as Darcy returned with the two strangers.

Dante was easily recognizable as a vampire. Pale perfect features. Long black hair pulled into a tail at his nape. Silver eyes that flashed with a bad-boy glint. Yummy body dressed in white satin shirt and black Chinos.

But who would ever guess the tiny honey-haired woman with astonishing blue eyes and impish grin was a powerful goddess?

She waited in silence as Darcy urged Abby toward her while Dante sauntered toward the waiting Styx.

"Harley, this is Abby." Darcy performed the introductions with a broad smile. "Abby, my sister."

"You're the Chalice?" Harley demanded before she could halt the words.

"I know." With a grimace, Abby ran a hand down her casual sundress. "I'm always such a disappointment. You'd think that if I have to be a goddess, I would at least get a crown and scepter."

Belatedly realizing just how rude she must sound,

Harley blushed, but thankfully Darcy was swift to take charge of the awkward conversation.

"That's what a queen's supposed to have, although mine must still be in the mail," she teased, obviously a BFF with the goddess. "You should have a halo or a glowy gown."

Abby laughed. "Instead I have split ends and PMS."

Darcy nodded her head in sympathetic understanding. "Thank you for coming. I hope my mate wasn't too overbearing in his invitation?"

Abby glanced toward the two men who were strolling in their direction.

"I'm accustomed to vampires. If they aren't being overbearing, then I know something's truly wrong. Unfortunately, I'm not sure how much help I can be. This whole goddess gig is still new to me, and I spend most of my time just trying to avoid causing mass chaos."

The two vampires moved to stand at the side of their mates, each wrapping a possessive arm around the women they so clearly adored.

Harley pretended she didn't notice that she was standing by herself. Or that her heart was clenching with something perilously close to envy.

She didn't need a man standing at her side, bristling and flashing fang if anyone came too close. She could take care of herself, thank you very much.

"You have no sense of a disturbance?" Styx asked, his alarming gaze trained on Abby. "A demon lord would not be able to entirely disguise his powers."

"The problem is that I'm not really sure what a disturbance would feel like," Abby ruefully confessed. "A pity that becoming the Chalice didn't come with a user's manual."

Dante tugged her protectively close. "We all know you are doing your best."

"Have you noticed anything out of the ordinary?" Styx pressed, impervious to his fellow vampire's growing annoyance.

One arrogant king was obviously just like another.

Whether they were vamp or Were.

Abby shrugged, her expression troubled. "It's not out of the ordinary, but I do sense something I can only describe as . . . evil. I've felt it ever since I became the Chalice, so to be honest, I've learned to ignore it."

"Do you sense which direction it comes from?"

"I can do better than that. I can tell you exactly where it comes from."

"Where?"

"The caves where we fought the dark prince."

Harley took an instinctive step backwards as the two vamps stiffened in shock. She didn't know anything about the caves or dark prince, but it clearly struck a nerve.

"Bloody hell," Dante muttered.

Abby shivered, nestling closer to her mate. "That's why I've always dismissed the creepy sensations. I assumed it was some sort of residual nastiness from the mages."

Styx narrowed his eyes. "The mages."

"They're dead," Dante said, his voice flat and cold.

Definitely a story there.

"Unless they had a backup team," Abby pointed out.

The suggestion was enough to make Dante's fangs lengthen and his silver eyes flash with an eagerness to kill.

"You think someone else is trying to open the portal between dimensions?" he demanded of his king.

"It's possible, although I think it more likely that a demon lord managed to discover an anchor in this world before the portal was closed," Styx said grimly.

A chill shot down Harley's spine. Holy crap. That couldn't be good.

"What's an anchor?" Harley asked.

"A lesser creature who accepts a portion of the demon lord's power. If the bond is strong enough it would allow the demon to continue to touch this world even after the goddess was summoned, although not directly."

"The King of Weres," Harley breathed.

Darcy regarded her in startled disbelief. "Salvatore?"

"No, the one before him. Mackenzie." Wrapping her arms around her waist, Harley returned to her pacing, attempting to remember precisely what Salvatore had said about the previous king. "Salvatore suspected that something was wrong with him before he died. But why would a demon lord give a Were power? What's in it for him?"

"The demon lord is capable of controlling his anchor and forcing him to do his bidding, but more importantly, he can siphon the life force of his victim," Styx answered.

Harley came to an abrupt halt. "Life force?"

Styx shrugged. "Chi . . . soul . . . whatever you want to call it."

"And it gives him power?"

"Yes."

Darcy moved to grab her hand, her eyes dark with concern. "What are you thinking, Harley?"

An awful, horrible dread curled through the pit of her belly. She met Styx's searching gaze.

"Caine always said that Salvatore's strength came from his position as king. Is that true?"

"Salvatore is the strongest of the Weres or he would never have been able to claim the throne, but he is able to call on his pack when necessary."

"So, he's connected to them?"

"Of course . . ." Styx bit off his words, his features bleak. "Damn. The bastard has been draining the Weres. That's why they've lost their ancient magic."

Dante nodded. "It would explain a great deal."

"But the previous king is dead, and I can't believe Salvatore is willing to deal with a demon lord," Darcy pointed out.

"He would never put his people at risk," Harley snapped, unconsciously rushing to Salvatore's defense. "It's Briggs who has the black magic."

Darcy gave her fingers a squeeze, but surprisingly it was Styx who offered reassurance.

"No one would suspect Salvatore of sharing power with a demon lord." His lips twisted in a humorless smile. "Hell, he's far too arrogant to share power with anyone."

"Which must make him a pain in the ass if there's a demon lord lurking out there," Dante said. "Not only does his position as king prevent the bastard from drawing energy from the Were packs, but he has enough innate strength to threaten to bring back the ancient powers."

"It would certainly be a reason for someone to want Salvatore dead," Styx agreed.

Dante snorted. "Just one of many."

Harley sent him a warning glare. "Hey."

The vampire lifted his hands in a gesture of peace, his earrings glinting in the light of the Venetian chandeliers. "Sorry."

"No one gets to kill him but me," she informed her companions, pulling away from Darcy as she was struck by the sudden, vicious sensation that Salvatore was in trouble. God. It might be ridiculous, but she could physically feel his pain. "As soon as I track him down. So if you'll excuse me. I really have to go."

She was headed toward the door when Styx moved to stand directly in her path.

"Wait, Harley."

With no choice, she came to a halt. She might like to think of herself as a badass, but she wasn't suicidal enough to try to wrestle her way past the most dangerous demon in all the world.

"Please, I've wasted too much time already," she whispered. The need to get to Salvatore was becoming downright unbearable.

"When I spoke with Salvatore, he said that the Were pursuing the two of you was a projection."

"That doesn't mean he's any less dangerous."

"No, but it does mean that his physical body has to be somewhere. My bet would be that he's remaining close to the protection of his master."

She frowned, attempting to follow his logic. "The caves?"

"Yes."

"It's strange," Abby muttered. "Why would this demon lord choose the same place to hide as the dark prince?"

"I suppose it's possible that a portion of the dark magic lingers and attracts evil. Or maybe the mages chose the location because the barrier between dimensions is thinner there. We shall soon discover." Styx grasped her shoulders. "Will you join us, Harley?"

Chapter Seventeen

Salvatore had to force himself to enter the labyrinth beneath the abandoned graveyard.

Dio, he was sick to freaking death of dark, dank tunnels. Once he killed Briggs he intended to spend the next century running beneath open skies.

Of course, such a cold, miserable setting seemed appropriate for the treacherous pureblood. He was a maggot who deserved to decay alone in the gloomy depths.

The long tunnel at last spilled into a barren cavern. Salvatore came to a halt, catching the unmistakable stench of rotting flesh.

His nemesis had to be near.

"'Welcome to my parlor, said the spider to the fly . . .'" he muttered as he glanced around the empty cavern with the walls that had been smoothed and polished over the years.

"An apt anthology," Briggs taunted from the shadows.

Salvatore grimaced, waiting for the spooky music to be cued. That was all that was lacking to complete the hokey atmosphere.

"I love what you've done with your crib," he drawled, folding his arms over his chest. "What do you call this? Post-Neanderthal?"

"It serves my current purpose."

"And what purpose would that be?"

"To watch you die."

Salvatore shook his head. He'd spent too long being jerked around by enemies who manipulated him from the shadows. This ended now.

"I don't believe you."

The chill in the air thickened. "You don't think I intend to kill you?"

"I think there has to be a hell of a lot more to it than just my death. You would never have gone to the trouble of kidnapping Harley and her sisters, or using Caine to keep me distracted if you were going to kill me." Salvatore shrugged. "At least not if you are as powerful as you claim to be. You could have struck me dead in Rome after your miraculous rising from the grave."

"But it's been so much fun watching you chase your tail," Briggs mocked, still keeping himself hidden behind his black magic.

"No doubt priceless entertainment," Salvatore said dryly, "but hardly worth wasting decades when you could have been sitting on the throne."

"My motives are none of your concern."

"But they weren't your motives, were they, Briggs? You're nothing more than a toady dancing to someone else's tune."

Through the darkness, Salvatore heard the rasp of Briggs's infuriated breath.

"Tut, tut, Salvatore," he said, his voice tight. "Be careful you don't annoy me."

"Or what? You'll talk me to death?" Salvatore sneered. "Too late."

"You want more action? Very well. Your wish is my command."

Salvatore lowered his arms, bracing for the attack. He had churned over the endless reasons he might have been lured to these caves since Briggs had demanded he come here. He hadn't come to a logical conclusion—surprise, surprise—but he was certain as hell that it wasn't going to be good for his health.

Still waiting for an unseen blow, Salvatore was caught off guard when there was an odd shimmer in the center of the room, and then the darkness seemed to part, like curtains being pulled back to reveal a stage.

With a frown, he watched as Briggs came into view. It wasn't the projection of his physical body that Salvatore was expecting. This was more of a . . . window. A glimpse of Briggs as he stood somewhere else.

Somewhere in the caves, Salvatore decided. Although that didn't precisely narrow down the possibilities. Even his limited ability to sense dark, creepy places could tell that the spiderweb of tunnels and caves were extensive.

Then Briggs gave a wave of his hand, and the vision widened to reveal that he was standing in a cave similar to the one to where Salvatore lingered. All bare rock and medieval torches. But that wasn't what captured Salvatore's attention.

No, it was the sight of the familiar Were who was kneeling at Briggs's feet, his blond head bowed, his slender body wrapped in heavy silver chains.

Max.

Salvatore clenched his hands in impotent fury. He'd been prepared from the moment he caught the scent of his servants outside the graveyard to have them used against him. But that didn't make the sight of Max being tortured any easier.

"You spineless coward," Salvatore hissed. "If you want to fight, then face me like a man."

Briggs laughed as he casually reached down to backhand the cur, snapping back his head and sending a spray of blood flying through the air.

"My house, my rules."

"What do you want from me?"

The crimson eyes flashed with the sort of impressive fury that took centuries to nurture.

"I want you to suffer before you die," he hissed, grabbing Max by the hair and viciously shaking him. "I want you to watch as I torture your servants. I want you to know that once I take your throne, I'll destroy everything you loved or cared for in your life."

The king in him demanded that he try to negotiate with the Were. It might piss him off to admit that Briggs held the upper hand, but for the moment it was the unfortunate truth.

The wolf in him, however, snapped.

A member of his pack was under attack, and it was his place as alpha to protect him.

"No, you bastard. I'm done with your games," he gritted, heading across the cavern to the tunnel on the other side. "You can't hide from me any longer."

"Stay where you are or I'll kill him, Salvatore."

"Not if I rip out your heart first."

"Salvatore. Come back. Salvatore."

Ignoring the furious commands, Salvatore charged through the darkness, his skin prickling and the glow of his eyes bathing the stone walls in shades of gold.

His wolf clawed to get out, eager for the taste of blood in his mouth and the feel of flesh tearing beneath his claws. His animal half was ready and eager to wreak havoc among his enemies.

Following the twisting tunnels ever deeper into the earth, Salvatore savagely beat back his beast.

Soon enough he would rip Briggs into tiny shreds and feed him to the rats. For now he had to keep his priorities straight.

Rescue his curs.

Discover who was behind the nefarious plot.

Mutilate and destroy Briggs.

In that order.

Passing through empty caverns, some obviously having been used as living spaces in the past and others as grim prisons, he ignored the strange energy in the air that muted his senses. He might not be able to follow Briggs's scent, but the spineless worm couldn't hide the nasty iciness that clung to him like a shroud.

Following the growing chill in the air, Salvatore at last came close enough to the bastard to smell the stench of rotting flesh.

He slowed, entering the large cavern with a stone altar and burning brazier set in the middle of the floor.

"I know you're here," he growled, checking the nooks and crannies that were shrouded in heavy darkness. The chill was thick enough to give him frostbite. "Briggs? I can smell your cowardice."

Briggs's laugh echoed through the cavern. "Always so full of yourself, Salvatore."

"Then come out of the shadows and let's put an end to this." The words had barely left Salvatore's lips when there was the sound of shuffling feet and Hess made an appearance from behind a stalagmite—or was it stalactite?—whatever. The important thing was the rigid expression on his servant's face, and the blank emptiness in his eyes as he charged directly toward Salvatore. "Shit."

"Don't blame me if you don't like the game," Briggs countered in sly tones, taking obvious enjoyment in watching Salvatore scramble to avoid Hess's attack.

Muttering beneath his breath, Salvatore crouched and watched as Hess abruptly shifted into his wolf form.

Cristo. This was exactly what he hoped to avoid. His soldier was completely under the thrall of Briggs, helpless to do anything but what the damned bastard commanded.

With a fluid movement, he jerked free the knife he'd tucked into his ankle holster before heading for these caves. It was silver, but it would do less damage than the silver bullets he'd loaded in his handgun.

Or at least that was the plan.

Balanced on the balls of his feet, Salvatore was prepared when Hess jumped forward, his massive jaws snapping at his head. Jerking back to avoid the fangs that could easily rip out his throat, Salvatore brought the knife upward, slicing a thin wound through the cur's upper chest.

He wanted to stop Hess with as little damage as possible.

Of course, what he wanted and what he got was rarely the same.

With the scratch of claws on stone, Hess scrambled to turn and squatted down as he prepared to pounce. The acrid scent of burned flesh filled the air, but Salvatore only had to glance at Hess with his eyes flashing crimson and his lips curled back in a snarl to know it was going to take more than a scratch to end this battle.

He clenched his teeth and prepared for another assault. He didn't have to wait long.

Familiar enough with his finest soldier's tactics, Salvatore was prepared when he feinted a strike high and then darted low to attempt to circle round and hamstring him. He swiftly turned and slashed with the knife, catching Hess on the muzzle.

The cur whined as the silver bit deep into his flesh, the blood flowing, his flesh burned by the silver. Shaking his head in a pained motion, Hess appeared briefly defeated, then with a sudden leap he hit Salvatore directly in the chest, knocking him to the ground.

Salvatore managed to yank his head to the side, avoiding the snapping teeth, but it left him vulnerable and he howled in pain as Hess sank his fangs into his shoulder. The cur tore a chunk of flesh from him before Salvatore managed to get a grip on the cur's thick coat, and with a savage thrust tossed him against the wall.

There was a nasty crunch as Hess hit his head against the unrelenting stone, falling boneless to the ground.

"Ah. What a beautiful sight," Briggs hissed as Salvatore lay flat on his back, the wound in his shoulder deep enough to take an effort to heal. "The mighty King of Weres wallowing in the dirt. Exactly where he belongs."

"Screw you," Salvatore muttered, swallowing his whimper of pain as he forced himself to his feet.

Instinctively his gaze went to the cur lying broken and bleeding on the hard stone. Hess. He lived, but he was seriously injured. Just another motivation to hunt down Briggs and make him pay for ever crawling out of his revolting grave.

Moving across the cavern, Salvatore hissed in frustration. His head ached from where it had bounced off the ground and his shoulder continued to leak blood as the flesh struggled to knit back together. The uncompleted mating bond was making it difficult to repair his injuries, but he wasn't going to wait.

Briggs had to be close.

He couldn't have held Hess in thrall unless he was.

Which meant that this time, he wasn't going to escape.

Trusting his instincts, he clutched the knife tight in his hand and circled the edge of the cavern.

"There's no one left to hide behind," he taunted, using the increasing cold to lead him toward a connected cave. "I don't fear you."

"You always were an idiot," Salvatore muttered, his skin prickling as a foul clamminess washed over him. God Almighty. Briggs was just . . . wrong. "Come out, come out, wherever you are." He abruptly halted, the overwhelming stench of rotting flesh breaking through the spell that had been muting it. "Bingo."

There was a cold rush of air and instinctively Salvatore ducked, growling as the sword whistled less than an inch above his head.

He'd been expecting magic, not mundane weapons.

And nearly got his head chopped off.

With a furious howl, Salvatore shifted.

Heat and magic poured through his body, altering and changing him from the inside out. His bones popped, his muscles thickened, and his skin shivered as his heavy pelt flowed over his body. A combination of pain and bliss exploded through him at the transformation.

It was a sensation that Weres craved like a drug.

The prickles in the air warned that Briggs was shifting as well, and Salvatore was prepared when the pureblood charged, knocking him to the ground. Turning his head, he sank his fangs into the wolf's front leg and was rewarded by a shrill yip.

His satisfaction vanished as the Were's blood, tainted with decay, spilled into his mouth. *Dio.* He tasted as bad as he smelled.

And that was saying something.

Releasing his grip, Salvatore gained his feet in time to dodge the teeth snapping at his throat. He growled, the days of frustrated fury searing through him as he coiled his muscles and attacked.

The cold that shrouded Briggs bit into Salvatore like tiny ice daggers, but he ignored the stinging pain, far more concerned with the savage swipe of the Were's massive claws and the fangs that were desperate to rip out his throat.

He was beyond battle tactics and campaign strategies.

This was going to be raw power against whatever vile magic Briggs could conjure.

Salvatore barreled straight into his opponent, sending them both rolling over the hard ground. He accidently hit the lump already forming on the back of his skull, and stabbed a sharp rock into his hind leg as they skidded across the empty cave, but his teeth managed to slice a deep gash in Briggs's chest before the Were blasted Salvatore with an invisible flare of magic.

Salvatore flew through the air, smacking into the wall with enough force to rattle his teeth. He was back on his feet in a heartbeat and charging across the floor of the cave without feeling his injuries. He'd waited for this moment for days.

Hell, he'd waited for years, although he hadn't known it was Briggs he was hunting. Nothing was going to stop him now.

Briggs darted to the side, no doubt trying to summon another burst of magic, but Salvatore again slammed into his wolf form. Screw this magic shit. He rolled Briggs closer to the opening of the cave, using his heavier body to firmly trap the Were beneath him. Then, before Briggs could guess his intention, Salvatore shifted back to human form, grabbing the knife he'd dropped earlier and plunging the silver blade into Briggs's chest.

It was a risk.

Salvatore didn't have a clue if he could kill the already dead Were. But he intended to give it his best shot.

He twisted the knife deeper, searching for a heart and listening with grim pleasure as Briggs's breath became a rattle. The pureblood's lips pulled back in a snarl, clearly in pain, if not actually dying.

The silver burned through Briggs's flesh, at last forcing him to shift back to his gaunt, fragile human body.

"No." The crimson gaze shifted over Salvatore's shoulder, as if searching for someone. "Master."

"Do you want me to wait so your big bad master can come save you?" Salvatore sneered. "Or do you prefer the whole resurrection process?"

"He'll never allow you to harm me."

"I'm willing to test that theory."

Yanking out the dagger, Salvatore was on the point of driving it back into the narrow chest that was already bleeding in a strange, sluggish way when there was the sound of a low hiss from behind him.

Salvatore jerked around, prepared for whatever was coming.

Except . . . nothing was coming.

At least nothing he could see or touch.

Was he jumping at shadows?

The thought had barely passed through his mind when a strange mist swirled around his head, and the sound of a bell echoed through his brain.

That was the last thing he remembered.

* * *

Salvatore discovered coming back to his senses was a slow, unpleasant process.

His head was groggy, his mouth as dry as the Sahara, and his entire body blazed with an agony that was explained once he opened his eyes to find he was currently stretched out on the stone altar, and held in place with a thick silver chain that wrapped around his body from his neck to his ankles.

Lifting his aching head a few inches off the hard stone, he took inventory of his situation, his breath hissing through his teeth as he noticed his own silver dagger stuck into his upper thigh. WTF? The chain was frying his skin with such intensity he hadn't even noticed the damned dagger in his leg.

His brows snapped together as he watched the steady trickle of his blood flow into a tiny trough that had been carved along the edge of the altar. Pooling at the bottom of the table, the blood slowly dribbled into the brazier below his feet, the blazing fire hissing with each drip.

"What the hell?" he muttered, his gaze searching the seemingly empty cavern.

He didn't know how long he'd been out, or where Briggs had disappeared to, or how he'd been carted back to this cave and trussed up like a sacrificial lamb.

All he knew was that he was in a boatload of trouble.

"Unfortunately, my servant is correct," an unfamiliar voice filled the cavern, powerful and yet oddly muffled, as if it were speaking through water. "As much as I have enjoyed watching you teach Briggs a lesson in humility, I still have need of him."

Genuine, undiluted alarm clenched Salvatore's stomach.

Whoever had hog-tied him wasn't any normal demon. The magic that hummed in the air was enough to make his hair stand on end.

"And you are?" he gritted, refusing to give into the urge to panic.

"Nilapalsara."

"Sorry. Doesn't ring a bell."

"It's an ancient and revered name, although in this world I was worshipped as Balam," the stranger smoothly answered, indifferent to Salvatore's taunting.

His heart slammed against his aching ribs, his hands clenching at his sides.

"Demon lord."

"You seem surprised."

Surprised? Not the word he was looking for.

"You were banned from this world."

Painful prickles raced over his skin. "The goddess certainly did her best to be rid of me. Thankfully, I possessed a deep and intimate connection to this dimension."

Salvatore grimaced. "Mackenzie."

"Very good."

"How did you trick him into accepting your bond?"

"There was no trick." There was the faintest hint of superiority in the voice, as if the demon lord wasn't entirely above petty emotions. "The pureblood sought me out when it became obvious that he wasn't the next in line for the throne."

Salvatore desperately wanted to deny the claim. The mere thought that a Were would sacrifice his people for his own gain went against everything purebloods held sacred. But he'd already accepted the previous king's treachery.

What was the point in playing dumb?

"You gave him the power to kill the legitimate heirs?" he instead said.

"I like to encourage ambition."

"Blind greed is not the same as ambition."

"Perhaps not to you, but they both suit my purpose."

It was that mysterious purpose that was bothering Salvatore. Demon lords didn't grant favors out of the kindness of their black hearts. Ignoring the ravaging pain and the sickening hiss of his life blood dripping into the flames, he struggled to think clearly.

"Mackenzie was given the black magic necessary to steal the throne; what did you get out of the deal?"

"He allowed me access to this world."

"There had to be more . . ." Salvatore ground his teeth as realization abruptly hit. *Dio.* How the hell had he been so dense? "You used Mackenzie to drain the souls of all Weres. You're responsible for the loss of our powers."

The demon lord's laughter echoed through the cavern. The sound was perhaps the creepiest thing Salvatore had ever heard.

"Very good, Giuliani. It took Mackenzie centuries to at last realize I was able to call on his connection to the packs."

Salvatore bit back his smart-ass comment as Balam's words sank through the fuzziness in his brain.

He'd never been close to Mackenzie, and after it was known that he was to be the next king, the older Were had become downright surly toward him. But there had been something different about him in the last few years of his life.

He was still secretive and bad-tempered and prone to treat Salvatore as the enemy, but looking back, Salvatore was beginning to suspect that Mackenzie had come to regret his choices.

Could he actually have been loyal in the end?

"And when he discovered you were draining the Weres, he tried to cut off your supply," he accused.

The air thickened with a tangible anger. "His last futile act as king."

"I assume Briggs murdered him before he could break your bond?"

"Such delicious irony. Mackenzie was horrified when it was discovered his son was not to be the next in line for the throne, and he was the one to bring Briggs to me for the power to defeat you."

Salvatore made a startled sound. Weres were more animal than human when it came to family. The entire pack raised the cubs, and bloodlines had no substantial meaning. Each pureblood was expected to prove themselves, not rely on their parents or grandparents to give them worth.

"He brought Briggs to you?"

"Yes, and in the end Briggs used the power to kill his own father."

He growled deep in his throat. "He wasn't so lucky against me."

"No. I will admit, I underestimated your power."

Salvatore was certain that the demon lord didn't intend to make that mistake again.

"I would be a lot more flattered if you hadn't planned for Briggs to kill me and take my throne," he muttered.

"It was nothing personal. You were an obstacle that needed to be disposed of."

"Nothing personal?" Salvatore snorted. "I happen to take attempted murder very personally, but maybe that's just me."

"And yet, here you are."

Something in the dark voice set off yet another rash of alarms in Salvatore. Astonishing he could feel anything beyond the scorching agony of the silver chains and his strength that was fading with every drip of blood.

"Yes, here I am," he rasped. "Odd. After Briggs's abysmal failure to rid the world of my presence, I would have thought you would have sent a new assassin. Briggs isn't the only one who would be happy to see me dead."

"My power in this world was limited when the goddess was summoned, and nearly destroyed when Mackenzie died, leaving me without the ability to call upon the Weres' energy." The demon lord surprisingly answered. No doubt he enjoyed revealing his clever scheme. "To bring Briggs back from the grave took years to accomplish, and drained me of what few powers I had left."

Salvatore grimaced. He at least knew why it had taken so long for Briggs to pull his Lazareth act, but it wasn't particularly reassuring to think he'd been so easily bested by an impotent demon lord.

"Obviously not all your powers."

"Ah, yes, a little gift from the mages who once worshipped the dark prince in these caves."

Salvatore swallowed a soft moan, his thoughts threatening to scramble at the relentless pain. He knew something about mages and caves, didn't he? Something about Dante's mate becoming the Chalice.

"The vampires killed the mages," he said.

"True, they failed in their efforts to kill the goddess and return their master, but their devoted sacrifices over the past decades have thinned the barrier between dimensions. When I recovered enough to once again touch this world, I realized that you might be far more valuable alive than dead."

Somehow, Salvatore wasn't remotely reassured.

There were all sorts of nasty things worse than death.

"Why did you send Briggs to raid my nursery?" he demanded, as much to head off the looming panic as to hear the answer to the question that had been nagging at him for the past thirty years.

"I simply requested that he find the means to lure you closer, while keeping you too distracted to realize you were on our leash."

Salvatore gritted his teeth.

Cristo, he'd been such an imbecile.

He had wasted years chasing shadows. If only he hadn't allowed himself to be sidetracked by the missing babies, he might . . .

Salvatore abruptly cut short the mental flagellation.

Even if he hadn't allowed Briggs to lead him around like a docile sheep, he would never have figured out what was slowly killing the Weres.

Who the hell would suspect a demon lord? They were supposed to be nothing more than a myth.

"Taking thirty years to lure me into a trap is a little extreme," he muttered, his pride as damaged as his body. "All he had to do was let me know the babies were here, and I would have happily rushed to my own doom."

"I had planned to await this moment until I was once again at full strength." The flames again flared with annoyance. "Unfortunately, my perfectly devised plan has been threatened by Briggs's obsessive hatred toward you, and your own annoying interference."

"Interference?"

"You can't be allowed to mate and bring back the ancient magic," the dark voice hissed.

Ah. So he wasn't going insane.

The powers were truly returning.

Salvatore briefly closed his eyes, allowing the wondrous thought of Harley to fill his mind. Instantly the scent of vanilla washed over him, her warmth battling back the ruthless pain as if she were near. Impossible, of course. Still, it was a comfort he readily clung to.

"So now you have me here," he husked. "What do you want from me?"

"Your blood."

Not a big surprise. He glanced down at the dagger stuck in his thigh, draining him like a butchered pig. He had already assumed it was his blood or soul that the demon lord desired.

"Perhaps I'm not inclined to share."

"I fear that's not going to be an option."

"I at least deserve to know what you intend to do with it."

The air thickened until Salvatore could barely breathe. "Deserve?"

"I assume I won't be around to appreciate the sacrifice."

"No, that much is guaranteed."

"Then what's the harm in sharing?"

There was a long pause, as if Balam was momentarily distracted, then his low chuckle swirled through the cave. Salvatore shuddered in revulsion.

"Very well," the demon lord agreed. "I intend to use your blood to create a portal and enter your world."

"Why not use Briggs's? He would no doubt be thrilled to donate to the cause."

"His blood will never possess the potency of yours. A knowledge that has plagued him for centuries."

Balam sounded as if he enjoyed Briggs's frustration at his potency shortfall. So much for honor among thieves.

"But he's good enough to be your stooge?"

"For now. Once I've passed through the portal, his services will no longer be required. I'll be able to take personal command of the Weres."

Fury blasted through Salvatore. Not for Briggs's

inevitable death at the hands of the demon lord. Good riddance. But the threat that his Weres might become mere fodder for the demon lord was enough to make him howl in anguish.

He had to find some means of stopping his blood from draining into the brazier. Unfortunately, at the moment his only hope was baiting Briggs into killing him before the portal could be opened.

"Have you shared that bit of info with Briggs?"

"I prefer to keep it a surprise."

"No shit. Where is the idiot?"

"He's gone to greet our uninvited guests."

Salvatore stiffened, a bad feeling inching down his spine. "Guests?"

"Your potential mate has arrived with several nasty leeches. She obviously needs to learn what happens to naughty Weres who intrude where they don't belong."

Harley.

How had she followed him? And more importantly, why?

Dio. He was going to kill Styx for letting her put herself in danger.

Indifferent to the excruciating pain, he jerked against the binding chains, desperate to get to his mate.

"You bastard."

"Forgive me, did you desire a tearful good-bye with your beloved?"

"I'm going to kill you."

"No, Giuliani, what you're going to do is set me free."

Tilting back his head, Salvatore screamed in terrified fury.

"Harley."

* * *

Harley's nerves were near the breaking point by the time they pulled to a halt at the long forgotten church.

It could have been the result of being squashed into the Hummer with several very large, very lethal vampires, a full-fledged goddess, and her twin sister. Or even the lightning speed with which they had made the trip.

But Harley was honest enough to admit that her stomach-clenching stress was entirely due to Salvatore Giuliani.

She could feel him, deep inside.

Like a nagging awareness that refused to leave her in peace.

Snarling with impatience by the time the vampires had thoroughly scouted the area and at last allowed her to enter the caves, her temper wasn't improved when she realized there was something suppressing her ability to follow Salvatore's scent.

Dammit.

When she wanted to be alone, she couldn't get rid of Salvatore.

Now it seemed as if the entire world was determined to put obstacles in her path.

Prowling through the upper caverns, Harley waited for Dante to return from his search and rescue mission. As much as it might irritate her, she had been forced to give her word to Styx that she wouldn't take off on her own.

On the point of telling Styx he could take her promise and shove it up his ass, her restless pacing was brought to an abrupt halt as Dante silently slid from one of the numerous tunnels and crossed toward Styx and the rest of the motley crew. Harley remained standing several feet away as the sensation of Salvatore continued to pull at her.

"Well?" Styx demanded, appearing even more ferocious

with the large sword he clutched in his hand. Talk about overkill.

Dante shook his head, frustration etched on his too-beautiful face.

"It will be impossible to track him."

"I can find him," Harley said, squaring her shoulders as all eyes turned in her direction.

Darcy lifted her brows in surprise. "How?"

"I . . . feel him."

Styx scowled. "This could be a trick."

Harley wasn't stupid. She'd already considered the possibility that someone or something was messing with her. And a part of her wasn't entirely adverse to the thought that this was a devious spell. Otherwise she'd have to accept that she had a connection to Salvatore that went way beyond a casual lover.

"It doesn't matter," she muttered, wrapping her arms around her waist as a cold chill raced over her. Damn, it felt as if the temperature had dropped by a dozen degrees. "I have to do this."

Styx shifted his attention to the goddess at his side. "Abby, do you sense anything?"

"Evil." Abby shuddered, her face paling to an unhealthy shade of gray. "God, it's so thick I can almost taste it."

"Take her home, Dante," Styx growled.

Abby jutted her chin. "No."

Dante ran a frustrated hand through his hair. "Abby."

"This is my duty." Abby pointed a warning finger in her mate's face. "You know it."

Dante threw his hands in the air. "That doesn't mean I have to like it."

Oddly fascinated by the sight of the mighty vampires

bending to the will of the tiny woman, Harley was caught off guard by the faint scent that briefly stirred the air.

Somehow sensing Harley's sudden surprise, Darcy took a step in her direction.

"Harley, what is it? Salvatore?"

"He's here." Harley breathed deeply, shaking her head when the scent evaporated as swiftly as it had appeared. "But I sense another presence."

"The demon lord?"

"No. It's familiar." Harley deliberately paused. "Like you."

Darcy's eyes widened at the implication another sister might be near.

"Oh, my God. Are you certain?"

Harley shrugged. The scent had been so fleeting it was impossible to be absolutely certain.

Moving toward the nearest tunnel, she attempted to determine where the smell had come from when she was struck by a sharp wave of panic.

She faltered, glancing around in confusion.

She would swear that Salvatore was attempting to warn her. But of what?

There was a baffled moment as she simply stood at the mouth of the nearest tunnel, wondering what the hell was going on. Then, as she once again shivered at the thickening chill in the air, realization belatedly hit.

Briggs.

Turning her head, she sent her sister a frantic gaze. "Run!"

Chapter Eighteen

Harley was remarkably unfazed as the flash of magic exploded through the cavern and the ceiling promptly collapsed. Of course, she'd endured a number of explosions and cave-ins over the past few days. Maybe she was becoming immune to disasters.

Sending up a quick prayer that the others had managed to escape, she darted into the tunnel and ran from the choking cloud of dust and debris. Only when she was certain that she was beyond the collapsing ceiling did she slow her pace and pay attention to the confusing warren of caves and passageways.

The burning need to find Salvatore continued to plague her, but she wasn't stupid enough to rush blindly through the dark. Briggs was somewhere crawling through the shadows, not to mention a demon lord, and who knew what other nasties.

Contrary to popular opinion, she didn't need anyone telling her to be careful.

Pulling the silver knife from the holster her sister had fitted around her ankle before leaving Chicago, Harley allowed the sense of Salvatore that echoed in her blood to lead her through the cold, oddly barren passageways.

She felt like a damned homing pigeon, she ruefully acknowledged, wondering if Salvatore was deliberately doing something to afflict her with this overwhelming need to find him. That suspicion was certainly preferable to the thought that this growingly desperate urge was coming from her.

Coming to a halt as the tunnel branched into three separate directions, she hesitated as she caught the faint whiff of cur. It was muted, but unmistakable.

Alarm raced through her.

She wanted to believe that the curs were Salvatore's servants who were here to rescue him, but that would be way too convenient for her current streak of luck. Besides, Salvatore had been adamant in not allowing his pack near. Not when they could be used as a weapon against him.

Which could only mean that they were either strange curs, or ones under the control of Briggs. And yet another danger to have to worry about.

Perfect.

Gripping the knife tightly enough to make her knuckles crack, Harley swallowed her reluctance and forced her feet forward. She wasn't opposed to killing a few curs who got in her way, but she suspected that Salvatore would blame himself if anything happened to them.

And that bothered her, why?

Harley gave a shake of her head. She might as well accept she was currently out of her mind. It would be easier than trying to make sense of her recurring bouts of crazy.

Prepared for an ambush, Harley cautiously followed

the sharp curve in the tunnel, halting in surprise when an oversized, bald-headed cur staggered toward her.

Her first thought was that he was stark naked, as if he'd recently shifted. Her second thought was that he was taking up way too much space for one man. His shoulders almost brushed each side of the passageway. And if his head hadn't been bowed and covered by his hands, she suspected it would have been in danger of bumping the ceiling.

Warily, she watched as he weaved and stumbled toward her, muttering beneath his breath.

Okaaaay. If this was an ambush, it was the strangest one she'd ever heard of.

The cur had nearly reached her when he belatedly realized he was no longer alone. Jerking his head up, his eyes flashed crimson and his lips curled back in a snarl.

"Just hold on, Rambo," Harley held up her hands in a nonthreatening motion. Well, nonthreatening if you didn't count the big knife. "I don't want to hurt you."

The cur tilted back his face to sniff the air, and Harley realized that he was bleeding from a wound on the temple and that the left side of his face was a painful shade of black and blue. He looked like he'd just come out the loser of a *Bully Beatdown*.

"You're not Darcy," he at last growled.

"No shit, Sherlock," she muttered, not entirely reassured by the knowledge he was familiar with her twin.

Would she be able to tell if he was under the influence of Briggs?

"Who are you?" the cur demanded.

"Darcy's sister, Harley. And you?"

"Hess." He sucked in a deep breath, coming back from the edge of shifting. Not that he was any less dangerous. "Why do you smell like Salvatore?"

Hess. The name clicked into place.

Salvatore's most trusted soldier.

She could see why. He was a freaking mountain of muscle.

"The idiot seems to think I'm his mate," she said.

His brow furrowed, as if stumped by her explanation. "Weres can't mate."

"Yeah, well, that's something you need to take up with your king."

"Salvatore." Instantly distracted, the cur slammed his fist against the stone wall, his expression twisted with regret. "Shit."

Harley instinctively stepped back. "What?"

"I attacked him. Christ, I knew he was my master and I still tried to kill him." He stepped toward her, his expression wild. "I couldn't help it. I swear to you, I couldn't help it."

Anger exploded through Harley. Damn Briggs. He had to know that forcing Salvatore to hurt his own pack was the worst torture that Salvatore could endure.

"Save your pity party for later. I need to find your master," she snapped, sensing that Hess was in need of a strong leader, not a shoulder to cry on. A good thing. She wasn't a touchy-feely kind of gal. "Where did you see him last?"

As hoped, Hess was jolted out of his shame and squared his shoulders in determination.

"I'm not sure," he admitted, the muscles of his jaw knotted as he struggled to control his emotions. "He knocked me out during our fight and when I woke up, he was gone, so I took off. I wasn't going to risk being used against him again."

Which explained the bruises and his stumbling.

"How did you get here in the first place?"

He growled, his eyes flashing red. "Caine."

Stupidly, Harley was caught off guard. It wasn't that she thought Caine was above using and abusing his fellow curs. He was so lost in his delusions of grandeur that he was willing to sacrifice anyone and anything to make his vision come true. But he usually preferred to leave the grunt work to others.

Precious Caine didn't like to get his hands dirty.

"Someday soon I'm going to rip out his treacherous heart," she muttered.

"Not if I find him first."

"Did Caine kidnap anyone but you?"

"Three others."

Harley grimaced. "Where are they?"

"The cur had us in silver cages before the whacko Were came to take me away." He waved a hesitant hand to the left. "That way . . . I think."

Harley didn't fault him for being confused. The place was like an endless maze of barren stone.

"Go find them and get them out of here," she commanded.

Hess instantly bristled. "No, if you are the mate of Salvatore, he'd kill me if I let something happen to you."

Harley swallowed the urge to tell him exactly what he could do with his macho bullshit. It didn't matter that she could kick this cur's ass with one hand tied behind her back. Just because she had a uterus rather than a cock meant he had to protect her.

Instead, she simply outwitted him.

Not a particularly difficult task.

"Do you truly think you would be of any use to me if Briggs decides to take control of you again?" she demanded.

Hess scowled. "He won't . . ."

"Look, we're wasting time," she interrupted, her tone warning he was taking his life in his hands to argue with her. "You know that it isn't safe for you to be around Briggs."

Hess folded his hands over his massive chest. "How do you know he can't control you?"

"My connection to Salvatore protects me," she blatantly lied. She wouldn't let herself consider the possibility. "Go rescue the others."

There was a brittle silence, then with a foul curse, Hess swept past her, headed for the entrance of the tunnel.

"I'm going to be pissed if you get yourself killed and I'm blamed," he muttered.

Harley rolled her eyes. "I'll keep that in mind."

Waiting until she was alone in the tunnel, Harley sucked in a deep breath and continued her nerve-wracking journey. She hated feeling as if she were buried alive in this endless web of caverns. The vamps could have the dark and dank, as far as she was concerned. She wanted the open sky overhead, and a fresh breeze filling her lungs.

Ignoring the growing chill that prickled over her skin, Harley headed deeper and deeper into the darkness, losing track of time and direction as a creeping sense of claustrophobia threatened to choke her.

She concentrated on keeping her heartbeat steady and one foot moving in front of the other, her years of training at last coming in handy as she flowed silently through the empty tunnels.

On the point of turning back and trying another path, Harley caught the unmistakable scent of smoke. It wasn't exactly proof positive that Salvatore was near, but it was the first indication she wasn't completely alone in the barren hellhole.

Following the smoke, Harley slowly entered the large

cavern, her heart coming to a complete and perfect halt at the sight of Salvatore laid out on a stone altar, his blood dripping into a blazing brazier.

A savage, astonishingly protective fury ripped through her. Christ, his body was being destroyed by the heavy silver chains wrapped around him, and his beautiful face . . . it was dangerously pale from the rapid loss of blood. Dammit. She wanted to rip off Briggs's head. She wanted to feed his putrid heart to the rats. She wanted . . .

Her heart twisted.

She wanted to snatch Salvatore off the ghastly altar and take him far away from this cavern.

Checking the impulse to rush across the seemingly empty cave, Harley forced herself to pause and use her brains. Hey, there was a first time for everything.

Spreading out her senses, she searched for any hint of danger. It should have been simple. Beyond the altar and brazier the vast space appeared to be empty. But she knew from bitter experience that Briggs had the ability to pop in and out without warning.

When there was no smell of rotting meat and the air remained chilly, but not icy, she took a cautious step forward. She had taken her second step when Salvatore's head abruptly snapped in her direction, his eyes widening with unexpected panic.

"Harley, no," he growled.

"Listen to him, Were," an ominous voice rasped through the air. "A step closer and I'll kill him."

Harley sucked in a sharp breath, belatedly catching sight of the shadow that hovered above Salvatore.

She knew instinctively that the . . . *thing* wasn't Briggs using his hocus-pocus. The thick power that suddenly pulsed through the air had nothing to do with Were, and everything to do with pure, undiluted evil.

This had to be the demon lord that Styx feared.

Or at least a portion of his essence.

She briefly stumbled, her mouth dry with sheer terror. Deep in her heart, she understood she was in way over her head. What the hell did she know about battling a demon lord? Or a zombie Were, for that matter.

Then gritting her teeth, she ignored her perfectly reasonable fear and instead concentrated on the scent of Salvatore that at last broke through the dampening spell.

"You're going to kill him anyway," she accused, continuing forward.

"True, but you can save your own life," the voice promised. "Just turn and walk away."

"No."

"*Dio,* Harley, do as he says," Salvatore rasped, struggling against the silver chains. "Get out of here."

"Listen to your mate, female," the demon lord warned.

"Go to hell," she muttered, her gut clenching as Salvatore abruptly screamed in agony, his body contorting as if it were being tortured by an unseen enemy. "Shit. Just hang on, Salvatore. Do you hear me?"

Despite his obvious pain, Salvatore's golden gaze never wavered from her.

"Please, go. I can't bear . . ."

"Shut up, Your Majesty. I'm not leaving."

Unable to halt her by punishing Salvatore, the demon lord turned his attention in Harley's direction. She was mere steps from the altar when a bolt of energy smashed into her with enough force to send her to her knees.

Salvatore cried out. "Harley."

She pushed herself upright, jerking as another bolt slammed into her. Pain exploded through her body, but she refused to go down. Just a few more steps. And then . . .

Then what?

She didn't have a clue what she was going to do when she actually reached Salvatore, she only knew that she had to get to him.

Jagged shards of agony burrowed into her bones, making her movements awkward, and black spots danced before her eyes, nearly blinding her. Distantly she could hear Salvatore's ragged breaths and the low moans that were coming from her own throat, but she refused to focus on anything but putting one foot in front of another.

Demon lord or not, she was too damned stubborn to concede defeat.

There was blood dripping from a dozen small wounds, and Harley suspected that more than one bone was cracked by the time she at last reached the altar.

Once there, she realized that Salvatore looked even worse than she felt.

The dark hair was matted with blood, and his face was an alarming shade of gray. And his poor body . . .

She shuddered at the charred flesh, unable to imagine the agony he must be enduring.

Instinctively she reached to offer comfort, her hand lightly touching his shoulder.

Her fingers had barely brushed his skin when the black shadow that had wrapped around her gave a bloodcurdling scream. Harley leaned protectively over Salvatore, convinced that her eardrums were about to shatter.

What the hell was the matter with the thing?

Trying to prepare for whatever the demon lord intended to throw at them, Harley barely noticed the tingling sensation beneath her palm. Why would she? She tingled whenever she touched Salvatore.

But as the tingling became more pronounced and a strange heat raced up her arm and through her body, Harley pulled back to meet Salvatore's startled gaze.

The shadow that had been tormenting her had seemingly vanished, although Harley didn't believe for a moment that it had truly disappeared. No doubt it was revving up for something even more horrible. But for the moment, she couldn't concentrate on anything except the warm awareness that flooded through her.

Good . . . God.

Her wolf impatiently prowled beneath her skin, growling with a need she didn't understand. It was as if her beast were anxiously searching for something just out of reach.

Shivering, she met Salvatore's glowing golden gaze. She could sense the power of his wolf reaching out to her, brushing over her skin and cloaking her in his familiar heat. But more than that, she could feel him flowing through her fingertips and into her bloodstream.

Like warm honey, the feeling of Salvatore poured through her, marking her in the most intimate way possible. Harley made a sound of shock, but deep inside, her wolf howled in satisfaction, the restless ache that had plagued her being replaced by a stunning sense of . . . rightness.

She was whole.

Complete.

The thought had barely passed through her aching brain when she realized there was more than just the essence of Salvatore racing through her blood. There was his power. More power than she'd ever dreamed possible.

Charging full throttle through her body, it washed away her weariness and healed her wounds at record speed.

With a moan, she leaned against the altar, struggling

to remain upright as her bones mended and her flesh knit back together at an insane rate. Holy crap. The patching up hurt nearly as much as the initial injury.

At last the deluge of power settled to something bearable, and sucking in a steadying breath, Harley straightened enough to stab Salvatore with a suspicious frown.

"What the hell just happened?"

Salvatore smiled with smug satisfaction. "Exactly what you think happened."

The mating.

It was complete.

"Oh, shit."

"Too late for regrets, *cara.*"

She bit back the urge to tell him that this mating didn't change a thing between them. Although Salvatore had done his own share of healing, the silver chains continued to burn his flesh and sap his energy.

"It might be too late, period, if we don't get out of here," she muttered, her attention shifting to the large silver lock that held the chains in place.

For all the power that tingled through her, she didn't think she could free him with her bare hands.

As if reading her mind, Salvatore jerked his head toward the shadows behind the altar.

"See if you can find Briggs's stash of weapons. He's always had an obsession with big swords. No doubt to compensate for what he lacked in other areas."

Harley shook her head. They didn't have time for her to go on a treasure hunt. Already the black mist was beginning to form over the flames of the brazier. She had to get Salvatore loose, and she had to do it now.

"I have a better idea," she muttered, bending down to lift a heavy rock from the base of the altar.

Holding the rock in one hand, she grabbed the lock, hissing as it instantly blistered her skin.

Salvatore struggled against the chains, his face tight with frustration.

"*Merda,* you'll hurt yourself."

"Turn your head away."

It was the only warning she gave him before she set the lock against the stone altar and lifted the rock to smash the stupid thing over and over. Sparks flew and the sharp sound echoed through the cavern, but with stoic persistence, Harley at last beat the lock to a mangled bit of metal that fell away from the chains with a reluctant clunk.

With a harsh growl, Salvatore shoved the loosened chains off him and leaped from the altar. Then, yanking the knife out of his upper thigh, he glanced at the smashed lock at his feet.

"Remind me not to piss you off."

"Too late," she muttered, anxious to get the hell out of the caves. She had reached the end of her tolerance for dark, cramped places and vicious enemies who enjoyed causing pain. "I think that blob of a demon lord is trying to make an encore performance."

With a nod, Salvatore clutched the knife and began to head back toward the opening of the cavern.

"Let's get the hell out of here."

On creepy cue, the blob shifted away from the brazier and headed directly toward them.

"No," the demon lord hissed. "We have not yet finished our business, Giuliani."

"Oh, we're finished," Salvatore growled, shoving Harley behind him as the mist swooped downward and attacked.

"Shit." Harley flinched as the pain smacked into her

with the force of a freight train. "How are we supposed to fight this stupid thing?"

Salvatore shoved the knife into the heart of the mist, making it shudder and pull back, but only for a moment. Before they could run, it was returning for another attack.

"He was taking his power from my blood," Salvatore gritted.

Blood? Harley glanced back at the altar, realizing that the blood Salvatore had lost was pooled in a small cavity at the end of the altar and continued a steady drip into the flames.

She didn't know jack squat about demon lords, but she had to try something.

"Keep him busy," she ordered Salvatore, making a dash toward the brazier.

Slashing at the mist with his knife, Salvatore snarled when the flames shot directly toward her.

"Harley."

"Trust me."

She tried again to approach the brazier, only to be driven back by the fierce heat. Dammit. There had to be a way.

Turning her attention from the blazing fire, she instead approached the altar. If it was Salvatore's blood that gave the demon lord his power, then she had to get rid of it.

Easier said than done.

She might still be buzzing from the mating with Salvatore, but the altar was massive. It would be nothing less than a miracle to move it by herself.

She was considering how best to tackle the daunting task when the feel of Salvatore's pain echoed deep inside her. A glance over her shoulder revealed the black mist had nearly engulfed him.

As if he sensed her hesitation, he sent her an impatient frown.

"Harley."

"I'm working on it," she said, putting her shoulder against the altar and shoving with all her might.

"Work faster."

"If you think this mating thing gives you the right to nag at me, then you better think again."

Her muscles burned, her legs shaking with the effort to shift the stupid lump of stone. She gained a smidge. Then a half an inch, but she could still hear the relentless drops of blood hitting the flames.

She gritted her teeth. Her muscles were on fire and her shoulder popped out of joint, but she refused to concede defeat.

Dammit, this had to work.

Focused on the altar, Harley barely heard Salvatore when he shouted in warning.

"Look out."

She grunted as the pain slammed into the back of her head, digging through her skull with nauseating force. Her knees went weak and knowing she was losing the battle, she glanced over her shoulders, relieved to discover that Salvatore was already headed in her direction.

"We're going to have to do it together," she gritted.

Something hot and dangerous flashed in the golden eyes. Something that would have sent Harley fleeing in terror if she hadn't been distracted by her pesky fear of imminent death.

"*Si*. Together, *cara*."

Using a running start, Salvatore rammed into the altar, making it shift another inch. There was a shrill scream of fury that filled the cavern, and the pain in Harley's brain became crippling.

The demon lord was clearly displeased with their efforts.

Which meant it had to be hurting the bastard.

"More," she managed to gasp, sensing they had only moments before the demon lord could gather enough strength to crush them like bugs.

Salvatore grunted as he placed his hands against the altar and pushed with all he was worth. Which happened to be a great deal. His muscles bulged and the veins of his neck popped out as he added his strength to hers.

The unnerving screeching continued, and the pain filtered from Harley's brain down her spine, threatening to drain the last of her strength. But with Salvatore at her side, they managed to keep the pressure on the altar, and with a deafening crack the bottom at last broke free of the stone floor.

Breathing heavily, Harley watched as the massive stone slowly toppled over, breaking into a dozen pieces. For a moment, Salvatore stood at her side, then with a low curse he turned and kicked the brazier.

The flames sputtered, the hot coals spreading across the floor like glowing gems. Immediately the ravaging pain disappeared and with a gasp, Harley sank to her knees.

"Is it gone?"

"I don't intend to stick around to find out." Reaching down, Salvatore scooped her off the ground and headed for the entrance to the cavern. "Time to go."

On the point of commanding that he put her down, Harley stiffened as a deep boom echoed through the air and dust trickled down from the ceiling.

"Why don't I think that's a good thing?" she muttered.

"*Cristo.*" Tucking her against his chest, Salvatore

sprinted through the tunnels. "I'm growing tired of having caves falling on my head."

"No shit," she muttered, feeling the tremors that preceded a full-scale collapse. "Next time you piss off a demon lord, could you make sure he has a lair on the Riviera?"

His laughter echoed off the crumbling walls of the tunnel. "I'll see what I can do."

Chapter Nineteen

Caine didn't know how much time had passed when he returned to the land of the living.

It had to be long enough for the worst of his injuries to have healed, although he wasn't ready to do any backflips. He was still weak, and his muscles groaned in protest when he forced himself to his feet.

Glancing up, he studied the tiny opening of the pit far above his head. One thing was for certain. There was no way to get out the way he came in. He was a cur, not a damned bat.

"He's right about one thing. I am a stupid prick," he muttered, recalling Briggs's mocking words as he'd plummeted through the air. "Stupid and oh-so-dead. Why did I ever believe that bastard?" He turned his attention to his stark surroundings. "Because I wanted to believe. I was convinced I was so freaking special. What a joke."

With a shake of his head, Caine headed toward the nearest tunnel. He could wallow in self-pity and walk at the same time. God only knew how long it was going to take to find a way out of the hellhole.

He traveled through the low tunnels, occasionally slogging through water that tumbled from God only knew where, and more than once he was forced to bend over nearly in half to keep from banging his head.

All and all, a perfectly miserable journey.

Over an hour passed before Caine at last caught the scent of something besides damp rocks. Coming to a halt, he peered through the crack in the tunnel wall that revealed a small cave on the other side.

"Hello? Who's there?" He sucked in a deep breath, testing the air. There it was again. The faint scent of . . . Were? "Harley?" There was a rustle of sound and he caught the glimpse of a shadow dart past the narrow crack. "Shit."

Unable to bust his way through the thick wall, Caine splashed down the tunnel, hoping to find an opening into the cave. The smell wasn't exactly Harley's, but it was close enough that the Were had to be her relation.

Why the pureblood would be down here defied his imagination, but the mere hope she might lead him out of the nightmare maze was enough to make him ignore the danger of decapitation from the low ceiling as he dashed recklessly through the dark.

The scent deepened, the hint of lavender tugging at his senses, leading him down a side tunnel. He didn't have a clue where he was going, but suddenly finding the Were had become the most important task in his life.

His pace instinctively slowed as the tunnel ended at the opening to a large cavern.

Unlike the rest of the lower chambers, he sensed that someone regularly spent time in this area. His gaze scanned the shadows, taking in the shallow stream of water that had cut a groove in the smooth floor, and the stones that had been chiseled to resemble chairs.

No bat did that bit of sculpting.

Caine stepped into the cave, already sensing the Were hidden behind one of the larger stalagmites.

"You might as well come out," he commanded.

There was a tense pause, then with a slow movement, the diminutive pureblood stepped into view.

The hint of familiarity in her scent had already prepared Caine for the female's striking resemblance to Harley.

Her hair was a paler shade, closer to silver than blond, and pulled into a braid that fell to her waist. Her skin was a perfect alabaster, smooth and silken. Her eyes were also lighter, green the color of spring grass and flecked with gold.

Her face, however, was shaped exactly like Harley's, and beneath the frayed jeans and sweatshirt her body was slender, but hard with well-honed muscles.

She had to be one of the four pure-blooded females.

The one that Briggs had taken after they were nearly discovered in Chicago.

The Were had told him he'd sent her to a cur pack in Indiana. He should have known it was a lie.

Nothing else that had come out of the bastard's mouth had been true.

Staring at him with wide eyes, she tilted her head to the side, as if listening to a voice only she could hear.

"You shouldn't be down here."

He took a step forward. "Who are you?"

"Nobody." She warily shifted backwards. "I'm nobody."

Holding up his hands in a gesture of peace, Caine took another step forward.

"Easy, love," he soothed. "What's your name?"

"I don't have one."

He frowned. Was she jerking his chain? Or was she just flat-ass crazy?

"Everyone has a name."

She shrugged at his disbelieving expression. "I'm still waiting to discover what it's going to be." She stilled, abruptly glancing toward the ceiling. "I have to go."

With the quicksilver grace of a fairy, the female spun on her heel and darted toward a narrow opening on the far side of the cavern.

"Hold on." She ignored his command. Of course. Being stubborn had to be coded into the sisters' DNA. Without so much as a backwards glance, she disappeared from sight. "Freaking hell."

Caine was in swift pursuit, ignoring the very real possibility that this was another trap devised by Briggs.

He had to find the female.

He didn't know why. He only knew that it wasn't an option to allow her to escape.

Turning sideways to squeeze through the narrow opening, Caine entered the small cave. It was no larger than most bedrooms, with a narrow cot next to one wall and a battered dresser beneath a broken mirror next to another wall.

His brows snapped together at the realization that the stark, desolate cell must be where the beautiful woman was kept. An unexpected and unstoppable fury exploded through him.

Completely irrational considering he had more or less held Harley hostage.

Still, after the past few days, he wasn't in the mood to be rational.

Intent on the silver-haired Were, it wasn't until she'd bent to light a candle that he was aware of the odd shimmers in the air.

"What the hell . . ."

His hair threatened to stand on end as his gaze slid over the foreign glyphs that covered the stone walls. In the flickering candlelight they glowed in a strangely hypnotic manner.

"You can't be here," the woman whispered, wrapping her arms around herself as she sank to her knees beside the cot.

"I hate to argue with a beautiful woman, but obviously I can," he absently muttered, moving toward the nearest wall. "What is this place?"

"It's a secret."

He halted just inches from the wall, studying the designs. "Did you do these?"

"Yes."

A peculiar sensation inched down Caine's spine as he realized that the glyphs weren't carved onto the walls as he first assumed, but instead floated just above the rough surface, occasionally shifting and changing color with a dizzying speed.

These weren't random works of art created by a bored pureblood.

This was . . . power.

Turning, he moved back to tower over her kneeling form. "What are they?"

"Pain, joy . . . death." She shook her head, fear rippling over her delicate face. "You have to go. He'll be mad if he finds you here."

Caine hadn't been feared among curs far and wide for no good reason. He could be cold, cunning, and calculating. He could also be brutal when the occasion demanded.

But something pierced his heart as he gazed down at the fragile woman. Something rare and perilous.

Without thought, he was kneeling in front of her, reaching to grab her chilled fingers.

"Who?" he rasped. "Who will be mad?"

"He'll kill you."

"Are you a prisoner?" he demanded. She ducked her head, and he hooked a thumb beneath her chin, forcing her to meet his searching gaze. "Look at me. Are you being held here against your will?"

"He won't let me out."

"Tell me who it is."

A shadow crossed her face. "I'm not allowed to say his name."

"Is it Briggs?"

"The dead Were? No." A small smile touched her lips. "He's frightened of me."

Caine couldn't hide his surprise. Briggs was the sort of nightmarish creature that would terrify any demon. Why would he be frightened of this tiny Were?

"Frightened?"

She shrugged. "He shouldn't have asked if he didn't want to know."

"Know what?"

"His future." She pointed toward one of the swirling glyphs. "There."

Caine frowned in confusion. "What is it?"

The pale green eyes stabbed him with an unnervingly piercing gaze. As if she could see into his very soul.

"Death."

"Christ."

Caine jerked in shock. Dammit. For decades he allowed himself to be blinded by a vision that his rational brain told him was impossible. Not only would it take nothing less than a miracle to turn him from a cur into a pureblood, but Briggs's claim that his black magic gave him the power to reveal the future was beyond crazy.

After all, most of the known prophets were under the control of the Oracles, and they possessed only random flashes of the future. Enough to grasp an overall image of various possibilities or pivotal events, but not a detailed revelation for an individual.

And now, when he'd at last accepted that he'd been a total putz to fall for Briggs's scheme, he was confronted by the most extraordinary of all creatures.

"You're a seer," he breathed.

She shook her head. "I don't see. I dream." She glanced toward the shimmering glyphs. "I dream and they appear."

Gently he shifted his hand, cupping her cheek. "Did you dream of me?"

The green eyes were abruptly veiled with a disturbing white as she gazed blindly at the wall over his shoulder.

"Your blood will run pure."

Caine didn't feel elation at the soft words. In fact, the chill that had been snaking up and down his spine now spread to lodge deep in his gut.

"You're certain?"

She placed her hand flat on the stone floor, her eyes still clouded. "Here."

"I don't understand."

"Your blood. So much blood," she husked, shuddering. "It's everywhere."

"Shit." Surging to his feet, he yanked her upright, his instincts on full alert. "We have to get out of here."

With a blink, her eyes cleared, revealing a poignant sadness that shook him to the very core.

"He'll never let me go."

"I don't intend to ask his permission," Caine growled, tugging her toward the crack that led to the outer cavern. There had to be a way out of the damned caves. "Let's go."

He only made it a few steps before she dug in her heels. Literally.

"I can't."

She was tiny, but she possessed all the strength of a pureblood. Snarling in frustration, Caine turned to glare at her.

"Can't or won't?"

"Can't," she said, her expression composed. "I'm tied to these caves until he's banished."

Well, of course she was. Hell would freeze over before luck was on his side.

"So who are you?" he demanded in frustration. "Cassandra or Repunzel?"

Seemingly indifferent to the danger that pulsed in the air, the female Were flashed a smile that arrowed straight to his heart. Damn the female. What was she doing to him?

He was a man who appreciated a beautiful female. Especially when there was a bed so conveniently nearby. But he wasn't the sort of sucker who allowed a woman to bewitch and bedazzle him.

With a shake of his head, he squashed the irrational thoughts. He'd puzzle out his idiotic behavior later.

Like when death wasn't actually looming.

"Cassandra." She said the name like she was testing it on her tongue. Her green eyes glowed with a sudden pleasure. "Yes, I like that name."

"Fine, you're Cassandra." He cupped her face in his hands and pretended he wasn't completely charmed. "What mysterious man keeps you here?"

Her brief happiness faded as swiftly as it had arrived. "Demon lord."

Caine dropped his hands, a bolt of fear nearly paralyzing him before he gained control of his rattled nerves.

No. Demon lords had been banished centuries ago. Someone had to be screwing with the poor female's brain.

"Impossible."

"Nothing is impossible," she softly countered. "Although some things are more probable."

He narrowed his eyes. "Just how long have you been down here?"

"An eternity."

"You . . ." His words were bit off as a chilling scream ripped through the caves, followed by a violent earthquake that sent Caine sprawling on the hard floor. Pressing a hand to the lump on the back of his head, he regained his feet and glanced warily at the ceiling. It was nothing less than a miracle that they hadn't been buried beneath an avalanche of rock. "What the hell was that?"

Standing in the middle of the cave as if nothing out of the ordinary had occurred, the pureblood pointed a finger toward the swirling glyphs.

"Crossroads."

Caine's sharp laugh echoed through the suddenly still air. The woman might be beautiful and fascinating, but she was as crazy as a loon.

"Is it in the prophet handbook that seers have to mutter complete crap?"

She blinked. "There's a handbook?"

"Christ." He shook his head. "What do you mean by crossroads?"

She again pointed at the designs that had started to pulse and churn with a nauseating tempo.

"Leave now and you have a chance of altering your future."

"And if I stay?"

She met his gaze squarely "You die."

Even expecting the prophecy of doom, her simple words hit Caine like a punch to the gut.

You die . . .

For the past thirty years he'd believed that immortality was in his grasp. Hell, he'd become downright cocky, taking insane risks.

Like trying to kidnap the King of Weres.

Now he smiled wryly as his mortality smacked him directly in the face. Obviously he should have been paying more attention to his rotten karma, rather than placing all his bets on a vision he'd completely misread.

"Of course I die," he muttered. "And what happens to you?"

She shrugged. "Fate."

Caine's brows snapped together. The thought of his imminent death pissed him off. The thought that this woman might be harmed . . .

Unacceptable.

"Well, screw fate," he growled, kicking off his running shoes.

Her green eyes widened with something that might have been female appreciation as he stripped off his T-shirt.

"What are you doing?"

He tugged off his jeans, tossing them aside. "I'm done trying to make an impossible dream come true."

Perhaps sensing his reckless determination to go down in a blaze of glory, Cassandra moved to frame his face in her hands, her expression troubled.

"I told you, nothing is impossible."

Her touch sent a shocking blast of awareness through Caine, nearly sending him to his knees. Christ, it was like being struck by lightning.

A damned shame he could sense something very large and dangerous charging through the tunnels toward them.

A gruesome death might be worth a night with this woman.

"Maybe you're right, Cassandra, my love." He savored the beauty of her delicate features, lingering on the vulnerable curve of her mouth. "After all, you're about to witness a miracle."

"What miracle?"

Bending down, he kissed her with a fierce regret.

"For once in my miserable life, I'm going down a hero."

He stole one last kiss, then, with a defiant howl, Caine shifted and prepared to meet death.

When Harley opened her eyes, she was briefly bewildered by the cupid-painted ceiling above her.

Lying on the oversized bed with silk sheets and a fluffy comforter that was perfect to burrow beneath, she battled through the fog still clinging to her brain.

She remembered being in the caves. Kind of tough to forget. It wasn't every day a woman had to fight a demon lord. Not even in her crazy world. And then there had been a mad dash through the caves, barely staying ahead of the thunderous cave-in.

After that . . .

She had a vague memory of stumbling over Darcy and the vampires in the upper chambers. They had swiftly bundled Harley and Salvatore in a Hummer and headed back to Chicago. And then there was nothing.

She had no recollection of arriving at the mansion on the outskirts of Chicago. Or being tucked in bed.

And she most certainly didn't remember being stripped naked.

The last of the fog was seared away as Harley became aware of the warm body laying next to her. With a jerk, she rolled to the side, not at all surprised to discover Salvatore.

Even without the heat brushing over her bare skin, she would have known he was near. The essence of him was branded deep inside her.

Unnerved by the sensation, Harley allowed her gaze to drift over the finely chiseled face, a familiar need stirring as she took in the thin aquiline nose and full sensuous lips. With his raven hair spilled across the pillow and richly bronzed skin glowing in late afternoon sunlight, he might have looked ridiculously pretty if not for the savage power that hummed just below his sophistication.

Intent on her survey, it took Harley a moment to notice the amused gold shimmering beneath his lowered lashes.

Her heart did an alarming flop and she instinctively tensed, preparing to scramble out of the bed.

As quick as she was, however, Salvatore was quicker.

Wrapping his arms around her, he hauled her against his equally naked body, a wicked smile curving his lips.

"Buon pomeriggio, cara."

She sucked in a sharp breath as an urgent desire charged through her. Her brain might be freaking out at the thought of being eternally bonded to Salvatore, but her body didn't give a crap.

He was near. He was naked.

He was freaking gorgeous.

Enough said.

Doing her best to ignore the treacherous excitement spreading through her body, Harley planted her hands against his chest.

"What are you doing in my bed?"

He arched a teasing brow. "How do you know this isn't *my* bed?"

"Dammit. Why are we in *any* bed together?"

His hands slid down to her lower back, pressing her close enough to feel his stirring erection.

"Where else would your mate sleep?"

Mate. Panic sliced through her and she struggled to put a bit of space, and hopefully a measure of sanity, between them.

"Just hold on, Giuliani."

"I'm trying, but you keep squirming." His warm breath teased over her cheek, sending bolts of pleasure through her body. "Not that I find it entirely unpleasant."

"Salvatore."

He nuzzled a path of kisses along the line of her jaw. "Yes, *cara*?"

She desperately tried to hold onto her train of thought. Not easy when her body was melting in anticipation.

"This whole mating thing is simple biology," she warned. "You understand that, right?"

He chuckled, his hands running a path from her hips to the curve of her breasts.

"There's nothing simple about biology, *cara*. It's complex and magical and far too often inconvenient as hell."

She forgot how to breathe as his thumbs lazily teased her nipples to hard, aching peaks.

"I'll second the inconvenient-as-hell part," she muttered.

"And the magical part?" he whispered, bending his head to tug one nipple between his lips.

The groan of bliss escaped before she could swallow it. "I'm trying to have a conversation with you."

"I'm listening."

"How can you be listening when you're groping me?"

He gently used his teeth to send shock waves of pleasure through her breast to the pit of her stomach.

"I told you. I can multitask."

No crap. He was the freaking master of multitasking. In fact, if he multitasked any better, she would be singing "Afternoon Delight" and seeing fireworks.

With a sudden shove, Harley rolled Salvatore onto his back, straddling his waist as she grimly reminded herself that they needed to get a few things straight.

She might have become his mate.

But that didn't make her his "little woman."

She pressed her hands to his shoulders, glaring at his amused expression.

"Pay attention."

The golden eyes glowed with a tangible heat, his hands skimming over the curve of her hips.

"You have my full and eager attention." He shifted his hips until his erection pressed against her backside. "Painfully eager."

Harley clenched her jaw. Holy crap. He wasn't the only one eager.

"We need to discuss our . . ." She struggled for the right word.

"Mating?"

"Relationship," she snapped. "Or more specifically, our lack of a relationship."

His fingers tightened on her hips. "Nothing seems to be lacking to me," he husked. "In fact, I couldn't be more pleased."

"Just listen," she commanded. "This whole mating doesn't mean I'm going to become your plaything."

"Of course it does." He flashed a decidedly wolfish smile. "And for the next few centuries, I intend to keep you barefoot and pregnant while you tend to my every need."

"Oh, yeah?" She leaned down until they were nose to nose. "I'll see you in hell first."

His hand tangled in her hair, keeping her from pulling back.

"Harley, the mating just happened. We have an eternity to figure out the relationship."

"After my first litter or two? Isn't that what you want from a female?"

"Madre del dio . . ." Unprepared for her accusation, his grip faltered and she pulled back to study his guarded expression.

"Darcy thought it was only fair to warn me that your sole interest in finding us was because of the babies we can produce for you."

Harley watched the irritation ripple over his beautiful face, knowing she was being a fraud.

Not that she was interested in becoming a mindless broodmare for this Were. No way. But she did understand his frantic need for pure-blooded children, and his willingness to do whatever necessary to have them.

He was king, and his first duty would always be to his people.

That was what she admired most about him.

No. She was merely using the convenient excuse to put a barrier between them.

"Remind me to properly thank her later," he muttered.

"Do you deny it?"

"I deny nothing, *cara,*" he grudgingly confessed. "My intention was to create pure-blooded females who could carry a litter to full term. But everything has changed now that you're my mate." His expression softened with a tenderness that smashed directly into her heart. "My personal miracle."

Harley stiffened, the unexplainable panic once again looming.

"Don't say stuff like that."

"That you're a miracle?"

"Yes."

"Why?"

"Because it's freaking me out."

"Harley." Reaching up, he grasped her face between his hands. "What's going on?"

Well, that was the question, wasn't it?

She licked her dry lips, trying to put her vague fears into words.

"For the past thirty years you've been the monster in the closet that gave me nightmares."

"Merda." The golden eyes flashed with outrage. "You think I'm a monster?"

"Of course not. My point is that Caine made me believe his lies. He controlled and manipulated me, and I was too stupid to realize it."

His expression remained grim. "Not stupid. You were young and vulnerable, and the bastard took advantage of you."

"I *let* him take advantage of me." She unconsciously squared her shoulders. "That's never going to happen again."

"You don't trust me."

"I barely know you." She rolled her eyes as a smirk curved his lips. "Sex doesn't equate to knowing someone."

Chapter Twenty

Salvatore was careful to keep his possessive instincts hidden behind his taunting smile.

This woman was his mate.

And nothing, not even Harley herself, was going to keep him from claiming her.

But he hadn't been born yesterday.

Or even a century ago.

He might not fully understand Harley's hovering panic, but he did know that a display of blatant machismo would push her over the edge.

It was a moment for finesse, not force.

"You know me." He placed his hand just above her breast, savoring the jump of her heart at his intimate touch. "Here."

Her eyes darkened with awareness of the bond forged between them, but she stubbornly shook her head.

"This is happening way too fast."

Salvatore allowed his gaze to dip to the perfect curve of her breasts. There was no point in arguing. Not when she was obviously in the mood to assert her independence.

Eventually she'd learn to accept their bond.

And until then, he had a perfect means of passing the time.

"Very well, *cara.* I can do slow," he promised, his hands moving to cup her breasts. He growled deep in his throat as her nipples tightened into tiny nubs and the air was scented with her arousal. "As slow as you want."

Her eyes darkened with ready passion, but her expression remained leery, no doubt sensing she was being deliberately distracted.

"Salvatore . . ."

"Harley, we just escaped from a demon lord," he protested, his fingers lightly circling her nipples. "Surely we deserve a few hours before we go searching for more trouble."

She shivered, her back arching beneath his caresses. "I don't have to search for trouble when you're around."

"So cruel," he teased, lifting his head to replace his fingers with his lips.

"You think you're so damned irresistible," she complained, even as her fingers threaded through his hair and she guided his mouth to her other breast.

He gently nipped her creamy skin. "I'm more interested in whether *you* think I'm irresistible."

"You're . . ." She groaned as his tongue flicked over the tip of her nipple. "Passable, I suppose."

His wolf stirred at the direct challenge. Without warning, he flipped her onto her back and covered her with his larger body, pressing her into the mattress.

"Passable?"

"Hey."

"My turn on top."

She was insanely beautiful with her golden hair spread across the pillows and her cheeks flushed, but it was the sensual anticipation that glittered in her eyes that made his muscles clench in painful need.

"Don't get used to it," she husked.

"We'll see." Her lips parted to argue, but her words faltered as Salvatore sank his cock deep into her wet heat, her low moan of pleasure filling the air. "There's an endless number of possibilities," he whispered, "and positions."

She sank her nails deep into his back, drawing blood as he slowly pulled back and then thrust forward. The pinpricks of pain only added to his pleasure, and pumping his hips in a slow, steady rhythm, he bent his head to capture her nipple between his lips.

"Yes," Harley breathed, wrapping her legs around his waist. "Don't stop."

Stop?

Madre del dio. There wasn't a force in heaven or earth that could make him stop. Not when her slick heat was clamped around his erection, her hips rising to meet his thrusts with the hungry demand of a female Were.

Muttering soft words of encouragement, Salvatore shifted to bury his face in the curve of her neck, the mating bond roaring through him. The sense of Harley was not just physical, but branded on his every emotion.

She was a part of him.

For all eternity.

Feeling the gathering power of his orgasm, Salvatore grasped the tender flesh of her neck between his teeth, gripping her hips as he drove into her with rapid strokes.

His entire body tightened with a fierce joy.

Si. This was what sex between mates was supposed to be.

Intense, thrilling, and wild.

With a sharp cry, Harley reached her climax, raking her nails down his back as she convulsed around him.

The sensation was enough to catapult him over the edge, and tilting back his head, Salvatore roared in pleasure, allowing his seed to pour deep inside her.

For a breathless moment, he remained poised above her, then with a shuddering sigh he collapsed beside her, gathering her tight in his arms.

"Admit it," he murmured, tenderly tucking a damp curl behind her ear.

"Admit what?"

"You find me irresistible."

She snorted, shifting so she could meet his teasing gaze. "I find cheesecake irresistible, but that doesn't make it good for me."

"Cheesecake." He studied her with a wicked smile. "Hmmm."

"Why are you looking at me like that?"

"I was just imagining how delicious cheesecake would taste served on this decadent skin." His fingers traced a path up the curve of her back. "What else do you find irresistible?"

She smiled with faux sweetness. "A loaded Smith and Wesson .357."

"Sexy."

Her eyes widened, then without warning, her choked laugh echoed through the vast room.

"For God's sake, is there anything you don't think is sexy?"

A poignant, entirely unreasonable warmth filled his heart at the genuine amusement shimmering in her eyes.

"Not when you're near," he husked.

"So predictably male."

He pressed her closer, his cock already stirring with a ready passion.

"A wolf is never predictable . . ." His words broke off as a cold, sweeping power filled the air.

"What is it?" Harley demanded.

"The leeches are stirring."

"Is that a problem?"

"I need to speak with Styx."

"About what?"

He shrugged. His conversation with the Anasso was not something he intended to share.

At least not with Harley.

"Unfinished business."

Her brows drew together in suspicion. "Could you be a little more vague?"

He brushed a light kiss over her lips. Time for a distraction.

"What about you, *cara*?"

"Me?"

"What are your plans?"

She stiffened in his arms, the wary expression returning with annoying predictability.

Ironic really.

Wasn't it traditionally the role of the male to panic at the mention of "happily ever after"?

"For tonight?" She deliberately misunderstood. "Popcorn and a movie in bed sounds pretty good."

It sounded better than good. It sounded like paradise.

A pity he had a few loose ends to tie up.

Which meant he had to leave Harley behind. At least for a few days.

He intended to make certain she would be safe until his return.

"Harley, you know what I'm asking," he said softly.

"I don't have an answer."

"Do you intend to remain here with your sister?"

"Perhaps for a few days."

"And then?"

Her expression hardened, her hands moving to press against his chest.

"That's my business."

Content with the knowledge that she was willing to remain with the vamps for at least a few days, Salvatore smiled. It shouldn't take more than a day or two to finish his business, and then he could concentrate on his obstinate mate.

"There's no need to jut that chin at me." He kissed the chin in question and then the tip of her nose. "I have no intention of locking you in my lair. At least not in the foreseeable future."

She frowned in confusion. "You're just going to let me go?"

Let her go? When hell froze over.

He merely smiled. "You're not my prisoner."

Far from stupid, she narrowed her eyes in suspicion. "This is some sort of trick, isn't it?"

"No trick."

"It doesn't bother you that your mate isn't going to be with you?"

"As I said, we'll figure this out in time." Sliding out of bed, Salvatore scooped Harley into his arms and headed for the attached bathroom. "For now, I need a shower."

She widened her eyes as he crossed the marble floor and entered the shower that could fit an entire army regiment.

"What are you doing?"

Setting her on her feet, Salvatore savored the scent of her sharp excitement that perfumed the air.

She could snap and snarl and pretend she wasn't destined to spend the rest of her life with him, but this . . .

This she could never hide.

Turning on the hot water to spill over them, he skimmed his lips over her cheek, his hands cupping the perfect curve of her breasts.

"You can't expect me to scrub my own back, woman," he teased. "That's what a mate is for."

"Creep," she whispered, a smile curving her lips as she plunged her fingers in his hair and kissed him with a hunger that had him pushing her against the ivory ceramic tiles and spreading her legs.

"And this . . ." With a slow, steady thrust, his cock was deep inside her. "Is what I'm for."

She groaned, wrapping her legs around his waist.

"Not bad, Giuliani," she whispered. "Not bad at all."

An hour later, Harley was settled on the bed wrapped in a terrycloth robe, aimlessly flipping the channels on the plasma TV that had appeared, with a push of a button, from behind a sliding panel.

Her skin was pruny from the hour she'd spent in the shower with Salvatore, and her body deliciously sated, but she felt oddly restless as she shifted on the silken sheets and adjusted the pile of pillows behind her.

It would be simple enough to blame her fidgets on the chases, cave-ins, and numerous near-death experiences she'd endured over the past few days. What woman wouldn't be twitchy?

Or even the fact that she was in an unfamiliar house, surrounded by dangerous demons who could call themselves family, but still were little more than strangers.

She knew, however, those weren't the true reasons she couldn't relax.

No.

Her inability to relax was directly due to Salvatore.

Or more precisely, the absence of Salvatore.

Damn the man.

After their prolonged, and deliciously erotic shower, Salvatore had dressed in one of the numerous designer suits that had been left in the walk-in closet, and pulled back his hair with a leather cord. Then with a lingering kiss, he'd taken off in search of Styx, leaving her to enjoy a quiet evening alone.

Exactly what she wanted.

So why did the humongous bed feel empty and the night stretch before her with a tedious boredom?

She clenched her teeth, jabbing her finger on the channel button of the remote control as she scrolled past infomercials, reruns of *Green Acres,* and a number of movies that involved an abundance of naked bodies and juvenile humor. There were a thousand channels. One of them had to have something worth watching.

She had just started on her third run through the channels when a light tap on the door offered a welcomed distraction.

Tossing aside the remote, she sucked in a deep breath, recognizing the scent of her sister.

"Darcy?"

"I come bearing gifts," she called through the thick wood of the door. "Can I join you?"

"Of course." Harley slid off the bed, her eyes widening in surprise as Darcy wheeled in a small cart that was overflowing with stacks of movies, bowls of popcorn, and large ceramic mugs. "How did you know . . . Salvatore."

"He mentioned you wanted popcorn and a movie. I thought we could watch together if you don't mind." Darcy flashed a charming smile, looking decidedly impish in her casual shorts and skimpy top, her blond hair spiked. "I brought everything from *Die Hard* to *You've Got Mail.*"

"Definitely *Die Hard,*" Harley said before she could halt the revealing words. Hoping to cover her ridiculous aversion to romance, she bent to peer into the ceramic cups. "Hot chocolate?"

"My weakness." Darcy perched on the edge of the bed as she waved a hand toward a delicately scrolled armoire. "There's whiskey in the cabinet if you want it with a kick."

Harley grimaced, joining her sister on the bed. "I prefer to keep my wits intact when Salvatore is around."

"Ah." Darcy tilted her head, studying her with an unnervingly perceptive gaze. "Very wise."

Harley ran a self-conscious hand through her still damp curls.

"Why are you looking at me like that?"

Darcy grimaced. "I'm sorry. Nothing is a secret in the demon world."

"What secret?"

"You've completed the mating bond."

Harley pressed her hands to her face. Was that a blush heating her skin? Frigging hell. She was an idiot.

"Yes."

"So, you're Queen of the Weres. Congratulations."

Disbelief jolted through her. Queen of Weres. She'd been so rattled by the shock of being mated to Salvatore that the rest of the baggage he brought with him had skimmed right over her head.

Until now.

She groaned, flopping back on the mattress.

"Oh, my God," she moaned. "What the hell have I gotten myself into?"

"Harley?" Darcy's worried face abruptly hovered over

her. "Forgive me. I have a habit of putting my foot in my mouth."

Harley heaved a sigh that came from the tips of her toes. "It's not you, Darcy. It's Salvatore Giuliani."

"Typical." Darcy scooted back so Harley could push herself up on her elbows. "Do you want to tell me what's wrong?"

"All of this," Harley muttered.

"Could you be a little more specific?"

Harley shivered, briefly closing her eyes. Even from a distance, she could sense Salvatore. He was in a room directly below her, pacing the floor with a barely controlled impatience that she felt as vividly as if it were her own emotion.

She lifted her head to meet Darcy's gaze. "I'm not sure I want to be a mate, let alone the freaking Queen of Weres."

Darcy's lips twisted at her plaintive, yes, maybe even childish, tone.

"Get in line," she said bluntly.

"Excuse me?"

"I seem to have this conversation a lot over the past few days," she said with a rueful shake of her head. "Harley, you aren't the first woman to be . . ."

"Unhinged?" she helpfully supplied.

Darcy chuckled. "Okay, unhinged, by the thought of being irrevocably bound to a male. Especially if that male happens to be an arrogant, overbearing, far-too-fond-of-giving-orders demon."

"You?"

"In case you haven't noticed, Styx tends to take arrogance to an epic level. He's quite convinced that he's been put on this earth to take command of everyone and everything. Including me."

"Why didn't you run?"

"I did."

Harley jerked in astonishment. Not even the most cynical demon could fail to appreciate the devotion between Darcy and her vampire.

"Really?"

Darcy wrinkled her nose, clearly recalling one of those memories that you could only laugh about later.

"Styx and I had our own share of troubles."

"Obviously you came back."

"Because distance doesn't change anything." Darcy shrugged. "My bond to Styx isn't just an ancient demon rite or sappy exchange of vows. He's a part of me." She pressed a hand to her heart. "Wherever I am."

The words did precisely nothing to reassure Harley.

"So you just gave up and let Styx take over your life?" she demanded.

Darcy's eyes widened before she fell backwards on the bed, her laughter bouncing off the vaulted ceiling and echoing through the priceless chandeliers.

"Only in his dreams," she at last managed to gasp, sitting up to wipe the tears from her face. "Actually, if you asked Styx he would tell you that I've completely taken over his life, and that he's not even allowed to step out of the house without asking my permission."

Harley frowned. The big, scary King of Vampires asking permission?

"I don't believe it."

"The truth is that we have both learned to compromise," she said. "Styx has grudgingly accepted that I'm capable of making my own decisions, and I've grudgingly accepted that his position as Anasso means that he has to put himself in danger far too often." She reached to grasp Harley's hand. "It doesn't mean that we don't still have our moments, but we've learned we can discuss the situation and find a solution we can both live with."

"Compromise? Salvatore? Yeah, right." Harley snorted at the mere suggestion. Salvatore would learn to compromise when pigs learned to fly. "I don't think so."

"Trust me, Harley. He will learn to compromise because he won't have a choice."

"You obviously don't know the pain-in-the-ass Were as well as you think you do."

Darcy leaned forward, her expression oddly serious. "I know that a male demon might be obsessed with his need to protect his mate, but he's equally obsessed with his need to make her happy." She caught and held Harley's gaze. "The moment that Styx senses his overprotective habits are suffocating me, he has no choice but to back off."

There was no doubting the sincerity in Darcy's voice. She truly believed a demon like Salvatore could be tamed.

Not that Harley actually wanted to *tame* Salvatore.

No. Of course not.

She wanted . . .

What?

A frightening ache unfurled in the center of her heart. An ache that was directly connected to Salvatore Giuliani.

Dammit.

He made her crazy with the thought of being mated. And at the same time, he made her crazy with the thought of ever leaving him.

In other words, he flat-out made her crazy.

Shifting uneasily, Harley turned her attention to the stack of movies on the tray.

"Actually, I just want to forget Salvatore and our . . . mating for the next couple of hours."

Darcy looked as if she wanted to press the benefits of being mated to an uberalpha demon with a throne, but easily recognizing the stubborn expression on Harley's face, she heaved a rueful sigh.

"That should be simple enough." She grabbed one of the mugs of hot chocolate.

Simple?

Harley lifted her brows, sensing she was missing something.

"Why do you say that?"

"When I spoke with Salvatore a short time ago, he mentioned he was leaving tonight and might be gone several days. We'll have plenty of time to get to know one another without being bothered by the King of Weres."

"Leaving?"

A sharp alarm had Harley off the bed and storming toward the door.

Salvatore hadn't said a word to her about a road trip.

So either he was making plans for her without asking her opinion.

Or he intended to leave her behind.

Either way, he was going to get his assed kicked.

Chapter Twenty-One

Salvatore didn't need anyone to tell him that he was an idiot.

What male, especially a male werewolf, would willingly leave the warm, welcoming arms of his mate?

Unfortunately, he was also a king, which meant he couldn't avoid his responsibilities. No matter what the temptation.

Reminding himself that the sooner he was done with his business the sooner he could return to Harley, Salvatore forced his reluctant feet to carry him down to the kitchen to briefly speak with Darcy, and then to the back of the mansion where he found Styx.

Entering the long narrow room, he lifted his brows in amused appreciation.

Like the rest of the house, the room was drenched with a profusion of ivory and gilt, with massive chandeliers that hung from a cavernous ceiling. But instead of delicate furnishings and expensive carpeting, the walls were lined with glass cases that held rows of weapons. Guns, swords, crossbows, maces, daggers . . . the only thing missing was a rocket launcher, and Salvatore wouldn't have been surprised if there was one or two tucked inside the wooden cabinets at the back of the room.

The floor was an expensive parquet affair, patterned in a sunburst, but there were also a half dozen workout mats tossed across the glossy wood, with casual indifference to the beauty of the craftsmanship.

Salvatore had his own armory and Olympic-sized gym in his Roman lair. What demon didn't? But the contrast between the frilly French décor and the brutal arsenal was absurd enough to bring a smile to his lips.

He took another step forward, his gaze catching sight of Styx in a far corner.

The ancient vampire was wearing nothing more than a loose pair of yoga pants, with his long hair pulled back in a braid as he whirled a massive sword through the air. His movements were fluid and perfectly measured, the mark of a true swordsman.

A predator.

Salvatore's wolf stirred in instinctive response.

Weeks ago, he and Styx had pitted their strengths against each other.

Styx had won that battle, arrogant bloodsucker, but Salvatore knew that things would be different now. With the demon lord dead and the power of his mating with Harley pulsing through his blood, he would prove a far greater match for the ancient vampire.

As if sensing Salvatore's thoughts, Styx turned to regard his guest with a piercing gaze, the sword held loosely in his hand. Then, with a faint smile, he reached to pluck a matching sword from the glass case on the wall and casually tossed it in Salvatore's direction.

Snatching the ornately carved hilt, Salvatore strolled forward, a growl of anticipation rumbling in his chest.

"Preparing for an invasion, Styx?" he drawled, gesturing toward the vast array of weapons.

"A good king is always prepared." A taunting smile curled his lips. "Besides, I never know when I might be challenged by an arrogant Were who doesn't know his place."

"My place?" Salvatore paused to strip off the elegant Gucci jacket and white silk shirt. Then, kicking off the shoes, he lifted the sword in a silent invitation. "Do I have to teach you my place?"

"You are welcomed to try."

Sweeping his sword upward, Styx attacked.

Salvatore was prepared, and with a swift motion he met the brutal flurry of strikes. His true strength was in his wolf, but he possessed enough power and skill with the sword to hold his own, even managing to get in a few blows.

Easily sensing Salvatore's increased ability since their last confrontation, Styx flashed his fangs in a lethal smile, slicing his sword through the air with a ferocious speed. Salvatore grunted as his muscles absorbed the merciless impact of the attack, flowing in a seamless dance from one side to another.

They sparred in silence, retreating and advancing to the sharp crash of colliding steel and a shower of sparks.

Astonishingly, Salvatore found himself enjoying the mock skirmish. As King of Weres, it was difficult to find a partner who could match his strength, let alone his expertise. It was stimulating to fight a worthy adversary.

Even if that adversary was a leech.

Shoving aside his fear at Harley's refusal to acknowledge their mating bond and the nagging certainty that Briggs was still out there somewhere, Salvatore lost himself in the pure pleasure of pitting himself against the immense vampire.

A mixture of sweat and blood from shallow wounds

coated their skin before both of them stepped apart in mutual agreement.

With a feral smile, Styx set aside his sword and moved through an open door at the back of the room. He disappeared for only a moment before he returned with two damp towels, tossing one in Salvatore's direction.

Salvatore put the sword on a nearby stand to be cleaned and oiled. Then he gratefully scrubbed away the sweat and blood. Whatever Hollywood director had decided that werewolves were savage, uncivilized beasts had never actually met a pureblood. No creature with such an acute sense of smell could be anything but fastidious.

Of course, not all Weres were blessed with his exquisite taste in fashion.

Styx leaned casually against a glass case, the wounds marring his broad chest rapidly healing.

"The mating with Harley has increased your strength."

"It has." Salvatore smiled wryly, realizing that the vampire hadn't just been casually sparring. He was the Anasso and he would make it his priority to know the precise amount of power the King of Weres could call on. No one, after all, could call him stupid. "Along with the death of the demon lord."

Styx narrowed his eyes, his expression hard with frustration.

"How the bloody hell could he have remained hidden from us all these years?"

Salvatore understood the vampire's anger. The demon lord had managed to deceive them all.

"Because he truly wasn't in this world." Salvatore shrugged. "Without Mackenzie and then Briggs, the bastard would never have been able to injure the Weres."

Styx grimaced. "They willingly allowed themselves to be anchors?"

"*Si*. Worthless cowards."

"Unfortunately, there are always those willing to sell their souls for power. You are certain the demon lord is dead?"

Salvatore took a moment to consider his answer.

During the confusion of the battle with the demon lord, followed by his hasty flight with Harley from the collapsing caves, he'd been too distracted to consider precisely what had happened to Balam.

All he knew was that the ravaging pain was gone, and that the bastard had at least been severely wounded. They never would have managed to escape if he hadn't been.

It wasn't until he'd awaken a few hours ago that he'd realized just how dramatically the world had altered.

"I'm not sure anything can kill a demon lord, but I know his connection to this world has been severed." His lips curled in a smile of satisfaction. "Already I can feel the strength of my packs beginning to increase."

"I can sense it as well." Styx regarded him with a steady gaze. "Soon the formidable powers of the Weres will no longer be just an ancient memory."

Salvatore didn't miss the hint of warning, and his chin tilted in defiance.

The Weres had spent too long in the shadow of the vamps. He intended to make sure they were given the respect they so richly deserved.

"We will rule as we were intended to," he said without apology.

Their gazes clashed in a silent battle of wills, then a slow smile curved Styx's lips.

Like all demons, he respected power.

"It should be interesting."

"*Si*."

"Do you intend to remain in America?"

"Once I've concluded my business, I will need to

return to my neglected duties as king. It's been too long since I've visited my packs." Salvatore grimaced, considering the number of months it would take to complete his task before he could return to his lair in Rome. Not that he had a choice. His connection to his packs was something that had to be cherished and nurtured. And the only means to do that was by spending time among them. "I hope Harley enjoys traveling."

"She is prepared to take her position as queen?"

"She's . . ." Salvatore reached for his shirt, yanking it on, although he left it hanging open. There were still a few slashes on his chest healing, and he wasn't about to risk staining the fine silk of his shirt. "Adjusting."

Styx's laugh echoed through the room, and moving to the back cabinet, he poured them both a healthy shot of whiskey, returning to press one glass into Salvatore's willing hand.

"Have patience, *amigo*. Female purebloods might be stubborn beyond reason, but they are well worth the trouble."

"You don't have to convince me of my mate's worth."

"Actually, it was more an offer of sympathy. Your life will never be the same."

Salvatore snorted. As if he needed a reminder. Already his gut was tied in knots as he struggled between the instinct to return upstairs and force Harley to accept her place as his queen, and his duty to hunt down and destroy the remaining danger to his Weres.

He'd been mated . . . what? A handful of days?

Cristo.

"For once we're in perfect agreement." Raising his glass in a mocking toast, Salvatore downed the whiskey in one swallow. "*Salute.*"

Styx drained his own glass, and his eyes narrowed. "There is something troubling you."

Salvatore snorted, setting aside the empty glass. "I thought Viper was the one famed for reading the souls of others?"

"It does not take a special talent to sense your distraction. Is it Harley?"

"Only in part," Salvatore confessed. "I need you to continue protecting her for the next few days."

"Of course. She is a welcomed part of my clan . . ." Styx deliberately paused, a wicked glint in his eyes. "Brother."

Salvatore shivered, not yet prepared to consider the repercussions of being so intimately connected to a damned leech.

"Merda," he growled. "Don't remind me."

Styx chuckled, thoroughly enjoying Salvatore's suffering.

"I assume your request has something to do with the unfinished business you mentioned earlier?"

"My curs were in the caves," he said, his jaw tightening at the memory of Max being tortured and Hess under the compulsion of Briggs. The son of a bitch was going to pay, and pay dearly. "I have to make sure they managed to escape the collapse."

"I could send my Ravens."

Salvatore blinked in surprise, acutely aware of the honor that Styx had just bestowed.

The Ravens were personal bodyguards to the Anasso, and the finest trained assassins ever to walk the earth. Styx didn't loan them out like they were Netflix.

"Grazie." He dipped his head in gratitude. "But they need my presence. Briggs did more than torture them. He invaded their minds. Only I can heal them."

Styx nodded. Salvatore's ability to share healing powers with his Weres and curs was no secret.

"And once you've rescued your curs?"

Hot fury poured through his blood like lava. "I intend to hunt down and kill Briggs as slowly, and with as much pain, as possible."

"You're certain he survived?"

"Certain?" Salvatore shrugged. "No. But my instinct tells me he's like a roach that refuses to die. Until I've seen his rotting corpse, I'm going to assume he's out there somewhere plotting more trouble."

"You intend to face him alone?"

"No one's allowed the pleasure of killing him but me."

"I am not disputing your right, but your reasoning." Styx held his gaze. "I, better than most, understand your desire for vengeance, but you cannot allow it to blind you. You have too much to lose to take unnecessary risks."

Hell, yeah, he had everything to lose.

A beautiful mate who filled his heart with joy, even when she was driving him nuts.

The opportunity to return the Weres to their former glory.

A new Lamborghini waiting for him in St. Louis.

But that didn't mean he could ignore his duty.

"There's no risk. Without being able to call on his master's powers, Briggs will be helpless."

"A cornered demon is the most dangerous creature on earth. And you cannot be certain that he has not prepared for such a turn of fate. He could have any number of nasty surprises waiting for you."

Salvatore's lips twisted. "Briggs is too arrogant to have considered the possibility that I might defeat the demon lord."

"*You* defeated the demon lord?" a female voice drawled with dangerous composure from behind Salvatore. "What a selective memory you have, Your Majesty."

Salvatore heaved a sigh as he turned to meet the furious gaze of his mate.

"Cristo."

A tight smile curved Harley's lips as Salvatore slowly turned, his beautiful face carefully composed to hide his guilt.

Oh, he was so busted.

But rather than gloating at having caught his lord and master off guard, Harley felt her mouth go dry and a blaze of heat explode through her body.

Holy . . . crap.

Standing in front of a half-naked Aztec warrior and a delectable Roman god, there was enough yummy eye candy to make any woman's brain turn to mush. Especially when it was obvious the two had just finished a sparring match that had left Salvatore's raven hair clinging to the damp skin of his face, and his eyes glowing with a fierce golden light.

A dangerous warrior who would never be fully tamed.

Perhaps sensing her lack of a functioning brain, Styx moved smoothly forward.

"Harley. I am delighted to see you have fully recovered. I trust you have everything you need?"

He reached to take her hand, only to come to a sharp halt when Salvatore's low growl rumbled through the air.

"Styx."

Styx held his hands up in a gesture of peace. "Easy, wolf."

Harley rolled her eyes. "Thank you, Styx. Unlike some, I appreciate your very generous hospitality."

The vampire's lips twitched. "You are welcomed to remain as long as you wish. Darcy is delighted to have you near."

Harley turned to stab her mate with a warning glare. "Right now my plans seem to be up in the air."

"Ah." Styx reached to pull on a loose black robe. "If you will forgive me, I have someplace I need to be."

"Where do you need to be?" Salvatore demanded.

Styx flashed a meaningful gaze at Harley's grim expression.

"Anywhere but here."

The King of Weres snorted. "Traitor."

"Self-preservation, *amigo*."

A thick silence descended as the vampire left the room. Caught between the urge to slug Salvatore and push him to the floor and tear off his clothes, Harley instead wandered the short distance to stroke her fingers over the hilt of the heavy sword propped on a stand.

She was supposed to be annoyed with the Were, not yearning to run her tongue over the exposed muscles of his chest.

"Been playing?" she demanded.

"Styx was in need of a sparring partner."

"Yeah, I bet."

Salvatore moved to stand at her side, his fingers tucking a stray curl behind her ear.

"I thought you intended to spend the evening watching movies?"

She jerked from his gentle touch. He wasn't going to distract her with sex.

A shame.

"And to make sure I did, you sent Darcy to keep me distracted," she accused in a tight voice.

"I sent her to keep you company," he smoothly countered. "As Styx said, Darcy is happy to have you as her guest, and I assumed you would enjoy spending time getting to know your sister."

"You wanted me too busy to notice when you slipped away like a Slugaugh demon."

He folded his arms over his chest, studying her with a brooding gaze.

"You were the one, *cara,* to make it clear that our mating was nothing more than biology," he reminded her. "What does it matter if I intend to leave or not?"

She clenched her jaw. She wasn't going to be deterred by logic or reason. She didn't have to make sense. If she wanted to be pissed off, then she was going to be pissed off.

"You're going after Briggs, aren't you?"

"My first priority is to make sure that my curs are safe. Briggs was holding them captive in the caves."

Crap. A pang of guilt twisted her heart. Of course he was worried about his pack. She should have told him that she'd seen the curs the minute they had gotten free of the caves. Unfortunately, she hadn't been thinking clearly on the trip back to Chicago.

One side effect of battling a demon lord.

She reached to place a comforting hand on his forearm. "I ran across Hess when I was searching for you. He was . . ." She abruptly halted, considering her words. Salvatore didn't need to be reminded that he'd been forced to beat the poor cur to a bloody pulp. "Disoriented, but I'm sure he managed to get the others free and lead them out of the caves."

His lips twisted with rueful amusement at her unusual attempt at tact.

"Even if they weren't caught in the collapse, they will need to be near me."

She couldn't argue with that. Salvatore could help heal both the physical and mental wounds the curs had suffered.

Luckily, there were any number of other things to argue about.

"You didn't answer my question. Are you going after Briggs?"

"It's my duty."

"This has nothing to do with duty," she gritted. "You want revenge."

A muscle twitched in his jaw. "I might have more than one motive, but the bottom line is that I can't allow the bastard to escape." The golden eyes glowed, his voice roughening with fury. "He nearly destroyed the Weres once. He won't get a second chance."

She understood his desire for revenge. She really and truly did. But that didn't mean she was going to let him stumble into a potential trap. Not when he was blinded by anger.

"What could he do without the demon lord to give him magic?"

"No doubt he's already attempting to discover a way to reopen the portal."

Her brows jerked together at the mere thought. "Good God. Is that possible?"

"I don't intend to find out."

Her lips tightened. "So your plan is to charge off like the Lone Ranger to capture the bad guy?"

A hint of amusement sparkled in his eyes. "Lone Ranger?"

"Do you prefer Batman? Hellboy? Incredible Hulk?"

He framed her face in his hands, peering deep into her eyes.

"Does it matter if I do charge off?"

"You're damned right it matters."

"Why?"

"Because . . ." She licked her dry lips. "Because it's stupid to take such a risk. You're supposed to be a king. You have an endless number of Weres and curs who can kill Briggs."

"Hardly endless."

"You know what I mean."

His gaze lowered to her mouth, his thumbs teasing the corner of her lips.

"I could send others in my place, but I won't be satisfied unless I watch him die with my eyes, preferably by my own hands."

Her heart faltered. Not at the jolt of need that clenched her stomach. Being near Salvatore would always stir her desire. No, it was the melting tenderness of his touch that was doing all sorts of dangerous things to her heart.

"Fine." She was forced to halt and clear the huskiness from her voice. Just like a starry-eyed romantic. Damn. She determinedly squared her shoulders. "But you can forget going by yourself."

His thumb feathered over her bottom lip. "Are you giving me orders, *cara*?"

"I'm a queen, aren't I?"

He stilled, his gaze sweeping over her upturned face with an unnerving intensity.

"You said you didn't want the position. Have you changed your mind?"

"I . . ." Her mouth was dry, parched.

With exquisite deliberation, Salvatore slowly lowered his head, brushing a soft kiss down the line of her nose. "Harley?"

"I'm going with you."

"Why?"

"Because."

Salvatore pulled back, regarding her with lifted brows. "That's your explanation? Because?"

She ignored the hint of smug pleasure in his voice. She didn't want to dissect her violent reaction to the thought of Salvatore leaving her behind.

All that mattered was that she kept him from doing something stupid.

"My explanation is that you're not going alone, and that's final."

"Hardly a reasonable argument," he countered.

"Fine." Her chin tilted. "Either I'm worthy of being your queen or not. If you insist on going after Briggs, then we'll go together."

He stilled, as if caught off guard by her words. Then, with a slow smile he bent his head.

"Si." His kiss was soft and savoring, as if she were the most precious treasure. "Together."

Chapter Twenty-Two

Caine didn't know how long he had been unconscious.

Actually, he didn't know *how* he became unconscious.

He remembered shifting as a black, malevolent fog had entered the cave. There had been pain. Not the someone's-going-to-pay-for-this kind of pain, but the holy-shit-I'm-going-to-die kind of pain.

He had wanted nothing more than to curl into a ball on the floor and whimper. Just like a beaten pup. And that might have been his fate if he hadn't seen the strange mist headed directly for Cassandra.

Instinct had taken over, and with a howl of fury, he had leaped directly into the path of the advancing fog. He didn't care what the hell the thing was, it wasn't going to touch the female pureblood.

And that's when things got fuzzy.

Groaning, he forced his eyes open, wishing he hadn't when the flickering candlelight sent a stab of pain through him.

"Am I dead?" he croaked.

There was a sweet scent of lavender and then Cassandra's face appeared above him, her hair tangled around her face.

"Not now."

Caine's heart forgot to beat at her somber words. "Is that a joke?"

"No."

"Christ."

He shivered, trying to laugh off her impossible claim. He was a cur, not a pure-blooded demon. When he died, that was it. Sayonara, baby. End of story.

A part of him, however, wasn't in the mood to laugh.

Something had happened to him.

Something vast and earth-shattering.

He could feel it to his very bones.

"Now I really know what it feels like to be 'death warmed over,'" he wryly muttered, laying his hands flat on the hard stone to push himself to a sitting position.

His head spun with a sickening dizziness, nearly sending him tumbling back into oblivion. With the speed of a pureblood, Cassandra had her arm around his shoulders, holding him steady.

"I'm not sure you should move," she chastised, her lips brushing his ear, sending an electric shock of awareness through him that proved that despite his recent introduction to death, everything was still functioning as it should.

"There are a lot of things I shouldn't do, but I never let that stop me. As I have so painfully proven," he muttered. Then his eyes widened as he caught sight of where he'd just been laying. "Oh . . . shit."

"Blood," Cassandra whispered.

"Yeah, I noticed."

He swallowed the urge to vomit at the sight of the thick red stains that spread across the floor and splashed obscenely up the wall.

It wasn't that he was squeamish. Hell, he'd slaughtered

a pack of hellhounds who had attacked one of witches with his bare hands. But it didn't take a doctor to realize that no creature could lose that amount of blood and survive.

"I told you to leave," Cassandra murmured.

"No one likes a know-it-all," he retorted, grateful to turn his attention to her pale, beautiful face. "Was it the demon lord who attacked?"

"Yes."

"Charming guy."

"Not particularly."

He smiled, ridiculously fascinated by her habit of taking his words quite literally.

"I have a vague memory of a dark shadow entering the cave, heading directly toward you." He shook his head, hoping to clear the remaining cobwebs. "Then the world exploded."

"I think the demon was injured. He tried . . ."

Caine frowned as her voice faded and her eyes clouded with a painful memory.

"Cassandra? Cassie?" He turned to grasp her shoulders and tugged her against his chest, relieved to discover his strength returning. Laying his cheek on top of her head, he sucked in her delicate scent of lavender, feeling it flow through him with a healing calm. "Hey, it's okay."

She burrowed against his chest, shivering. "He tried to use me to keep his essence anchored to this world, but you attacked him and he had no choice but to leave."

Caine ran a soothing hand down her back, caught off guard by his fierce urge to protect this female.

She was a Were, for God's sake. A pureblood.

Way above a worthless cur like him, even presuming Salvatore hadn't put out a death warrant on him.

With a shake of his head, Caine thrust aside his inane

thoughts. The only thing that mattered was getting out of the hellhole.

"So he's gone?" he demanded. "Really, truly, never coming back gone?"

"He's gone."

"And you're not hurt?"

She pulled back, and before Caine could guess what she intended to do, she lifted her shirt to study the flat plane of her stomach.

"I don't think so."

Caine choked back a groan at his instant, painful reaction to the sight of her smooth alabaster skin and the lower curve of her bare breasts. God, if he could just get that slender body beneath him . . .

His erotic fantasy was brought to a rude end as his gaze caught sight of the small tattoo that marred the skin just beneath her belly button.

He leaned forward, studying the crimson hieroglyphic that flickered with the same unsettling shimmer as the designs on the wall.

"What's this?" he demanded, cautiously brushing a finger over the tattoo. His muscles clenched in alarm at the unpleasant chill that clung to the mark.

Whatever it was, it couldn't be good.

Her grimace confirmed his suspicion. "The mark of the demon lord."

"Bastard. What does it do?"

She turned her head, as if attempting to hide her expression.

"He used it to keep me bound to these caves."

There was something more.

"And?"

"It allows me to . . ."

He captured her chin between his thumb and finger and turned her back to meet his searching gaze.

"You can tell me."

"It's hard to explain."

"Try."

"I can touch the other side."

"The other side?"

"Heaven, hell, another dimension . . ." She shrugged. "Whatever you want to call it."

Unease snaked down Caine's spine, and with an abrupt movement, he was on his feet.

Dammit. He had to get them out of there.

He didn't know who Cassandra was connected to, but he did know it couldn't have her.

She belonged to him.

Period.

"Are you stuck down here?"

"No, that spell has been broken."

"So you can leave the caves?"

She rose gracefully to her feet, her gaze deliberately shifting to the narrow opening of the cave.

"If we can find a way to dig ourselves out."

"Dig?" He froze, praying she wasn't implying what he thought she was implying. "What do you mean?"

"The tunnels have all collapsed."

Well, hell. Of course they had collapsed.

Maybe he had died, after all. He'd always known that he was destined for hell, and what could be worse than an eternity in this dark, barren cave?

Of course, it wouldn't be true torture so long as Cassandra was near, a traitorous voice whispered in the back of his mind.

"All of them?" he rasped.

A white cloud floated eerily across her eyes, then a tranquil smile curved her lips.

"Don't worry. We'll get out." There was a short pause. "In time."

Caine clenched his hands, his temper flaring. Had she been stuck so long in the cave she didn't understand the danger they were in?

"I don't have time," he snapped. "Unlike you, I'm not immortal."

She moved toward him, laying her hands lightly on his chest.

"Are you certain?"

He grasped her hands, his brows snapping together. "Enough with your cryptic . . ."

"Don't you feel it?" she interrupted, studying him with an intensity that made him pause.

Don't you feel it . . .

A bolt of terror shot through his heart.

He did.

Waking up, he'd been too weak and disoriented to pay attention to the strange sensations that pounded through his blood. Or the powerful vitality that was swiftly repairing his battered body.

Hell, even if he had noticed, he wouldn't have assumed he'd been magically transformed into a pureblood.

It was freaking nuts.

But now, he couldn't deny the subtle change in his scent and the growing power that was altering him with every beat of his heart.

He stumbled backwards, glaring at the woman who stood there with her Zen smile and aura of pure innocence.

"Is this a trick?" he demanded.

She tilted her head to one side, her hair spilling over her shoulder in a curtain of pale silver.

"How could it be a trick?"

Caine clenched his teeth, ready to suspect the entire world was out to scam him.

Paranoid? Nah.

"Briggs deceived me for the past thirty years," he bit out. "I'm not going to be a putz again."

"Deceived you?"

"He made me believe in a vision . . ."

"That came true," she softly interrupted.

"No." He shook his head. "It's impossible."

"I've told you . . ."

"I don't care what the hell you told me," he retorted, his nerves wound so tight he felt as if he might shatter. "A cur doesn't die and come back from the dead as a pureblood." His breath hissed through his teeth as he was struck by a hideous thought. "Oh, my God, I haven't turned into a zombie like Briggs, have I?"

She studied him intently, sniffing the air as if testing for the stench of zombie.

"No, you're very much alive."

"Then how?"

"It has to have something to do with your battle with the demon lord." Her brows puckered as she considered the various possibilities. "He's been draining the ancient magic of the Weres for centuries. A portion of his essence must have been left in you."

Caine shook his head.

Not in disagreement—hell, it was as good a theory as any—but in sheer bafflement.

Good God, was it possible?

Had he somehow been transformed into a pureblood?

And if he had . . . then why?

Muttering a savage curse, Caine paced the narrow

floor, trying to wrap his brain around the staggering implications of his transformation.

He might have what he always desired, but it wasn't the glorious revolution that he had dreamed it would be.

Actually, he felt more alone and uncertain than he had since giving up his human life to become a cur.

"Damn." He shoved a hand through his hair, longing to fill his lungs with fresh air. A long run beneath the moonlight was just what he needed to clear the fog from his brain. "This was not how it was supposed to be. I thought the vision meant I was destined to be the savior of the curs."

Her smile dimmed, a haunting pain darkening her eyes. "Visions are rarely what you believe them to be. They're deceptive and dangerous."

"No shit."

"I try to warn people, but they never listen." She shivered, wrapping her arms around her too-slender waist. "They always want to know."

Caine wrenched himself from his dark thoughts, belatedly noting Cassandra's stark pallor and the bruises beneath her eyes.

He wasn't the only one who'd had a nasty day.

Gently he cupped her face in his hands, acutely aware of the fine shiver that shook her body.

"What people?"

"Briggs would bring some to the church or cemetery above us and demand I share the visions. Others would pay him to come and visit his 'seer' in person."

"God." Caine thought back to when he'd supposedly been "blessed" with his vision. For the most part, the night remained lost in fog, no doubt Briggs's doing, but he did have a clear memory of being in a vast, empty room. "I was blindfolded, but Briggs must have brought me to the church."

"Yes."

"Are the visions still with you?"

She bit her bottom lip, her expression troubled. "Yes."

Caine grimaced, knowing she *should* be troubled.

For all his frantic need to be out of the caves with the wind on his face, he was beginning to realize the dangers of plucking Cassandra from the depths of obscurity.

A true seer was . . .

Fucking priceless.

Entire demon nations would go to war for the opportunity to gain control of her visions. Others would go to any lengths to kill her and bring an end to her ability to see into the future. After all, when you were plotting evil deeds, you didn't want to have to worry they might show up, shining like a beacon, on some female's wall.

And of course, there was no telling what the Commission would do to her.

The mystical Oracles who ruled the demon world might decide she was beneath their notice, or they might make her disappear. Cassandra wouldn't be the first demon with rare powers to be isolated from civilization for the safety of all.

And no one would dare try to save her from their prison.

At least no one with even a pea-size brain.

"Damn."

"What's wrong?"

"Do you want a list?" he muttered, moving the short space to take her chilled hand in his own. He would worry about keeping Cassandra safe once they managed to escape from their current disaster. "Come on."

"Where are we going?"

"Now that, pet, is one hell of a question."

* * *

With Viper's extensive automobile collection at his disposal, Salvatore decided on the sleek red-and-black Alfa Romeo. It would have made more sense to take a Hummer or Land Rover, but Salvatore enjoyed tweaking the nose of the vamps. He didn't doubt that Viper would be pacing the floor until Salvatore returned his precious baby to his underground garage.

Plus, he couldn't deny the satisfaction of roaring through the Chicago streets in the elegantly engineered machine. He was a Were who enjoyed the finer things in life.

No, not just the finer things.

The very finest.

His gaze slid to Harley's profile as she watched the passing scenery flow from Midwest suburbia to clusters of warehouses, and then finally, flat farmland.

Smug pleasure settled in his heart.

His protective instincts might howl at the thought of deliberately taking his mate into danger, but a greater part of him understood that this was how it was meant to be. As mates, the two of them were stronger together than apart.

Besides, she had made an irrefutable point.

The Queen of Weres was not an empty title.

Harley would be judged as much on her strength and ability to protect the packs as her skill in leadership. The Weres respected power, and there would be no sympathy for her inability to shift, or the years she'd been held captive by Caine.

She would have to earn their loyalty.

Not that he doubted for a minute that she would.

There was a ruthless strength in Harley that was hidden beneath her fragile beauty. *Dio,* she'd faced a demon lord, hadn't she? Something that would have sent any other creature screaming in fear. She would rise to whatever challenge she might face.

Not to mention the fact that she was as stubborn as a mule.

Reluctantly easing off the accelerator, Salvatore slowed the car from light speed to a mere crawl, and forced his attention to their surroundings as he exited off the highway and onto the dirt road that had once led the faithful to the forgotten church.

In a wash of moonlight, the overgrown cemetery slumbered, seemingly undisturbed for decades. His gaze traveled over the wrought-iron gate that hung open, no longer bothering to protect the bodies that had long ago turned to dust. Behind the fence, the broken marble statues and crumbling mausoleums peeped through the weeds, as if refusing to concede total defeat.

Just beyond the graveyard loomed the abandoned church, the once grand structure now an empty shell of stone and decaying wood.

He halted the car behind a patch of trees. The entire neighborhood was vacant, but humans were always straying where they didn't belong. The sight of the expensive car in the middle of nowhere would stir the kind of attention he hoped to avoid.

At his side, Harley shook her head in wry resignation. "It looks like an abandoned set for a Rob Zombie horror flick."

"Briggs never did have any taste." Salvatore shook his head in disgust. "He's the sort who gives werewolves a bad name."

"I don't think it's a matter of taste that gives werewolves a bad name," Harley said, shoving open her door and climbing out of the car.

With a chuckle, Salvatore joined her at the side of the road.

"True," he agreed. "Maybe I should hire a good PR firm."

"Yeah, right." She rolled her eyes. "You love knowing that the demon world quakes in fear when a werewolf enters their territory."

Salvatore couldn't argue. Being the biggest, baddest, predator in the room had its benefits.

"It does tend to avoid confusion," he said smugly.

"Everyone knows you're the king, and everyone must bow before you?"

"Something like that."

"Good God," she muttered, flicking her gaze over his expensive suit and Italian loafers. Hunting or not, he liked to look good. "You were arrogant before you came into your full powers. Now you're going to be impossible."

He bent his head to capture her lips in a swift, possessive kiss.

"Not when I have a beautiful queen who is always eager to keep me humble," he husked against her mouth.

She reached up to tangle her fingers in his hair and returned his kiss with enough heat to start a nuclear reaction.

"I suppose that's true enough," she whispered.

Salvatore briefly considered the logistics of removing her jeans and stretchy shirt to get her naked before reluctantly pulling back.

Dio. He couldn't allow himself to be distracted from their urgent business. Not with his curs missing and Briggs still a threat.

They would have an eternity to enjoy making love beneath the moon.

"Ready?" he demanded, his voice thick with frustration.

She nodded. "I'll go right, you circle left."

"Harley . . ."

Her eyes flashed with warning. "Don't start."

He swallowed the lecture that trembled on his lips and instead tugged on the end of her ponytail.

"Be careful."

She smiled, reaching behind her back to pull out two Glocks loaded with silver bullets.

"Always."

With a silent grace, she disappeared into the bushes that surrounded the graveyard, and Salvatore turned to head toward the church. Again Salvatore felt that surge of pride.

His mate.

Strong, beautiful, fearless.

Perfect.

Then, with a shake of his head, he concentrated on the scents and sounds that filled the night.

He took a quick pass through the church, then concentrated on the circle of trees that surrounded the yard.

Hundreds of scents clung to the thick bushes, but Salvatore easily shifted through them, dismissing all but those that held the familiar musk of Were and cur.

Finding nothing among the trees, he headed toward the graveyard and the entrance to the caves. More than once he caught the scent of Hess and Briggs, but the trails were too old to have been made after the collapse of the caves.

Cristo, were they trapped in the tunnels?

The thought was enough to make his blood run cold.

The curs had been tortured, mind-raped, and abandoned by Briggs. Being trapped in the caves might be enough to send them over the edge.

The last thing he wanted was to have to put them down like savage dogs.

Ruthlessly, he crushed the thought.

He was going to find his soldiers, and then he was going to kill Briggs.

He wouldn't accept any other outcome.

Weaving through the long forgotten graves, Salvatore joined Harley as she stood beside a marble mausoleum at the very back of the property. He frowned at her distracted expression.

"Did you find something?"

"I thought I caught Caine's scent, but it . . ." She broke off her words with a shake of her head.

"What?"

"It couldn't have been him."

"Why not?"

"It was the scent of a pureblood."

Salvatore lifted his brows, instantly aware of the significance in her words.

Caine had been so confident that he was to become a Were. Could he possibly have seen the future?

Could the vision have been real?

"Merda," he breathed, dismissing the unpleasant image. The dark lord had massacred anyone claiming to be clairvoyant a millennium ago. There were occasional prophets and those who were sensitive to premonitions, but there weren't any true seers left in the world. "It can't be."

Harley shrugged. "It doesn't matter."

"Not tonight," Salvatore readily agreed. "But eventually I intend to track down the cur and repay him for all those years he held you captive."

"I would say he's already been punished. He thought he was destined to be a great Messiah, and instead he's lost everything."

Salvatore's lips twisted. Caine had been a willing partner in Briggs's near destruction of the Weres. Not to mention, he had dared to treat Harley as a pawn in his self-serving games.

"I prefer a more tangible method of punishment," he growled.

She grimaced, knowing better than to try to change his mind. There were some things that couldn't be compromised.

"Did you find any hint of Briggs?"

"Nothing fresh." He glanced toward the silent fields beyond the graveyard. "If he came out of the tunnels, then it wasn't here."

"There has to be more than one way out. We need to widen our search."

That had been Salvatore's thought as well.

"We'll go together."

"Giuliani." She narrowed her eyes. "If you wanted a female who likes being treated as if she needs a big, strong male to protect her, then you shouldn't have chosen me."

Salvatore heaved a sigh. Then, bravely ignoring the handguns that could cause a number of nasty injuries, he brushed his thumb along the line of her stubborn jaw.

"There will never be a moment when I won't need to protect you, *cara*. I can't change that."

She stepped back, her expression grim. "My entire life was controlled by Caine. I won't be leashed again."

Her voice was flat, emotionless, but Salvatore knew that she meant every word.

"And I thought battling a demon lord was going to be difficult," he muttered. "I'll meet you back here in an hour."

Chapter Twenty-Three

Aware of the urgency that beat through Salvatore's blood, Harley moved swiftly past the broken fence of the graveyard and into the cornfield beyond. She should be annoyed. It was difficult enough to deal with her own jumbled mess of emotions without adding a direct, wireless connection to Salvatore's. Tonight, however, her only thought was making sure that the stubborn Were didn't end up dead.

And that meant finding Briggs before the freak-of-nature could regain his strength.

Crisscrossing the field to make sure she didn't overlook any hint of Briggs or the curs, Harley was headed toward the adjoining field when a low whistle cut through the air.

Salvatore.

With a smooth turn, she was running toward the narrow dirt road on the far side of the field, crouched low to the ground, her guns held ready. She sensed Salvatore's flare of fury and she intended to be prepared.

For anything.

Salvatore was in a deep culvert by the road, staring at

a heavy rock that had been pushed aside to reveal a large hole in the ground. Obviously an opening to the caves below the surface.

She scrambled down the side of the culvert, catching the unmistakable stench of rotting meat. Briggs had come out of the hole.

"You got him," she said, her satisfaction cut short at the unmistakable smell of cur blood. "Shit."

Salvatore's face was set in bleak lines as he followed the scent down the culvert and then up to the road. Harley stayed close to his side, keeping watch on their surroundings so Salvatore could concentrate on the trail.

Her gaze scanned the seemingly empty fields and clusters of trees that could hide any number of nasty creatures. Her senses told her that there was nothing near, but her finger remained on the trigger.

She'd had a stomach full of unwelcomed surprises over the past few days. She'd be damned if it was happening again.

Perhaps a mile down the road, Salvatore bent and touched the ground, his brows drawn in a frustrated frown.

"They took off in a vehicle," he muttered.

"Can you follow it?"

He tilted back his head, dragging in a deep breath. "On foot."

"Then what are we waiting for?"

Straightening, he considered her for a long minute, clearly wanting to demand that she return to the safety of Styx's mansion. Then, proving he wasn't completely without a functioning brain, he heaved a deep sigh and pulled his cell phone from the inner pocket of his jacket.

"As amusing as it would be to leave Viper's car for the nearest chop shop, I might have need of the leeches before this is done," he said, punching in a series of numbers and holding the phone to his ear.

He exchanged a few abrupt words with Viper and then slipping the phone back in his pocket, he grabbed her arm and urged her into a steady jog down the dark road.

"Do you consider vampires your enemy?" she demanded, slipping the guns back into the holsters that hung at her lower back before easily falling into step beside him.

"I did."

"And now?"

He didn't immediately answer, and Harley was startled by the vague sense of foreboding she could sense deep in his heart.

"Now, I'm beginning to suspect that we must negotiate a truce," he grudgingly admitted. "Times are changing and we must change with them or perish."

"Do you mean technology?"

"That's a part of it." He grimaced. "The humans' ability to detect our presence increases with every passing year, as does their ability to harm us. It's foolish to assume our natural superiority will protect us."

Harley lifted her brows. Few demons were willing to admit that lowly humans might pose a threat, despite growing proof of the danger.

"And the other part?"

"I'm not sure I should share." He shook his head, his expression hard. "You might think I've lost my mind."

"I assumed that you'd lost your mind the minute you crashed into Caine's basement," she assured him.

He chuckled, the golden eyes glowing in the darkness. *"Grazie."*

"What's bothering you, Giuliani?" She held up a warning

hand as his lips parted to blather some useless denial. "And don't tell me it's nothing. I can sense it."

His lips twisted. "This mating is going to take some getting used to."

She snorted. "Ya think?"

His eyes narrowed. "Harley . . ."

"Just tell me what's bothering you," she interrupted.

His jaw tightened, his gaze returning to the road and the faint tire tracks that were still visible.

"The ancient magic is returning. I can feel it flowing through my blood."

Harley slowly nodded. She'd felt the potent magic stirring since they'd escaped from the caves.

"Yes."

"And it's whispering to me of danger."

A chill inched down her spine. "The demon lord?"

"No."

She studied his grim expression. What could be worse than a demon lord?

"Salvatore?"

"I don't know, *cara*. It's as if . . ." He shook his head in frustration. "The world is holding its breath, waiting for something that will change us all."

"You're scared?" she breathed.

"Cautious," he said softly. "It seems wise to consolidate my power base."

"The vampires?"

"For a start."

"The Weres and the vamps working together." Her voice held an edge of teasing. It had never been a secret that the two species had often attempted to exterminate the other. "The demon world is going to think that hell has frozen over."

"I told you you'd think I'd gone mad." He glanced in

her direction, his brows pulling together as she stumbled to a sudden halt. Turning, he cupped her chin and lifted her face to study her troubled expression in the moonlight. "Harley?"

"I just remembered there was an elderly witch who Caine hired to create hexes of protection for his labs. She spoke of warning signs. At the time . . ."

"You thought she was nuts?" he asked wryly.

Harley grimaced. "Maybe a little."

"What did she say?"

Harley had to strain to recall the old woman's ramblings. She'd always liked Anastasia, but the witch had often creeped her out with her dire omens.

"She claimed that a new Oracle had been discovered."

"*Si*. Anna Randal, an Elemental. She's mated to a vampire."

"She seemed to think that was some sort of portent of coming upheaval."

He slowly nodded. "There is an old legend that a new Oracle is only discovered during times when the need is the greatest. Vague mumbo jumbo, like all prophecies."

"She also said . . ." Harley's eyes widened. "Oh."

"What?"

"She said that the wind spoke of ancient powers returning."

"The Weres?"

Harley shrugged. "I don't know."

He narrowed his gaze. "Do you think she was a seer?"

Harley laughed. She might have been sheltered from the world, but everyone knew that seers were extinct.

Like dragons and leprechauns.

Well, everyone but Caine, who'd been stupid enough to believe in visions.

"No, she didn't claim to read the future, only the various omens and signs that she could see around her."

"Did she say anything else?"

Harley searched her mind. "Most of it was gibberish, but I remember she said something about the rise of Gemini."

"The astrological sign?"

"That's what I assumed, but she didn't really make much sense."

Salvatore lifted his head, his brooding gaze turned toward the moon as he considered her revelation. Watching the spring breeze ruffle the raven hair that framed the proud lines on his face, Harley's heart forgot to beat.

He was so stunningly beautiful.

So magnificently powerful.

So . . .

Hers.

Utterly and completely hers.

Harley jerked in surprise at the raw, primitive sense of possession that blasted through her.

Where the hell did that come from?

Thankfully unaware of her cavewoman impulse to drag him off and give him a reason to howl at the moon, Salvatore heaved a resigned sigh and resumed following Briggs's trail.

"Obviously, the sooner we're done with Briggs and back to the safety of our lair, the better."

Disgruntled by her savage awareness of Salvatore, Harley kept a determined space between them as they ran through the darkness.

"*Our* lair?"

"Do I look like a fool?" He flashed a wry grin. "You would have castrated me if I'd said *my* lair."

"Okay," she grudgingly conceded. "Valid point."

"I'm learning."

For a time they moved through the darkness in silence, Harley absently noting that the tidy fields were being left behind and replaced by a tangle of underbrush and trees. Hard to believe that the road could lead to someplace even more isolated than the abandoned church and graveyard.

"I've never been to Italy," she abruptly muttered.

Salvatore's lips twitched, although he was careful to keep his attention to their surroundings.

"I think you'll like the palazzo," he said, his voice carefully bland. "It's old, but it's been magnificently restored."

Palazzo?

As in palace?

Oh, that was just fan-freaking-tastic.

"Is it huge?"

"Fairly huge."

"With marble?"

"*Si,* there's marble." He sent her an amused glance. "Do you have an irrational dislike of marble?"

"No, but I have a very rational dislike of becoming a joke among the Weres."

The smile disappeared as his expression hardened with a haughty outrage.

"I assure you, *cara,* no one will ever dare laugh at you," he said with the absolute confidence that his word was law.

And why not?

His word *was* law.

She shook her head, thinking back to her unconventional childhood. Caine had certainly never prepared her to become a sophisticated lady. Hell, she was more comfortable at a firing range than a ballroom.

"Maybe not to my face, but I'm going to look like an idiot in some fancy palace." She pointed a finger in his direction. "And don't think for a minute you're getting me into a slinky dress and high heels."

His husky chuckle brushed over her skin. "I'd rather get you *out* of a slinky dress. Although you can leave on the high heels."

The image of her standing naked in front of Salvatore with a pair of crimson high heels sent a hot flash searing through her body.

Good . . . God.

"I mean it, Salvatore," she managed to croak.

"No, you don't," he countered with annoying calm. "You're just trying to find another reason to convince yourself you shouldn't be my queen, and I won't play. I don't care if you run through the palazzo stark naked or wearing Prada."

Her lips parted, and then snapped closed, as she accepted that he was right.

Salvatore was her mate.

She could feel it to the very marrow of her bones.

And her instinctive need to rebel against his claim on her was becoming downright childish.

Not that she intended to become his doormat, she wryly acknowledged.

Not all the ancient powers combined could perform that impossible task.

But it was time to be done with fighting the knowledge that her destiny was forever, irrevocably connected to Salvatore Giuliani.

"You think you're so damned smart, don't you?" she muttered dryly.

A muscle twitched in his jaw. "If I were smart then Briggs would never have crawled from his grave, and we would be spending the night having hot, sweaty sex beneath the moon."

Sensing his annoyance was directed at himself, Harley reached out to touch the rigid muscles of his arm.

"We'll find him."

"Si."

They once again fell silent, their pace slowing as the stench of Briggs became more pronounced. Instinctively, Harley reached behind her back to pull the guns out of the holsters.

The tangle of brush and trees had thickened until it was impossible to see beyond a few feet from the road, and while her senses told her there was nothing but the usual wildlife scurrying through the shadows, she wasn't going to take any chances.

Rounding the curve in the road, they both halted at the sight of the small cabin that looked in dire need of a match and some kindling.

Tilting precariously to one side, the paint had long ago peeled from the wood planks and the small front porch sagged with weariness. If there had ever been shutters, they had long ago disappeared, along with several wooden shingles from the roof, and at least one window.

Of course, the cabin looked almost habitable when compared to the shed with a rusty tin roof, built behind it.

Cue banjo music.

Harley resisted the urge to roll her eyes. At least it wasn't another cave.

Breathing in deeply, she closed her eyes and sorted through the barrage of near overwhelming scents that filled the air.

It was easy to pick out Briggs's odor that wafted from the cabin. Rotting meat was pretty tough to miss.

Not that he could have hidden his presence, even if he

could disguise his god-awful stench. The frigid chill in the air would always give him away.

Taking in another breath, she ignored the vile presence of Briggs and concentrated on the scent of curs. It was no surprise to find their scent laced with a combination of fear and frustration. Even for curs, who always lived on the edge, they'd been put through hell over the past few days. It was a surprise, however, to realize their scent came from the shed, rather than the cabin.

Why wasn't Briggs using them as a shield? More important, why would he leave them where they could so easily be rescued?

There was only one explanation.

A trap.

Salvatore moved to whisper directly in her ear. "The curs are in the shed."

"I smell them." She turned to meet the golden gaze that glowed with a savage anticipation. "You know he's expecting you? This is a trap."

"Bene."

She clenched her teeth, torn between the urge to shake some sense into him and knocking him over the head with the butt of her gun.

Unfortunately, neither of them would keep him from waltzing straight into Briggs's ambush.

"Salvatore, if you get yourself killed, I'm never going to forgive you," she hissed.

With a feral smile he bent down to claim her lips in a kiss she felt to the tips of her toes.

"You're never getting rid of me," he whispered against her mouth.

Arching against his hard body, Harley momentarily allowed herself to savor the feel and scent of him. Then with a sigh, she reluctantly stepped back.

"What's the plan?"

"You release the curs and get them out of here."

"While you battle Briggs by yourself?"

He shrugged. "It has always been inevitable."

"No, it's not . . ."

"*Si,* it is." He framed her face in his hands. "I have to do this, Harley. And I need to know that Hess and the others are far enough away that Briggs can't gain control of them."

She wanted to argue. It was insanity for Salvatore to confront Briggs alone. The Were was not only Hannibal-Lecter-nuts, but he was already dead. How the hell did you kill a zombie?

But in the end she bit back her words.

This wasn't just Salvatore's macho need to prove his superiority over the other male.

Briggs hadn't just been an enemy to Salvatore. He had violated the entire Were nation with his bargain with the demon lord. And he'd come far too close to destroying them all.

As king, it was Salvatore's duty to make sure the traitor suffered the ultimate punishment.

"Fine."

He brushed one last kiss over her lips. "Take the curs back to the church. I'll join you there once I'm certain Briggs is dead."

Salvatore barely waited for Harley to disappear into the shadows before efficiently stripping off his expensive suit. He had every confidence in her ability to free the curs and lead them to safety.

Even if she did want to give him a black eye.

It wasn't the first, and it certainly wouldn't be the last time he annoyed her.

The gods willing.

His smile faded as he shifted into wolf form and silently padded toward the cabin.

He wasn't going to underestimate Briggs. The Were was a flaming nutcase, but he had to know he was no match for Salvatore without his demon lord to hide behind. Which meant he must be confident that whatever trap he had set was capable of destroying Salvatore.

Circling the cabin, Salvatore allowed his superior animal senses to search the area for any hint of danger.

Predictably, the presence of werewolves had frightened off the local wildlife, and the nearest human was miles away, but there were a few lesser demons in the vicinity. A pack of hellhounds sniffing through the underbrush. A tree sprite dancing through the branches. A distant hag.

Nothing that could offer a threat.

Which meant that Briggs's trap must be magical.

Naturalmente. The worthless hound wouldn't recognize a code of honor if it bit him on the ass.

Accepting there was nothing physical to battle, Salvatore shifted back to human, moving through the overgrown backyard to peer through a window.

He could see a small kitchen with a worn linoleum floor and cabinets that had once been painted a hideous yellow. The appliances had been removed or stolen, leaving behind broken pipes and exposed wires.

Salvatore grimaced. Even without Briggs, the place was a deathtrap. He could only hope that the electricity had been turned off.

As if on cue, a bloom of candlelight filled the front room beyond the kitchen, revealing a battered sofa and matching chair that was the only furniture. Although it would be generous to label the rotting pieces of junk as furniture. More a post-apocalyptic nightmare.

His eyes narrowed as the shadowed outline of a cloaked figure was suddenly visible. Briggs. How convenient. Just the sleazeball he'd been looking for.

Climbing the back steps, Salvatore kicked in the door and rapidly crossed through the empty kitchen. If there was a trap, then so be it. Tiptoeing through the place wasn't going to help.

He made it into the front room, headed straight for Briggs, when the expected snare was at last tripped.

A cold breeze prickled over his naked body, then invisible bonds wrapped around him, slamming him into the wall with enough force to shake chunks of plaster from the ceiling.

Salvatore grunted in pain, but he didn't panic.

Briggs might be able to conjure a portion of his black magic, but his strength had to be failing with the death of the demon lord, while Salvatore's power had never been greater.

Proving his point, Briggs pushed back the hood of his cloak, revealing his face that was barely more than a skull, with drooping bits of gray flesh and a set of crimson eyes that glittered with a rabid hatred. *Cristo.* Salvatore had stumbled across genuine zombies who looked better than this Were.

And the stench . . . Salvatore shuddered in disgust.

"You just never learn, do you, Salvatore?" Briggs taunted, strolling to stand directly before Salvatore.

"It's not a matter of learning." Ignoring the pain, Salvatore managed a smile. "I simply don't fear you."

Fury flashed over the Were's emaciated face before he managed to regain his smug composure.

"I knew that arrogance would be your downfall."

Salvatore shrugged. "It might be eventually, but not tonight."

Briggs halted directly in front of him. "We'll see about that."

"What are you going to do, Briggs? Your master is gone, and without his powers you don't have a chance in hell of beating me."

The Were laughed, waving a hand toward Salvatore's body pinned to the wall.

"Obviously I'm not without resources."

"You can't hold me here indefinitely. So, unless you have another demon lord tucked in the cellar, you're screwed." His eyes narrowed. "I do have one question."

"You want to know why," Briggs mocked.

"No, I know why. You're an amoral, spineless son of a bitch who would willingly destroy your own people rather than accept the fact that you weren't worthy of being their leader."

An icy burst of pain exploded through him, reminding Salvatore that while Briggs might look like a corpse, he wasn't in his grave.

Not yet.

"I'm more worthy than you'll ever be," the pureblood hissed.

Salvatore's humorless laugh echoed through the empty shell of a cabin.

"Not even in your sick and twisted brain can you still believe your own lies."

"Without you . . ."

"Without me the Weres would have become extinct. I'm not only their chosen king, but their savior," Salvatore deliberately prodded. "My name will become legend among the purebloods."

Briggs's composure cracked, his eyes flashing with an insane fury. Reaching up, he smacked Salvatore across the face with enough force to split his lip.

"Bloody bastard."

Salvatore calmly turned to spit the blood from his mouth. "What I want to know is, was it worth it?"

"Worth what?"

"Was it worth sacrificing your pack, your loyalty, your sense of honor for a futile attempt to sit on a throne never intended for you?"

There was another blast of icy pain, and Briggs's face twisted with insane hatred.

"It will be worth every sacrifice once you're dead."

Salvatore's muscles clenched at the arctic assault, but through the pain he sensed Briggs's magic beginning to falter. The bonds holding him against the wall were deteriorating, and the chill biting into his flesh lessening.

Thankfully, the bastard was too distracted by his own anger to realize the danger.

"It's a shame really," Salvatore drawled, quite happy to stir the bastard's temper. "The Weres' ancient powers are on the cusp of returning, and you won't be around to appreciate our glory."

The stark truth of his words was the last nudge needed to send the maniac over the edge.

"Enough," Briggs roared, throwing off his cloak to reveal his skeleton body. "Hell's waiting for you, Giuliani. Give my regards to Mackenzie."

Salvatore braced himself as Briggs shifted, the sound of his low growls and popping bones unnaturally loud in the isolated cabin. The candlelight flickered as his face elongated, his fangs lengthening to deadly daggers and his eyes flashing with crimson fire.

Crazy or not, he was still a lethal predator.

Which he was swift to prove as he launched his attack, using Salvatore's immobility to strike straight at his throat.

Dio.

Straining against the invisible bonds, Salvatore barely managed to avoid the death blow, instead taking the violent impact on his shoulder. He felt his collarbone snap and the fangs rip deep into his flesh, but he survived.

This time.

Hot blood gushed from his wounds and the clinging magic made every movement a lesson in torture, but gritting his teeth, he managed to force himself from the wall and confront the Were as he once again pounced.

Plowing directly into Salvatore's chest, Briggs's attack sent them both rolling across the uneven wooden floor, his fangs once again biting deep into Salvatore's shoulder. Agonizing pain jolted through him, but Salvatore barely noticed. He was intent on forcing his awkward body to obey his commands.

With a merciless growl, Briggs scrambled to regain his balance, his fangs dripping blood, and his eyes smoldering with a deadly promise.

Sucking in a deep breath, Salvatore prepared to shift. It was much easier to call on the power of his pack in werewolf form. Not to mention the fact that he was more than ready to rip out Briggs's throat.

Reaching for his beast, he abruptly growled in disbelief, stunned to discover that his powers lurked just out of reach. His wolf snarled, but remained frustratingly leashed by Briggs's magic, as if trapped behind an invisible barrier.

Just as his connection to his pack was cut off.

His gut twisted with dread as he shoved against the unseen wall, searching for a means to break through.

Dio.

Briggs's spell had not only affected his muscles, but it had stolen his wolf.

Ignoring the urge to howl in frustration, Salvatore instead forcibly calmed his racing heart and stopped his futile struggles against the black magic. His wolf was currently impotent, but as his mind cleared, he realized there was something else inside him . . .

An unwavering power that had nothing to do with his position as king. Or even his strength as an alpha werewolf. This force came directly from his heart, and had everything to do with Harley.

The sound of Briggs's claws scraping against the wooden planks was the only warning as the Were charged forward, his fangs snapping just over Salvatore's head as he called on Harley's powers and managed to throw himself to the side.

He rolled toward the sagging sofa, cursing as he heard Briggs's howl of rage echoing through the cabin. The bastard wasn't going to be satisfied until he'd ripped out Salvatore's heart, and Salvatore couldn't depend on dumb luck to keep him alive.

Time to do something.

A pity he didn't know what the hell that was.

Harley had been horrified when she'd entered the shed.

Predictably, the four curs were chained to the walls with silver shackles, the stench of burning flesh enough to turn her stomach, but it was the sight of their ragged appearance and the wretched defeat etched on their filthy faces that made her heart twist in fury toward Briggs.

They had quite literally been broken by the evil Were.

Damn the bastard.

She hoped Salvatore ripped out the pureblood's heart, chopped it into pieces, and fed it to the rats. Then raised him from the dead and did it all over again.

Her grim mood didn't improve once she had the curs released and was leading them through the tangle of trees in a straight path back to the church.

She'd expected to have a brawl on her hands when she told the curs that they were leaving without Salvatore. Actually, she expected a mutiny, even after telling them that their king had ordered them to go with her.

It was disturbing to have them follow behind her with mute obedience, their heads hanging and their spirit lost.

Once in the empty church, she'd settled them on a rickety pew, her heart twisting as they huddled together, needing the physical contact to ease their fear. A part of her felt a befuddled need to do something to comfort them. She was supposed to be their queen, after all. It seemed like it should be her duty.

Unfortunately, she didn't have a clue what to do.

She didn't think a pat on the head and a "there, there" was going to help.

Another part of her, however, was consumed with her relentless awareness of Salvatore.

Since their mating, the sense of him always hummed through her. More like a background noise than an intrusion. Now she found herself restlessly pacing the empty vestibule, the feel of Salvatore so acute it was almost painful.

Unwittingly rubbing the spot just over her heart, Harley walked to stare out a broken stained glass window. Something was wrong.

And it terrified her.

Turning back, she caught sight of the large bald-headed cur regarding her with a melancholy expression.

With a lift of her hand, she gestured for him to join her. "Hess."

Despite his bulky muscles, the cur moved with a fluid grace as he crossed to kneel at her feet, his head bowed.

"Your Majesty."

Harley reached out and hastily urged him back to his feet, disturbed by the cur's groveling. Respect was all fine and dandy, but she was never going to get used to very large predators bowing and scraping.

"Please don't do that," she muttered. "My name is Harley."

He grudgingly nodded his head, not pleased by her refusal to follow tradition. A cur of the old school, obviously.

Bleck.

"If that is your wish."

She frowned at the sight of violent bruises and raw burns that marred his bare chest.

"Are you hurt?"

"Nothing that won't heal."

His dull, lifeless tone warned Harley that the worst of his wounds weren't physical.

He needed Salvatore.

Hell, they all needed Salvatore. Herself included.

"Tell me what happened," she demanded. "How did Briggs get you to the shed?"

"I was leading the others from the caves as you commanded when Briggs found us."

"Predictable. He has a talent for always being at the wrong place."

"He . . ." Hess licked his lips, his expression haunted. "He said he needed to make sure Salvatore would follow him."

Well, at least now she knew why the curs had been left

in the shed. They had been expendable once Salvatore arrived.

"You were bait."

"Yes." His glance briefly shifted to the other curs still huddled together on the pew. "We couldn't fight him. He gets in our brain and makes us do things."

She reached out to touch him, surprised to discover she could sense the mass of anger and confusion that tormented the cur.

"No one blames you, Hess," she said softly. "There was nothing you could do."

"I blame me," he growled, his hands clenching. "I have failed my master over and over. I'm not worthy to be his servant."

Harley frowned, her sympathy being replaced with frustration. Okay, Hess and the other curs had been through hell. She got it. But right now Salvatore needed them to be strong.

And that's what they were going to be.

Without giving herself time to think, she reached up and slapped the cur with enough force to snap back his head.

"Stop that."

Hess growled deep in his throat, the dull shame in his eyes being replaced by a spark of anger.

Thank God.

"It's the truth."

"Whether it's the truth or not, Salvatore needs his warriors, not a bunch of self-pitying whiners," she snapped.

He flinched at her brutal accusation, a meaty hand lifting to rub over his bald head.

"You said Salvatore had ordered us to leave."

"He did."

"Then obviously he understands that we are useless."

"He's concerned about Briggs taking control of you."

"Because we were weak."

"For God's sake. That's enough." She stepped until they were a mere inch apart. The cur might be twice her height and three times her weight, but she was a pureblood and her strength would always be superior. "Salvatore needs us."

"What can we do?" Hess demanded. "If we get close to Briggs, he will just use us against Salvatore."

Hardly a newsflash. She'd already realized the danger of allowing the curs near the cabin. Which was the only reason they weren't charging to the rescue. But she wasn't prepared to sit around doing nothing.

"We don't have to be near. Salvatore's the king. Can't he use you as a boost to his powers?"

"Yes. But . . ."

Harley's heart faltered at the sudden scowl that marred Hess's face.

"But what?"

"I don't feel him."

"You mean he's not calling on your powers, or you can't feel him at all?"

His hand shifted to press against his chest. "I can't feel him at all. There's something blocking our bond."

"Magic?"

"It has to be."

Damn Briggs. He obviously still had enough black magic to interfere in Salvatore's connection to his pack.

"Why do I still sense him?"

Hess shrugged. "It must be the mating bond."

"A fat lot of good that's going to do," she muttered, then her eyes widened. "Wait. Can Salvatore use it to gain strength?"

"Only from you."

"Shit." Harley returned to pacing, the ball of fear in the pit of her stomach becoming unbearable. "This is bad."

"Really bad," Hess agreed, his voice grim.

"There has to be something." Her steps slowed as she was struck by a sudden realization. "Wait. I'm the queen."

Hess regarded her warily, as if wondering if she was laying some sort of trap.

"Yes."

"Then I should be able to do the whole . . ." She waved her hands. "Sucking power thing, shouldn't I?"

He stiffened, his obsession with formality offended by her casual manner.

"You shouldn't make fun of our bond with Salvatore," he rasped, his unwavering loyalty to the King of Weres shining in his eyes. "It's an ancient tradition."

She bit back the urge to tell the cur that the feudal days were long gone and the serfs had been freed.

She was slowly beginning to accept that the rituals and customs that were so important among the werewolves weren't just an antiquated means of keeping the curs enslaved, as Caine had always claimed. They were a tangible expression of the intimate bonds that held a pack together.

"You're right, but can we worry about political correctness later, Hess?" She reached to lay her hand on his stiff arm. "I need to know if I can be a . . ." She searched for the proper word. "A conduit to share your powers with Salvatore."

Hess gave a helpless lift of his hands. "I don't know."

She made a sound of impatience, her fingers digging into his arm.

"Then help me try," she charged. "I don't even know where to begin. How does Salvatore do it?"

"He just . . ." Hess halted, clearly at a loss. "Does it."

Does it?

Well, that helped a butt-load.

Biting her bottom lip, Harley tried to ignore the gnawing sense that Salvatore was in danger. Instead, she concentrated on the vague tingle of distress that she was certain was coming from Hess.

She didn't know how she could feel it, but she did know that she hadn't noticed it until she had actually touched the cur.

"Okay, I want everyone in a circle," she said, ignoring the frowns of the curs as she urged them into the center of the vestibule. "Now take the hand of the person on each side of you."

"If you think I'm going to sing "Kumbaya," then you're out of your mind," the blond-headed cur muttered.

"Shut up." She glanced around the circle, grabbing the female cur's hand on one side, and Hess's on the other. "If you want to help Salvatore, then I need you to concentrate."

"Concentrate on what?" Hess demanded.

Wondering how the hell she'd gotten in so far over her head, Harley closed her eyes and filled her mind with the image of Salvatore.

"Me," she muttered. "Concentrate on me."

Laying facedown on the ground, Salvatore planted his hands on the floor and willed his stiff limbs to cooperate. *Dio.* He could already hear Briggs digging his claws into the floorboards as he prepared for another attack.

Now was the time for the grand heroics he had planned.

If only he could get to his feet.

He turned his head, preparing to push himself upright,

when a glint of silver caught his eye. Pausing, he pressed his head back to the filthy floor, peering under the sofa.

Of course.

Briggs's stash of weapons.

He never left home without them.

Now, the question was whether he could battle through the black magic still clinging to his body and find the strength to get his hands on the weapons before Briggs killed him.

Blood dripped from his shredded shoulder and he had at least a half dozen broken bones, but he managed to get to his knees. He would crawl if he had to.

Intent on reaching the sofa, it took Salvatore a moment to notice the stench of Briggs was being replaced by a hint of musk and pure, rich earth.

The scent of pack.

Fear jolted through him. *Merda.* His curs couldn't be stupid enough to risk coming to the cabin. Not when they had to know that they would be used as weapons against him.

It took a long moment to realize the scent was coming from him. And that it was strong enough to have made Briggs hesitate in wary confusion.

Painfully rising to his feet, Salvatore felt an unexpected heat flow through his blood, searing away the vile magic and healing his body. He shuddered as sensation returned to his deadened body, deepening his connection to his mate.

Harley.

This had to be her doing.

Somehow she had tapped into the power of the pack and allowed it to flow through their mating bond.

Clever woman.

Perhaps sensing his prey was no longer helpless, and

worse, about to kick his ass, Briggs threw back his head and howled with a fury that shook the rafters. Then, bunching his muscles, he launched his massive body through the air.

Salvatore was already moving.

No longer hampered by the black magic, he swiftly grabbed the nearby sofa and smashed it into Briggs, sending him flying into the far wall.

There was a sharp yelp as the Were hit with enough force to crack the wall, but Salvatore's attention was on the pile of swords and silver daggers that had been hidden beneath the nasty sofa. Reaching down, he snatched a long sword from the pile, and whirling toward the center of the room, he spread his legs and balanced himself on the balls of his feet.

He would be stronger and faster if he shifted, but removing the bastard's head would be easier with a sword than with his fangs, if not quite as satisfying. He no longer wanted to drag out the death of the traitor with a slow, painful torture.

He wanted the world rid of Briggs.

Now.

Prepared for the next attack, Salvatore watched Briggs regain his footing, his crimson eyes flashing with hatred, and his fur bristled with a battle lust. The Were was crazed, with a combination of pain and frustration, and obviously incapable of rational thought.

Otherwise he would have fled the cabin and prayed he could find a deep dark cave to hide in.

Crouching low, Briggs pulled his lips back to reveal his fangs that dripped with Salvatore's blood. Then, remaining low to the ground, he charged, his jaws snapping open as he prepared to hamstring Salvatore.

Salvatore didn't hesitate.

The sword flashed downward in a smooth arc, slicing deep into the werewolf's shoulder. It wasn't a killing blow, but the blade cut through muscle and tendons, crippling the Were. Briggs snarled, but he was too far gone to give a crap that he was badly wounded.

Sinking his fangs into the back of Salvatore's leg, he tried to yank Salvatore to the ground, snarling in frustration as his wounded leg buckled, refusing to give him leverage.

Salvatore grimaced in pain, using the hilt of the sword to smash into Briggs's muzzle, ripping his fangs from Salvatore's thigh and breaking the pureblood's jaw in the process.

"It appears that my reunion with Mackenzie will have to be postponed," he taunted, his sword already swinging toward the Were's throat. "But I'm sure he'll be happy to welcome you back."

With a belated attempt at self-preservation, Briggs scrambled backwards, the putrid scent of rotting flesh thick in the air. Gagging at the stench, Salvatore never allowed his stroke to falter, putting his full strength behind the blow.

Cristo. Enough was enough.

With deadly accuracy, the sword hit the Were directly on the neck, the impact jolting through Salvatore's body even as the blade slid through the flesh and bone.

There was no sound as Briggs's head toppled from his body, his crimson eyes still filled with his twisted loathing. Grimacing, Salvatore swiftly cut out the bastard's heart and backed away as a sluggish trickle of blood oozed from the life-ending wounds.

Merda. Briggs's carcass smelled even worse dead.

Salvatore would have bet good money that wasn't possible.

And more disturbing, there was a nasty tingle of black magic that was beginning to swirl through the air.

Holding the sword as if it could keep back the unpleasant chill filling the cabin, Salvatore unconsciously shook his head in denial.

No. He couldn't rise from the dead again.

Not without the powers of his demon lord.

Logically accepting that the nightmare was at an end, however, didn't keep Salvatore from continuing to back away as he waited for Briggs's body to return to its human form.

He'd been played and manipulated like a mindless putz for centuries.

He wasn't taking anything for granted.

The sound of Salvatore's breathing was the only sound to break the thick silence. Then, at last, a faint shimmer covered the mutilated corpse.

Expecting the transformation back to human form, Salvatore hissed in shock as the head and body began to darken and then disintegrate, as if it were turning to ash before his eyes.

Dio. The bastard was . . . dissolving.

Salvatore resisted the perfectly sensible urge to flee in horror. He could only assume that this was a consequence of the spell that had brought Briggs back to life. After all, he'd been nothing more than a pile of ash after Salvatore had been done with him the first time. It was, perhaps, only to be expected that he would return to his original form once he was no longer a puppet of the demon lord.

Salvatore had never been particularly squeamish, but he found his stomach heaving as the last of Briggs vanished into a pile on the floorboards.

It was a suitable end to the traitor, but still unnerving as hell.

At last accepting that there wasn't going to be another Lazareth act, Salvatore tossed aside his sword and crossed the barren room to grab the candle set in the windowsill.

Then with a brief prayer, he tossed the candle to the center of the room and walked out the front door.

He'd barely reached the edge of the tree line when the cabin was consumed in flames.

The end of his past.

And the beginning of his future.

A smile of anticipation curved his lips.

Epilogue

It was approaching midnight when Harley wandered through the hallways of Styx's Chicago mansion.

It had been over a week since she and Salvatore had escaped from the demon lord, but this was the first time she had ventured out of the massive guest rooms.

A smile of pure satisfaction curved her lips.

Actually, she'd barely been out of bed for the past week.

Why should she have?

She had everything she needed.

A gorgeous, totally edible mate who devoted himself utterly to keeping her satisfied. A hot tub to soak away the sore muscles after marathon bouts of sex. Fabulous food delivered to the door by a discreet vampire.

Nothing less than nirvana.

Tonight, however, was a full moon and Salvatore had taken off at sunset for a wild run through the surrounding countryside. He'd urged her to join him. Even if she didn't shift, she could feel the tug of the moon and the desire to be out in the night, running free, but she had firmly declined.

As much as she'd enjoyed the past few days, she knew

that they were stolen moments that were swiftly coming to an end.

Salvatore was the King of Weres, and while he'd spent a portion of each day speaking with various pack leaders on the phone or by computer, she understood that he couldn't remain in virtual isolation.

And she had her own duties, she reminded herself with a faint grimace.

Somehow during her efforts to link her powers with the curs to help Salvatore defeat Briggs, she'd bonded the poor schmucks to her. A stroke of luck since the whole bonding thing managed to heal their broken spirits, but a bit unnerving since they had decided they were now her personal guards, and refused to leave the mansion without her.

At some point she had to decide what the heck to do with them.

First, however, she wanted to spend some time with her sister.

So, giving Salvatore a lingering kiss, she'd sent him on his furry way and pulled on a pair of jeans and tank top to go in search of Darcy.

A half hour later, she managed to stumble across her in a peach-and-ivory room that had been converted to a private theater, with a huge plasma TV and several overstuffed couches. Darcy was curled on the center sofa, a tray beside her that held a large bowl of popcorn and a large thermos.

Sensing her arrival, Darcy pressed a button on the remote to pause the movie and gestured for Harley to join her.

Walking across the ivory carpet, Harley settled on the couch, tucking her feet beneath her in a mirror image of her sister.

"I'm not interrupting?"

"Good grief, no. I hoped you would join me tonight." Darcy reached for the thermos. "Salvatore has been entirely too selfish with your time."

Harley laughed, a delicious heat racing through her blood at the memory of Salvatore's insatiable hunger.

"He's not entirely to blame."

Darcy flashed a wicked smile. "Good for you. Hot chocolate?"

"Sounds perfect." Allowing her sister to press the large mug into her hand, Harley glanced toward the TV, her brows raising as she realized what her sister was watching. "*Terminator*? I would have guessed you were more a *Singin' in the Rain* fan."

"Are you kidding me?" Darcy waggled her brows. "A chance to see Arnold naked? Priceless."

"True." Harley held up her mug in a toast to man candy everywhere. "To a naked Arnold."

Darcy touched her mug to Harley's. "Here, here."

Sipping the creamy chocolate, Harley settled into the soft cushions.

"I assumed Styx would be with you."

Darcy grimaced. "He's busy on his throne."

Harley gave a choked laugh. "Excuse me?"

"He's having an official powwow with Dante and Viper. I think even Cezar stopped by."

"Trouble?"

Darcy's smile faded, concern darkening her eyes. "Levet is still missing."

"But . . . I thought he'd been captured by Caine."

"Apparently not. Your curs said that they found no trace of him."

"Damn." Harley frowned in dismay. She'd only known the tiny creature a short time, but she'd become attached to him. "He helped to save me and Salvatore from Caine's cell. I hope he's okay."

"So do I. He acts tough, but he's not as indestructible as he wants others to believe."

Harley reached to grab her sister's hand, offering what comfort she could.

"I have to admit I'm surprised that Styx and the other vampires would be bothered by Levet's disappearance. I had a fairly strong feeling they found him annoying."

Darcy squeezed her fingers, her smile wry. "Styx knows how much Levet means to me, but the vampires are far more concerned with the disappearance of Tane."

"Tane?"

"Yet another vampire."

Harley had a vague memory of Salvatore mentioning the vampire, but nothing more.

"What does he have to do with Levet?"

"Levet said he was following Tane's trail the last time we heard from him."

Okay, that didn't sound good.

Still, it wasn't like a babe lost in the woods.

"There's not many things that can hurt a vamp," she pointed out.

"Especially not Tane," Darcy readily agreed. "He's a Charon."

Charon? Somehow Harley didn't think he was a ferryman.

"Is that some sort of ubervamp?"

"I suppose you could call him that. They're trained assassins who hunt down vampires who have gone rogue."

"Yikes."

"Yeah, my thought exactly."

Harley sipped her hot chocolate, wondering what would

induce a vampire to choose such a dangerous position. It certainly wouldn't make him popular among the clans.

"It's not much of a surprise he would vanish. He has to have a lot of enemies."

"Actually, he wasn't on the job, so to speak," Darcy confessed. "He was with Salvatore when they discovered the presence of a jinn. He followed her trail while Salvatore continued his pursuit of Caine."

"Oh." Setting aside her mug, Harley rose to her feet, a scowl marring her brow. She'd forgotten that Caine's demon had disappeared during his disastrous journey to Hannibal. Now she felt a pang of fear for the poor creature. "Why would he care about a jinn?"

Darcy tilted her head to the side, clearly puzzled by her sister's concern.

"From what I understand, it's the fact that she's a half-breed that has everyone all wound up."

"Why?"

"Their powers are supposedly unstable."

Salvatore had mentioned his fear of the jinn, but it hadn't occurred to her that the vampires would be hunting her down as if she were an animal.

The thought made her heart twist in sympathy.

Despite the fact that Caine had always kept the jinn at a distance, Harley had always felt an unspoken bond with the beautiful creature.

They both had their reasons for hiding from the world.

"What will they do to her if they find her?"

With an abrupt motion, Darcy set aside her mug and rose to her feet, crossing to grab Harley's hands.

"I'm sorry, Harley, I never even thought about that. Was she a friend of yours?"

"Not exactly a friend. Caine kept her isolated from the

rest of us," Harley corrected. "But I don't think she would be a threat to anyone. She always seemed so . . ."

"What?"

"Frightened."

"Frightened of Caine?"

Harley shook her head. The few occasions she'd seen the jinn in the company of Caine, she hadn't picked up any vibes that the pretty demon was scared of Caine. But there had been something that haunted her eyes.

"No, I don't think so." Harley shrugged. "He kept her locked in a private lair, but she wasn't his prisoner. At least no more than I was."

Anger rippled over Darcy's face at the mention of Caine's role in protecting the bastard who had stolen them from the nursery. Not to mention putting her sister Regan through hell. Then, with a shake of her head, she returned her attention to the missing jinn.

"What do you mean?"

"She left more than once and returned of her own free will."

Darcy sucked in a startled breath, her eyes wide. "Then she might be trying to get back to Caine?"

Harley chewed her bottom lip, debating whether to tell a lie. She didn't want to be responsible for the death of the poor jinn.

Then again, she was fairly certain that Darcy would sense any attempt at deception.

"It's possible," she grudgingly admitted. "I think he has a way of keeping her hidden."

"I have to tell Styx." With a brief kiss on Harley's cheek, Darcy was headed for the door. "He'll want to track down Caine and find out if he's seen the jinn."

"Darcy, wait." Harley called.

Her sister halted in the doorway. "What is it?"

"Would you ask them not to kill her until they find out for sure whether or not she's dangerous?"

"Of course." Darcy paused, a slow smile curving her lips. "Harley?"

"Yes?"

"If they manage to find Caine, do you want him brought back to you? Styx would be happy to tie him up with a bow if you want."

Harley rolled her eyes. "Only if Salvatore doesn't find him first. I'm assuming he already has his pack out looking for Caine."

"Ah, you know me so well, *il mia amore*." The dark, richly masculine voice filled the room as Salvatore pushed open a French door behind her and stepped in from the garden.

"I think that's my cue to make myself scarce." With a wink toward Harley, Darcy had disappeared down the hallway.

Harley barely noticed her departure.

Who could blame her?

What female on the face of the earth wouldn't be entranced by Salvatore prowling toward her wearing nothing more than a pair of faded jeans he'd obviously just pulled on after shifting?

She breathed in his rich, musky scent, allowing her gaze to savor the magnificent sight of his smooth bronzed skin stretched over chiseled muscles, and the spill of raven hair that framed his lean, starkly beautiful face.

A sexy, dangerous predator that made her heart skip and her blood heat.

Easily sensing her appreciation for his raw masculinity, Salvatore wrapped her in his arms and studied her upturned face with a promising glow in his eyes.

"I like the way your sister thinks."

"Yeah, that's kind of obvious." She wiggled against the hard thrust of his arousal. "Behave yourself."

"I'm trying." He buried his face in the curve of her neck. "Mmmm. Sweet vanilla."

Harley's eyes fluttered closed as a heady rush of pleasure exploded through her, the feel of his teeth nipping at her vulnerable throat nearly sending her over the edge. But with effort, she forced herself to arch away from his exquisite nibbles.

Salvatore was way too talented in distracting her.

"So, do you have a hit squad out for Caine?" she demanded.

His eyes narrowed. "Would it bother you if I did?"

Would it?

"I . . . don't know."

Salvatore scowled, not pleased by her hedging. "The bastard nearly helped to destroy the Weres, not to mention holding you hostage for the past thirty years."

Harley grimaced. Hell, she wanted revenge as much as the next person. She'd been used and manipulated and terrified by the damned cur.

But that was all in the past.

Nothing mattered now but the future.

Her future with Salvatore.

"I could care less about Caine, but he does have a large number of curs who are loyal to him." She framed his face in her hands. "It's time for peace, Your Majesty."

He heaved a rueful sigh. "There's no hit squad. I've simply made it clear that I would be pleased with anyone who could give me information on the cur's current location."

She snorted, well aware that any pureblood who managed to get their hands on Caine was going to make his life pure misery.

"You make it sound so very civilized."

He arched a raven brow. "You wouldn't be implying that I'm a savage, would you?"

Her thumb brushed the sensuous curve of his lower lip. "When you want to be."

The gold of his eyes flooded the room as he studied her with smug pleasure.

"You can be something of a savage yourself, *cara.*"

She chuckled. It was true. With Salvatore's urging, she'd become downright aggressive in bed.

With stunning results.

"I haven't heard you complaining," she murmured, draping her arms around his neck.

"Never." His eyes darkened with a tender emotion he kept hidden from all but her. "You are perfect in every way."

"I'm your mate. You have to say that."

His hands skimmed up her back, pulling her close as he gazed deep in her eyes.

"Not just my mate," he husked. "What we have between us is more than biology or ancient powers, Harley. I adore you. I crave you. And most of all, I love you."

Her heart clenched with a joy she'd never dreamed possible. "Forever?"

"Beyond eternity." He bent to brush a gentle kiss over her lips.

Her knees threatened to buckle. Damn him. He knew how emotional she became when he was all sentimental.

"I love you, too, Salvatore Giuliani," she husked, her voice thick with tears.

With a last lingering kiss, Salvatore pulled back, a teasing smile on his lips.

"Naturally."

She punched his arm, but secretly she couldn't deny

a flare of relief. It was going to take time for her to become comfortable with the mushy stuff.

"Your modesty overwhelms me."

He chuckled, his eyes flashing with wicked amusement. "I have a better way to overwhelm you."

Amen to that.

She shivered, but once again she resisted the urge to give into temptation.

"Do you intend to wait here until Caine is discovered?"

His smile faded. "I know you wish to spend time with your sister, *cara*, but the packs are anxious to meet their new queen. We must begin our grand tour soon."

Harley wrinkled her nose. "Grand tour?"

"Our mating has brought back traditions nearly forgotten by the purebloods." He kissed the tip of her nose. "In the ancient days, the King of Weres would perform the *Sylnivia* when he became mated."

"And just what does this . . . *Sylnivia* entail?"

"Nothing too outlandish." He shrugged. "We will travel to meet our various packs and receive the blessing of our people." He paused, the smile slowly returning to his mouth. "It's supposed to ensure our fertility."

Harley abruptly cleared her throat.

She wouldn't get a more perfect segue.

"Actually—" She licked her suddenly dry lips. "I don't think we're going to be needing help in the fertility department."

Salvatore froze, his hands gripping her with a sudden tension. "Harley?"

She shifted, feeling awkward beneath the searing intensity of his gaze.

"When I woke up this morning, I felt weird." She unconsciously pressed a hand to her stomach. "At first I assumed it had something to do with our bond. It's been . . . a little erratic."

Looking decidedly shell-shocked, Salvatore obediently nodded.

"I'm still struggling with my powers," he muttered absently.

Harley smiled. That was the understatement of the century. Over the past week, Salvatore had accidentally shorted out the electricity, yanked the bathroom door off its hinges, drained Harley of her power one minute, and the next filled her with such energy she was nearly bouncing off the walls.

Which, of course, explained why she had first dismissed the bundle of warmth her wolf sensed in her womb.

As the day passed, however, she could no longer ignore the truth.

It was the spark of life.

Actually, her werewolf was whispering that it was several sparks of life.

Barely more than a few days old, but already growing strong.

"Yeah, I've noticed," she teased.

"Harley." He stopped, clearly struggling to breathe. "Are you saying . . . ?"

She went on tiptoe to press her lips to his. "You're going to become a proud papa, Salvatore Giuliani."

"Papa." For a crazed moment he swayed as if he might pass out. Then without warning, he sank to his knees, pressing his face to her flat abdomen. "I knew you were my savior, *cara,* but now you have given hope to the entire race of werewolves." Tilting back his head, he gazed at her with such profound respect that Harley had to fight back the urge to weep. "You are a miracle."

She gently threaded her fingers through his raven

hair. "I think you might have had a little something to do with this particular miracle."

His fingers brushed over her stomach, treating her as if she were as fragile as spun glass, even as his face darkened with sudden concern.

"How are you feeling? Are you sick? We have to get you to a doctor . . ."

"Salvatore, I'm fine," she interrupted, belatedly realizing that her mate's protective instincts were about to kick into hyperdrive. Frigging hell. She would be smothered if she didn't nip a few of them in the bud. Firmly she tugged him to his feet and laid her head on his chest, taking comfort in the steady beat of his heart. "Obviously we'll have to find a doctor who will help me through the pregnancy, but I'm not the first woman to have babies. It's all perfectly natural."

He pulled back to glare at her casual tone. "I don't care about other women, only you. We'll travel straight to our lair in Italy tomorrow. I have a number of doctors at my disposal, as well as a full staff of servants to make sure you have nothing to worry about but taking care of yourself."

She frowned. "But what about the *Sylnivia*?"

He blinked, looking at her as if she'd lost her mind. "Naturally, it will have to be postponed."

"There's no 'naturally' about it." She caught and held his gaze, her expression warning. "I told you I feel fine, Salvatore, and if you try to treat me like a mindless child who can't decide what's best for herself, you're not going to like the consequences."

His lips parted, then snapped shut as he studied her stubborn expression. Finally he heaved a sigh of resignation and pressed her head back to his chest.

"I will *try* to be reasonable," he grudgingly promised. "But it's not going to be easy."

"And our grand tour?" she demanded.

"We will decide on the *Sylnivia* after you've seen a doctor."

She knew it was as good as she was going to get. "Fine. We can no doubt find a competent doctor here in Chicago."

"I'll speak to the local pack master." There was a pause as Salvatore ran his hand gently over her hair. "Harley?"

She tilted back her head to meet his wary gaze. "Yes?"

"Are you . . ."

She frowned as his words faltered, his expression oddly uncertain. It wasn't like her arrogant mate to be anything but supremely self-confident.

"What's wrong?"

"Are you happy?"

She frowned at the ridiculous question. Her heart felt as if it might burst with joy.

"Of course I'm happy."

"Not so long ago you accused me of wanting you only for the babies you could give me," he softly reminded her, his gaze watchful. "I don't want you thinking I . . ."

Harley grabbed his face and yanked it down so she could halt his words with a kiss that was filled with all the love and wonder that flowed through her heart.

"Salvatore, I said a lot of stupid things over the past few days," she murmured against his lips. "I was scared and stubborn . . ."

"Insanely stubborn," he clarified.

"Don't push your luck, wolfman." She nipped his bottom lip, chuckling at his low growl of approval. "I was an idiot, but now I can't imagine anything I want more than to have you as a mate, and our home filled with children."

"Wait." His tension eased from his body, although his expression remained wary. "Just how many children are you talking about?"

"Five."

"Cristo." He blinked, clearly stunned, then with a loud crack of laughter, he wrapped her in his arms and twirled her around the room. "You're the most amazing woman."

"Amazing or not, I'm going to be sick if you don't put me down," she teased.

Instantly she was back on her feet, Salvatore's fingers threading through her hair as he kissed her with exquisite tenderness.

"You do know what this means, don't you, *cara*?" he whispered.

"You're going to have to learn how to change diapers?"

He pulled back, the golden eyes flashing with wicked amusement.

"*Si*. And also how to appreciate the rare moments when I have my mate's undivided attention." His fingers traced a path of fire down her back. "They will soon be few and far between."

"Hmmm. Did you have something in mind?"

His eyes were lit with a golden hunger that sent a shiver of anticipation down her spine.

"We could always return to our rooms."

"But I was just getting ready to watch the movie," she said, her expression one of faux innocence.

He glanced toward the screen, his brows lifting in surprise.

"Terminator?"

"Hello. Arnold naked." She gave a startled squeak as Salvatore scooped her off her feet and firmly headed toward the door. "What are you doing?"

"I have something better for you to look at."

She wrapped her arms around his neck. "Are you certain?"

He smiled with smug assurance. "Nothing but the best for the Queen of Weres."

And it was . . .

Please turn the page for an exciting sneak peek of
DEVOURED BY DARKNESS,
the next installment in Alexandra Ivy's
Guardians of Eternity series!

Laylah was tired.

She was tired of the dark, cramped tunnels that she'd been running through for the past two days. She was tired of being chased by an enemy she couldn't see. She was tired of her stomach cramping with hunger and her limbs screaming in protest at her relentless pace.

Reaching a small cavern, she came to an abrupt halt, shoving her fingers through the short, spiky strands of her brilliant red hair, her black eyes searching the shadows of her pursuer.

Not that she expected to actually catch sight of the frigid pain in her ass.

Vampires not only possessed supernatural speed and strength, but they could shroud themselves in shadows, making them impossible to sense, even to most demons. It was only because she had the power of jinn blood running through her veins that she could detect the relentless leech following her mad dash through the tunnels.

What she didn't know was . . .

Why.

She shivered, her mouth dry. Christ. She'd thought

she was being so clever when she'd initially allowed the vamp to catch her scent She'd hoped to lure him, along with the other intruders, away from Caine's private lair.

Not that she gave a damn about the cur, but she had hidden her most precious treasure at his estate, and she could not afford to allow any creature with the superior senses of a vampire, or even a full-blooded Were, near her secret. She'd thought the demons would give chase for a few hours and then grow tired of the game, hopefully returning to Hannibal or even St. Louis.

But her hasty plan had fallen apart right from the start.

The Were had continued on his path to Caine's lair, and the vampire had refused to give up, no matter how far or how fast she had run.

Now she was too weak to call upon her teleporting powers, and too far from Caine to call for his help.

"Oh, screw it," she muttered, planting her hands on her hips and tilting her chin in unspoken defiance. "I know you're following me, vampire. Why don't you just show yourself?"

A warning chill thickened the air, prickling painfully over her skin.

"You think you can give me orders, half-breed?" A dark, sinfully beautiful voice filled the cavern.

Laylah's heart missed a beat. Even with her demon blood she wasn't immune to the ruthless sensuality that was as much a part of a vampire as his lethal fangs.

"What I think is that I'm done running," she gritted. So either kill me or go chase someone else."

"Ah. Then you're confident you've managed to lead me far enough away?"

"Away?" Laylah stiffened, licking her suddenly dry lips. He couldn't know. No one knew. "Away from what?"

"That is what I'm wondering," the voice drawled. "It must be of great importance."

Laylah forced herself to suck in a deep breath, refusing to panic. The stupid vamp was simply trying to press her buttons. Everyone knew that they loved to toy with their prey.

"I don't know what the hell you're talking about."

"Hmmm. Have you ever watched a quail?"

She felt unseen fingers brush her nape, the cold touch ironically sending a bolt of heat straight to the pit of her stomach. She whirled around, not surprised that the predator had disappeared.

"The bird?" she rasped, belatedly wishing she was wearing more than a pair of cutoff jeans and a muscle shirt. Having so much skin exposed was making her feel oddly vulnerable.

Not that clothing would halt a determined vampire.

It wouldn't matter if she were wearing a suit of armor.

"When a predator approaches the nest, the mother quail will feign a broken wing and dash away to lure the danger from her chicks," her tormentor murmured, his voice seeming to speak directly into her ear.

She instinctively stumbled backward, her mouth dry with a sudden fear.

"The only quail I care about are baked and served on a bed of rice."

"What are you trying to protect?" There was a deliberate pause. "Or is it who?"

"I don't know what the hell you're talking about."

"Is it a lover? A sibling? A child?" His soft chuckle grazed her cheek as the sharp leap of her pulse gave her away. "Ah, that is it. Your child?"

Laylah bunched her hands into fists of frustration. He was getting too close. She had to distract the bastard.

"I thought vampires were known for their courage," she deliberately taunted, willing to risk a battle she couldn't win if it would keep her secrets. "Are you such a coward you have to hide in the shadows?"

The chill thickened, the danger a tangible force in the air. Then, the shadows directly before her stirred, and the vampire slowly became visible.

Laylah reeled, feeling as if she'd just been punched in the gut.

All vampires were beautiful. And sexy.

Wickedly, indecently sexy.

But this one . . .

Reminding herself to breathe, Laylah allowed her gaze to skim over the elegant features that revealed his Polynesian ancestors, lingering on the slanted eyes that were a brilliant shade of honey and the inky black hair that had been shaved on the side, leaving the top to form a Mohawk that fell past his broad shoulders.

Her gaze lowered, that vicious awareness only intensifying.

The aggravating creature was wearing nothing more than a pair of khaki shorts, leaving his body on full, wondrous display. Her fingers actually twitched with the desire to stroke over the smooth muscles of his chest. Or down the flat plane of his stomach.

No doubt aware of her helpless response to his sensual beauty, the demon stepped far too close, his fingers casually stroking along the curve of her neck.

"Have you never been told the dangers of provoking a vampire?" he murmured.

A chill inched down her spine, but she forced herself to meet his hypnotic gaze.

"Do you intend to drain me?"

His lips twitched. "Tell me about the child."

"No."

"Is it yours?" He paused, his fingers drifting to the pulse that hammered at the base of her throat, an intense concentration etched on his beautiful face. "No. Not yours. You are as pure as an angel."

Genuine fear speared through her heart. Damn the interfering leech.

"Leave me alone," she breathed.

The honey eyes darkened with a dangerous hunger. Laylah wasn't sure if it was for blood or sex.

Maybe both.

"A beautiful angel," he husked, his arms wrapping around her to yank her hard against the strength of his body. "And I have waited too long to have a taste."

Unable to halt her panic any longer, Laylah's unpredictable powers lashed out, the electrical charge that filled the air enough to make the vampire leap back in wary surprise.

"I said, leave me alone," she hissed, wrappimg her arms around her waist.

The golden eyes narrowed. "Well, well. You like to play rough?"

"I don't like to play at all," she snapped. "What do you want from me?"

"My first intent was to capture you so you could be brought before the Commission."

She jerked at the threat, her powers abruptly faltering. She'd been hiding from the official leaders of the demon world for two centuries. To be taken to the Oracles that made up the Commission was nothing less than a death sentence.

I have done nothing to earn such a punishment," she attempted to bluff.

"Your very existence is worthy of punishment." The

vampire smoothly countered. "Half-breed jinns have been forbidden."

Laylah squashed the familiar anger at the sheer injustice. Now was not the time to debate whether or not she should be exterminated for the sins of her parents.

"You said that was your first intent," she said, her voice thick. "Have you changed your mind?"

A dangerous smile curved the vampire's lips as he reached to trace the plunging neckline of her shirt, his touch searing a path of pure pleasure.

"Let us say I'm willing to postpone our journey with the proper incentive."

"Incentive?"

"Do you need me to demonstrate?" he murmured, his lips softly brushing over her mouth.

"No . . ." she choked, attempting to deny the piercing need that clutched at her heart.

God. She had been alone for so long.

So very long.

"Tell me your name," he whispered against her lips. "Tell me."

"Laylah."

"Laylah." He said her name slowly, as if testing it on his tongue. Pulling back he studied her pale features, his hands skimming down her sides to grasp her hips and boldly press her against the hard evidence of his arousal. "Exquisite."

Laylah clenched her teeth, ignoring the sizzle of excitement racing through her blood.

"I assume you have a name as well?"

There was a brief pause. Not surprising. A name in the hands of a magic-user could give them power over a person. Then he shrugged.

"Tane."

It suited him. Ruthless. Powerful. Stunningly male.

"Great." Placing her hands against the steely hardness of his chest, she arched her back to meet the honey heat of his gaze. "Let me make this perfectly clear, Tane. I don't use sex as a bargaining chip. Not ever."

Expecting him to be angered by her blunt rejection, Laylah was unnerved when his lips curled into a smile of pure anticipation. Hauling her tightly against him, he spoke directly into her ear.

"Now let me make this perfectly clear, Laylah," he whispered. "When we have sex it will only be after you have begged me to take you."

About the Author

Alexandra Ivy lives with her family in Ewing, Missouri. She is currently working on the next installment of her Guardians of Eternity series, *Devoured by Darkness*. Readers can visit her Web site at www.alexandraivy.com.